THE CROWN OF A FALLEN QUEEN

AN ENEMIES-TO-LOVERS ROMANTASY

CURSE OF THE FAE
BOOK FOUR

ANYA J COSGROVE

BANISHED

"Violet Devilyne Eros, you have been found unfit to rule. You are hereby banished from Faerie. From now on, you'll live as a mortal. Should you ever attempt to escape this fate, you'll be met with nothing but agony and suffer a slow, tortuous death."

CHAPTER I
SOS
SETH

20 miles off the coast of the Summerlands, Faerie

It takes only one big rock to sink a boat. One stupid, badly-placed rock, and *bam*, you go from being captain of a sailing boat to a very fucked, very pissed off castaway.

And that weird mist—where the hell did that come from?

Water skims my knees as I wade through the cargo hold. The gurgles of sea water being sucked in through the gaping hole in the hull are counting down the minutes until my little brother drowns. Wooden crates slosh around the cramped space, Luther rolling his eyes at me as I make my way toward him.

"You sunk my ship?" he grumbles, unimpressed.

I grab the first shackle chaining his wrists and ankles to the floor of the boat and twist the key into the lock, freeing his left hand. It took a lot of manpower—and frankly, a bit of luck—to get him into those cuffs, and the growing pressure in my chest fills me with dread. But I don't want him to die, and I haven't got many other options at the moment.

I kneel down to free his leg, but in my haste, I accidentally tug on the chain. The rowan spikes embedded inside the cuffs sink deeper into his skin, drawing a sharp, pained gasp from him.

"Fuck," he hisses under his breath. "Those shackles hurt like hell. Be careful."

I manage to liberate his left leg and move quickly to the other, but it's tricky with the water rising. "You chained me down here first, as I recall. I was only repaying the favor."

"I only tied you up because you were being unreasonable."

"Shut up," I mutter, my tone more amused than I'd like.

He cracks a grin, and I grin back. No matter how far he's fallen, he's still my baby brother.

But that smile fades as quickly as it came, replaced by the cold, hard stare of the revolutionist—the "do whatever's necessary, kill or be killed" warrior he's become.

"When are you going to accept that you and I aren't on the same side anymore?" His voice is low, yet steady. I can feel the distance in it, and how easy it is for him to detach himself from his old life.

I pause, trying to keep my hands from shaking, and finally uncuff his other leg. "Oh, there are sides now?"

"You made it very clear you don't want to join the tides."

I stand to work on his other wrist, and the flicker of hurt in his eyes twists my heart.

"So, if I'm not with you, I'm against you?" I say.

He grunts at that, like I'm playing with words. "Seems obvious enough." There's that edge again, the one that makes me feel like I've already lost him.

A heavy sigh escapes my throat. "You're still young, Luther. Your so-called allies are exploiting your idealistic views." The words hang in the air, laced with something I can't quite name. Regret. Love. A mix of both. "They're using you."

The last cuff comes undone, and he rubs his wrists in turn. His magic crackles over the surface of his skin, no longer held back by the silver and rowan alloy. Electricity zaps up and down the muscles of his arms.

"And you wonder why we don't get along anymore," he mutters. "When you always treat me like I'm too young to know my own mind." He shakes the thunder off his shoulders. "You know what that mist means, don't you?"

My brows furrow as the thick, murky mist that derailed our voyage slithers inside the cargo hold. "Bad weather?"

His focus shifts, and he climbs over the barrels and crates bolted to the sinking ship. His accomplice, Imogen, is tied up in a similar fashion in the back of the cargo hold, and I join them on the other side.

The water is rising quickly in this section, too. Imogen struggles to find traction on the wood, the boat slowly tipping over, forcing her to balance herself on her tiptoes to relieve her bound arms.

The slender woman with short black hair grunts in relief as Luther blasts her restraints off with his juiced-up magic and slides down her gag.

"Well done sinking the ship, Seth," she snaps.

Electricity sparks along her arms, but Luther braces his hands on her shoulders to pacify her. "Meet me at the rendezvous point, Gen." He tosses his head in my direction. "I'll deal with my brother."

Half-brother, really, but I've always been more comfortable in a storm than in the luxurious halls of the Spring castle. While my magic straddles the line, my personality is more compatible with darklings, and no one has ever been truer kin to me than Luther.

Imogen nods gravely, still as loyal to him as she was when they were Faen playing pirates in the Storm Court's catacombs. She disappears into a cloud of rain, and a familiar ache settles in my chest.

For years I've been obsessed with finding Luther, and now that he's finally here, finally within reach, I'm about to lose him again. Maybe for good this time. It's heartbreaking to search for someone who doesn't want to be found and being desperate to help him even though he doesn't want to be helped. It's a fool's errand, really, but I had so much *hope*. I thought I could get through to him, or say the right thing at the right time, enough to tip the scale and bridge our differences.

I've failed.

Luther turns to face me, his eyes flickering with a thirst I know all too well—one I even shared, once upon a time. "The tides are rising, Seth. The Storm King is dead. I feel it in my bones, and with any luck, all his buddies went with him." The bottomless greed in his voice makes my heart pound. If he's right, and all the monarchs of Faerie perished tonight, then the whole Fae Continent is at war.

"It's troubling how you speak of your father's death as though it's something to be celebrated," I say quietly, beating the thickening fog with my arms to keep it at bay.

His brows raise, calling me out for my hypocrisy. "He was your father, too, and you don't sound at all choked up."

I look away from his youthful face, well-aware of the part I played in souring their relationship. "Let's be honest, he was more your father than he ever was mine."

Luther's lips curl in a bitter pout. "Because he was weak. Always scheming to keep us in the dark, trying to control us." He raises his arm in my direction. "War is coming. What have the seven crowns ever done for you but laugh in your face and reject your power, all because you're a little too dark for the light folk, and too much of an extrovert to keep to the shadows? You have to join us, brother."

The thought of war, of irreparable bloodshed, ices my soul.

"All this violence. All this hate. It's not you, Luther," I croak, trying to hold him back, to keep him from his darkest desires, to save him from a path that'll no doubt chip away the last remnant of the boy I once knew. But I fear he's already gone.

"Where you see darkness, I see potential. Where you see conflict, I see change. And the sooner you accept that, the happier you'll be." He grips my head with both hands, pressing a loud kiss to my forehead. The loving touch feels both overdone and sincere. "Though I would have loved to have you on my side again."

Then, just like that, he vanishes into a silver, powdery cloud.

CHAPTER 2
MONSTERS
DEVI

All monsters look normal in the dark.

Creatures that aren't supposed to exist can't exactly walk around in broad daylight—especially not in a place that hasn't completely forgotten about the Fae.

The busy streets of Inverness are empty at this hour. Even the drunkards stumbling out of bars and taverns have gone home. The tourists yearning for a change of scenery are still tucked in their warm hotel beds, while the lively shops, cafes, and restaurants remain closed.

It's the perfect time for outcasts like me to do business.

The glare from the shops' windows stabs at my retinas, and I pull my hood lower over my red locs, turning away from the wide, reflective glass panes. In these uncertain times, you never know who might be watching.

My army boots echo off the stone pavement as I stride toward the shadowy back alley leading to the banks of the river, where I'm to meet Nick's friend. The scent of fresh blooms and cheap beer gives way to rain-soaked earth and a hint of something metallic that reminds me of industrial steel.

The man I'm meeting is tall but lean, with a scruffy red beard and wearing too much leather for his own good. His brows knit together when he sees me coming. He's nervous, twitchy, his fingers drumming against his thigh.

"Oh, you're havin' a laugh!" he grunts, eyes to the sky.

"Beg your pardon?"

"How old are you?" he scoffs, like he can't quite believe his bad luck.

"Older than I look, I assure you." My eyes narrow just as my lips stretch in a sly smile, daring him to contradict me.

The man pinches the bridge of his nose. "I told Nickolas I needed his very best. It's a very *delicate* operation."

I can't believe Nick stuck me with a rookie. He knows better than that. But even my rebellious godson can't pick and choose which of his sources will lead him to the most precious cargo. I usually don't handle middlemen, but after hearing Nick's claim about the shipment being moved through *my* city, I had to come and see for myself.

I ram my hands in my jacket's pockets to keep from flipping the stranger off. "I'm here as a favor to him. But if you don't want me around..." I move to leave, unimpressed by his attitude, his Londoner accent scraping my ears.

He raises a hand in my direction. "Wait. I trust Nick, so I'll trust his judgment on this."

Typical boy club stuff. Ugh.

"You better." I walk all the way into his bubble, relishing the way his pupils dilate, and the bob of his Adam's apple.

A good look at him tells me he's in love, the soft glow of his mortal heart about as obvious as his wedding band. And it's a strong bond, too. But there's something else lurking underneath this love. Indelible pain. The unexpected depths of his sorrow soften me up to his rude behavior, and I pull down my hood.

He shifts uncomfortably from side to side, no longer irate. "Are you meant to protect me, or distract them?"

I throw him a knowing wink. "I excel at both."

He swallows hard. "Do you have the talisman?"

I reach inside my cleavage and unveil a long golden chain, tugging on it until the Aurelian talisman slips from my neck and dangles in the space between us. The polished piece of engraved metal is opalescent under the night sky, its very own light shining from within.

Even though it's a priceless artifact, the man's gaze is glued to me. "You're one of them, aren't you? A Fae?"

I chuckle darkly in the affirmative before passing him the necklace, and he staggers. "Wow," he breathes with a sudden, reverent head tilt. "I didn't believe your lot still walked this earth until just now." He works the chain around his neck. "I've been raised in the city, despite my heritage. You have to forgive me."

"Don't worry about it."

"You're so beautiful..." he trails off dreamily, his eyes glazing over.

I rein back my lure, trying to spare him the conflicting onslaught of lust, but he's a mortal man without any magic to shield himself. He's bound to go a little nuts in my presence. "Let's not get carried away. Where are they being kept?" I clip.

"Err— Right." He clears his throat. "I'll take you there now."

He leads me to a boat beached on the muddy riverbank. The engine growls to life, and the sharp scent of burnt gas clogs the air as he steers upriver, past the Ness Islands and under the Holm Mills Bridge.

He's in over his head, and we both know it. Still, I can't begrudge a thirty-something mortal on some idealistic crusade. Most of them would rather sell the talisman on the black market, not borrow it to save captive witches.

"They're being held in a barn off the river. There are cameras everywhere—hence the talisman," he explains, stopping near a steep, grassy cliff. "You should wait in the boat."

"How chivalrous... How did you plan to break in?"

A grim line drags his features down. "I have the code."

"And what if it's been changed since you acquired it?"

"That's where this comes in handy." He slips a slug shotgun from a hole in the boat's hull meant for fishing poles. By Eros, this man looks ready to barrel through an organized crime operation all by himself.

My eyes narrow. "Easy there, big guy. How did you hear about this place?"

"The man who runs it... I've been investigating him for a decade."

"You're a police officer?"

"I was." His gaze darts to the ground for an instant. "I got kicked out for not following protocol. The man who owns this place, he's into all sorts of trade, but he's particularly interested in witches, and he finally managed to get his hands on a couple."

The dark circles under his eyes, the sunken shape of his cheeks beneath the beard, are telltale signs that he hasn't been eating or sleeping enough.

I try to stay out of other people's affairs as a rule, but this is different. "What does she look like? The one you're looking for?" I ask.

"They took her to punish me. My daughter." He slides a picture out of his wallet and presents it to me.

The frayed edges somehow make the freckled, redheaded girl look even younger. She must be about ten years old. Her toothy grin reminds me of my goddaughter Maxine at that age, and my stomach cramps.

"Let's find her, then." I step off to the riverbank first, and a mix of rocks and gravel crunches under my feet. The farm's lights are just ahead, partially hidden behind a line of trees.

This is no ordinary place. It's too quiet—no animal sounds, no chatter, no movement. Only the subtle hum of cameras, their lenses most likely trained on every corner of the property. A series of electric floodlights illuminates the area, bathing the farmhouse, barn, and outbuildings in cold white light.

I stop before crossing the broken down fence, the grass beneath my feet still saturated with rain, making the terrain muddy and slippery. There'll be no chance to conceal our escape path, not until we reach the boat. I slip my hood back over my head and motion for my unlikely partner in crime to activate the talisman.

His knuckles clench around the chain, his entire body shaking with nerves and rage, his silhouette blurring as the magic of the talisman envelops him. He's not completely invisible, but in the dark, he's just a shadow. And it will definitely ensure the cameras don't pick up his presence, the mortal technology easily diverted by the subterfuge.

"Don't be a hero, alright? Your daughter will need you when this is all over," I whisper.

"As long as we get her out," he chokes out, forging ahead.

The magic I inherited from my sire—a magic I keep secret from my kin—allows me to become completely invisible as I follow the ex-cop's muddy tracks to the seemingly abandoned barn. The doors and windows have been boarded off, but the methodical, secure way it was done hints at the sinister truth of it.

We pause by the only door that's still in use.

"I can open the door, but their security system will see that it's open. Unless they're snoozing on the job, we won't have a lot of time," my companion warns.

"We only need a minute."

Inside, the illusion of a barn is gone. Sweat, blood, and urine assault my senses, mixing with the acrid smell of fear that clings to the concrete floors. The original barn walls have been reinforced with plywood, the added layer meant to muffle the prisoners' cries and shouts. Two rows of cheap, metal beds litter the space, with twenty or so women and girls sleeping—or not sleeping—in them. A series of cameras surveil the interior of the barn as well.

"There's too many of them," I whisper quickly.

A makeshift bathroom in the back, separated only by a curtain on a rail, offers no privacy. This isn't some witch hunter cult, but a full-blown human trafficking operation. Young women are herded here like cattle, waiting to be sold to the highest bidder. My heart pounds in my chest.

I will end this.

The bite of power coming from the two little girls near the front confirm Nick's suspicions that real witches are amongst the prisoners. They can't be older than nine, holding each other for dear life. Even though I do not share their blood, my heart aches for them.

Escaping quietly isn't an option anymore, not when there are two dozen hostages, and I let the invisibility fall, revealing our presence to the prisoners—and the cameras. I shouldn't do this, but I can't help myself. I'm exhausted from all these covert, inefficient operations. Sneaking, stalking. Barely scratching the surface of a well-oiled machine that trades women and children. These men need to be punished for once.

Hiccups of surprise and fear echo through the barn, the women unsure whether I'm friend or foe, probably thinking I'm just here to feed them. Or buy them.

"Change of plans. You better call the cops, Roger," I clip, making up my mind about what I need to do, no matter the consequences.

"My name is William, actually."

He might be an ex-cop, but he's still a stranger to my world, still a mortal, and I roll my eyes. "You should never tell a Fae your real name, William."

He wrenches the talisman from around his neck to break the spell. "Angie? Angie, darling, are you in here?"

A little girl, still tucked under the grimy, pitiful covers of her cot, shrieks and leaps out of the bed. She runs headfirst into my companion.

Shouts, hurried footsteps, and the clicks of shotguns reach my ears, coming from outside. "Now, close the door behind me, get these women away from the walls, and call for backup," I order. "I'll give these men what they deserve."

I slip outside the barn, but William follows.

The cold night air swirls in strings of mist in front of his face as he says, "You can't possibly face them alone—"

I shoot him a death stare, demanding to know why he's resisting my command, and let my true power rise to the surface.

His eyes bulge. "Yeah, yeah, alright!"

He doubles back inside and slams the door shut behind me. Relief licks my ribs as I hear him barricade it from the inside.

There must be ten or fifteen men heading my way, trickling from the farmhouse and adjoining garages, and I cradle a whip of light in my hand, a weapon made out of pure energy.

I don't care what it costs me. I'll kill them all.

I let the light pass right through me, becoming invisible again.

My breaths are steady, my heart pounding with a smidge of elation as I crack the whip, the sharp *snap* of the popper echoing in the silence. Light floods the path and cooks their retinas through, incapacitating them all at once. The men howl in surprise and stagger backward, clutching their faces. A flurry of gunshots ricochet off the barn walls, striking down a few with friendly fire. One bullet buries itself in my shoulder, but I ignore the sting of pain and condense my magic into a dagger.

The man closest to me falls first with a swift strike to his heart, collapsing before he can shout a warning. I glide toward the next, my fingers tightening around the hilt of the blade. One by one, they drop, their confusion and fear palpable in the moments before darkness takes them. They will never know what hit them, only that their reign of terror ends here, tonight, at my hand.

When I call for William to open the door again, the ex-cop is pale as a sheet, his daughter curled up in his arms. Her sniffles and cries are muffled by the fabric of his jacket, the talisman's chain now sticking out of his pocket.

"It's done. You're all safe now," I announce loudly, becoming visible once more.

The other women are huddled in the back of the barn, and I congratulate myself for wearing dark clothes, the blood staining my sleeves and jacket not too obvious. I can't afford to comfort them any further, not if I want to survive the night.

William takes one step out of the building, still cradling his daughter, and takes in the scene of death and destruction I painted with wide eyes.

He deposits his precious Angie on the ground, but she just curls around his thigh, never looking in my direction. He looks so winded and weak, I fear he might topple over. "Who are you?" he croaks, his voice trembling.

"I'm Devi Eros."

William falls to his knees. "I am honored and humbled by your presence here today, Your Majesty."

I grip his sleeve and pull him up by the arm. "By Eros, I'm not a proper queen anymore. Stand up."

The little girl steals a glance at me then, like she's heard of me, too. Somehow, the thought that mortals still whisper my name in reverence is heartbreaking—but also oddly comforting.

"Me and my family are forever in your debt." He hands over the talisman, and I cram it deep into my pockets.

"Go back in there and wait for the cops, William. I'll stay close by until they arrive, just in case."

These women need nurses and social workers, now. I've done my part, though I'm going to get a nasty scolding from Mabel for murdering so many mortals and putting my life at risk. I figure I have about half an hour to spare before hell rains down on me.

It was worth it, my inner self snickers.

I bury my hands in my pockets to hide the bloody streaks marring my skin and begin to walk away, but William shouts, "Wait! What should I tell them about the bodies?"

I shrug, steeling myself against the shivers that rock my spine, the inflamed flesh around the bullet hole in my shoulder throbbing painfully at the motion. "Tell them to recover the footage from the cameras. They'll see these men were stricken down by an invisible force you couldn't possibly control."

There's a moment of silence before he adds, "Thank you."

Other men might judge me for what I've done, but he doesn't, and I offer him a tense nod. "Nick will be in touch to take the witches back home."

They should have been allowed to train in the Red Forest, but instead, they suffer here, in a world that either denies their existence or tries to destroy them. They've been cast out, shunned from their rightful place in the worlds, just like me.

My gaze falls on the young girl glued to William's side, now staring at me with the kind of directness and wonder only a kid can muster. "I wish you both the best," I tack on, rusty when it comes to goodbyes and eager to smooth over the memories that little girl is bound to keep of me.

I've lost faith in people, mortals and Fae alike, but it's no reason to further traumatize a child. After they stripped me of my crown, after the monster who killed my mother managed to have me banished, I barely survived.

If I'm never to set foot in my native land again, never to be allowed to rule over the mortals' hearts like I was meant to, maybe revenge should be my next calling. I could rebrand as a sort of avenging, invisible spirit.

Eros knows I've got enough anger simmering inside me to sustain such a life.

CHAPTER 3
WITCH HUT
DEVI

T he first sign of trouble is the rumbling of thunder in the distance. The previously cloudless sky darkens, burgundy clouds rolling in from the West. I need to head home, and pronto. Invisible, I tuck my head and shoulders in, waiting for the officers to arrive.

Two police cars pull up, keeping at a safe distance, their two-tone sirens casting red and blue hues against the dark fields. They radio for backup before finally stepping out of their vehicles, their weapons drawn as they take stock of the rampage I caused. Beads of sweat shine on their foreheads, and their pulses flutter at their necks. They're afraid whatever creature killed those men is waiting for them in the dark.

Once more, the crackle of the radio pierces the air, followed by muffled voices, urgent and clipped.

I use a zap of magic to unlock the car that's closest to the road and ease my way inside the abandoned sedan. Slipping into the seat without a sound, I take great care not to slam the door. The leather creaks under my weight as I grip the steering wheel and twist the key into the ignition. The engine roars to life, and shouts resonate behind me, but I'm already on my way.

I drive straight from the fringes of the countryside to the heart of the city and ditch the car a mile from my house, walking the rest of the way. The unusual storm clouds are almost blood-red now. My eyes flick to the sky every few seconds, searching for the shadows I know are bound to rain down on my head. The faint sound of wings flapping in the distance sends a glacial chill through me.

Bloody hells. They found me. That didn't take long. Then again, I wasn't being very discreet.

As Mabel has warned me many times, I'm playing with fire. Refusing to heed my fate as a no future, has-been queen. Freya couldn't take *all* my magic away, but she made it deadly to use it. I've fucked up this time. Used too much, too far away from the protection of rowan wood. I bled, making it easier for the cupids to track me.

Cupids are sneaky little beasts, originally created by my grand-sire to play tricks on mortals by briefly sparking their passions. They feed on the chaos they create, and when cupids come flying by, they're not here to help anyone find true love.

But I've got my own special brand of cupids chasing me. Every time I use my powers, they come, and those little bastards are vicious.

I flatten myself against the brick wall, pulling two obsidian crystal knives from the inner pockets of my jacket. I don't know much about my monsters, except that their assault is mostly propor-tional to the power I used, and that my magic, whether it's forged as a whip, a dagger, or a bow and arrows, is useless against them. They are born from it and immune to its influence.

My jacket scratches against the brick wall as I rush from corner to corner toward the entrance of my shop, keeping close to the wall to avoid an attack from behind. The rowan wood and spells I used to ward my home will protect me, but first, I need to get there alive.

A flock of one-foot-tall cupids descends from the sky, their wings beating the air in rapid flutters. Shadows made flesh, born of a curse that's haunted me for decades, and they won't stop until they rip me apart.

Their bodies are grotesque, with oily, tar-like skin stretched tight over round buttocks. They resemble overly muscled, creepy toddlers —if toddlers had long, sharp claws designed to carve out a heart.

And people wonder why I stay away from children.

The cupids' sole purpose is to hunt me down, shred me to pieces, and take my heart back to their mistress. But it's their wings that get me every time, their black feathers so similar to my own.

They move too fast and form blurry projectiles streaking toward me. I barely have time to react before the first one slashes my arm with its long claws. The pain is sharp—a burst of fire in my muscles, and the gash is no doubt deep enough to join the flurry of old scars marring my skin, if it's ever allowed to heal.

I don't have the luxury of screaming as another cupid flies at my left side, teeth bared. I twist away just in time to avoid the bite, but its claws catch the hem of my jacket, tearing the fabric as it spins off behind me. I swing one of my knives at it, but it dodges my attack at the last second.

Another one sinks its teeth into my leg, and a sickening jolt shoots through me. I strike it down with a hiss, gritting my teeth together. The cupid shatters, breaking apart into dark, opaque pieces of glass that skitter across the paved alley. Each time I take one down, another appears.

Evading them is the only viable option, but it soothes my raw nerves to feel the crunch of their monstrous bodies under my feet. I stagger forward, blood gushing down the side of my leg, my body screaming in pain. They feed on it. They're getting stronger, more frenzied, more rabid.

The shop is visible now. The *Pat's Pottery, Pots, and Potions* sign swings on its hinges as a chaotic burst of wings blurs my vision. The cupids move together—coordinated, fast, relentless. One needles my arm, while another slices my stomach, in the exact spot where the Mark of the Gods stands. Its nail gouges the flesh of my abdomen as if it means to peel off the tattoo in one sharp swipe. The mark brands me as Eros' true heir, and I won't surrender the last remnants of my crown so easily.

They aim for my heart next, for that ultimate trophy.

Twisted laughter fills the air, and I push myself forward, determined to escape, barely staying on my feet as I press a hand to the torn flap of skin and muscle hanging from my belly. It's too much. Blood soaks through my clothes, and I know—I know—they're hungry for it.

Almost there.

I won't let them win. Not when it means Freya will inherit what's left of my God-given magic, the part that sank deep into my bones, a power so rooted in me that even she couldn't grasp it. I'd suffer a thousand deaths before legitimizing her claim to the throne, allowing her to become the rightful Spring Queen instead of the usurper she is.

The door to the shop opens, my faithful Percy hovering in the air, sensing my arrival. The sight of his round, purple melon hat fills my eyes with tears.

With every ounce of strength I have left, I run. I only need one more second.

One more step forward.

I stagger over the rowan threshold, my breath coming in painful rasps. The cupids that dare to cross with me immediately shatter into a cascade of polished glass beads, which scatter in a cacophony of *tinks* across the floor, rolling deeper into the shop, carried by their own momentum.

I made it.

Molten heat engulfs me as I fall to my knees on the varnished wood. My antique shop doubles as a tea and divination parlor, and the familiar warmth of the hearth feels eerie. The gentle glow of the fire is meant to soothe the chill of early morning, not to heal the brutal treatment I suffered at the hands of the monsters who butchered me in the streets.

I'm on all fours, shaking and retching from the stench of my own blood, but the shallow drizzle of red in my wake is nothing compared to the pool forming beneath me. Sweat clings to my skin, mingling with the sweet-dill fragrance of the tea I brewed late last night.

There's no place to die but home, right?

In the far corner, three round tables with tall stools allow my customers to exchange stories, while the bar counter separates the front area from the kitchenette. Shelves cluttered with glass vials and mismatched jars line the walls.

The flames crackle softly, the only sound in the room besides my uneven breaths, until Percy slams the door shut behind me. "Blimey! You swore—you swore you wouldn't use too much magic—"

I shrug off his scalding tone, sliding down to press my forehead to the cold wood, then rolling to my side, my world spinning. "Didn't you see 'almost being mauled to death' in the schedule? You're slipping, my friend."

He lands on my thigh, his arms braced on his tiny hips. "I would've noticed if you'd added something as meaningful as a botched suicide attempt into my planner."

I grin, desperately holding back a chuckle as Percy starts healing my wounds. Laughing is agony when your intestines are threatening to spill out of your abdomen, but the sting quickly wanes.

Percy's a great healer, the one power I've always failed at. Healing, whether myself or others, from cuts and scrapes or a broken heart, is beyond me. Percy fixes what I destroy, and it's always been that way. My loyal Faeling excels at what I do worst by divine irony. The only skill we share is our flippant, sarcastic, and downright mental sense of humor, but I can see his smile doesn't quite reach his eyes.

"You almost did it this time. Almost came home in too dire a state for me to fix." A heavy sigh whistles through his lungs. "Is that what you want? For our story to end like this, in a dark corner of the new world, forgotten by most and reviled by the rest?"

"*Reviled?* Are you trying to cheer me up or finish me off?"

Now, he laughs, pleased with himself, and my chest warms at the sight.

"Don't lose faith, *diamatay*," he murmurs.

In his language, it means more than friend. More than family. More than heart.

"I'm exhausted, Percy. If I can't use my magic, what am I good for?"

He fixes the torn flap of muscles and skin next to the Mark of the Gods until only a faint web of silvery scar remains and wraps his hands around the tip of my index finger, giving it a heartfelt squeeze. "Anything you set your mind to, *diamantay*. Anything at all."

I fight back the pesky tears again. I don't do tears. Never. But as Percy pieces me back together, I wonder, how much longer can I go on when I'm only scraps of what I was before? Banished from my home. Unable to use my abilities. Forced to hide in a world that has no use for me.

Percy's vibrant bite of power dulls, but he still tugs on my jacket to access the gash in my arm. The blood makes the fabric cling to my skin, and I clench my jaw, steeling myself against the pain as I peel it off, discarding the shredded jacket to the side.

Percy fusses, his iridescent wings sagging against his back as he takes stock of the long, deep zigzagging cut running from my wrist to the underside of my arm. He's pale, his skin almost gray in the light of dawn.

"I'm good. This isn't fatal by any means." I crawl to a seat, testing the newly healed muscles of my abdomen. I'm pleasantly surprised to find everything in perfect order. "You can get to it later."

"I'm not finished," he insists. "You're still bleeding."

I arch a brow, daring him to fight me on this when he's clearly on the verge of collapse. "But you're exhausted."

"It's my job to make you whole, *diamantay*," he says in a breathy, almost desperate rasp.

The corners of my lips curl up, and I give my oldest friend—my forever family—a resigned chuckle to ease his sorrow. "Oh, Perce. You know I haven't been whole in decades."

"I know." He hovers near my arm. "It's killing me that I can't do the one thing I was born to do. But I can fix those cuts. Stop the bleeding. Let me at least do that."

I draw a sharp inhale at how emotional he sounds. "Alright, you can heal this one, but the leg will have to wait."

He inclines his head in agreement and lands on my arm, his boots leaving prints in the half-dried blood staining it. I track his movements closely. The span of his hand barely covers the width of the cut, so it takes him a minute. He shouldn't be so hard on himself. No one could fix me as I am now. The gashes in my spirit, my soul, run deeper than cupid claws could hope to reach. I chew on my bottom lip and wait for my Faeling to finish, watching for signs of further exhaustion on his part, ready to catch him if he falls.

"There. Good." He nods to himself, a bit of life returning to his cheeks.

"Thank you, Perce." I move to stand, but the blood loss dizzies me for a moment, so I brace myself against the wall at my back. Despite Percy's incredible work, I'll need a bit of time to adjust.

He takes one dark look at me and steals my cell phone from the pocket of my destroyed leather jacket.

I raise a hand in warning. "Don't you dare call Mabel—"

"I'm calling Mabel."

"Percival Arthur Batten, you leave that phone alone!" I growl, infusing the order with as much power as I can muster, still leaning against the wall not to collapse.

Percy lets out a satisfied huff at my failed attempt to bend his will. "You're too weak to control me. Serves you right." He extends his small hand to the screen of my phone and taps in the password, but before he can do anything else, a powerful knock at the door spooks us.

My pulse spikes as we both turn toward the entrance of the shop.

"Percy? Percy, it's Mabel. Are you in there?"

Say her name out loud, and she appears. That witch. Shit. Did she already hear about my murder spree?

"Weren't we supposed to meet in town for breakfast? Why are you so early?" I shout through the door, calculating the chances that she caught a whiff of the cupids' bite of power.

"Open up, child. Or the stink left behind by your chubby visitors will trigger my migraines."

My eyes screw shut, and I rest my head against the wall. Caught red-handed. So much for keeping it a secret.

CHAPTER 4
MABEL
DEVI

Percy flies to let Mabel in while I lean against the wall in a relaxed, natural way, still feeling a little too weak to stand without help.

"Hey, Mabs, what brings you in so early?" I say.

"Bad news, I'm afraid."

Percy scans the street behind her, checking on the cupids, and a cold wind gusts into the room.

The bite of Mabel's magic settles over my frayed body like a weighted blanket as she tightens her hold on the handle of her black umbrella and shakes it over the carpet. The accessory quickly melts into a cane.

"What possessed you to throw a party for those vicious beasts? I smell what, twenty? Thirty? What in the Dark One's name did you cook up in here to summon a haze storm of cupids at your doorstep?" Her gaze darts from the pool of blood at my feet to the deep bite in my leg before she rests both hands on the raven-shaped pommel of her cane. "Oh, I see. You went out again."

A judgmental throat-clearing sound escapes her, bringing heat to my cheeks, and I offer her a sheepish grimace.

"It was worth it."

Mabel fixes her bun, her white hair tied neatly at her neck. "And how long do you figure you'll be stuck within two blocks of this place?"

As soon as I step outside the safety of the house, the cupids will track me down, and it takes them weeks to vanish back to the hell they crawled from.

"A month? Maybe two? Max can bring me groceries. It'll be fine."

"*Hmprh.* Should I fry a few of them before I go?"

I cross my arms over my chest, finally letting go of the wall. "Don't bother. They won't stay down for long anyway."

While the cupids created by the curse are completely immune to my magic, they are merely hindered by anyone else's. They can't be killed. Period. When one is struck down, its body breaks apart, and another appears in its place—only buying me time to get away.

Mabel walks across the room to the kitchenette, leaning her cane against it before filling the boiler to the brim. "I've received dire news from the continent."

Mabel doesn't share my longing for the motherland that chewed us up and spit us out, but her web of spies still keep her informed, so she can better protect what's left of her people. She's always watching over her shoulder, trying to protect me and her other protégés.

I raise a curious brow. "Spill."

She glowers at my breezy attitude. "Max is parking the car. You should probably clean yourself up."

Maxine, Mabel's adopted daughter, is a mortal. As young and sheltered as she is, growing up in this world, she's not used to seeing me in pieces. And the Fae Continent is as intangible to her as the nightmares that keep me awake at night.

I join Mabel in the kitchenette, careful not to step on the glass beads still littering the floor. "I'll take a quick shower before Max gets here, but you can't tease me with gossip of that magnitude and not spill the details. Just tell me."

She twists on the portable stove. "The Eternal Chalice has been destroyed."

My heart skips a beat. "But how? What happened?"

Percy gets to work cleaning up my blood from the floor with a rag almost as big as he is, listening in on our conversation.

"The Lord of the Tides melted it off, and both Eliza Bloodfyre and Thorald Storm perished during the attack on the capital." She clutches the tea chest with both hands. "Freya survived, but I heard she's in pretty rough shape."

I try not to smile or pump my fist in cheer and concentrate on more pressing details. "What about Elio? And Damian?"

"Both alive, I think." She presses her lips together. "Though I couldn't say for how long."

My mouth dries up, my tongue parched. A searing hope weasels its way inside my heart, potent and dangerous. If the Eternal Chalice has been destroyed, it means the only thing standing between me and my rightful crown is Freya Heart.

By Eros...

"Hurry up. The kid can't see you like this, not if you still want to hold on to your secrets," Mabel warns, waving me off.

The shop's doorbell chimes at Maxine's arrival. She rushes through the front door with her jacket held over her head to protect herself from the rain, and I slip behind the curtain of glass beads separating the shop from my private quarters to stay out of sight.

Percy flies to welcome her. "Ah, my favorite goddaughter."

"I'm your *only* goddaughter, Percy," Maxine deadpans, leaning in for him to kiss her cheek.

I enter the bathroom and close the door behind me before peeling off the rest of my bloody clothes and throwing them in the hamper. Inspecting the bite wound on my leg, eager to clean it up, I wince at how deep the teeth indentations are—four puncture marks to add to the growing collection. My skin is riddled with similar scars, old and new, each one a reminder of the price to wield magic.

Faded yellow wallpaper peels from the wall in the corner next to the sink, the diamond-shaped tiles chipped and stained with age. The small window above the bathtub lets in just enough light to showcase the grime that sticks to the creases in the windowsill, in spite of my best efforts to rub it off.

The aging house is proof of how much time has passed, while my body remains plump and youthful, at least on the outside. If it weren't for the growing number of scars, no one would be able to tell I'd lived at all.

When I come out of the bathroom, dressed in fresh clothes and my leg bandaged to keep the wound from prying eyes, Maxine and Mabel are already waiting at the table in my private area of the shop, a steaming cup of tea set out for me.

The crystal ball I use to play tricks on the mortals who visit my divination parlor sits at the center of the round wooden table, goops of wax dripping down the side of the lit candles surrounding it.

"Devi! I'm so glad to see you." Maxine abandons her seat and rams into me with one of her bone-crushing hugs.

"Hey, Freckles," I whisper, my eyes closing for a moment. There are very few people I like in this world, but Maxine and her brother Nickolas are the exception.

"How's the new job going, Maxie? Do tell all," Percy prompts her.

"Any jerk I need to deal with?" I add with a wink before taking my seat.

She rolls her eyes. "*No*, everyone's been very nice."

Mabel clears her throat. "She met a man."

"Mabel!" Maxine cries out.

The old queen waves dismissively. "She thinks she's in love."

I could tell from one glance, but act surprised all the same. "A hottie, I hope?" I eye the diamond ring on her finger.

Percy loses his shit, wings flapping behind him. "Oh my Eros, Maxie! You're engaged?"

She squeezes my hand, her beaming gaze darting between us. "I'm getting married next month in Glasgow, and I want you both to come."

"Next month? Wow!" Percy grips Maxine's ring with his tiny hands, grinning.

My gaze slides from the bride's bright smile to the frown pulling at Mabel's brows.

"So soon," I murmur.

Maxine grunts. "Now, don't start. I'm a grown woman."

Mabel purses her lips together. "What about asking Devi to vet the union first, darling? Like we talked about?"

"No!" Maxine glowers, her sharp green eyes darkening with a hint of magic, the temperamental witch about to lose her grip over her unstable powers. "I don't want any magic involved."

"Wouldn't you prefer to know now if the love arrow wasn't strong enough for your marriage to last?" Mabel insists.

Maxine holds a decided finger in the air. "Please, Devi. Don't use your magic. And I don't want to hear another word about love arrows."

I don't have to use my magic to know that her marriage won't last. One look at her was enough. But I know when and where to keep my mouth shut.

"My lips are sealed." I pick up my tea cup and blow on the steam rising out of the amber, honey-glazed liquid.

"Your eyes say everything," she mumbles. "You obviously disapprove."

I hold my arms up in surrender. "Freckles, I'm butting out of your love life. I promise."

If I've learned one thing about mortals, it's that they don't like to be told bad news—especially when it concerns their fiancé. Fae distrust mortal love as a rule. Most attachments in this realm are formed because of an archer's meddling, but Maxine is only half-fae. She doesn't know any better. And mortal marriages can be dissolved, unlike ours.

"Well, I'm famished. How about I cook us all some fried eggs?" she offers, the hot-blooded young witch struggling to stay idle for more than a minute, desperate to change the subject.

"I have some sausages in the fridge upstairs. Go nuts."

Maxine climbs the narrow stairs two at a time, entering my loft.

Mabel leans in close to my ear. "Tell me the truth about this *love* of hers," she asks in a tired wince.

Percy's wings flutter at his back the way they always do when he's negotiating the narrow path between his morals and his bottomless hunger for gossip. "If Max doesn't want us to meddle, we should talk about something else."

I throw Percy and Mabel a wink. "I won't tell if you won't."

Percy suppresses a smile, the corners of his mouth tilting upward despite his efforts. "But this stays between us three."

Mabel grins at my Faeling. "Of course, little man."

"Their marriage won't last," I reveal on an apologetic grimace. "The love arrows used by the archer were subpar."

Mabel curses under her breath. "By the Dark One, the arrow carvers are really getting sloppy without you."

"Bad romances might just drain the mortal world of hope if that usurper isn't careful." This botched job wouldn't have been tolerated under my watch. "Using a side-notched arrowhead to try and make up for the flimsy shaft was just plain stupid. They're bound to cut deeper in one person than the other. Mortals need flings and memorable heartbreak as well as true love, but they don't need damaging, asymmetrical entanglements. Maxine got hit pretty hard, but I doubt her fiancé fared the same."

Mabel's wrinkled hand clenches around the porcelain handle of my roses-and-crowns tea set. "You have to tell her."

Percy's eyes bulge, and he opens his mouth to protest, but I beat him to the punch.

"And have my head bitten off? I don't think so," I grumble. "Maxine was very clear with her boundaries, and I won't alienate her *weeks* before her wedding. I'm her Faerie Godmother."

Mabel huffs at my attempt to *be modern*, as she calls it. "Despite the liberties she's taken with her life, she's meant to lead the coven one day. And contrary to what you both seem to believe, I won't live forever."

A knowing smile tugs at my lips. "You still have decades to live."

"Even you can't make an old, destitute queen live forever. I need to know Max is ready to face her responsibilities, and tying herself to a mortal man who has no idea who she really is—that's reckless."

Though she's much older than I am, Mabel and I are kindred souls. And we've both long-forgotten what it's like to feel young.

"Max was born and raised here, in the new world. She doesn't know anything different."

"Nickolas was raised here, too, and he doesn't shy away from magic." A sharp exhale rocks my friend's lungs, and her hazelnut eyes fly to the ceiling.

"Twins share a special bond, but those two are like blood and water. How is dear Nickolas? He hasn't visited since—"

Mabel cuts me off. "He's never been more involved in the family business, yet he still refuses to come home. That boy will be the death of me, I tell you."

I take a careful sip of tea. "Max still struggles with being a witch. Nickolas might not be physically here, but he's got his head in the game. You can't expect her to take up your mantle anytime soon, not with the way things are going."

Mabel presses her lips together, her fleeting smile wiped away in favor of a grave pout. "Speaking of unwanted baggage, I brought something with me. It's in the trunk. Let's get it now."

CHAPTER 5
ONE STORMY NIGHT
DEVI

"I could ask Max to bring the crate inside if you prefer," Mabel offers.

I tiptoe out into the street, scanning the sky for any signs of the cupids. "I'm good."

After an attack, they usually fly back and forth over the city, tracing my steps back to where I first used my magic. What they lack in intelligence and strategy, they make up in speed and brute strength. I can't feel their nauseating bite of power in the air at the moment, but I know they haven't gone far.

Mabel twists her car keys in the trunk's lock and lifts the lid. "I can't keep it at my house any longer," she announces on a heavy sigh.

A wooden box the size of a milk crate rests on top of Mabel's reusable grocery bags. She pricks her thumb on the lock to open it. The rowan wood has been burnt to withstand the test of time, and the whines of the rusted hinges bring goosebumps to my neck. This box hasn't been opened in a long, long time.

My breath catches. "Is that—"

"Yes."

Inside the box lies a golden spindle. Intricate Fae runes swirl across its surface, some ancient patterns etched into the shaft, and the carvings decorating the whorl's beveled edge are impossibly smooth and precise.

As the worlds' most talented arrow carver, I cannot even begin to understand the power and craftsmanship that went into making such an artifact. A dizzying flare of magic sparks from the crate, zapping my fingers as I inch my hand toward it, as though the spindle aches to be claimed and mounted upon a wheel once more.

A spindle rumored to alter the course of destiny.

"You've had the Spindle of the Gods in your attic all this time?" I say quietly, my fingers numb from its proximity, my tongue dry.

"It wasn't an issue as long as nobody knew it was there," she grumbles.

My gaze darts over to her. "And who knows now?"

"No one yet, but I can't afford to keep it with me, not anymore. A new Mist King has been crowned the second the Eternal Chalice melted."

My head swims at the news. "Do you know who he is?"

"No, but I felt his presence, as surely as I'm talking to you now. It won't be long before he seeks me out."

When she was young, Mabel was married to the Mist King, and her first husband almost destroyed the Fae when he tried to seize control of the continent. She lost her queenly powers when he died, but a part of him, along with a fraction of his magic, stayed with her.

"Why would he come for you? It's been centuries since you've stepped foot on the Islantide."

"We both know well how the magic of a realm is infused with certain...flavors of the past. Like muscle memory. The new Mist King will be eons younger than I am, but I'm still to blame for his realm's downfall." Mabel's lids flutter closed, her face pale and riddled with grief.

"You only meant to stop Armand. You never condoned any of the cold-blooded murders that followed his demise."

Deep lines appear around her tight mouth. "No, but my actions still led to a realm-wide genocide. If Armand had married anyone else, he would have become the one and only King of Faerie, and the Summer King wouldn't have slaughtered all his people."

"The slaughter of the Mist Fae was an unforgivable crime, and everyone involved was severely punished for it," I say quickly.

"Were they?" Mabel muses, deep in thought. "When their children are still reigning over the realm?"

"They're all dead, at least," I negotiate.

"That they are." She tightens her hold over the raven-shaped pommel of her cane, her knuckles white. "I'm the last Fae alive who lived through the Mist Wars. Even if the new king of the Islantide doesn't blame me for how they ended, he will seek me out, if only to know what facts were left out of the history books. But whatever happens next, he must not be allowed to use that spindle."

Mabel is my best friend, and I won't let some psycho king imbued with the powers of the most deranged leader in history hurt her.

"I will keep it—and you—safe. Hells, you should move in here until the fucker shows his face."

The corner of her mouth quirks. "I've never known you to be quite so sentimental."

"You know how much you mean to me, Mabs, despite all my shortcomings. I couldn't love you more if you were my own flesh and blood."

She pats my arm. "And I love you, my Devi. But I don't need a bodyguard, no matter how heartfelt the offer is. By the Dark One, you might be in worse danger than I am."

I nod. As much as it thrills me to be closer than ever to reclaiming my stolen crown, it also means I've become a target for those who drove me out of Faerie. "Freya must be freaking out. With the chalice gone, I could easily take back my crown, if not for that wretched curse."

"Don't underestimate her. Or the curse. And don't get any ideas about using the spindle. Not all wheels spin all yarns, and the tapestry of the gods is not meant to be altered—" Mabel stops, her wrinkled eyes narrowing on a dark silhouette barreling down the cobblestone sidewalk on the other side of the street.

Jonas Campbell strides toward the shop through the drizzle, rain dripping from the edges of his leather jacket. He slows down as he approaches, his green eyes as sharp and watchful as ever, and crosses the street to meet us. He looks good. He always does.

"What are you doing outside in this weather?" he asks, never quite able to turn off his suspicious nature.

"Come and see for yourself," I shoot back.

Rain patters against the car's roof as I skirt away from the open trunk, allowing my old flame a look inside. The Spindle of the Gods might be one of the most powerful Fae relics, but it doesn't look like much. Its wood is dark with age, and though the pointed rod is made of gold, it's hardly the kind of object that makes a homicide detective stop in his tracks. By mortal standards, it's not valuable enough to matter, and as an antique shop owner, it's perfectly reasonable for me to collect such things.

He raises a brow, his eyes dancing with humor. "Can I ask what it is? Or what's it's for?"

I offer him a genuine smile, not unhappy to see an old friend after the day I've had. "Depends on how badly you want to waste your time."

Our gazes lock, and he draws in a sharp breath. "Long time, Devi." He squares his shoulders, burying his hands in his pockets, and takes an awkward, very deliberate step back. "We need to talk."

Jonas Campbell. If I'd been in a position to ever fall in love with a mortal, it would have been him. But if he's here today, it's not to rekindle anything.

"I have company, detective."

Jonas turns to Mabel. "I'm sorry, madam, I've forgotten my manners. I'm Jonas Campbell, Detective Inspector, Police Scotland."

A warm, old-womanly smile stretches across the witch's lips.

"We're about to have breakfast. You're welcome to join us inside, Detective."

Jonas takes a long look at her white hair, wrinkles, and cane, then shakes his head. "Thank you, madam, but I'm on the clock." He shifts his weight from one foot to the other. "I'll come back after my shift, alright?"

"Mm-hmm," I nod.

He leaves, and Mabel leans in, her voice conspiratorial. "When did you stop sleeping with the handsome detective?"

I pick up the spindle crate and hold it to my chest. "It's been years, now."

"But you know why he's here," she muses.

"I'm afraid I do."

She nods and hurries me along. "Let's eat, then we'll be out of your hair."

Back inside the shop, she pauses, her gaze flying to the bronze ceremonial lantern in the corner.

"Since I'm leaving the spindle in your care, I'll take my Starlight's lantern back with me. I'll appreciate the occasional company now that Max has officially moved out. And maybe it'll do him some good to get out more. I know you two don't exactly get along..."

Goosebumps rise on my neck as my eyes flick to the lantern. "He's been pretty quiet lately," I admit.

"Well, thank you for taking care of him as long as you did."

"Not at all. He's my responsibility."

The corners of her eyes crinkle, her smile stretched a little tight. "Maybe, but he's my grandson."

AFTER MY LAST PATRONS HAVE GONE, JONAS FINALLY STEPS INTO THE SHOP.

His blazer, tie, and dress shirt still look neat despite the late hour, so he hasn't stopped by the pub before coming to see me.

He doesn't waste time with pleasantries, his voice low, "We need to talk, Devi." His eyes scan the room, landing on me with a look that tugs at something deep inside my dead heart. As soon as our eyes meet, he looks away and rubs the arch of his brow, his breath catching in his throat. "I'm serious."

I'm wearing a black dress with a scoop neckline, a fitted bodice, and a flared skirt for the occasion—and nothing else underneath. Shiny black army boots complete the look. Bet that'll distract him from his detective duties.

I finish washing the teacups from my last customers. "I'm all ears."

He approaches the bar. "We got a strange call this morning, by the river. I've got about twenty dead men and the picture of a bonnie lass..." He presents the picture to me, and it's blurry, so I give him a pep-filled shrug.

"How are you so sure it's me?"

A shadow drapes over his brow. "William told me," he grumbles, glaring at me with his inquisitive, serious detective stare, yet I catch him sneaking a glance at my bare thighs.

I shake off the nerves and reach for the top cupboard, pulling down Jonas's favorite teacup. The earthy green ceramic feels steady in my hand, the smooth matte surface cool and achingly familiar against my fingers. "Tea?"

He clears his throat. "It's...been a while."

My eyes dart to the empty seat in front of me. "You want answers, don't you? Sit down."

He shrugs off his leather jacket and hooks it on the coat rack, but he doesn't obey. Instead, he licks his lips, his strong, powerful arms crossed in front of his chest. "You can't keep killing people."

I wave away his concern. "Criminals."

"And I can't keep covering for you."

I walk around the counter and press my hip into his side. "But you will."

Our gazes meet, and a heavy sigh whistles out of his lungs. "You're one complicated woman..." He shakes his head and hides his hands in his pockets. "I'm too old for this."

I huff. "Old? You're barely forty."

"And yet you don't look a day older than the night we met."

I grip the counter, my jaw clenching at the familiar reproach. "So you've told me many times before."

Jonas and I met during one of his patrols. He was a young, 22-year old constable with killer abs and a sweet, heartwarming passion for doing the right thing. We dated on and off for almost a decade.

He stopped seeing me after we crossed paths with one of his new detective friends. The bastard scolded him for dating a girl barely out of puberty. I assured him I was of age, but the accusation shook the then freshly-promoted detective to the core. It's a sore subject between us, and one of the most painful reasons why mortals should never fall in love with a Fae.

"We shouldn't do this. You could pass for my daughter, now." He traces the shoulder strap of my dress with the back of his index finger, and the soft caress spreads from my chest to my belly, warming my whole body.

"Come on. You know I'm older than you, Jonas," I scold him.

"I know."

I stand on my tip-toes to nuzzle his nose. "It's just us, here."

"I can't." His breath warms my lips, and the hunger stirs inside me. He strokes the curve of my waist back and forth, his actions a sharp contrast to his words. "I have to go."

Who is he trying to fool? He's not going anywhere.

"I really need a friend tonight," I whisper in his ear.

He dips his head down with a lopsided smile. "Is that what you need? A friend?"

"With some benefits."

His tongue darts out to touch my lips, and I hum against his mouth, pulling him down for a fast, almost famished kiss.

It's been so long since I indulged my cravings. I've been so disciplined about not using magic the last few months, a good girl through and through, but a flicker of Spring magic couldn't possibly worsen my situation tonight, not when there's already a throng of cupids buzzing up and down my neighborhood.

Spring Fae are always horny, but ever since my crown was stolen, I've had this...maddening ache inside me. A dull twinge that never completely fades away. I was born to crave attention, devotion, but most of all, the sweet throb of a lover's cock buried deep inside me. The only thing my people value more than true love or raw power is that tethering cliff that precedes an orgasm, that sharp intake of breath before the nervous system crumbles down in sweet, sweet capitulation.

A common misconception about Spring Fae is that we need sex to sustain ourselves, but that's not true. We simply wither when celibate, everything else bleak in comparison when we go too long without it, and I've been starving myself for *months*.

It's so *easy* with Jonas. He knows exactly what I like and how I like it.

The cupids not only stripped me from a few pints of blood, but also the semblance of freedom I've fooled myself into thinking I had. The need to reclaim my body, my flesh, as my own and not their chew toy, drives me to pull Jonas past the bead curtains and up the stairs to my loft.

His nostrils flare as we pause at the top of the stairwell, and he traps me between his body and the wall. "You've ruined me for all other women," he grunts, tracing the shape of my lips with his thumb. "And you don't feel at all guilty about it."

"Why would I? Sounds right to me," I tease with an edge of anger, tugging on his belt.

The bob of his throat.

The embers of lust in his eyes.

The soft tremble of his hands on my waist.

I live for them. With a thousand scars on my body and my pride and spirit broken, I can still bring this clever, beautiful, and kind man to his knees. Make it so he craves me beyond reason. I peel away the layers of pretences between us, of regrets and reproach and disappointment, as well as his shirt. The grooves of his chest feel heavenly beneath my fingers, and he snakes a hand under the mini skirt of my dress to kneed the flesh of my ass.

"Fuck. There's no one like you. Not even close."

"Mm. Keep talking." I close my eyes.

Jonas leans down to ravage my neck, his kisses impatient as he unzips his trousers.

He loves me still, in spite of his best judgement, in spite of his efforts to move on.

He loves me *always* because such is the fate of a mortal man who falls for the Queen of Hearts. I might not have a kingdom to rule, an army of archers to command, or a true home, but I still have that.

"You're the most beautiful—" He stops cold, the loud creak of the stiff venetian blinds drawing our attention to the opened window.

Jonas squints at the loose cord flying in the strong night draft. "You left a window open in this storm?"

The heat that had built in my chest is extinguished by the drizzle of rain splashing inside the room, and my brows furrow. "Definitely not."

Bloody hells.

I push Jonas off me and stride toward the window just as an airy, rainy cloud seeps inside, the intrusion prompting me to slip out the crystal dagger hidden in my boot. The cloud drifts closer and closer. Until it condenses into a tall, dark-skinned Fae.

CHAPTER 6
INTERRUPTUS
DEVI

"What the fuck?" Jonas reaches for his belt, struggling to put his pants back on.

The stranger stands a couple of inches taller than my lover, and while the detective is all muscle and brawn, this man is leaner, more athletic, but no less intimidating. He doesn't look away from our disheveled appearances, nor does he apologize for his rather impolite and ill-timed interruption. Instead, he holds himself even taller, and the roguish curve of his mouth stretches all the way into an impish smile. That, combined with his unwavering poise, tells me he's well-born and bred, with the arrogance only a Fae royal can muster.

The undertow of his magic threatens to swallow me whole, so I steel myself against his bite of power and reflect a glimpse of the queen I used to be upon him, in lieu of warning.

"So...you're Devi Eros." His pupils dilate, and he lets out a low whistle. "The monks weren't kidding when they warned us about you." His tongue darts out to touch his bottom lip, his gaze gliding down my body in the most deviant way imaginable. I'm accustomed to men's lustful stares, but this Storm Fae doesn't leer the way others do.

Instead of appraising my body, he watches me as if I'm both his hell and salvation, a rare, cursed treasure he's spent a lifetime searching for.

"You are every bit as ruinous as the stories implied," he rasps. The hushed, terrible compliment quickens my pulse before he shakes off my show of power with a full-bodied shiver.

The click of Jonas's gun resonates in the air, but the intruder isn't rattled in the least, so I grip the hilt of my weapon and press the side of the blade to his neck. "Who are you?"

He raises his hands up in surrender, his grin widening. "I'll tell you if you remove the knife."

I motion for Jonas to stand down with my free hand, my eyes never leaving the intruder as I scan him for clues. His brown skin is smooth, untouched by time or imperfection. His short, dark hair is tousled just enough to suggest he doesn't care, or that he can't quite tame the wind he carries with him.

An array of silver earrings marks the curve of his pointy ears, and his wet, embroidered black and gray ensemble clings to his muscles like a sexy unitard. Any other man couldn't pull that off, but his disheveled appearance only enhances his mystique. He's a figure fresh out of some dark, forgotten fairytale, the kind where the prince isn't meant to save anyone but himself.

A shade of clear, unnatural purple swirls in his eyes, and I tighten my grip around the hilt of my dagger. The more handsome the Fae, the more trouble I'm in.

"Who are you?" I repeat. "I'll slit your throat if you don't tell me."

"How can you be sure that would kill me?" he cracks.

"Ugh." I slide the blade across the cocky Fae's throat, willing to check, and he lets out an audible gasp.

He dissipates into mist and reappears on the other side of my bed, arms held in front of him. I suspect he hadn't expected me to actually attack and that he won't give me another opportunity to get that close again.

His jaw hangs open on an incensed scoff as he runs his thumb over the fresh laceration in his throat. "Not messing around, eh? Freya warned me that you were a bit of a lunatic."

My eyes narrow. "You're on first-name basis with the bitch who stole my life?"

A dark-skinned Storm Fae with enough power to melt into a rainy cloud in the blink of an eye, and with enough gall to mention Freya can only mean one fucking thing.

My uninvited guest smiles from ear to ear. "Not really. I usually call her Ma'am. Or *Mother*."

Yep.

"You're Seth Devine."

The corners of his eyes wrinkle at the mention of his name. "It's a wonder we've never met, isn't it? The two most hated Spring Fae alive."

Freya's only son...in my bedroom. The lure of the dark, handsome stranger fades at the knowledge that this otherwise very attractive man actually came out of the woman who stole my crown. When life hands you the only child of the queen you spent most of your time plotting against, and the best of your days loathing, you make lemonade out of his very blood.

My brain calculates the quickest and cleanest way to kill him. Maim him. Filet his entrails and nail them to Freya's door.

He's as gorgeous and dissolute as the gossip suggested. The only physical attribute he got from his mother is her darker skin, whereas his bone structure and build is the hallmark of a Storm Fae. Thorald Storm—the Jackal—broke too many hearts in his prime, and his first-born, legitimate son Maddox is renowned for his rugged looks. Seth is the black sheep of the family, the illegitimate child whose turning of age rocked not one, but two royal marriages and precipitated a decade-long feud between Spring and Storm.

He slicks his wet hair over his head with crafted nonchalance. "Elio Lightbringer sent me."

The mention of the Winter King brings me pause.

Seth can't lie. I wouldn't put it past him to invoke Elio's name in vain, but it does make me curious as to why the Winter King would even deign to speak to him. He's not a very social person. "Elio knows better than to send strangers my way in the middle of the night."

"According to him, you're the best tracker in this realm."

I huff. "I'm the best tracker in all the realms."

"Then you're the woman I need."

Ah! If I had a dime for every time a man hunted me down to use me in some shape or form... I let my weapon fall at my side.

"Not if I kill you first, pretty boy," I mumble, turning my back on him in a display of self-confidence, as if I can't be bothered to track his next move. Then I face my nervous lover. "You should go, Jonas."

He raises his hand, signaling for Seth to stay back. "Not before you tell me what's going on."

"Is that your boyfriend? A police officer?" Seth teases.

"Detective," Jonas corrects him.

The two men stare each other down until a wistful smile stretches the Fae prince's lips. "Isn't he a little young for you?" he cracks.

Jonas's jaw clenches, and he exhales through his teeth, biting back whatever he was about to say. The answering twinkle of victory in Seth's gaze boils my blood, but I school my face into a mask of boredom. Seth can't know the handsome detective means anything to me, or he might use it to his advantage. And, despite all his bravado, Jonas knows he's outmatched. That's the other reason why magic-less mortals should never fall for a Fae.

Deep down, all of them regard us as freaks of nature.

"I want you both downstairs, now," I order.

"Your wish is our command," Seth quips, motioning for Jonas to lead the way.

I inhale deeply before following them down the stairs and guide my lover out through the front door without much fanfare or apology. "See you around, Detective."

If he was having second thoughts about fucking me tonight, this intrusion is certain to drive the nail into our friends-with-benefits coffin.

"Text me later, alright?" he whispers, his eyes never leaving Seth.

He leans in to peck my cheek, but I brace myself against the open door, keeping my distance.

"I'll be fine."

The door slams shut at the dismissive answer, and my heart pounds in a wild, unexpected rhythm. I spin on my heels to face Seth, lifting my chin as I eye the small puddle of blood-tinged water at his feet. "Are you going to offer me some context as to why you're drenched to the bone?"

"Nope." He shrugs off his wet jacket. The white dress shirt underneath is see-through and offers an enticing view of his stomach. "Gods, I pity the man, really. Having to stop seconds before entering you... The poor guy might never recover. You're really as cruel as the legends say."

I huff and move to the kitchenette area to prepare some tea. "Your bad timing did this. Not me."

He watches me fill the kettle with a dubious smile. "What did you expect me to do? Stand by and watch?"

I click open the portable stove and bite my bottom lip, still percolating with different brutal scenarios, all ending with Freya mourning her precious weed. The wound I carved into his neck is still gushing.

Seth pushes back through the glass bead curtains, their soft clatter echoing in tandem with the scrape of his boots against the floorboards. "It's harder to concentrate with blood raining down my neck. Give me a sec."

He heads straight for the washroom, and I follow. I don't like strangers poking around my things.

Seth picks up a fluffy white hand towel, and holds it to his wound.

I click my tongue. "This isn't some wayward inn where you can just—"

"Fix my bleeding throat?" He twists open the faucet with his free hand, rummaging through the cupboard until he finds the bandages I used earlier to patch up my leg. "I thought even a banished old witch wouldn't deny me that."

Old? My red locs tumble over my shoulder as I spin around and return to the kitchenette. I dump a spoonful of tea leaves in the infuser. "A witch, am I? Funny, I thought it was *your* filthy blood dripping all over my floor."

He's not entirely wrong, though. I've picked the perfect tea for him—poppies and skullcaps, a blend that'll dull his wits and kill his libido.

He crams his wet, tainted shirt into the stacked dryer and presses the power button. The quick, mechanical *beep* raises goosebumps on my arms.

A half-naked Seth joins me in the main room and shakes off his hands, droplets of water splashing onto my chest. "You've been out of Faerie for a long time, and from what I've heard, keeping witches as friends, family, and lovers. Who knows what malevolent blights you might have picked up?"

It's not every day a Fae prince I've never met invades my little corner of the world. It's even rarer for him to rattle me. "So...you're the kid Freya so desperately wanted to have."

His dark skin gleams under the dim light, faint traces of electricity crackling along his arms like the first whispers of a storm. "And you're the rebel granddaughter—"

"*Step*-granddaughter," I correct him, reminding him in no uncertain terms that we have no blood relation at all.

"—the rebel *step-granddaughter* who used to wear her crown."

"You mean *my* crown."

He matches my smirk tenfold. "By the spindle... You're as beautiful and delusional as they say."

I roll my eyes in response, but the back-handed compliment squeezes my belly.

This man probably grew up in a world that couldn't stop whispering about me, and that thrills me more than it should. To know he heard my name, synonymous with beauty and guile and revelry. An object of many forbidden fantasies. Outlawed. Taboo.

Only minutes ago, I was about to get fucked against a wall. Naughty promises were made. My body expected sex. It's the only reason why I'm attracted to this prince of nothing. Not the fact that his sculpted abs are on full display, or that he's the only darkling I've ever met who also possesses the lure of a Spring Fae.

I'm a sucker for tall, dark, and emotionally unavailable men, and Seth can probably smell the arousal between my thighs. That's a recipe for bad decisions, and he strikes me as the kind of man who excels in disastrous choices.

His gaze flicks to the swell of my breasts. The cold draft he dragged in—along with the weight of his stare—makes the peaks tighten beneath the black spandex. "That's some fatal attraction mojo you've got going on... Should we get it out of our system now?"

I meet his offer with an overly magnanimous smile. "Oh Seth... I'm *never* having sex with you."

"Hey, it's in our blood. We're bound to be at each other's throats, all wired and restless, until we fuck." He arches a brow, inching closer. "If it had been me up there with you earlier, I would've done things quite differently."

The fresh, airy scent of rain mingles with a metallic tang of steel at his closeness.

"And what would you have done, pray tell?"

His husky voice is full of greed and confidence as he answers, "I would have fucked you against that wall, window opened or not, storm or no storm." He rests his thumb below the angle of my jaw, right over my pulse point. "Fed you my cock in one hard stroke. Hard enough to soothe the unsatisfied hunger in your belly. Deep enough to leave a mark on your soul. Isn't that what fucking the most beautiful Fae in the worlds is all about? For her to remember you for all eternity?"

Damn... I like how he thinks.

A quickie with Jonas would have been nice, but a night of unscrupulous sex with a Fae as powerful as Seth would soothe the ache in my bones for *days* to come. Bloody hells, he's probably a very talented lover.

But I hate this man, and everything he stands for.

I lick my lips, unable to stop myself from picturing it. "And what if we were being attacked?"

"Then our attacker would've had the privilege of seeing the rapture on your face before I killed him."

I tilt my head to maintain eye contact as he draws closer, his body heat radiating from his tall, muscular, and completely off-limits frame. He grazes my waist over the soft fabric of my dress, and the small, yet incredibly intimate touch goes straight to my overheated core.

I shudder all over, dizzy with the possibility of letting him claim a prize he's clearly been daydreaming about for years, and nudge his side with my hip. "So cocky... Don't you know what having you as a hostage could buy me?"

He steadies my hips, holding me to him in a gentle but brazen manner. "You want to tie me up that badly?" he asks, his gaze fixed on my bottom lip.

I drum a slow rhythm over his pecs. "Believe me, pretty boy... If I tied you up, it wouldn't be pleasant. Not for you." I slam my open palm to the middle of his chest and shove him back, forcing him to retreat by several inches. "Now, stop wasting my time and tell me why you're here."

Bottomless lust burns in his gaze, but he doesn't bridge the gap between us. "I'm here to offer you a deal, Devi Eros."

I cross my arms over my chest. "By all means. Dazzle me."

"Oh, but I might." He flashes an annoyingly perfect row of white teeth. "Faerie is in upheaval. The magic is going haywire, and if we want to avoid an all-out war, we need to mend all the torn fences. Come back to Faerie with me, and I'll find a way to end your banishment."

When a handsome devil offers you what you crave most in this entire universe, it's hard to say no. But what is he playing at? What good would it do me to return to Faerie when I can't use my magic?

Curses do what curses will. Freya wove that curse, but she couldn't take it back even if she wanted to. Only the gods themselves would know which loose thread could unravel it and rid me of my monsters.

Perhaps Seth doesn't know a thing about the curse.

CHAPTER 7
SCOUNDREL
SETH

The gossip around the Royal Academy was that meeting Devi Eros for the first time was like being kicked in the nuts while a nymph went down on you. Nymphs are vicious beasts that don't exactly cater to the sexual needs of the Fae, so I've always struggled to understand the comparison.

But I do now.

A wild cascade of red locs flows down her back, burning as fiercely as the woman herself. Some claim she moves like an ensnarer vine, others like a serpent, but all agree on one thing—no one walks away from her unchanged. She's dangerous.

Her freckles scatter across her face like embers left behind by a dying fire. They form a constellation of deep-brown clusters across her cheekbones and the bridge of her nose, as if the gods themselves had traced their fingers there, marking her as their kin.

I wish I could kiss each and every single one of them.

The fitted bodice of her black dress molds her luscious curves, while the airy, flared skirt shifts just enough to reveal the alluring shape of her buttocks. By the looks of it, she's not wearing anything underneath. The scent of her arousal lingers in the air, and my mouth dries up, thirsty for it.

"Tea?" she asks, handing me a tiny, steaming cup with no handle.

An intricate white and blue fleur-de-lys adorns the sides, and I swallow hard. I'm in a witch's hut, being offered tea by a woman who wants my entire family dead, but still, I bring the cup to my lips. "Sure."

Steam curls into the air, carrying the earthy smell of the burgundy, honey-tinged liquid. The first breath is bright, citrusy, with a freshness that lingers at the back of my throat. Beneath it, a quiet bitterness is threaded with the taste of crushed stems and dried hay.

My cock pulses in my trousers, and while my interest lies solely in the tea I could drink off her body, I welcome the calming balm it brings. The aftertaste of poppies blooms on my tongue, faintly sweet, a whisper of something floral, like petals left to wither in the sun.

I take another sip. "Do you want to lull me to sleep, Violet?"

"Never call me that," she clips, her tone sharp.

My brow lifts. So far, she's been careful not to let me glimpse any emotion besides irritation. I can tell she's a talented poker player from the cold way she dismissed her lover and the fake, sugary smiles she uses to cover up any hint of humanity.

I offer her a dismissive shrug. "It's your name."

Violet "Devi" Eros is a name spoken like a curse in my mother's court, a myth draped in flesh and blood. Growing up, the men whispered about her beauty, even though the mere mention of her name was treason. They said her piercing eyes could worm their way through a heart with a single look, and that her smooth brown skin glowed under the sun.

Devi might have lost her crown, but she's still the one and only Queen of Hearts.

The tea helps with the lust, the pain in my groin subsiding, which I suspect was the whole point. But her matching cup tells me I wasn't the only one that needed to simmer down.

She moves away from the bar, retreating to the farthest corner of the kitchenette, her hands curling around her cup. "You're bluffing. Freya would never let me come back. She'd send her armies after me the second she learned of my return."

"She's fond of me, you know. I'm her only child."

"That's not enough."

I tilt my head. "How isolated are you? Have you heard from Faerie recently?"

Devi lifts the cup to her lips without taking a sip. "I heard about the chalice being melted, if that's what you're hinting at."

I shift to brutal honesty. "If my mother doesn't survive the wounds she suffered during the attack on the capital, it's likely that her magic will revert back to you."

Devi chews on her bottom lip, eyes half-mast, then breathes, "How do you figure that?"

"Educated guess."

She finally drinks her own brew, relieving me of the fear it might be poisoned. "Seems like I only have to sit tight and wait for her to croak, then. Why should I risk my life and return to Faerie now?" She braces her elbows on the counter between us, the motion dragging my attention down to her cleavage.

Being presented with the ultimate model of beauty and lust is a test of will. I have to play this right, or I might fall into the trap I've been running from my entire life: lusting for something I'll never be allowed to have.

I know she's my enemy, and if I ever forgot, the grievances pulsing in her silver-flecked irises would beat me over the head with it. But I can't help myself.

She's the embodiment of rebellion, wildness, and recklessness. Everything I grew up being warned against. A criminal, a temptress.

I can't look away.

"What happens if you, the Fallen Queen, regain power?" I let the words settle. "My mother's advisors once served you. They're terri-fied of reprisal. Each of them commands an army of archers, and I hear they'd rather not risk your ire. In a matter of days, it'll be open season for you. And the one who brings home your head will be hailed a hero." I set my cup down with a deliberate *clink*. "If you don't believe me, ask Elio. He wants me to escort you to Wintermere, so he can protect you."

Devi's fingers tighten around her cup. "That's why Elio sent you." Her voice is quiet now. "But why not kill me yourself?"

A humorless laugh scrapes my throat. "Err—Elio didn't just mention your tracking skills. He told me about your past. How you almost sided with the Lord of the Tides, once upon a time."

Her spine stiffens. "Elio should mind his own secrets and leave mine unspoken. You can show yourself out."

"Wait. Elio only told me because my brother is the Lord of the Tides' second-in-command, and I'm desperate to find him."

She pauses mid-turn, one brow lifting. "Maddox? That's hard to believe."

"Not Maddox. My younger brother. He's barely of age but power-ful. He was recruited into the Tides by your old friend, Morrigan."

Devi bares her teeth but sinks back onto the stool. "Rye isn't my friend. Not anymore."

Morrigan "Rye" Quinn was the reason Devi stood trial, the reason she lost everything. If she hadn't been Oberon Eros' only living heir, they'd have killed her outright.

"But you were one of them, weren't you? A Tidecaller?" I ask, testing the waters.

She purses her lips. "The Lord of the Tides used to be a close friend of mine, that I'll admit."

"Could you find him?"

"Mm. Maybe."

I tap the knife's edge of my hand against the table, knowing this is my last chance to pitch. "Faerie is splintered. Winter, Shadow, and Summer stand on one side, while the Red Queen has renewed her alliance with Ethan Lightbringer. My mother will cling to her crown until her dying breath, and she's close with Ethan, too. Storm is poised to break the tie. The winning side will decide how the rebels are dealt with, how our laws, alliances, and magics will be reshaped now that the Eternal Chalice is no more. Whatever happens in the next few months, Faerie will never be the same again."

"You've got that right." She pauses like she's choosing her next words carefully. "The Tidecallers used to advocate for democracy, but the way magic works makes passing down crowns impossible."

I take another swig of tea. "I don't disagree that democracy wouldn't work, but why impossible? You passed down your crown, didn't you?"

Some secrets never make it into books. They say becoming king is like having your eyes opened to the Faerie sight a second time, and Devi is one of the only people alive, besides the seven reigning monarchs, who truly knows what that means.

A shiver quakes through her. "Let's just say that for the magic not to fester, the roots running through the earth and culminating at each realm's Hawthorn need a living vessel to enact their gods' will. Whether that's a king or a queen, the vessel is bound to it forever, no matter what. And as long as the seven crowns exist, people will fight over them."

"Seven crowns are better than one. Doing away with them altogether would bring nothing but ruin. We saw what happened when the Mists' Hawthorn was scorched. I wouldn't wish that on my worst enemy." I pause, thinking of what the Mist Fae endured. "My brother is chasing a pipe dream. Destroying the Eternal Chalice wiped out our only chance to elect new rulers. Now, the gods' will determines who takes the throne." I lean in, almost reaching for her hand but stopping at the last second. "We have to lead by example, show that even enemies can come together for the greater good."

She doesn't soften.

I clear my throat, wary of her distrust. I don't want to oversell it either and make it seem as though I'm trying to manipulate her. "I'm a pragmatist, and I don't want to live in a world where Ethan Light-bringer and his Red Priestesses rise to power again. Do you?"

She purses her lips. "Are you plotting against your own mother?"

"I'm saying that with your help, we might sway the crowns' response, negotiate a truce with the Tidecallers, and end this war before it begins."

"And what do you get out of it?"

I catch a grin from surfacing. "Aren't I allowed to have strong, altruistic beliefs?"

She snorts.

I tilt my head back, my gaze flying up to the ceiling in surrender. "Ugh. I love my brother. I don't want him executed, and I certainly don't want to see Faerie razed by war, but I have no real seat at the table as it is." I wet my lips. "With you by my side, the Spring Court will be united once more, and stronger for it. The High Fae that are still secretly on your side will rally, and when my mother dies, you'll be queen again."

Her eyes slip shut, and she licks her lips, the scenario I'm proposing both sweet and forbidden. "But you wouldn't want Freya to die at my hands," she murmurs.

"Of course not. But she's not at her peak anymore, and we both know what happens to monarchs who aren't. Her days are numbered either way."

Her gaze strips me bare. She's not looking at me as a man but as something to be used, measured for worth in her grand scheme. The cold precision with which she studies me is unsettling, like she's already decided what I am. A stepping stone. A tool. A means to an end.

She's not at all the tamed, reasonable, and defeated monarch people believe her to be. She's hungry for more. In her eyes, I'm just another piece to be moved. But gods help her if she thinks I'll let her control me that easily.

"How would you propose getting around the issue of me being banned from Faerie?" she asks.

"You've been back since your banishment."

"Never long enough for it to matter."

I lick my lips in anticipation. "There's one thing Spring folk value more than power. My mother included."

"A good fuck?" Devi cracks.

I know she'll think I'm mad for mentioning it, but she'll be forced to recognize my genius. "True love."

"But we don't love each other," she counters, as amused and skeptical as I expected her to be.

I step closer, my voice softening, magic sparking from my skin. "Nobody knows that but us."

"We couldn't lie about it," she says, her pupils dilating despite her calm, dismissive tone. She narrows her eyes, leaning in, her breath warm against my cheek. "Or are you proposing I shoot you with a love arrow?"

Her heavenly scent floods my senses—a rose set ablaze, spiced with saffron, kissed by sunlight, and shadowed by a trace of ash.

"I'm offering you my hand in marriage," I declare with a verve I didn't know I had. "You must have thought about it before now." I gesture to the hearth and the rowan-paneled walls. "You've been stuck here, brooding in this... dump for eight decades. True love reigns supreme in Spring, and marriages have saved more than a few Fae from ruin. If you were married, even just for show, to Freya's only son, how could anyone deny you a second chance?"

"Your brain is awfully skewed by your own sense of self-importance."

"I'm right, and you know it. What do you say, Devi Eros? Will you marry me?"

She smiles, her voice warm with the rumble of a genuine laugh. "In your dreams, pretty boy."

"I'll take that as a *maybe*." It was a little reckless to phrase it like that, and not ease into like I'd planned, but my lips twitch.

"Is this a habit of yours? Tying up all your romantic relationships with a quid pro quo?" she asks.

"Deals are easier to manage than feelings."

She nods in agreement, but before I can sell her on my idea further, a ball of movement the size of a fist zooms toward me, almost hitting me square in the face.

"Who do you think you are, you sleazy dick?" the ball shouts, inches from my face. "Talking about marriage as though it's on the table, when we don't even know you? The nerve!"

Electricity crackles along my skin, fading as I register the intruder as a small Faeling.

Devi's Faeling.

I've read about him, but I didn't expect him to be so...outspoken.

He wears a deep purple frock with golden embroidery on the lapels and cuffs, paired with a neatly buttoned waistcoat. A crisp white shirt peeks out from beneath, fastened with a miniature cravat pinned by a bronze brooch. His trousers taper into polished little boots, while leather cuffs encase his hands, adding a roguish touch to his otherwise refined look. Delicate wings shimmer at his back, peppered in Faerie dust.

Faelings are born out of a royal Fae's first laugh and are tied to their masters for life. The needs and flaws of the one they serve shape their personalities, and their souls are so entwined that Faelings wither when separated from their master for too long.

"You should kneel before her, if you have any respect at all," he adds.

"Percy..."

"She's Devi Eros, the Queen of Hearts, the devil of Spring, the most powerful archer, carver, and groomer these realms have ever seen. Her blood flows with the beauty and vitality of the Secret Spring, as well as the li—"

"Percy," Devi cuts in.

"And way above your league," the Faeling corrects himself, but I take note of the strange exchange.

"And who are you?" I ask, half-amused, half-terrified.

"I'm Percival Batten."

I incline my head in greeting, the proper and polite way to address him, as so many other Fae treat them like annoying little pests. "Nice to meet you, Faeling. I'm Seth Devine."

"I know who you are and what you're after, prince of nowhere at all."

"Be good, Percy," Devi scolds him. "Seth's harmless."

The corners of my mouth fall. *Harmless? Ouch!*

"Are you serious?" The Faeling waves a dismissive hand up and down me, with the snobbery of a royal stylist. "Him?"

Devi shrugs, her gaze softer than before. "Why not?"

"You've lost your mind." The little ball of disapproval flies off in a huff, and I follow his blurry shape until he disappears into an alpine weather house, where both the blonde girl holding an umbrella and the sunny gentleman take refuge inside the bauble.

"Percy is very protective of me," Devi explains.

I give her an understanding nod. "As any Faeling should be. He's not wrong that his mistress inspired legends."

Her smile vanishes in a flash. "You know the thing about legends? They're all set in the past. I'm ready to live in the present again and return home."

"I'm your ticket back to Faerie, if you're smart enough to take me up on it."

She gives me that look again, the one that sends a shiver down my spine. "It appears you are."

"Let's do this again. Properly. To appease your loyal servant." I kneel in front of her, and as soon as my knee touches the ground, her eyes dance with greed—and something else. More serious than amusement, but more subtle than surprise. Something that makes my gut squeeze under her scrutiny, her beauty even more obvious from this angle, as if her face was chiseled to be idolized from just this view.

"Devi Eros, Queen of Hearts, devil of Spring, and most illustrious magic wielder. Will you marry me?"

A quiet, offended sigh tears out of the alpine weather house. "That was only *slightly* better," Percy whines.

Devi bites her bottom lip, and I'm almost sure I'm about to lose her, so I pivot. "We don't have to get married right away," I say quickly.

She stands on her tip toes to open the highest cupboard, and the movement calls attention to her perfect waist. The angle allows me a particularly scandalous view of her smooth thighs, all the way up to the curve of her bare ass. "Hold on. If we're truly about to discuss a scheme of this magnitude, I'm going to need a stronger drink."

A giddy smile threatens to break across my face, but I rein it in, unwilling to betray my emotions. I think I've just convinced the most beautiful, powerful, and criminal Fae to be my fiancée. It's not every day you get engaged to a living legend, let alone one you've fantasized about since puberty.

I've always been a scoundrel, but this might be my best con yet.

CHAPTER 8
TWISTER
DEVI

My heart pounds in my ears as I pour two glasses of Nether cider. "Careful, pretty boy. You might just fall for me for real."

"Not a chance," he says warmly. "But, was that a yes?"

"First, we need ground rules."

"I agree." He staggers back to his feet, his brows pulled together at the effort. I bet he thought it would be easy to stand after kneeling in front of *me*.

It's not the first time I've pretended to be engaged, so it shouldn't be too hard to pull off. Only Seth is my nemesis, not my friend, and I still want him dead.

Details for future me to deal with, I guess.

"First rule: If we don't want the other royals to brand you as a traitor, too, we have to convince them that we actually have feelings for each other. This can't be viewed as *just* a political scheme, or they'll fight us at every turn."

Seth's jaw drops, but he quickly shakes off the shock of my statement. "And what if my mother asked us to wed immediately?"

I raise a brow. "I think Freya will hope to change your mind, no?"

"I don't know. I wouldn't put it past her to agree to the marriage only to have you killed after the wedding night," he says with an apologetic grimace.

"I wouldn't put it past you, either. You'll have to earn my trust, first."

His gaze flies to the sky. "You can rest easy. If I betrayed you, Elio would have my head."

"That's a small relief, indeed." I chuckle, but it's a low, dangerous sound. "You're not the first to come to me with such a proposition, you know. The current political landscape could prove a unique opportunity for us both, but we have to be ready for anything."

A strangled huff whizzes out of his lungs.

Freya will *burn* when she hears this. The humiliation... to have her precious son, illegitimate or not, parading around Faerie with the one woman she loathes above all others. Him advocating for the criminal she banished, the fallen queen she tried so desperately to replace, but fell short at every turn. The young girl she betrayed making a comeback decades later, smarter and more beautiful. I'm salivating.

The thought fills me with a dark, sinful pleasure. Her lover dead, her political influence crumbling, and her only child chasing *me*, the very embodiment of everything she despises. This bogus engagement will be a deep thorn in her side.

But for it to work, Seth has to believe he actually has a chance to rule by my side, even though I'd rather die than marry Freya's heir. Still, I'm not lying when I say this is a unique opportunity.

"Second rule: No side pieces. No lovers. You'll have to keep it in your pants until this arrangement falls apart, or until the wedding night, whichever comes first." I keep the wording deliberately vague, unsure whether I want to include myself in that rule.

"And does that no-sex until marriage rule include you?" he challenges me.

I craft an enigmatic smile. "There's no marriage without consummation, no? We'll have to get naked at some point."

He tries very hard to hide it, but I see the way his pupils dilate, the way his abs tighten... He's interested, as he should be. I'm Devi Eros.

"But not before?" he insists, forcing me to take a stand.

"Not before."

While he waits on the wedding night, I can trust he won't sink a blade between my ribs. I'll keep him dangling, half-starved, for as long as it takes. I'm not naive enough to think this isn't some tangled scheme to get my powers. Whether or not his mother's in on it, Seth wants my magic. But if I hope to win at this game, I'll drive him to want my body more.

And the off-chance possibility of breaking his heart for real? Delicious.

He keeps staring, and I can practically see the dirty scenarios playing in his mind.

"You're not going to rock my world, you know? Very few men have," I taunt him.

He licks his lips. "I take that as a challenge."

"That no-sex-with-other-women rule is non-negotiable, so I'll need you to swear to it," I add, suppressing a grin.

"Are you a very possessive woman?" he teases.

"I'm the Queen of Hearts. It wouldn't be believable for my fiancé to have a wandering eye."

"Fine, but I won't be bound by that promise if, as you say, the arrangement falls apart. If we aren't wed in let's say...a year, or if you break it off, this no-sex rule falls apart."

He doesn't want me to trick him, but I'm baffled he'd offer a year. He doesn't strike me as a Spring Fae who's ever been celibate for long, so he probably doesn't understand the toll abstinence can take.

"Alright," I concede.

"Then I swear I won't touch another woman until our wedding night, or until the aforementioned terms are met," he says the words lightly, as though it doesn't cost him anything, and my heart skips a beat. He certainly didn't include me in that promise.

Magic pulses between us, sealing his vow.

The late night bleeds into the early hours of the morning as Seth and I sit in my shop, working out the minutia of our deal. How to play it in front of the other royals and arguing whether we should ease them into it or not. The dim glow of the hearth flickers over a growing pile of empty bottles and the verdant glint of Nether cider in our glasses, the air thick with distrust and intrigue.

The dryer finally dings, and Seth stands up to retrieve his shirt.

"I'm supposed to take you straight from here to Wintermere. An emergency meeting is planned between the seven crowns." He rubs the curve of his jaw. "Elio thought it best to summon them before paranoia completely settled in."

"Elio doesn't know about your insane proposal, does he?"

"No."

"Good. He's not a big fan of arranged weddings."

"Funny coming from a man who's had dozens." Seth huffs out a laugh. "But that's all in the past. He's in love now, and his new wife is a doppelgänger of my cousin Iris, did you hear?"

I tip my chin in affirmation.

"She's quite something." A secret smile touches Seth's full lips, his eyes cast down, and I get the feeling he's fond of this woman. Maybe even enamored with her, which irks me, given the circumstances. Iris was gorgeous, of course, but her affair with Elio's brother ended with her dead, and the fallout dragged everyone involved into decades of misery.

I send a discreet sliver of magic forward, probing Seth's heart, searching for the depth of his affection, but he's harder to read than most. Storm Fae keep their emotions hidden behind the clouds, their magic shielding them from scrutiny. I catch only brief, shallow glimpses of his emotions, not enough to hold onto. It leaves me unsatisfied, unsure if he's hiding the truth or if there's nothing deeper to find.

"Do you have a thing for Elio's wife?" I tease, still unsure how to interpret the faint traces of jealousy emanating from him. "That's dangerous territory to tread."

"Not a crush, no." He tilts his head. "But I envy their marriage. Elio's a lucky bastard. He's known true love not once, but twice."

"His first marriage wasn't so lucky, trust me. As much as I loved Iris, she really destroyed him. Spring folks worship true love, swear by it even, but how many of us manage it in our lifetime? Very few, and the rest are stuck longing for something they'll never have."

Seth quiets down even more. "Is that why you crafted love arrows strong enough to pierce a Fae's heart? Are you a romantic?"

"I crafted the arrows because it had never been done before. Because I had to prove myself at every turn. No one could accuse *me* of being a romantic."

"Don't you see how flawed it was, in hindsight, to manipulate your peers?"

"We manipulate mortals' feelings every day, and they don't live meaningless lives because of it."

"When the archer does their job right. Otherwise, it's not a gift, but a curse." He pauses for a moment. "And mortals don't know they're being manipulated. That counts for something."

I shake my head. He's totally missing the point. "I didn't mean for anyone to steal my arrows and use them for their own greed. I was matching consenting couples, which is entirely different from an arrow thief swindling an unsuspecting Fae king into marriage. My arrows were designed to ease the loneliness of arranged unions, but like all powerful tools, they can be misused. I shouldn't have been blamed for what Rye did, and if Freya hadn't been scheming against me—if my lieutenants had any backbone at all—I wouldn't have been banished.

Seth devours me with his eyes as though he finds my rant... delectable. "You're so passionate. I've known quite a few princesses, but none seem to spark the same fascination—"

"I'm no princess," I interrupt him. "I was *Queen*."

The corners of his mouth quirk, but he doesn't argue. He leans back on his stool, swirling the last of his cider, watching me.

My stomach flip-flops. It's been years since I've gossiped with a Spring Fae, let alone one as powerful and objectively attractive as Seth.

"How come you're named Devine and not Heart?" My exile started before he was born, and I never understood why Freya refused him her surname.

Seth waves dismissively. "Oh, it was all part of her strategy. She pretended I was the illegitimate child of her mortal lover, Garrett Devine, hoping to protect my real father's reputation and marriage. Mortal lovers and their bastards are not so unusual in Spring, as you must know. They don't count, so to speak."

"What made her change her mind?"

He rubs his jaw, looking more defeated than pensive. "She admitted to me being a full-blooded Fae when my Storm magic manifested. The Royal Academy doesn't invite half-Fae to their trials and requested proof of parentage. With me being a dual-wielder, my mother decided to put my future above her lover's need for secrecy and admitted publicly to the affair."

I nod, remembering all too well the elitist rules of the academy. "You think she acted out of love? I always thought she was too proud not to show you off, or that she hoped to destroy Thorald's marriage in the process."

His lips purse to the side, and I get the feeling he's actually considering the question and not at all ticked off by it. "Who knows why my mother does what she does? She wasn't wrong about me having the pedigree to pass the academy's trials, though." He takes a long, dejected gulp of cider. "I was an outcast there. Too frivolous for the darklings, and too dark for the Light Fae. That's when they coined the 'prince of nowhere at all' nickname. It's difficult to have the power but not the pedigree to become king. Must be hard to grasp for a first-born, golden child."

A sardonic grimace tugs at my lips, but I lean back in a stretch to hide it.

I don't pity Seth for his fucked-up childhood—I beat him in every aspect—but it reinforces my belief that the very concept of illegitimacy is idiotic at best and toxic at worst. I could never tell him, but we have more in common than he realizes.

My intoxicated gaze keeps drifting to him. His posture is effortless, yet there's an unspoken readiness in the way his shoulders are held, as though he's always prepared for a brawl. The fabric of his shirt pulls taut across his chest, and the line of his jaw sharpens when he speaks.

I shouldn't notice these things, so I gulp down the rest of my cider and climb to my feet. "We should get going. I need a minute alone. Just...wait here."

The stairs creak under my weight as I make my way back upstairs. The loft bedroom is quiet, but my pulse thrums loud and fast, dizzy with the promise of impending change. For eight decades, this room has been mine. Cracked walls. Scuffed floorboards. Shelves lined with books I've read three times over just to dull the sting of time.

I crouch beside the bed and pry up a loose floorboard, revealing the hidden cache beneath. Glass vials glint in the moonlight. Tinctures. Ingredients. Tools of a witch's trade, wrapped in handkerchiefs or tucked into velvet pouches. I retrieve them with careful fingers, checking each one, then tuck them into the small leather overnight bag I used to carry around when Jonas and I were still a couple. Funny how it's the only piece of luggage I own. But I was never meant to leave for long—not without risking my life.

For years, this place was a cocoon. A place to wait. To grieve. To heal.

But I didn't come here to wither and die.

I might not survive what comes next—and I'm weirdly okay with that. I slip Nickolas's invisibility amulet into the bag first, followed by my Shadow mask, a vial of Spring water, and a few other trinkets I've collected over the years. Each one a spell in disguise, a carefully chosen weapon. Many Fae sneer at such tools, dismissing them as parlor tricks. But I can't use my own magic without conjuring monsters from the ether, so I'll survive on whatever scraps I can borrow.

My fingers brush over Mabel's spindle. For a moment, I consider taking it with me. Instead, I tuck it deep into my warded cache, out of sight but not forgotten. It'll be safe there, warded against tracking spells and out of sight.

Percy hovers beside me, wings twitching. "We're really going with him, huh?"

Dim city light filters through the window, painting long shadows across the wooden floor. I move to the window, scanning the street below for any sign of the cupids. Timing my escape is crucial. "We've been waiting decades for an opportunity to get back in the game. This is it."

He hesitates, his tiny arms crossed. "You should discuss it with Mabel first."

"Mabel has already given up on Faerie."

"She has a point."

I shake my head. "We can't stand by while our homeland is under attack. If a war is coming, we have to help the common folk so they don't get caught in the crossfire of ambitious, ruthless, and privileged royals."

Percy huffs. "But we don't need him."

"We'll use him, that's all."

"I saw how you looked at him earlier." His voice drops. "You want to hurt Freya through him, but it's not going to make you feel better. You're letting your double-H guide you."

"Double-H?"

"Hatred and horniness. You crave two things, *diamantay*—sex and vengeance. And not necessarily in that order. Seth is the embodiment of both. You have a crush on him, I can tell."

"A crush? I *stabbed* him."

Percy raises his hands in a mix of defeat and incomprehension. "Foreplay, apparently. You're totally attracted to him."

I freeze, my fingers tightening around the strap of the bag. "Am not."

"Are too."

I glare at him, but Percy never backs down.

"You want to mess him up, yet you fancy him. It's a rubbish plan," he insists.

Arguing with him feels like arguing with myself. He's not exactly a voice of reason—too protective, overly cautious at times. Yet he becomes downright murderous when we're under attack, playing both angel and devil on my shoulder. He knows me better than anyone, so whenever we disagree, I feel this annoying pang in my sternum.

But I'm done waiting. I've spent too long rotting in exile, watching the world move without me. Faerie is calling me home, and this time, I won't be checked out of my own chessboard.

"Seth's hot, but I'm not about to fawn over Freya's son. We'll use him as long as he serves us and discard him when the time comes. Besides, the crowns will never give their assent for us to marry."

"And what if they do?"

"They won't."

"Stranger things have happened..."

Again, the possibility of being linked for life to Freya's son sets my teeth on edge. But a new, insidious scenario pops into my brain. If the seven crowns somehow gave permission for us to wed, I'd be free to shut this gorgeous Fae's mouth with a kiss and ride his cock to my broken heart's content...

"Be good," Percy says quickly, like he followed my thoughts down the gutter.

I change from the skimpy dress, opting for a form-fitting burgundy turtleneck and black jeans, and meet Seth downstairs.

The dark Fae is inspecting the saggy tea leaves at the bottom of the teapot as though he's hoping to read his future in them. His gaze darts up from the pot, and he raises a skeptical brow at the ruby-incrusted mask covering my face. "Didn't they confiscate your Shadow mask when you were banished?"

"Of course they did." The weight of the mask over the bridge of my nose sparks excitement in my blood. "This is a new one."

Seth studies me. The moonlight streaming through the bay windows of the shop deepens the purple flecks of his irises, and I swallow hard.

"You used to fuck him, no? The Shadow King," he asks.

"That's old news."

"And Elio?"

I roll my eyes, suppressing a disgusted grimace. "Are you slut-shaming me right now? I thought you were a modern, enlightened man, not one of those silly Storm Fae traditionalists—"

"I'm not judging you," he says quickly, tipping his chin. "Just wondering how any of them could let you slip through their fingers. You're a catch, witch. Makes me wonder what's wrong with them."

"Who says I wanted to marry?"

He shrugs. "Every Fae wants to marry. It's a double-your-power-for-free card, and very few resist the appeal for long."

He's not wrong. When a king dies, the magic they inherited from the realm's Hawthorn leaves their significant other forever, but the magic they were born with stays with their spouse for life. That's how Freya inherited my grandsire's god-given power and became strong enough to compete with me.

It's hard to refuse the hand of an old king when you know you'll get to keep his magic forever, when every dead husband means accu-mulating power. I've always judged Freya for the way she rose to power and held myself to higher standards, but old, serial widows are not regarded with the same distrust as single, independent women. What a world.

I slip into my rain coat and pull the hood over my head, tying the sash at my waist.

"There's no mirror here, I gather. Not even a warded one," Seth muses.

I let out an amused huff. "Who do you think I am? I'm not stupid enough to keep a mirror in my home."

He tugs on one end of the loose knot in the sash of my raincoat. "Don't bother with that, I can get rid of this weather—"

"No," I answer too quickly. The heavy storm will make it harder for the cupids to track me. "Leave it be."

I keep the breast pocket open for Percy, who flies into it with a resentful pout. "We love the rain," he adds for Seth's benefit. Faeling can lie, a fact that is not well-known amongst the Fae.

Seth observes us with a trace of wonder and curiosity. "As you wish."

Heavy rain glides down the waterproof fabric as we make our way down the street. The dim glow of the street lamps casts menacing shadows across the cobblestones, each of them surrounded by a halo, and I glimpse at the red clouds overhead.

The distant hum of wings on the wind rakes through my core. Seth's expression darkens, and the energy shifts around him. His fingers twitch, barely a movement, but enough for me to know he picked up on it.

We finally reach the laundrette, and Percy flies out of my pocket to make the window panes permeable, allowing us to slip inside unnoticed. The scents of old detergent and bleach assault me.

Four rows of washers and driers are separated by two alleys, and a huge mirror gleams against the far wall.

"Ready?" Seth asks.

"Let's make it quick."

He plasters his own mask over his eyes, but just as we're about to cross the mirror, he grabs my arm, stopping me. My breath catches. *Shit. They're almost here.*

"Third rule: you have to trust me. We can't hope to fool a bunch of powerful royals and convince them that we're engaged if you're constantly shutting me out. Just now, you were checking the street for something, and those red storm clouds are suspicious as fuck. What are they? I can keep a secret."

"So can I," I mutter, trying to move past him.

His hand curls tighter around my upper arm. "What was that sound before? Tell me."

I shove him forcefully through the mirror, catching him off guard, and leap after him into the frozen depths of the sceawere. Thick, insidious ribbons of mist ghost along my cheeks, spooking me.

The sceawere, the space between worlds, is usually frosty and clear, like a sunny, windy winter afternoon, but not today. An eerie, creeping mist gathers around us, its silvery rolls swallowing us deeper with every breath, each step heavy and sluggish. The thick fog blurs my vision, and the ground beneath me shifts with an unsettling fluidity.

"I might be cocky, but you're downright mental," Seth chokes out, peeling himself off the bottom of the in-between.

My skin prickles, a chill running down my spine. Seth's jaw is clenched, his masked face scanning the haze, his breaths shallow. There's no sound, no sign of movement, but the hairs on the back of my neck stand on end.

"Whatever you were running from followed us," Seth whispers.

"That's impossible."

Cupids can't follow me through the glass to enter the sceawere. That's their one weakness. This is something else. A growl echoes through the mist, too close and yet coming from all angles at once. My pulse spikes, the ensuing silence raising goosebumps on my arms. Seth and I instinctively press our backs to one another, searching for the source of the sound.

The nightmare preying on us starts as a shadow, creeping into the edges of my vision like a growing stain on a glass mirror. A monstrous wolf takes shape, its spiky fur shimmering, its eyes burning with malice. The edges of its body are slightly translucent, but the crack of its joints as it lowers into a hunter's crouch leaves me no doubt that the apparition is solid enough to maim and kill us.

It lunges at me without a second's hesitation. I raise my arm in front of me to protect myself, and the sharp edge of its canines tears through my jacket, taking hold of my arm with its powerful jaw. A dull ache spreads across my arm, but I clench my fist, sending a burst of light forward to blind the wolf. The beast whimpers, opening its jaw and stumbling back, but the flash is quickly swallowed by the heavy mist, and only provides a quick diversion.

Seth swerves around me, his hands crackling with energy. Lightning snakes from his fingers, the bolt-shaped arches slithering toward one another and merging into a sword of pure electricity. He swings the newly-formed blade at the beast but misses the mark, a meaningless chunk of fur separating from the creature.

I check on my bite wound, relieved to see the nightmare's teeth only punctured the skin instead of tearing it off the bone. Hopefully, using my magic in the in-between will not create special, sceaware-adapted cupids, but I've never tried it. I never had to.

I dig the balls of my feet into the almost-liquid terrain, gasping for breath, and summon a long Light dagger in my palm. Fighting here is like wading through mud. Each movement drags, and my limbs tremble from the effort. The swings of Seth's lightning sword are slow and labored, but the glowing, crackling weapon draws the beast's attention away from me.

The wolf leaps toward Seth, but he manages to side-step away from the beast and retaliates with a quick strike. A splash of black blood sprays his face, coming from the wolf's front limb, and the nightmare howls, jerking around to leap again.

I dash under the wolf as it flies through the air, angling my blade up to slit its jugular vein and carotid artery, using its own momentum to cut deep. The dagger shakes in my grip, but I hold on, knuckles white. Tar-like blood drenches my hands and arms and freckles my masked face.

Seth's sword cleaves the nightmare's body in two as it collides at his feet, reducing it to shadows that dust into the air.

Mist still presses around us, but the beast is gone.

I dismiss my weapon, my entire body shaking from the cold and sheer claustrophobia of it all. "By Eros, you weren't exaggerating when you said the magic was going haywire."

"Didn't you believe what I said? Faerie's fucked."

I tug on my raincoat's pocket, Percy still tucked safely inside. "Are you alright, Percy?"

"Five by five."

Seth's gaze falls to my right hand. "You're a dual wielder too? How did I not know that?"

"I dabble in Light magic," I grumble.

He frowns at my grumpy answer. "Is one of your ancestors from the Sun Court?"

"None of your business."

"You really don't trust me at all."

"What can I say? I'm not a very trusting person."

"Good job with the wolf." He reaches for his neck and swallows hard, as though he remembers exactly how close I came to slitting his throat, too. "You don't shy away from violence, do you?"

"I inherited an unhealthy taste for bloodshed and destruction from my sire."

Seth's brows lift. "Sire? Ouch. I'm the bastard son of a king who disavowed me, and I still called him my father."

I press my lips together, debating whether or not to elaborate, but I can't hold it in. "Believe me, the man who sired me isn't worthy of the name."

He tilts his head to the side. "Wasn't he a crow, your father? Some common Fae from the Shadowlands? Is that why you're so... direct?"

He means rude, and I crack a smile. "Maybe."

No one can know who my true father is, but Seth's been told the well-crafted lie my grandfather had catered to for decades before he died.

"I heard he lost his marbles after your mother died, started spewing venom about the seven crowns, and died in some prison or another?"

"If that's what you heard, then it must be true." I grab the strings of glass inside the sceaware to *play* the address for the Winter castle, much as one would play a melody on a violin, using the tattoos inked on my lower arm.

Seth hovers closer. "Let me do it. I just came from Wintermere."

I brace the tips of my fingers on his upper arm and shove him off in a precise and deliberate fashion. "I'm perfectly capable of finding my way, thank you."

But, as it turns out, I'm not quite as efficient as I'd hoped in locating Elio's study. Despite my attempts to enter the passage I use every year when I visit the Winter King, I can't find it, which means it's either been destroyed, or a new set of wards is blocking the way. I keep my face relaxed not to let Seth know anything is wrong and continue my search. But after many failed attempts, my pulse quickens, and I handle the strings a little harder, making the many glimpses of the different portals leading to Wintermere blur together.

"Are you sure you don't want my help?" Seth cracks, all smiles.

"Gods, stop breathing down my neck, I'll find it," I grit through my teeth.

Traveling the sceaware takes much skill, concentration, and patience, but it's also a bit of an art. For the life of me, I can't find the mirror I'm looking for, warded or not. I keep landing back at the one right next to the Winter castle, like I'm being forced in this direction by some unknown power, and I motion for Seth to move forward. "Let's get out of here before another wolf shows up."

Seth leans in. "That wasn't an answer. About your father."

I give him a nasty side-eye. "It was as much of an answer as you're going to get."

"Oh, this," he waves a hand between us, "is going to be fun."

CHAPTER 9
WINTER BLUES
DEVI

Seth nips at my heels on our way out of the sceawere. The sensation that comes with stepping out of the glass isn't what it used to be. Less icy, but just as uneasy, and more claustrophobic. Mist gathers on all sides, briefly blinding me, and I feel as though I'm being both cradled and smothered by a cloud. When the smoke clears, I suppress a cough.

The wrought-iron gates separating Tundra, the winter capital, from the castle grounds tower high above me as I blink away the strange lull, the glacial air of Wintermere immediately numbing my extremities.

Two twelve-foot-tall mirrors flank the ornate gates, embedded in the stone walls on either side, one of which we just threaded. The gate isn't truly meant to keep anyone out, but to separate the living from the dead. The reapers that walk in and out of the castle aren't meant to cohabitate with the villagers, and they use the network of tunnels underneath the mountain to do their duty before returning to their Ice City.

The scent of spiced wine and roasting meat soothes my pulse, and the rhythmic crunch of snow under heavy boots chases away the ominous blur of the sceaware.

The city sprawls at the foot of the mountains. Thousands of common Winter folk—or Moths, as we call them—live here, steps away from the most powerful Fae King. It's not the middle of the night here, but close to sunset. The narrow streets are alive with merchants and children fresh out of school. Dozens of miners in thick fur cloaks make their way home or to the taverns after a grueling day of work.

The Winter Castle looms over the city, its three snow-crusted towers obscuring the light of the dying sun, turning gold to blue. A fortress as old as Faerie itself, it's a place where power is not measured in courtly games but in endurance—in how long one can withstand the cold without breaking. Here, death is only another rite of passage, not an ending.

Moths do not whisper prayers to keep the darkness away. Instead, they welcome it and weave it into the fabric of their stories and songs. Even the children are not kept out of death's reach, playing hide-and-seek in the graveyard that's sandwiched between the forest and the castle walls. They run among the tombstones of their ancestors, their laughter echoing through the air like a hymn to the inevitable.

Four castle guards in sleeveless gray bodysuits accost us, emerging from the guardhouse next to the gates. As they approach, their hands settle on the hilts of the swords strapped to their hips, grips tightening with each step.

The leader flaunts a Royal Guard insignia and braces his arm across his chest. "Please identify yourselves."

The streets of Tundra are amongst the safest in the realm, so it's unusual for this neighborhood, the one closest to the castle and home to the wealthier classes, to be so well-guarded. I remove the hood of my rain jacket, unveiling my red locs and a face that the moths in these parts will not soon forget.

The royal guard pauses, his gaze immediately flying to the ground. "Your Highness. I'm sorry, I didn't recognize you."

Anywhere else, I'd be greeted with torches and pitchforks, but Wintermere's soldiers know their king is fond of me.

I rub a bit of warmth back into my hands. "Take us to the king."

"At once, of course." The man bows at the waist and escorts us past the gates and up the hill.

The buzz of the city fades as we ascend the winding staircases of the first battlement to reach the castle parapet. Despite the cold, I can't help but wonder at the sight before me. The Lake of Souls stretches out in the distance, a vast expanse of turquoise ice gleaming in the fading sunlight, its surface as smooth as the glass of a giant mirror. Watching it, I wonder if I was born in the wrong kingdom. Would I have thrived here, where power does not come from alliances and politics, but with one's ability to face death head-on? A blue rose?

Then again, I was always too hot-blooded for ice magic.

The guard leads us inside the maze of tall cedar hedges, the firs offering shelter from the wind. Its twists and turns take us to the king's gardens and the Hawthorn, toward the place where my friend Iris rests for all eternity, not far from where I saw her die. The ice statue erected in her name stands tall on the other side of the clearing, and I pause.

The guard takes a sharp right toward the closest entrance, but Seth hangs back, waiting for me.

My heels dig into the snow as I glimpse at Iris's coffin, the transparent glass pane on top turning orange in the twilight. I'm tempted to march over there to pay my respects, but with Seth watching, I feel intensely vulnerable.

Before I can make up my mind, the guard clears his throat to get my attention. "The royal chief of staff is right in here, Your Highness."

"Are you okay?" Seth asks quietly.

"I'm fine." I shake off the nostalgia and enter behind Seth into Sarafina's office.

The guard holds the door open for me, but he doesn't follow, and quickly closes the door behind us.

Sara looks up from her white birch desk. "Seth! You found her!" She jolts to her feet and sweeps her shoulder-length silver hair behind her ears. "Elio will be so pleased."

Seth beams at the royal chief of staff. "Hope you're glad to see me, too, Sara."

Sara comes over to peck his cheeks, and an uncomfortable itch blooms between my shoulder blades. *Are they friends?*

"You sent a man after me, Sara? I thought you were woman enough to do the chasing yourself," I tease.

She blushes at that, greeting me with an awkward handshake, her life-long crush on me a constant obstacle between us. "Welcome, Devi. I wish I could have come for you myself, but I couldn't leave Wintermere as things are," Sara explains in lieu of an apology. "Seth might have told you, but we're expecting the seven crowns by tomorrow."

"So Tundra is to be the next capital of Faerie? What does the new Summer King think of that?" I ask.

Sara braces both hands on her hips, clearly irked by the subtext of my question. "Aidan understands that Wintermere offers a prime strategic meeting point in any or all further dealings with the Tide-callers. It's not like there were other options—the Solar Cliffs are too hard to reach, males are not welcome in the Red Forest, and night-mares spilled out of the Dreaming even though we're done with Morheim, making the Shadowlands very dangerous indeed. Spring politics are weakened by Freya's injuries, and Storm's End is still reeling from the loss of their King. It's not like we planned this, you know. Elio couldn't care less about Wintermere being the next capital."

I open my palms in surrender, suppressing a smile. "Easy, I'm just messing with you." Sara's so easy to rile up, it's hard to resist, but I take the edge off and add, "I also heard you finally got Elio to stop being a baby and fess up on his true feelings. Well done."

"Well... You know how he is," she stammers at the praise.

I hide my hands in my raincoat's pockets. "I sure do. You're a Saint to put up with him."

Sara kept me from making a terrible mistake with Elio when the Winter King asked me to shoot him with a love arrow. I only wanted to offer his yearly Yule Pageant bride a sweet wedding night—some fireworks before the eventual funeral. But turns out Elio was secretly in love with another woman. A love so pure it broke the curse he was under. Though, until his new wife beats the odds and survives the whole year, I'm not sure I'll quite believe it.

Compared to his curse, mine is quieter and more private. It touches only me, and no one else suffers the cracks I keep hidden.

Sara holds her arms to her chest, covered in a deep-red blush. "The Tidecallers are rumored to be positioned on a remote island near the fringes of the Breach, and we are ready to take the fight to them. We just need to get the other crowns to agree."

My brows scrunch together at the news. "And you know who the Lord of the Tides is?" I need to fact-check their intel before I say too much.

Sara frowns. "If you mean to say that she's, in fact, a woman—one we know you've had quite a few dealings with—we do."

"Is that why I couldn't find my way inside the castle? Did you think I'd switched sides?" I muse, a little hurt.

Is that why I'm here? So Elio can keep an eye on me?

Sara eases my doubts with a straight-cut answer. "Not at all. All direct entry points inside the castle are now warded against everyone but the king and queen."

"That's inconvenient," Seth winces.

Sara gives a heavy sigh. "Immensely. It's a total zoo, here and everywhere—"

Elio enters through the door on the opposite side of the room, interrupting her sentence. His platinum blonde hair is in disarray as he hurries over to me, the chill of winter he usually carries with him tame by comparison. "By Thanatos, I'm so glad to see you in one piece, Devi. How was your trip?" He wraps me up in a heartfelt hug, and the silky lapels of his midnight-blue suit brush my cheek.

I draw back and meet his gaze. "Eventful."

His expression darkens, and he motions us toward the little nook at the back of Sara's office, where four periwinkle armchairs surround an oval-shaped coffee table. He looks good. Better than I've seen him in decades. The patch of snowflake at his neck has melted, and the permanent frown stuck between his brows has been smoothed away. The light beneath his skin shines bright, just like it used to back in the day.

I hold my breath, my heart in my throat. So alive and healthy, he reminds me of the old Elio, the man he was before he left for the Winter Court. Before the ugly business with Ethan happened, and his wings were so brutally clipped off...

"We were attacked by a nightmare," Seth says, jolting me back to reality.

Elio unbuttons his jacket and sits beside Seth. "I was afraid of that. Damian's trying to isolate a small portion of the sceawere to allow safe passage between a few key locations. Until the Shadow King reclaims his playground, no one should step into the in-between unless absolutely necessary. For now, I'm afraid most travel across the continent will be limited to sea and land routes."

I rub my neck and exhale a loud, "Bloody hells," shocked by how much the worlds can change in the span of a few days.

I knew all of this, in theory. We've all studied the previous wars in school and argued different points of view or decisions made during those difficult times. No matter how much we enjoy playing warlords, trying to fix past conflicts after the fact, it's not the same as living through them in real time. It's easy to think we could have done better when we already know the outcome. All students of history, no matter how passionate they are, want to believe the same horrific patterns their ancestors wrestled with won't get repeated.

That the people in charge have learned from those mistakes, when they seldom have.

We all want to believe the world as we know it cannot change as drastically as that.

That war is *not* coming.

But, cutting off easy travel between realms is war-room 101— straight out of every Fae rebel-slash-dictator playbook there is. I finally drop into the cushy armchair, landing with a sigh. "The Tide-callers have done it this time. Started a full blown war."

Seth winks in a playful manner. "I told you so."

The rest of us exchange a heavy glance, and we all sit in silence for a minute. When I agreed to Seth's *terms of engagement*, I was only thinking of revenge. I was focused on using him to take back my crown. Take back my life. I never stopped to consider that the monarchy might not survive. If Faerie falls, there won't be any crowns left to fight over.

Seth presses his thumb to his bottom lip. "And the Lord of the Tides? He's a *she*?"

Elio nods. "Willow Summers, the Summer King's sister."

"Didn't she die a long time ago?" Seth asks.

The look Elio gives me says it all—he knows I hid the truth from him, and he resents me for letting him believe Willow was dead. There's no anger in his voice, but his icy gaze burns with quiet reproach. "When you told me Willow had once approached you with wild, revolutionary plans, and that you had been tempted to join her, you failed to mention she was in leagues with the Tidecallers."

Heat rises to my cheeks, and I lick my lips. One of my best-kept secrets is now common knowledge, and while it's hard to hold Elio's accusatory gaze, it's also a relief not to have to hide this from him anymore. The weight of the lie, of all the half-truths and omissions —finally slips off my shoulders, leaving me raw but lighter.

"And not only in leagues with them. She probably resurrected them, stoked their ideology back to life in any pocket of unrest she could find," Sara adds.

I chew on that possibility. Sara's probably right, but my friendship with Willow transcends such things as politics. We've been through hell together.

Most people, present company included, see crowns as symbols of order and safety, but I've seen first-hand what power does. How it corrupts and consumes. It makes me feel like a traitor among them that I don't immediately flinch at the thought of tearing it all down.

"Our political system is rotten, and I almost joined the Tides, that is true. Willow was a smart, charismatic leader, with a lot of wonderful ideas. She understood that the magic, the gods, the very fabric of our world, needed regional monarchies to prosper. Her dream was not to get rid of them entirely, but to make the system fair to everyone."

"Why didn't you join her?" Seth leans in, looking genuinely curious.

"She was a succeed-at-all-costs kind of leader. She didn't mind sacrificing anyone—even herself—to the cause. She wholeheartedly believed true change couldn't be attained without tremendous loss of lives. I was all for killing Freya, Ethan, and a few other political monsters, but Willow didn't care about collateral damage, only the end result—"

Seth gives my elbow a soft nudge. "You're still bleeding." He grazes the back of my arm, and the faint caress is too careful and too intimate for me to keep a straight face. "Are you alright?"

I'm caught off guard by the intensity of his gaze. "It's nothing."

He stands and moves behind me, curling his hand around the lapel of my raincoat and giving it a light tug, as if he were helping a lady out of her coat at some grand ball.

I huff and shrug off the jacket. Percy flies out of my pocket and lands on my shoulder as Seth inspects the wounds on my arm.

The prince drums his fingers next to the marks where the wolf's teeth tore through my long-sleeved shirt and pierced my skin. The area is now sealed by bright red clots, and his brows knit together. "Doesn't look like nothing."

"It's definitely *something*," Percy clips.

"Now, don't fuss. It's not that deep," I warn them both.

My Faeling flies up to the puncture wounds and grimaces, shaking his head. "I can't heal them."

Seth's grip tightens around my lower arm. "Nightmares' teeth and claws can carry an array of poison." He turns to Elio. "Send for the palace healer."

Elio squints at the prince, his ice-blue gaze raising goosebumps on my skin. He's not used to being ordered around in his own kingdom, but his look holds more curiosity than annoyance.

Sara hurries out of the room. "Right away."

Seth's fingers hover for a moment in the wake of Sara's departure, then gently trace down the length of my arm. His gaze follows the silvery scars zigzagging across my skin. I'm covered in them, but they're faint enough to escape most people's scrutiny.

Very few people notice them—fewer still understand what they are.

Seth does.

I jerk back and cradle my arm against my chest. "You're fussing."

"Am not."

"Are too."

Elio links his long fingers in his lap, still observing us with his head cocked to the side. It won't be easy to sell him on this whole 'engaged to my mortal enemy' thing. Maybe I should have discussed an exception to the rules with Seth, so I could let Elio in on our secret, but before I can goad the Winter King into speaking his mind, Iris's doppelgänger enters the room.

I freeze, gobsmacked, as Elio leaps to greet her.

I've never seen him smile like that since he joined the Winter Court—or maybe ever.

He looks simply radiant as he slips his hand in hers and leads her over to me, eyes bright with excitement and pride, the happiest I've ever seen him.

"Lori, this is Devi Eros. Devi, this is my wife, Lori."

CHAPTER 10
RAVENOUS
DEVI

By Eros... I hold my breath, my fingers digging deep in the armrests of the chair. I'd heard of the resemblance, of course, but I wasn't prepared for Elio's new wife to be an exact, carbon copy of my Iris.

She's *exactly* like her—but younger, untouched by the burdens of time, the sadness of being stuck in an arranged marriage, and the weight of her mother's expectations. The same luminous brown skin, the same elegant arch of her brow, the same graceful, slender figure. The way she carries herself is familiar, yet not. Her posture is more fluid, her movements more assured, and her clear gray eyes are joyful.

She holds my gaze like few others have ever done upon first meeting me, as if we're already well-acquainted. "I can't believe I finally get to meet the famous Devi Eros. It's an honor." She extends her hand, which tells me she was raised in the new world.

I stand and shake it with the faintest hesitation, half-expecting my fingers to pass through air. But Lori isn't cold or translucent or untouchable. She's warm and solid. Flesh and bone.

A strange wave of nostalgia crashes over me, tangled with a

sharp pang of loss. It feels like I'm staring into a twisted, phantom mirror of the past. This girl is alive and unscarred, while Iris is dead and I'm just a shadow of who I used to be.

My jaw falls open, but I quickly shut it. In one glance, I can tell the heart of this stranger is hopelessly devoted to Elio, but there's a shadow hovering over it.

A dark soul—a leech—eels its way through the woman's spine, curling itself around the delicate fibers of her spinal cord. The silent intruder feeds on the connection between her mind and her body, and the way it nestles there turns my stomach. I can't admit to seeing it in front of Seth, not without revealing my darkest secret.

I swallow, forcing my mouth shut to hide my turmoil. This woman is not only a copy of Iris. She carries her battered soul within.

"You were close with Iris, yes?" Lori asks.

"Yes," I answer, my voice thick with tears.

Fuck.

Iris's soul fled after her death, and I hunted it for *years*, taking incredible risks and visiting parts of Faerie that chilled me to the core. I had to give up the search not to kill myself in the process.

Why is it here now? How? It's buried deep in Lori—too deep for me to extract. I need to speak with the newlyweds alone.

Seth clears his throat, stepping into our intense tête-à-tête. "Hey, Lori."

He kisses her cheeks like they're old friends, and my gut cramps. Does he know about Iris's soul? *What in the seven hells?*

Before I betray my emotions, the window closest to us ripples with the arrival of a Faeling. Dressed in a tight-fitting navy tuxedo, with slicked-back hair and round glasses, he carries an air of snobbery I'm all too familiar with. I refrain from rolling my eyes, a grunt threatening to rise in my throat.

Byron almost drops his precious clipboard at the sight of us. "By Thanatos." He swallows hard, hovering high in the air with his iridescent wings beating furiously at his back. "Percival Batten. How dare you show your face here?" he squeaks.

Percy lets go of my injured arm. "Hello, Byron."

Byron hikes his tiny round glasses up his severe nose. "Well...you don't look good, I dare say."

The Faelings stare each other down like they're about to duel, and Percy tips his chin in defiance. "Still bitter, I see."

Byron clutches his clipboard to his chest. "*Me*? Bitter?"

"Precisely," Percy huffs. "I was just doing my job."

"Sure felt personal."

Seth leans in and whispers, "What's with them?"

"Byron and Percy used to date," I explain.

Seth's jaw slacks, but he quickly schools his gaze back to neutral.

"Did you cross paths with a nightmare on your way over?" Lori asks, settling into the armchair previously occupied by Sara. We all return to our seats, leaving the ex-lovers to squabble over old grudges.

"Yes, a wolf, and it wasn't very friendly. The first step in taking control of the continent is isolating us from one another, and populating the sceaware with nightmares is an efficient way to go about it," I say, rubbing my face down.

Percy's high emotions tug at the link between us, bringing on a ginormous headache.

The corners of Seth's mouth curl down. "Wolves are Luther's thing. He must be the one weaving them."

Lori clutches her side. "I bet Morrigan taught him how to weave nightmares. Lucky we have her in custody, or we'd be dealing with venomous spiders on top of everything."

I arch a brow at the easy admission that Rye is indeed here in Wintermere, at their mercy and yet alive, when plenty of time has passed since I learned of her capture. Enough time for a trial to be held, and for a guilty sentence to be carried out. "I'm surprised you let her live. Damian must have demanded her head on a stick."

The Winter Queen's expression twists into a pensive frown. "It's complicated. Do you want to see her?"

My nose wrinkles at the notion. "Never."

"She might have usable intel. Can't you rekindle your friendship for the sake of the realm?" Elio suggests.

"Rye knows me well enough to see through any attempt at manipulation on my part. Besides, the only Fae who has any real power over her is the Shadow King, and maybe her grandmother..." I search Elio's gaze, almost certain I'm missing a vital piece of information, some reason why Rye is still alive. If the rumors are true, she should have been put to death for her involvement with the rebels and the attacks she carried out on the Winter and Shadow Courts. Reading between the lines, I'd say they need to pick her brain about some grand scheme. "Have you thought of asking Mabel for help?"

"Mabel has helped us quite a lot already, but I'm wary of asking her to betray her own granddaughter," Elio says. "And she doesn't want to come back to Faerie."

"Have you tried saying *please*?" I quip, well-aware that Mabel could not refuse her grandson's pleas if he put some heart into it.

Elio's gaze drops to the ground. Some things are contagious, I guess—like stubbornness.

Sara returns with the healer in tow, cutting off our conversation. Her eyes widen at the sight of Percy and Byron bickering, and she winces, shaking her head. Our eyes meet, and I know from that one glance she's just as worried as I am about them rekindling their courtship, considering how the last round ended.

The young brown-haired healer hurries to my side, her oversized burgundy robes hanging from her gaunt frame. Her gaze falls to my injured arm, but she hesitates. "Hi, I'm Leona."

"Thank you for coming to my rescue, Leona. I'm Devi."

"Devi Eros, I know." Her cheeks flush a deep shade of red. "Can I take a look?"

"Go ahead." I gesture for her to proceed.

She kneels beside me, setting her healer's bag on the ground with a soft clatter. Her fingers move quickly as she rummages through its compartments, pulling out a pair of scissors to cut off my torn sleeve.

"What kind of creature bit you?" she asks.

Percy hovers in the air above her head, lips pursed with worry. "A nightmarish wolf."

Leona uses a small bottle filled with a blue-tinged liquid to wet a bunch of white gauze and cleans the wound, her touch gentle despite the sting.

The bite marks beneath the clots become visible, and she sucks her bottom lip into her mouth. "This might fester if it's not properly cleaned." Her hands move swiftly, wrapping the wound with cling wrap, concealing it from view, and securing the temporary bandage with a metallic pin. "You'll need to come with me to Tundra's sanctuary. I'll also need every detail you have on this wolf."

Seth rises from his seat. "I'll come with you, witch."

"Do you want to meet us for dinner afterward?" Lori asks.

I rub my hands down my thighs, trying to push the exhaustion away. "It's late for us. Can we pick this up tomorrow morning?"

Lori nods. "Of course."

"I'll prepare two guest rooms in the East Wing," Sara adds.

Seth looks like he's about to say something, one corner of his mouth curled in an impish smile. I cut him off before he finds the gall to ask for only one room. "That works, thanks."

"And here," Sara picks a winter fur coat from the rack beside the door. "Wear this."

It's one of those enchanted garments that completely repels the cold.

"What about me? Am I to freeze to death?" Seth says.

Sara rolls her eyes and hands him a dark wool blanket.

I slip on the coat and head for the door, my heart pounding in my chest. Back home, I'd convinced myself it would be easy to sell everyone on the idea of Seth and me being in an actual relationship, but I hadn't anticipated that everyone would be so well acquainted with my *fiancé*.

He's exactly my type—Nemesis aside—but I don't do relationships. I hadn't expected my emotions to be so volatile around him, or for his wit and mischievous grins to get under my skin so easily.

Percy cowers in the large inside pocket of my coat once we step outside Sara's office, and I let the healer take the lead as I fall into step beside Seth.

"How do you know the castle so well? Or Sara and Byron, for that matter?" I ask, my tone slightly dry, wondering what else he forgot to mention.

"I stayed here every year for a few weeks during the Yule pageant as the Spring seeds' sponsor."

"Oh."

Seth's casual mention of sponsoring the Spring seeds during the Yule pageant sets a chill down my spine. That age-old barbaric tradition of parading young women like trophies, to judge their worth based on lavish gowns and pretty faces, never sat right with me. If he's so comfortably woven into that world, it doesn't bode well for how he truly views women or marriage.

We backtrack along the same path we used on arrival, night creeping in fast. The healer strides ahead through the maze, her small figure full of purpose. Seth and I walk shoulder to shoulder behind her, the rhythmic crunch of snow beneath our boots falling into perfect synchrony.

"How did you get involved in the pageant?" I ask.

"My mother didn't want anything to do with Wintermere after Iris's death and tasked me with it." Seth wraps the wool blanket tighter around his broad shoulders as we reach the castle gates. "But Elio was equally annoyed with her, so my seeds never made it far. Until Lori."

"That woman is no Spring seed," I clip.

"You're right," Seth chuckles softly, like this is all part of some heartwarming inside joke. "She's one of Damian's spiders. I schemed to get her enrolled in the Yule Pageant so she could spy on Elio for me, and the rest, as they say, is history."

I nudge his shoulder with my own. "So you have a knack for making convoluted deals with desperate women."

He bumps me back. "But with you, it feels new again. And I'd never use that word—desperate—to describe you."

"What would you use?"

He stops for a breath, and I glance at his face.

"Ravenous," he murmurs to the chilly breeze, and the word slithers through a tight, jarred crevasse in my soul.

That I am.

The guard from before nods in greeting as we pass the gates. Beyond them, the city is now dark and still. The snowy streets ahead twist downward in curves, their paths lit only by the mystical glow of blue Nether oil flames flickering on every porch. Dozens of chimneys release white smoke to the sky, the heavy fumes swallowing the twinkle of spiraling snowflakes.

Tundra feels smaller at night. The street narrows on our way down the slopes, the townhouses huddled closer together near the heart of the city. Their snow-capped rooftops cast long shadows on our path.

A few locals pass us by, their hurried footsteps confident and without thought, their faces half-hidden beneath scarves and hoods. I've never seen this part of Tundra, never ventured beyond the shops nestled outside the castle gates. Royal Fae usually travel between different parts of the kingdom using the sceawere, and it's bizarre not to simply step into one mirror and out of the next. The coming war will force the rulers of the continent to reinvent their entire way of living.

The easy banter from before has given way to an insidious silence, and I steal another glance at my companion. The mischievous prince who trespassed into my shop is gone, replaced by a brooding Storm Fae.

Tundra's main sanctuary rises at the center of town, its dark stone walls covered in droves of twisted, leafless white vines coated in frost.

Leona slows before the large doors and presses her hand to the wood, activating some kind of hidden mechanism. With a low groan, the ancient wood stirs and cracks open just enough to allow us entry. Seth and I follow a pace behind her, our shoulders brushing.

"You didn't have to come along, you know," I whisper without missing a step.

The frost-carved runes etched into the doors shimmer as we pass through the threshold, and Seth huddles closer. "I know."

I wait for him to add some justification. Maybe say he came to maintain the illusion that we're becoming fast friends, laying the groundwork for whatever comes next. But he remains strangely quiet.

The healer leads us past the waiting room and welcome counter into a large area in the back that's sectioned off into a dozen cubicles by tall partition screens. She guides us to the nearest one. A simple chair is set up near the cubicle's entrance, and I tip my chin toward it. "Stay here."

Seth's mouth curls down. "I have to tell them about Luther's wolves. It might help."

"You can tell them from this side of the screen."

I'm not sure if he's being nosy or just doesn't like being left behind, but I sure as hells don't know what to do with the caring look on his face.

"Oh, alright." He sinks into the uncomfortable seat, and I hand him my fur coat before following the healer to the other side, Percy perched on my shoulder as we enter the cubicle.

The healing room is a striking blend of modern and traditional fixtures. A deep sink stands beside a sleek white countertop, and a special ever-burning lantern—no doubt enchanted by the Sun Court —casts light rivaling the brightness of a cloudless day. A cushioned leather examination table, designed for the patient to sit on or lie flat, takes up most of the space, flanked on either side by a myriad of drawers in various sizes.

Leona removes the makeshift bandage she secured earlier and

cleans my wound again, then hikes up my sleeves to examine my cupid scars. This woman has the keen eye of a healer, and my skin tingles under her scrutiny.

"Don't mind them," I say quickly.

Her rich brown eyes search the depths of my soul. "Do you know what caused them?"

"Of course I do."

My curt tone discourages further discussion, but she presses on, lowering her voice. "Scars of that number and magnitude usually suggest a difficult childhood...or a violent lover." Her gaze shifts to the partition screen for a split second.

I take the edge off our conversation with a small smile. "I'm alright. Seth isn't violent. Just annoying."

Fae can't lie, so she's relieved to hear it, I'm sure.

Leona presses her lips together and squints at the scars once more. "If you told me what they were from, I might be able to help."

"I'm beyond help where those scars are concerned," I say firmly.

"Just sit here, then. I'll get the Master Healer."

She adjusts the partition screen to give me a bit of privacy and grills Seth about his brother's wolves before heading off in a flurry of faint footsteps. Healers are a class of their own. They come from every Fae Court, known for their exceptional selflessness and good nature.

The silence hums in my ears, and I'm acutely aware of Seth's presence a few feet away.

The legs of his chair scratch the floor. "What's going on in there?" he says.

"Oh, just come in."

I dangle my legs from the ledge of the exam table as he slips inside the room with his brows pulled together. He runs a hand up my bare arm, tracing the silvery scars, and his pupils dilate, his purple-flecked eyes overshadowed by a tempest of black swirling clouds. "What happened to you?"

"Don't start. It's none of your business."

"I make it my business. There's so many of them... Like your arm got chewed up by a Razorback Mauler before being tossed through a shredder. In my book, whoever did this to you deserves to die—"

"Shush," I cut him off.

Leona returns with two colleagues in tow, and Seth steps in behind me, the heat of him radiating against my back as he rests a hand on my shoulder. His grip is both comforting and aggressive—his fingers digging in as though he wants to press the name of my tormentor out of me, like juice from a blood orange.

I could taunt him with the truth—that his mother's curse is the root of it all. It'd make for a perfect jab, but it's too personal, and I won't reveal my inability to use magic without summoning all hells, not if I can help it.

The three healers examine my arm before the one wearing a dark grey robe adorned with a gold-threaded sash clears her throat. "You're lucky, the venom hasn't entered the bloodstream. We're going to clean the bite with frost apple juice, but I'm afraid it'll be very painful and unpleasant. To be blunt, it'll feel like we're sawing it off, but combined with our healers' magic, it should rid you of the scars, too—the ones in that region of your arm that is."

"Isn't there a less painful or unpleasant option? Analgesia, maybe? " Seth asks flippantly, his breathy tone stirring the sensitive hairs on my neck.

The healer focuses all her attention on me. "No. And we have to do it now, before the poison spreads."

"Do it." I wave Seth off. "You can go."

He inches closer. "I'm staying."

"You're not one of those controlling men, are you? Because I could never marry a man like that."

"Is it controlling to keep you company?" he deadpans.

"I just don't get what use you are."

The healers apply a cream to the rest of my arm to protect it from the treatment. "Do you want him to go?" one healer asks.

My mouth opens to tell him off, but before I can speak, he slips his hand into mine like it's the most natural thing in the world and whispers into my ear, "Just hold my hand, witch."

I press my lips together.

"If we are going to convince my mother that you like me, even a little, you are going to have to get used to physical contact," he adds quietly before turning to Percy. "What about you, Perce?"

In the blink of an eye, Seth's scowl vanishes—replaced by a cocky, devil-may-care smile. My Faeling opens his mouth to scold him for using the pet name, but Seth adds, "B-man looked pretty flustered when he saw you. I'd never seen him like that. He looked about to faint."

Percy grins from ear to ear. "He did, didn't he?"

"And that greeting? So squeaky. If he wants us to think he's moved on, he's not fooling anyone."

They exchange a conspiratorial glance and share a snigger. A shiver runs through me. Blimey... Percy and Seth getting along? That's a surprising twist I didn't see coming.

They gossip happily about Percy's ex-boyfriend, and I suspect they're both trying to take my mind off what's happening to my arm.

The master healer spreads an icy mixture over the bite marks under the watchful eyes of her colleagues, teaching them as she goes. I grit my teeth against the white-hot pain. The semi-liquid juice worms its way into my flesh like a living thing, frosting the edges and freezing the rest. A trickle of nausea slithers up my chest.

Ice burns deeper than flames.

Seth squeezes my hand, and to my horror, I squeeze back. The heat of his palm brings a shred of comfort, which I hate. I'm not used to relying on anyone or showing vulnerability, especially not in the presence of strangers, and I've got half a mind to throw him out of the examination cubicle before I completely embarrass myself, but the pain stops suddenly.

"All done. You did phenomenal. Most patients faint or scream, or both," the master healer says.

"Thanks," I grumble.

I'm used to pain, but I chew on my lips not to say so, unwilling to discuss my scars further.

"Can we go now?" I ask curtly.

The woman presses her lips together at my rudeness, but she nods. "Yes."

Seth lets out a small chuckle on our way out. "You're not used to saying thank you, are you?"

"I'm not used to asking for help." I bite the insides of my cheeks. "Or getting it."

The words taste strange, like admitting to a flaw I didn't know I had. I'm a grown, independent woman, used to facing life head-on and not expecting any favors from anyone.

Seth doesn't say anything else, and we return to the castle in stilted silence. His hand comes dangerously close to the small of my back a few times as Percy guides us through the maze toward the guest wing, a section of the castle I visited during my time as queen.

Sara's waiting for us on the parapet. "Byron warned me of your arrival. Is everything good with your arm?" she asks.

"No need to cut it off just yet," I joke.

She takes us through a side entrance, where long white marble hallways snake around a few lavish apartments. The sharp smell of ice and pine hangs in the air, cold and clean.

"Good," she says with humor. "I'll show you to your rooms."

We follow her to the end of the corridor. "Here for you, Devi. Seth, you're right at the end of this hallway." She hands us each a key. "Can I get you anything else?"

Seth grabs my hand, brings my knuckles to his lips, then twists it over and pecks the underside of my wrist. "Closer rooms?"

"Goodnight, Seth." I push him off, and he chuckles softly as he heads down the hall.

"Looks like he's found a new mountain to climb," Sara quips.

"Is that what he does? Climb *mountains*?" I enunciate slowly, my mouth pasty from the lack of sleep and the painful healing session.

"I'd say you're the most famous peak there is, but yes."

I brace my hands on my hips, watching Seth turn the corner. "I'm not opposed to a brave adventurer planting his flag on me, as long as he's nice to look at..." I trail off, sowing the seeds of what's to come. It's easier to play the flirt when he's not encroaching on my personal space. I hate that he gets to me, but Seth is right. If I want to convince everyone—including Seth himself—that we're engaged, I need to put on my game face.

A heavy sigh whistles out of Sara's mouth. "I wish I could relate, but to me, all men look the same."

I chuckle wholeheartedly at that and pat her shoulder in commiseration. "Good night, Sara."

CHAPTER II

BREAKFAST CLUB

SETH

I awake to sweaty, rumpled sheets and unfulfilled fantasies, but the cold doesn't bite the way it used to as I make my way to the castle's private sitting room.

Every other time I stayed here, it was as a sponsor for the Yule pageant. I wasn't important enough for the guest wing, and definitely not breakfast-with-the-Winter-King material.

The parlor is quieter than the ballroom and warmer than the dining hall. A few windows are open to the courtyard, letting in air that smells of loosened earth and fresh sap. Beyond the stone arches, Wintermere's sacred Hawthorn stands tall, its bone-white branches no longer locked in frost. Red buds freckle the tips, defiant and tender. The tree is waking up from a long slumber.

The crust of snow that blanketed these grounds for fifty years is finally giving way. Melting in uneven patches, it reveals slivers of vibrant emerald-green grass. Moss campions peak out from underneath the thinning snow, pink and bright.

All because of Lori.

"Good morning, Wintermere," I say, startling Sara as she serves herself coffee.

She reaches for a cloth napkin and wipes up the spilled drink. "Morning, Seth."

Sara is more of a friend than an employee, a fact made clear by her permanent residence in the guest wing. As the daughter of the previous Winter King, it was generous of Elio not to run her out of her childhood home.

I'm surprised to see Devi already here. I expected her to be asleep, and with good reason. She suffered through hell last night, and the memory of her squeezing my hand as though I was her last tether to this life is still raw. In the brief time we were apart, I thought of nothing else.

Lori and Elio greet me, but Devi just stares over the rim of her ceramic mug, glaring. Not exactly the warm welcome I was hoping for, but alright.

I walk to the buffet and grab a plate. "How's the arm?"

"Good. Fine."

I sit beside her and squint at her dismissive behavior, trying to see past the fallen queen persona to the woman beneath. How much of it is really her, and how much is bravado?

The Queen of Hearts, holy and ruined all at once.

My cock tingles from the erotic dream I had while I was sleeping. In the dream, she tasted of wildfire honey, sweet and searing. I can still taste her skin under my tongue.

The line of her jaw where I placed so many imaginary kisses taunts me. Her mouth was parted, like she's halfway between biting back a thought and speaking her mind. Her lashes cast thin shadows on her cheeks as she looks down at her hands.

The flex of her fingers on the handle of her coffee mug fascinates me. The curve of her spine when she shifts in her chair.

I can't look away. The dream still lingers behind my eyes, rushing through my blood, hot and vivid. I shouldn't be thinking about it, but in the span of one night, I made love to her. Revelled in the beauty of her smile at the altar. Felt her tremble in ecstasy beneath me. Built an imaginary life with her that shattered in the blink of an eye.

What I suffered through this night should be outlawed, because now that I've gotten a taste, I crave it.

I want all of that and *more*.

Zeus help me, Devi Eros was never meant to be anyone's. Yet, I want her to be mine. If this is the power of dreams, then the Shadow King is the most powerful king there is.

"I...dreamed," I say, stabbing my fork into a sausage. "I'd forgotten what it was like."

The threads of the Dreaming aren't supposed to allow visitors from Faerie, but the destruction of the Eternal Chalice has changed the continent's magic in ways we don't yet understand.

Devi shifts in her seat, hugging her knees to her chest. "It's nothing special to me."

"Not a morning person, are we?" I crack.

"Just a fact. I've been living in the new world for decades."

I grab the pitcher of water and pour myself a glass. "You've been having sex dreams for decades? That must be distracting."

She narrows her eyes but keeps her tone light, as if she knows how much I like to rattle her and is working overtime not to give me what I want. "There are other kinds of dreams."

The corners of my mouth twitch. "I wouldn't know."

Devi clearly isn't used to being vulnerable. As one of the most powerful beings in the new world, I bet she's forgotten what it's like to be on equal footing with anyone.

"Where's Percy?" I ask.

She plays with the silverware, the knife in her hand casting glints of light on the walls. "Sleeping in. He's exhausted."

If only she'd meet my gaze, I know I could thaw that icy exterior, the way I did yesterday.

Elio clears his throat, cutting through my botched flirting attempt. He stands, tossing his napkin over his plate. "Seth. A word."

He steps through the passage leading to the courtyard, and I follow him outside. The day is pleasantly warm, the bright sunshine keeping the cold at bay.

The sun hits his face, and his eyes flutter shut. "I asked you to get her here in one piece. Not try to seduce her."

I shrug off his concerns. "She's Devi Eros. I'm smitten."

More like besotted. Delirious. Obsessed.

"Ugh." Elio pinches the bridge of his nose.

I tuck my hands in my pockets, stealing a glimpse of Devi and Lori through the windows. My abs clench.

Her dark skin glows with an inner light, every inch of her crafted to enthral and provoke. There's perfection in the way she exists. I've spent most of my life trying to emulate such effortless confidence, but looking at her, I know I've always fallen short.

The stories warned me about her charisma, her power of fascination, luring hundreds of men in just so they could kneel at her feet. I thought I was above such manipulation, but in the brief time we've been acquainted, I've come to realize resistance is futile.

I *will* fall in love with Devi Eros. It's just a matter of when. And how much of my soul will be lost to her forever.

The window frosts over, cutting my line of sight, and my gaze flies to Elio.

"She's not like other women. She won't be impressed by your seductive smiles and vapid jokes, so behave," he says sternly.

A frown overpowers my face. His attitude reeks of disapproval, reminiscent of the blatant animosity that used to exist between us. I thought we'd moved past our mutual dislike.

"If I didn't know any better, I'd think you were jealous."

He sucks in air. "Don't be ridiculous."

"Yet there's something here, isn't there? What is Devi to you? An old flame?"

"Mind your own business."

"You're being uncharacteristically touchy about this, which says a lot given your baseline grumpiness. Devi's a grown woman. She can make up her own mind about me."

"I'm not—" He rubs his face and finally shakes his head. "Just stay away from her, Seth."

Well, well. The plot thickens.

I watch him return to his wife's side with a dubious smile and head off into the Winter gardens.

The soft ground shifts beneath my boots on my way to visit Iris, but I can't help but be in awe of how the space has been transformed since I was last here. Even the sky is lighter, as though the weight of years of sorrows has been lifted from the land.

I thread to the statue watching over Iris's grave. Elio's first queen is entombed in her glass coffin, her hands folded over her stomach, her painted red lips disgustingly vibrant compared to her chalky skin. The world around her may be waking up, but she remains frozen in the shade of the Hawthorn, untouched by the sun. A knot tightens in my chest as I read the bronze plaque underneath.

True love transcends crowns, blood, and flesh. It doesn't care for common sense and doesn't play by the rules. Love has no masters, only slaves.
- Elio Hades Lightbringer

Devi appears beside me without a sound. She gazes down at the bed of white feathers cradling Iris's body but doesn't flinch or turn away.

"Do you agree with that?" she asks, tracing the effigy.

"I bet you're the type who thinks we have complete control over our hearts. Or rather, that *you* control them."

"Mostly, yes. But I have to admit, no one can completely master true love."

My gaze shifts to the three towers. The single window at the top of the tall, crooked keep where the king's apartments are situated sends a shiver down my spine.

"I was there when Iris fell from the tower, you know," I whisper.

"So was I."

My eyes widen, and I open my mouth to ask how that's possible, but she adds, "I kept to the shadows, of course. Freya wouldn't have tolerated my presence. I came through the mirror to wish Iris a happy birthday—" She stops abruptly.

"Do you know how she fell? I hated Elio my whole adult life because I thought he pushed her," I say.

"As I was exiting the sceawere, I heard a commotion and rushed upstairs...only to catch a glimpse of Iris's dying form in the middle of the gardens." She keeps her voice steady and calm, with no trace of emotion, and I know she's rehearsed that speech many, many times before.

"But how did no one see you? Tons of people were watching the tower from below. My entire family was there—"

"It's nice to have family." There's a sharp edge to her voice, like I'm somehow to blame for her having none.

She probably thinks I got everything handed to me on a silver platter, apart from the family name.

"You forget, I grew up in the shadows as the bastard son of an adulterous Fae queen. For me, the concept of family is, at best, complicated," I say.

"It's laughable, really, that Freya ever hoped to get away with it. How did she plan to explain herself when you stopped aging?"

My eyes dart to the white, unripened frost apples dangling from the Hawthorn. "My mother and Iris had it all figured out. Iris had received a Frost apple after her wedding to Elio, and she'd eaten it, but she told everyone she'd given it to me. Of course, that lie was debunked the second I dissipated into a cloud, but their plan was actually clever. If I hadn't been a dual wielder, people would have continued to think of her as a full-blooded Fae, and me as the halfling, and no one would have been the wiser."

She moves away from Iris's grave, her top lip curled in disgust. "Ugh. I'm so sick of your mother's convoluted schemes."

I chase after her. "Hey, at least she didn't disavow me like my father did. I'm curious, you know. Sometimes, I wonder what would have happened if my mother hadn't become queen. If you hadn't been stripped of your title, maybe I would have had a completely different life."

She digs her heels in the snow. "Your mother would have worked herself to death before she gave up scheming against me. If I hadn't lost my crown, chances are you'd never have been born." She picks up the pace, heading for the entrance of the maze.

Devi's angry with me. Angry at my mother, angry at the world for all the damage it's done to us. I don't blame her. Maybe she deserves to be angry, but I'm not my mother, and I need her to see that.

"Elio wants me to keep my distance," I confess.

Her brows raise.

"He warned me off you. Like a jealous lover," I add, watching her reaction.

The corners of her eyes wrinkle with warmth. "Imagine that."

"I told him you were old enough to make up your own mind about me."

She chuckles softly, without thinking, and my chest swells with joy. I'm already hooked on that sound.

"Why did you act like a blushing bride at breakfast? Isn't it time to put our plan in motion? Or are you holding back because of some old romantic tie with Elio?"

"I'm as much a blushing bride as you are a wallflower," she jokes.

"You're shying away from our deal. We don't have much time."

She opens her mouth, then closes it. "You're right." She laces our fingers and pulls me toward the entrance of the labyrinth. "Let's take a quick walk, shall we?"

"Inside a frozen labyrinth?"

A dimple appears on her cheek. "Haven't you noticed? It's springtime."

Devi isn't a rose waiting to be picked, but a carnivorous plant in a field of simpering flowers. She doesn't want a man with titles or a polished smile. She wants the marrow. The kind of power that sinks into the soil and grows teeth.

A dark shard of me bristles at the chance to show her exactly how wild and beautiful a storm can be.

"Byron's watching," she mouths quietly.

"Where?" I tilt my head toward the sky, but she tugs on my coat lapels, scolding me.

Be still my heart. I block her path, trapping her against the hedge. "So you're into me now?"

She loops her arms around my neck. "Only for appearances."

I lean in just a little. Her smooth brown lips gleam in the light. "What if we catch feelings?"

"You said there was no chance."

"We just agreed that love has no masters," I remind her.

She digs her nails into my scalp. "If you fall for me, it'll destroy you. So don't."

"Consider me warned." My gaze dips down to her cleavage, to the smooth expanse of skin there, and I trace the constellation of freckles running down her collarbone. "But what if you fall for me, first?" I breathe, inches from her lips.

"Don't worry." She boops my nose with a finger. "I'd kill you before that happened."

It's a game. A good one. If I kissed her here, beneath the cedar hedge with snow crunching beneath our feet, I'm almost certain I could win.

Her clever eyes remain locked on mine, unyielding. I should walk away, but she's just so damn magnetic. I'm pretty sure she doesn't actually plan to marry me. She thinks she can back out when the time comes.

I'll change her mind.

Given her electric personality, I'll certainly enjoy the challenge.

CHAPTER 12
STYLE
DEVI

We're nearly out of the labyrinth when Lori steps into our path. The shadow huntress is dressed in black leggings, a sports bra, and an unzipped hoodie, like she's about to go for a run. The sight is jarring. Iris wouldn't have been caught dead in lycra, and she wasn't exactly athletic. It explains the difference in their bodies, though. Lori is built like a weapon, all lean muscle and sharp edges while Iris had been femininity and silk.

I drop Seth's hand like I've been caught doing something shameful. Which is ridiculous. People are meant to see us together. That's the whole point of this charade.

But no—apparently my instinct is to panic like a schoolgirl.

Gods. What are we, fifteen? Next thing you know, I'll be doodling his name in the margins of my war plans. Mrs. Devi Devine. Disgusting.

I cross my arms, pretending I was never holding his hand. That I'm above all this.

"Hey. Can I speak with you for a moment?" Lori asks, eyes flicking to Seth. "Alone."

He groans dramatically, like we're star-crossed lovers being torn apart.

"Don't worry," she says. "I won't keep her long."

He mutters something under his breath and heads into the dining room.

It's bizarre seeing Lori so soon after visiting Iris's grave, and an icy shiver runs down my spine. I don't believe in the afterlife. I think that when our souls return to the gods on the solstice, they scatter into the cosmos like stardust—gone.

I've never been one for superstition. There's no heaven, no seven hells, just oblivion.

The dark souls that refuse to go with their reapers and stick around longer than what's good for them become dangerous, and that's why the Sun Court hunts them down. Still, there's something deeply unsettling about the doppelgänger business. About living alongside someone who's both dead and alive. A ghost with warm skin and a beating heart.

She fidgets with her fingers, eyes cast down. "Elio speaks very highly of you. He told me how much you helped him, how you risked your life every year to soothe his pain and offer his brides a moment of reprieve." She chews her bottom lip like the words don't fit right. "I want us to be friends."

The way she won't meet my gaze sets off an itch between my shoulder blades. "Elio and I were never lovers."

She blinks, knuckles white. "No?"

"Never."

Her shoulders ease, the tension bleeding out. "Then why is he being so weird about your flirtation with Seth? Why didn't he just deny it when I asked?"

I cross my arms. "Before I explain, I have a few questions about Iris."

Her eyes widen. "Iris?"

"I know about your current condition. I...sense her in you."

She draws a sharp intake of breath, scanning the gardens before lowering her voice. "How? I thought only soul catchers could see dark souls."

"I have the power." I hesitate. "Do you...talk to her?"

Lori's gaze softens. "You loved her like a sister, I know. And she loved you, too. Maybe that's why I'm so eager to get to know you," she says quickly. "You never blamed Elio for her death, which he's very grateful for."

I start walking away from Iris's coffin. It feels disloyal somehow, to discuss this in front of her grave. "Listen... Iris was never meant to be queen of Winter. When she told me she was entering the Yule pageant to get a frost apple, I begged her not to. She didn't care about duty, and she was secretly fucking Elio's brother. Loved him, even. Her marriage to Elio was doomed before it even started."

"I've shared memories with her—relived parts of her life while sleeping," Lori says. "I've seen things. Seen you. I feel like I've known you all my life, to be honest."

"It must be hard to carry a dark soul." I lick my dry lips. Iris might be listening in, and it's bizarre and unsettling, but I've got to say my piece. "She'd hate me for saying this, but she never should've run from her reaper. No dark soul stays intact once the tether to its body is cut. Possession isn't a viable path to immortality. Dark souls strong enough to overpower their hosts rot from the inside out until nothing's left but scraps of who they were." A rough sigh slips out of my lungs. "Fae aren't meant to survive death."

Dark souls don't survive—they infect. And what's left of Iris will keep festering in that woman until it consumes her.

Lori's mouth tightens. "Can you do anything about it?"

She wants, with good reason, to get rid of Iris.

"No," I say too quickly. "And even if I could... I'm not sure I'd be able to destroy what's left of her. Even if I think it's the right thing to do."

Lori squeezes my lower arm, her sad eyes exactly like Iris's. My heart pounds in my chest, and I'm desperate to change the subject, but since we're in painful territory...

"I know Morrigan Quinn is in your custody, but I don't get why Elio is keeping her alive."

Her nose wrinkles. "Aren't you glad? Elio said you two used to be friends."

"She's the reason I lost my crown. I wouldn't mind seeing her dead. Has Damian asked for leniency or something? Because I thought she'd be executed the minute she was caught."

Lori's frown deepens. "Believe me, I wouldn't mind seeing her dead, either, but we're at an impasse. I can't tell you the details, but she cast a blood spell that makes it impossible for us to kill her. Seth called you a witch last night... Would you be able to help us?"

I shake my head. I've never heard of a blood spell that makes someone impervious to death, but if it exists, I wouldn't put it past Rye to find it. "Don't let the red hair fool you. I'm only distantly related to witches. Seth was joking."

"Too bad. I was kind of hoping we could get rid of her before Luther Storm comes knocking."

"Mabel Bloodsinger might be able to help," I muse, thinking if Elio's too stubborn to ask, maybe his wife can make him see reason.

Lori nods at that, and excuses herself. "I'm going for a run. Wanna come with?"

"No thanks."

Lori waves goodbye before running toward the maze entrance, and I watch her turn the corner. How does Elio plan on saving her before it's too late? Maybe he's still cursed after all.

Extracting Iris's soul from Lori will take more Light magic than Elio possesses. The King of Light would have the power, but Lori is better off as she is now than in Ethan Lightbringer's company.

A LITTLE WHILE LATER, I MEET SETH BACK IN THE PARLOR, AND HE PATS THE empty seat next to him. "You and Lori apparently had a ton to discuss," he says, his inquisitive eyes asking a million questions. "Anything interesting to share?"

I stop by the buffet and pour myself a fresh, hot coffee. "With you?" I taunt.

His plain shirt hugs his body in all the right places, the fabric stretching tight across his large shoulders. His dark skin is simply flawless. Compared to my scar-riddled shell, the smoothness of his is hypnotic. It makes me angry, envious, and horny all at once. I wish I could touch it. Cower into his heat after my long walk in the snowy gardens.

Spring Fae are meant to lure their prey in, but when two carnivorous plants meet each other, they know not to trust the beauty in front of them. It doesn't make it less tempting.

His eyes darken in a way that sizzles through my belly. "Trust goes both ways, you know," he warns.

"I asked her about Morrigan," I explain, trying to appease his suspicions without revealing anything about Iris's dark soul.

A muscle twitches at the corner of his jaw. "I'll breathe easier when that witch is dead and buried."

"I guess we'll both have to get used to disappointment." I size him up, wondering if his anger is genuine or just another move in the game.

"Weren't you and Morrigan friends once? Before she stole your arrows to enchant Damian Sombra?" he asks.

My eyes fly to the sky, my temper rumbling inside my throat. "When will everyone stop rubbing that in my face? Rye used to be the life of the party, before we all realized she was insane. *Everybody* was friends with her. But don't fool yourself, pretty boy. What happened between Damian and Morrigan was just an excuse to steal my crown."

Seth comes to sit next to me, dragging the chair closer so that his knees almost bump my left thigh. "How so?"

I didn't plan on saying so much, but the words keep leaking out of me, stolen by his calmness or patience or beauty. "I was too popular, too powerful, and too free from politics and bribes. Plus, I was the only Spring Fae strong enough to craft a love arrow that could pierce a Fae's heart. That made me a threat. Threats don't get to keep their crowns, especially women. Gods forbid a woman, a Fae royal, be happy alone. Maybe if I had married some dumb prince from another realm back when I was queen, the others wouldn't have been so quick to banish me." I play with my fingers, keeping them firmly tucked in my lap.

Seth's gaze drops down to the repetitive motion before he covers my hands with his, and all the stress coiled in my body evaporates. "When you put it like that, it sure hits differently," he whispers.

Long lashes frame his purple irises, mesmerizing. *Damn him and his beautiful skin.*

"I'm just stating facts. But of course, banished royals don't get to write the history books."

I should hate myself for even considering marrying Seth, as if a man with a dubious title could be some magic fix-all card. The stupid rules high society made up disgust me, but as Mabel says, we are all forced to live in the times we were born in.

Seth's lips quirk in a sad smile. "It was very unjust, what happened to you. And I don't need a revised history book to see that."

I slip my hands out of his grasp to brush a rebellious strand of hair away from his forehead. It's incredibly soft to the touch.

My gaze falls to his sculpted, masculine lips.

He's the son of a queen. Looking like that, there must've been some girl he was supposed to marry. Some Spring High Fae ready to fawn over that eight-pack and his Royal Academy degree. I wonder what ghosts hide behind his compassionate expression.

I take a long swig of coffee, the hot liquid grounding me against the desire to erase the sadness on his face with a kiss. Two royal Fae single past fifty... maybe Seth and I aren't so different after all. "Why did you never marry? You seem like the type."

He blinks, caught off guard. "I'd never met anyone I wanted to marry. Before now."

My chest tightens. *Well, damn.* I believe him—believe he's not just playing with words to butter me up. Maybe I'm having a crisis of faith. Or maybe I'm just tired.

Either way, this is new.

I probably just need more coffee.

Byron flies in, interrupting our conversation. He doesn't say anything but hovers in the back, and I know he's really waiting for Percy to show up.

Lori comes back from her run and unhooks her earbuds. "Where's Elio?" she asks.

"Three of the seven crowns have arrived, Your Majesty. The King has gone to greet them," Byron answers.

Her face falls. "Oh."

Just as Lori's about to say more, Elio enters the room with Sara on his heels, the royal chief of staff scribbling furiously on her clipboard.

Elio pours himself a drink and slumps into a chair, slicking his platinum-blond hair back with a quick sweep of his hand.

"I'm already exhausted," Sara clips, still taking notes. "Freya wants peaches for breakfast, for Thanatos's sake. Where am I supposed to find peaches in Wintermere?"

Byron flies to her ear to whisper something.

I swallow hard. "Freya's here?"

Seth raises his brows. "Doesn't she know the sceawere has been compromised?"

Sara rolls her eyes, the question clearly stretching the limits of her patience. "She doesn't seem to want to let a *detail* like that get in the way of her *peaches*."

Elio rubs a hand down his face, having already gulped down the Nether cider. "With three crowns in attendance, we're still two short of a quorum. Damian still hasn't returned from the Solar Cliffs?" he asks Byron.

The Faeling gives a decisive slice of the head. "Not yet, Your Majesty."

"Ethan hasn't set foot in Wintermere since you became king, right?" I ask.

"Right."

Considering how Ethan cut Elio's wings in punishment for leaving the Sun Court—scraping the roots clean off the bone—their relationship is disastrous at best.

Lori pats her husband's arm. "He doesn't have a choice."

"We might all be better off if he refuses to come," I grumble.

"Seeing as the summit can't take place immediately, I organized a matinée ball to occupy them while they wait," Sara says.

A big, unladylike grimace twists Lori's face—an expression I'd never seen on Iris. "Is that really necessary? This is hardly the time for a party."

Sara nods in the affirmative. "The Reds, Spring, and Summer delegations are less likely to tear each other apart—or us, for that matter—if they're kept entertained. The new Red Queen looks even more lethal than the last one." A full-bodied shiver rocks Sara from head to toe before she checks her planner. "The Reds sent eight High Fae to protect their queen, same with Spring, but the Summer King trusted us enough not to bring bodyguards, thank Thanatos."

A knowing smile stretches my lips. "Typical Aidan, thinking he's too powerful for bodyguards."

"We all should get dressed and meet in the ballroom in half an hour. We can't keep the other crowns waiting too long," Sara says.

She leads by example and exits the room, Byron perched on her shoulder, and Seth and I stand up to follow.

"Lori, do you have a minute?" I ask the queen, preventing her departure.

She meets me in the middle of the room, and Seth lingers in the doorway behind her before finally disappearing from view.

I lower my voice in case he only pretended to leave. "I noticed your makeup... Especially around the eyes. You can access Iris's magic, right?"

Lori's cheeks turn crimson, like she's embarrassed to be caught using a magic that doesn't belong to her. "Only a little."

"I can't use mine, a fact that I'd rather not share with anyone else. Elio already knows, of course, but he can't exactly help me do my hair..." I trail off, trying to infer the predicament I'm in. I'm a Spring Fae who can't do what most Spring Fae are best at: doll up for a ball.

Our eyes meet, and her voice trembles in a breathy, "I'd be honored."

She accompanies me to my room, and I lock the door behind us, not wanting Seth or anyone else to sneak in and witness how far I've fallen. Unable to weave my own dress, or even style my hair right. The shame.

The guest room holds an understated warmth in spite of the muted palette. The walls are paneled in pale stone, accented with soft gold trims that catch the light from the chandeliers. The furnishings are carved from white birch—sleek and elegant—with a high-backed chair near the hearth and a writing desk facing the tall windows. Heavy drapes, the color of late-winter dusk, are drawn back to reveal a sweeping view of Tundra below, its spires and chimneys dusted in snow. A thick fur blanket covers the bed, and I run my fingers through it, imagining what marvels I could craft with a piece of this size if I weren't cursed.

"Any special request?" Lori asks.

I bend down to grab one leg of the cushioned ottoman at the foot of the bed. "Do your best."

Dragging the velvety piece of furniture in front of the large freestanding mirror, I sit on it, offering her easy access to my head. She starts with my makeup, pairing smoky cat eyes with dark red lipstick.

"May I?" Lori motions to my hair next, and I give her a quick nod.

She bites her bottom lip and tentatively reaches for my red locs, running her fingers through them to familiarize herself with their texture.

Her lids drop, and magic prickles across the sensitive skin of my scalp. The locs unravel and twist back together, the process taking no more than a minute. I catch a glimpse of myself in the mirror and draw in a sharp breath.

My hair is now styled in tight, precise micro braids. Hundreds of them, small as thread. Just the way Iris used to style them. The weightlessness of them is so eerie and yet familiar. Their luscious glide over my shoulders when I turn my head feels like a kiss from beyond. The way they whisper against my skin twists my heart.

I haven't styled my hair this way in more than fifty years.

Percy stirs awake on the windowsill and lets out an audible gasp. "Oh my..."

"Does it look wrong?"

Lori pulls her shaky hands away, and I meet her gaze in the reflective glass. "No. No, it looks just *right*," I say softly.

Her hands fall to my shoulders, and she gives them a soft squeeze, but just as I'm about to address Iris directly—to reach her inside the body of a stranger—she slips back out of reach.

Lori's tear-filled eyes dart to the ground, and she jolts away from me, clearly spooked by the phenomenon. "I— I wouldn't know where to start with a gown... But I'll bring you one. And other clothes, too. Just wait." She rushes out of the room, the shadows around her almost palpable.

I sit on the ottoman for a moment, feeling vulnerable, helpless, and simply...bereft.

Percy perches on my shoulder and caresses the shell of my ear. "I love you, *diamantay*."

Tears glass over my eyes, and Percy opens his mouth to add something, but a soft knock at the door is quickly followed by the creak of the hinges. In her haste, Lori didn't close the door all the way, and an elegantly dressed Seth steps inside my bedroom, oblivious to what just transpired.

Sin dipped in velvet, his midnight-black coat highlights the shape of his shoulders, the collar high enough to frame that chiseled jaw I've already stared at for too long. His waistcoat is decorated with gold brocade, and the crisp white of his shirt opens just enough at the collar to make my pulse skip, revealing the shape of a rectangular, metallic pendant. No cravat, no apology. Just him, standing there like he knows exactly what he's doing to me.

I turn my back to the thick white door to hide the tears.

Percy braces both hands on his hips and stares down the intruder. "You, again."

"Afternoon, Perce." His voice grows louder as he draws closer. "I came for a preview of your Mistress' splendid ballgown. I've heard wonders about her capabilities."

"Bet you could do better, right?" Percy cracks, goading him and buying me a bit of time.

I stare out the window and force my eyes to widen, keeping the tears from spilling out. I haven't cried in decades, and now twice in two days? What the fuck is wrong with me?

"I might," Seth says with humor. "I've got style."

I arch a brow, spinning my problem on its head. "Then prove it. Make me a dress, pretty boy."

"You'd let me dress you?" he murmurs behind me.

"Why not?" I shrug as though it's no big deal and walk over to him, the tears all dried up.

"Isn't that too *controlling*?" he says in jest, one brow arched. He clearly thinks there's a catch, but he's also hooked on the idea.

"Are you chicken?"

The playful taunt hangs between us, our gazes locked until Percy clears his throat, inches from my ear. *Shit.* I'd completely forgotten that my Faeling was still on my shoulder, and my cheeks warm.

Percy flies off in a hurry. "I'll be back in a jiffy, lovebirds. I need to look my best to remind Byron what he's missing."

"Take your time." I wave goodbye, not looking away from Seth, waiting for Percy to be out of earshot before I ask again. "Tongue tied, pretty boy?"

I grab the pendant hanging around his neck and play with the rectangular piece of metal, gliding my thumb against the sleek dark piece of jewelry. I know these have to do with Storm magic, but I can't remember what they do.

Seth raises his hands to my bare arms, giving them a gentle, almost tentative squeeze. "Never. Just hold still."

Spring magic tingles across my arms, neck, and chest as Seth's power coats my entire body, and I instantly regret my offer. It's too personal. Too intimate. He undresses me with his magic, melding the red fabric of my turtleneck and black jeans and using them to line the dress.

Threads borrowed from the silk pillows, the fur, the drapes, and molten gold from the chandeliers drift toward us. Unwoven fibers and liquid metal glide against my skin to form golden rose petals that sew themselves together.

I spy on his progress in the mirror.

The opulent gown is springtime frozen in gold. It clings to me at the bodice, petals and metallic vines mirroring the candlelight. The off-shoulder sleeves threaten to slip, and the thigh-high slit draws attention to my legs. I don't wear this dress—I weaponize it. The plunging neckline dips down to reveal the curves of my breasts in a soft V-shape framed by a delicate floral appliqué. Alluring but classic. Daunting without being overly flashy. The kind of dress that lures stares in instead of shouting for attention.

A lavish fur coat hugs my shoulders, warm and soft. It cuts off just above my waist, leaving the full skirt of the gown untouched. The shoes are nude satin with a block heel, and two delicate straps snake around my ankles.

Fae don't let things like the end of the world get in the way of throwing a good party. If anything, they dress *louder* for it.

Seth comes to stand behind me, the fabric still humming with the last traces of his magic, and I end up flush against him, my back to his chest. We both freeze at the sight of our reflection. His hands settle on my waist under the pretense of checking the fit, his thumbs grazing the curve of my hips. He drinks me in with his eyes, proud of what he's made.

Subtle twines of gold are braided into my hair, reminiscent of a crown, and I swallow hard.

This is the filthiest fantasy brought to life. I can't stop staring at the two of us together. We look good—more than good. Royal.

His large hand settles on my belly, and my core pulses. This dress didn't come with underwear, and it'd be too easy for him to slip a hand underneath and find out exactly how aroused I am. I wouldn't stop him if he tried.

"I thought you were more of a little black dress type," I say to break the spell.

A zap of electricity goes straight to my heat, and I don't know if it came from him, or if it was just static, but I'm panting.

Seth winks at me in the mirror. "Any man that wouldn't cover you in gold is a fool."

CHAPTER 13
READY FOR IT?
DEVI

"Welcome to Wintermere, cousins," Elio announces, his voice carrying down the hallway just as Seth and I prepare to make our entrance.

The prince extends his arm, and I take it, eager to ruin Freya's day. Inside the ballroom, the checkered windows stretch nearly to the ceiling, their panes clear for once, offering an unobstructed view of the gardens beyond. Crystal chandeliers hang from a vaulted ceiling painted with the Fall of the Mist-King mural—the same one we have in Spring. Once a reminder of past mistakes that nearly destroyed the Fae, it now lurks above our head ominously, with a new Mist King ready to claim a power that laid dormant for generations. A long bar, carved from ice, stretches along one side of the room, the bottles behind it glowing in shades of orange, blue, and green.

The delegation from the Red Forest is already here, huddled in the back and cloaked in layers of fine silk and brocade. A bunch of Winter High Fae make up the numbers, some of them already dancing.

Percy flies to meet us, looking enchanting in his fresh midnight-blue suit. His hair is slicked over his head, and Seth whistles beside me. "Looking hot, Perce."

Percy ignores the compliment. "The new Red queen is here."

I examine the Red Fae at the center of the katana-wielding body-guards. She's a stranger, but the infamous Red circlet sits on her head, the accessory propped like a bloody halo atop her smooth auburn hair. Living ironwood roots from the Lorntre tree are weaved in its frame, intertwined with bands of dark metal. Crimson sap glimmers along the twigs, matching the deep red stones set at the front.

Males do not grow on Red soil, so all pure-blooded Red Fae are females. How they manage to have more children is a mystery, and even Mabel never revealed that detail of her heritage. The Lorntre, the sacred tree of the Red Forest, has been sealed off ever since the new religion declared war on the witches of Lorntre's Hollow. Long before I was born, Mabel had no choice but to flee into exile with her kin to escape slaughter.

This could be an opportunity to discover more about the Red priestesses and help Mabel avoid their scrutiny, but they say the secrets of the Red Forest can only be written down in blood.

Percy points to the other side of the ballroom. "The Summer King and Queen have also arrived, but there's no sign of the usurper."

"You mean my mother," Seth corrects him.

Percy turns up his nose at my improbable fiancée. "No sign of Seth's mother, *the usurper.*

Seth lets out a dramatic sigh. "I thought we were becoming friends..."

"I just call it like I see it."

"Be good. Both of you," I warn them.

A couple of familiar faces near the buffet plasters a dubious smile on my lips. *I'll be damned.*

Seth steers me over to Elizabeth Snow, interrupting the new Summer Queen just as she samples the buffet. "Betty Snow. How is married life treating you?" he asks warmly.

She holds a hand to her mouth and swallows, her dark brows lifting. "Seth. Devi. Hi."

I roll my eyes at the amity between them. "Hey, moth."

Beth and I have a very adversarial relationship on account of her being too straight-laced, but I'm happy for her. The fiery bite of Summer power radiating from the Winter Fae tells me she's finally married her sweetheart. Her heart is glowing, bursting with happiness, and it's a relief to see those two finally tied the knot.

"Congratulations," I say.

"Thank you." Her alabaster cheeks flush, and her gaze darts to her feet. "I'm surprised to see you here, Seth. I thought you were sailing to Storm's End. For that *errand*, you know?" she adds, speaking in code.

"Bad weather derailed my voyage, and I lost my *cargo*," Seth answers in the same cryptic manner. "Mist completely overtook the ocean, and the boat hit a big rock. There was nothing else I could do but untie my *load* and make it to the coast safely."

Beth's frown deepens. "We've heard reports of that mist, too. A bunch of fishermen had to be rescued off the coast of Augustus on account of the bad visibility. Do you know what might have caused it?"

"It's obvious, no?" I quip.

Both of them turn to me, and I let them dangle for a minute, stealing a couple of grapes off the bushel and biting down on them before I add, "The power of the Mist King had been imprisoned in the chalice for centuries, and the chalice is gone."

"Are you saying there's a new Mist King?" Seth breathes.

"Or queen," Beth adds quickly, clearly already in the know.

"Precisely."

Aidan Summers, the new Summer King, rejoins his wife's side. With short brown hair, amber eyes, and sun-kissed skin, he's the very picture of a Summer Fae, his fiery aura burning hotter now that he wears the crown.

"Seth. I didn't expect to see you here," he says.

Beth melts into his side, her luscious black waves spilling over her shoulder as she twists her neck to look at him. "Seth lost his cargo."

From the worry on her face, I gather that Seth's *cargo* poses some danger to her—and what else could they be talking about but Seth's revolutionist brother?

Aidan's brow knits together. "What, you lost him an hour after we parted?"

"Three. And only because of the magical armageddon that went on in *your* castle," Seth says with a hint of reproach.

"This Luther guy scares you, moth?" I taunt Beth.

"As he should." She rubs down her arms and takes refuge in her husband's embrace. The look they share does nothing to appease my suspicions that Seth's baby brother is a force to be reckoned with.

Seth entwines our fingers, pulling me away from the royal couple. "Can I have this dance?" He sounds rushed, and his gaze flies over my head for a moment. "My mother has arrived," he whispers.

"Did she see us? Does she look angry?"

"Not yet." A lazy smile curls his mouth, and it's contagious.

Blimey. Seth is about as excited for this as I am. He wants to rebel, and hell if I don't love breaking the rules and being the center of attention. He leads me inside the fray of other couples, where we swing to the rhythm of a slow-building but energetic tune.

The dancers make way for us, whispers and pointed fingers flagging our arrival as Seth whisks me into a series of languorous spins.

"You want to make a scene," I say.

Seth laughs, the sound warm against my cheek. "Anything less would be unworthy of you."

The waltz is a classic piece, but we take up a little more space than the other dancers and hold each other a little too close. Each sway is an excuse to brush against one another. We're the most attractive couple in the room, and definitely the only one tangled in unresolved sexual tension.

Everyone's watching, now. The music cuts off abruptly, the musicians too busy staring to keep track of the melody.

Instead of letting me slip away, Seth wraps an arm around my waist. His eyes are wild and tormented, yet full of life, like waves crashing at the foot of the Zepharion Fortress. I hold my breath when he cups the side of my face with his free hand and bends to kiss me.

The motion is smooth as hell.

I can't push him off, not with everyone watching. By Eros, I only wish I could keep my eyes open and see the disgust on Freya's face. The thought fills me with unbridled joy. A sinister yet blinding sense of happiness hums through me, and I deepen the kiss, slipping my tongue in Seth's mouth.

I truly, madly, deeply hate him, but we're both Spring royals. The best kissers in the realms. The most beautiful, treacherous lovers in the worlds. The rage coalesces in my blood and spices this interlude with a bittersweet sense of butchered pride and inedible envy.

Tongue fighting.

Hands gripping.

Hearts pounding.

It isn't soft. It isn't sweet. It crashes into me like a natural disaster tearing through brick walls, leaving nothing untouched. It's a contest: who does it better, who riles the other up a wall, and who knows exactly how to make the other moan the loudest. Breathe the hardest.

From Seth's heavy hand on the small of my back and the steely ridge of his erection pressing into my hip, I figure I'm winning, which makes the contest even more fun.

"Are you ready to yield, pretty boy?" I taunt him.

Seth drags his nose in the dip between my jaw and ear, inhaling deep. "You pretend to be above this, but you're the fallen Queen of Hearts. You remember what it's like to rule, and not suffer the same emptiness every single Spring Fae reckons with. You were the most desired woman in all the worlds, and men would line up for miles just to steal a glance of you. You *love* this."

He slips an arm around my shoulders and leads me off the dance floor.

I'm in awe of how natural he looks, taking hold of my hand.

"I don't need you—or any man—to kneel in front of me to feel whole," I whisper quickly, the sweet edge of victory fading.

A smile colors his rogue, talented mouth. "Maybe it's your turn to kneel, then."

My throat bobs, the suggestion rolling off his lips like a promise.

I see Freya half-running toward us, one hand clutching the rumples of her black skirt and the other cramped around her folding fan. Hatred rises in me fast and hot, the kind that never fades, no matter how long it festers.

The black dress and veil look eerie on her. She's grieving the loss of her lover, but I won't let that soften my anger. If she'd run off with Thorald Storm when she had the chance—instead of plotting away my crown—we wouldn't be here.

The rumors Mabel heard were right. Freya is a ghost of her former self, with red, inflamed burns stretching across her cheeks and arms. The many overlapping layers of loose skin indicate that her groomers tried to fix the marks in vain, over and over again. With her skin marred like that, her outside finally matches her rotten soul. She can't pretend to be the fairest of them all anymore.

"Hello, step-grandmother," I say.

The sound of my pep-filled voice shocks her, because she stops short, knuckles white, eyes refusing to meet mine. "The nerve! I'll have your head this time, Devilyne." Her voice is tight, full of worry and disbelief, like she's hoping if she keeps it low enough, I'll just disappear.

Percy zooms over to us and perches on my shoulder, crouching in a defensive stance. "Stay back, old woman."

Seth adjusts his position so his body creates a slight shield between us. "Mother, please. Let's be adults about this."

"I will not stand for this. She's a criminal."

The music stops, and Elio hurries to Freya's side, his hands raised in a calming manner. "We're in my court, Freya, and I have the final say on who's welcomed on my lands."

My smile curls at the edges, all sugar and knives.

Seth raises our linked fingers for Freya and all the Spring delegation to see. "Devi and I... We've decided to get married."

Outraged cries erupt from Freya's entourage, the same cowards and sheep who stood idly by when my crown was stolen. I bet they're all shaking in their boots at the mere thought of me returning home.

Freya's jaw hangs open. "It's ludicrous—" She slaps her son's free arm with her folded fan. "She must have used one of her disgusting love arrows on you."

"I wasn't hit by a love arrow, Mother. I went looking for Devi, and one thing led to another... We're more alike than we first thought." Seth glances amorously at me, his act perfectly balanced and sounding more genuine than I'd hoped. "She's the most beautiful and dauntless woman I've ever met. A real *queen*."

My insides squeal in victory, and Percy applauds Seth for his jab. I'm so pleased I could kiss him again, but Freya lunges in my direction, then thrusts her arm forward.

Quick. Efficient. A bit desperate.

I catch a flash of light over metal and instinctively leap away from her incoming blade, but it's not the shine of any dirk or knife. Not the tapered glint of steel or the regal lines of a wedding dagger, no.

The terrible, greenish glimmer of iron and silver alloy veined with rowan wood flips my stomach. The luster of certain death.

Seth grips his mother's wrist, his nostrils flaring, his other hand flying to her shoulder to stop her momentum. Dark clouds swirl inside his eyes, deep enough to drown in. Lightning sparks along the grooves of his muscles as the edge of an end-all blade hovers inches from my side. Only Seth's raw strength is keeping me from the grave, and he's shaking.

So am I.

One scratch from that blade would've poisoned me to death.

CHAPTER 14
FAMILY TREE
DEVI

The crowd gathers in a wide, careful circle around us, many Fae turning white at the sight of the weapon. Elio entombs the blade in ice, and Seth twists Freya's arm, forcing her to relinquish the hilt.

The ceremonial blade drops to the ground, its frozen casing shattering on impact, freeing the deadly weapon once more. Elio bends to pick it up, his top lip curled in a snarl. "You brought an end-all blade to my court?"

Lori rushes to his side, her ballet flats soundless over the marble. She's the only woman not wearing a dress, but her black pantsuit fits her like a very chic, very sexy glove, the path between her breasts deliberately bare. The way she moves reminds me of the Shadow King, her grace sharpened by stealth and flexibility.

I have no doubt she could win a fight against any man here.

"Easy," she says, calm but firm. "There's no reason to murder each other."

Freya spits at my feet. "There's every reason."

"Every reason, indeed," I shoot back, keeping my cool, my grin widening.

Elio rubs the arch of his brow. "Guards, please escort the Spring Queen to my private library. She needs to calm down."

A few murmurs rise from her entourage, but none loud enough to matter.

"She's the criminal, not me. I'm allowed to defend myself. Your father will back me up on this," Freya argues.

"You brought a concealed end-all blade to my ballroom. You'll be lucky to leave here alive," he rasps, the cold power of a glacier icing his deep voice. "Take a moment to compose yourself. We'll be joining you shortly, and we'll see what the others think of your unprovoked *defense*."

The guards lead Freya off the dance floor under Elio's watchful eye.

She messed up. Badly. She'll be punished for bringing a blade like that into the Winter King's castle, of all places. And as much as she might've liked to scratch me with it, she didn't bring that dagger because of me. She had no idea I'd be here.

Who did she mean to kill?

I couldn't have dreamed up a better opening chapter for my revenge. My blood thrums with adrenaline and the sweet burn of karma. Justice, at long last, is being served.

My body tingles with all flavors of *just desserts*, and I lean into Seth, my fingers digging into his coat. "You're not the mama's boy I thought you were," I say quickly.

Whatever love exists between them, they have issues.

My savior combs a hand through his short, tempestuous black hair and shrugs off the violent interlude with a click of his fingers. A flying tray zips over to us, and he grabs two glasses of Feyfire wine, offering me one. "I'll drink to that."

Bubbles spill over the rim, and the scent of honey and cinnamon set ablaze drags my thoughts down the gutter. I'm too fragile to ingest the most potent aphrodisiac in existence, but I'm also incredibly thirsty for it.

"Cheers." The soft *clink* of our glasses shivers through me. "That was quite a performance. I'm impressed."

The cocktail is slick and warm, enough to scorch my insides.

Seth's gaze lingers on my lips. "I bet you'd like to pretend there's nothing more between us than a performance." His gaze dips down to my stomach, his hands heavy on my waist. "But I can smell your arousal from here, witch. I bet your sweet heat throbs at the mere thought of my cock. Because I'd know exactly how to fuck you to make you scream, my *queen*," he says with an affable smile, as though we're having a perfectly innocent discussion on the fringes of the dance floor.

I blink, shaken by the molten wave of lust gripping my gut, and take another sip of wine. "You surprise me, pretty boy. I thought you were more of a gentleman."

He presses a hot kiss at the junction between my ear and neck. "You wouldn't know what to do with me if I were."

My lids flutter. The High Fae on the outskirts of the dance floor are all watching—pointing, whispering. I can't lose my head now.

I twist my hands in Seth's hair, nails sinking into his scalp, and swallow his next breath with an end-all kiss. It's the appropriate reward for his chivalrous rescue, but each time our tongues meet, my high wavers. Why does it feel like I'm losing this game?

The rush of humiliating Freya so thoroughly, so publicly, after dreaming of it for years... I should be flying. Instead, I'm unraveling.

Because as much as I enjoyed seeing her squirm, I've exposed myself as nothing more than a glittering jewel on her son's arm. As though I've fallen for him, as though I *belong* to him. That's the price of arranged marriages. Never mind that the engagement makes political sense. Never mind that Seth has fallen under my spell. The woman is the one seen as less-than.

What if the attack was planned, somehow? A ploy to win my trust? Even to me, it sounds like a stretch.

The trouble is, ploy or not, I've never wanted to jump his bones more. I'd give anything to be indifferent to him, to shrug off his gaze, his games, the flames he stokes in me, but alas...

Every fiber of my being still aches from the way he kissed me like I was already his. I want to strip him of his ambiguous smiles, his clever quips, and the nonchalance he wears like a crown. His clothes, too. I want to peel them off slowly, until there's nothing left between us but skin, hunger, and the knowledge that I'm the one in control.

Seth groans into the kiss, the ridge of his erection digging into my stomach, and I finally pull away.

Most of the High Fae are staring now, and I don't shy away from their fascination. Their tongues dart out to wet their rosy lips, blushes creeping along many of their cheeks. A Winter Fae's throat bobs with a quick, uneven swallow, just as her companion's fists clench at his sides. Sex is on their minds, curiosity hanging on their breaths, envy coiling in their bodies.

I'm Devi Eros. Every one of them is picturing themselves in Seth's place, women included. They all want to know what it's like.

Seth strokes my back, his callused thumb slipping under the material of my dress. My spine feels like a fuse, channeling heat deep and low, but the insidious caress stops abruptly.

"Uh-uh. Party's over," Seth warns.

I glance over my shoulder just in time to see Damian Sombra and Ethan Lightbringer entering together through the ballroom's main entrance, and the sight stops me cold.

I'd heard rumors that the Shadow King was back to his full power, but seeing him whole makes my heart bleed with joy and regret all at once. By Eros... His bite of power ripples across the room, shadows licking his sculpted shoulders, his black hooded tunic lacerated in various spots and revealing the tanned skin underneath.

Next to him, Ethan slicks his long platinum blonde hair behind his pointy ears, looking more disheveled than usual. His white waistcoat is freckled with dark, oily blood.

A bitter tang fills my mouth at the sight of him, and my core muscles cramp in disgust. Every inch of him turns my stomach, from his long, imperious nose, to the hollows of his cheeks and the arrogant cut of his jaw. Ethan Lightbringer's beauty is a menace, a thing of too-perfect angles and too-quiet calm. But it's the cruelty in his ice-blue eyes that gives him away. Anyone staring into those eyes can plainly see that the light inside him burned through and left nothing behind.

The vicious man I abhor above all others—the monster who raped my mother.

Every time I see him, I dream up new ways to kill him. Some quick and clean. Most slow and messy. Yet somehow, he's still walking around like a nightmare stitched into fine clothes.

The dancers all pause, and the royals gather closer, Seth ushering me forward, too. The signature smirk Ethan wears in public disappears when he spots me, and a glint of anger burns in his gaze.

"We should find a quiet place to talk," Damian announces, the low pitch of his voice echoing deep in my belly.

Elio nods, forced to play referee despite his own grievances. "Cousins, I prepared my private library so we can discuss things further between us." He doesn't want any political incident to derail this summit, but it must cost him a lot to keep a level head when Ethan is near. "Come with us, Seth," he adds quickly.

The prince narrows his eyes. "Me?"

"Yes. Go ahead, I'll catch up in a moment. I need a word with Devi first," Elio says, waving for Seth to leave without him. The Winter King's chest heaves, and he leans in, his posture almost menacing, though his voice remains perfectly amiable. "Lori told me you could feel Iris's soul inside her," he whispers.

To anyone but us, it must look like he's scolding me for the scene I just caused.

"I'm amazed you couldn't," I say with a fake, contrite pout.

"My Light magic dimmed when I left the Sun Court—you know that." He ushers me to the door where Seth and the other royals just exited and holds it open for me. Lori is still trying to settle the crowd in the ballroom, but her eyes dart over, wide with worry, just before we cross into the hallway.

A twinge of guilt stirs in my stomach. "Your wife assumed we were lovers. You should tell her the truth."

"I can't. Not while Iris hears everything I'm saying." He lowers his voice. "Dark souls destroy the bodies they borrow. I need to rid Lori of Iris for good. Mabel said only the King of Light could pull her soul out without harming Lori."

I blink, gobsmacked that Mabel already knew about Iris and Lori, and didn't tell me. "She's probably right."

"Willow is hell-bent on killing Ethan. If she succeeds, Helios will have to name a new king, and whoever is chosen will determine whether my wife lives or dies."

Helios, the God of Light, is fond of hereditary monarchies and almost always marks one of the children of the dead king as his new heir.

"It couldn't be you, you're already King," I assure him.

"Could it be you?" he deadpans.

My hand flies to my ribs to graze the Mark of the Gods tattooed on my stomach. "I don't think so. I'm not...free of Spring, really. I still bear Eros's mark."

Elio exhales loudly, rubbing his neck back and forth. "Last time you were here, you hinted that Ezra was not only alive, but that you knew where he was hiding... If you have a way of communicating with him, tell him now would be a good time for him to get his head out of his ass and return to Faerie. If he shows up as the new King of Light without a word beforehand, I'll assume he wants war."

A heavy sigh quakes my chest. "Don't fret. Ezra is not coming back to Faerie, and he's not going to be the next king of the Solar Cliffs." I hide a wince behind my palm, unwilling to open that particular can of wiggly, fucked-up worms. "That's all I can say."

Elio walks away with a nod but pauses at the foot of the staircase heading up to the towers. "What about Seth?"

"What about him?"

"You're not really going to marry him, are you?" He says on a pleading, childish pout.

I grab the skirt of my dress and walk backward toward the ball-room, never breaking eye contact, feeling as lawless and mischievous as the first time I shot him with a love arrow. "Why not? Seth's sexy as fuck."

Elio turns green. I simply *love* to tease him. For all the horror of my birth and the secrets that plague my bloodline, I'm happy he's my baby brother.

CHAPTER 15
SIX OF CROWNS
SETH

E lio confronts me as we climb toward the shortest of the three towers. "I told you to leave Devi alone. How did you strong-arm her into an engagement?"

"She's a grown woman, and I'm hot for her," I say. "Marrying me makes us the next in line for the Spring throne—even if my mother hates it. And it puts Devi under my protection. Why are you so upset?"

Why is he being such a prick about it? Even if he and Devi were lovers, he's happily married now. Why does he care so much?

The Red Queen glances over her shoulder, and Elio lowers his voice. "You must've blackmailed her into it. Like you did with Lori when she joined the Yule pageant."

"I didn't."

He growls under his breath. "We'll talk about this later."

I don't care how much he scowls. Devi will be mine. I want her bare, breathless, stripped of every little defense. I want her to beg—for pleasure, for mercy, for *atonement*. Because no one gets to toy with men the way she does, no one leaves that many wrecked hearts in their wake, without consequence.

She kissed me back, and not for the crowd. She wanted it. I felt it in the way her mouth parted, in the way her fingers clutched my coat like she was holding herself back from ripping it open. Saw it in the way she sipped her wine afterwards, carefully inching away, trying to hide the pounding of her heart, the heat rising in her cheeks, and the spicy edge of the desire leaking between her legs.

I drag a hand down my face to get my head back on track, willing my cock to soften the hell down. The last thing I need right now is to mix violent politics with raging erections.

The Winter King's private library has been rearranged in a hurry. Seven chairs of different colors form a circle around a round table in a rough replica of the Hall of Eternity that was destroyed. Light pours through the turret windows, cold and bright. It's not meant to impress, but rather to allow seven people who detest each other to put aside their differences and save the Fae Continent.

The three monarchs in front of us filter in one by one, with Elio and me closing the march. Freya is already inside, waiting, and the Winter King shuts the door behind him. Ice spreads across the room, frosting the windows, dimming the sunlight, and sealing the crack beneath the door, cutting us off from the outside world completely.

The arrangement of chairs has been altered from its original setup, reflecting the current state of Faerie politics: Summer, Winter, and Shadows now face the Sun, Spring, and Red Courts.

I graze the armrest of the stand-in for the Storm throne, a gray chair squeezed between Spring and Summer.

The swing vote.

With a bit of swagger, I unbutton my jacket and sit with them, an action that earns me a scowl from every one of them—especially my mother.

"You have no standing here, boy," Ethan enunciates in a deadly manner.

Elio clicks his tongue. "Seth is here at my invitation. As the only one of us who spent some real time in Storm's End, his perspective could prove invaluable."

"Let him stay, Ethan," Freya clips, her amity for Ethan cooled by his blatant show of disdain toward me.

The King of Light shows his teeth in the cruel imitation of a smile. "I saw Devi Eros in the ballroom. Have you taken another lame duck under your wing, Elio?"

My fists clench at the satisfaction curling his lips, but the Winter King keeps a straight face, clearly used to his father's antics, and definitely not as hot-blooded as I am.

"Helping people is only a sin in your book, Father," he says.

Ethan links his long, skeletal white fingers over his knee. "Not a sin, but weak. Devi Eros needs to be thrown into a cell until such time as the rebellion has been squashed."

Freya nods emphatically at that, but Damian clears his throat, commanding attention. The shadows hovering above his shoulders are twice as thick as usual, tendrils of smoke hugging the shape of his body.

"Enough squabbles, cousins. I have dire news to share. I can't get anyone in or out of Storm's End—and not because of the wolves prowling the sceawere." His tone is low and growly, making every word sound more ominous. "My sources say the new Storm King allowed an armada of boats into port and ordered all mirrors destroyed in Zepharion."

"As it's been foretold... another Fae court has fallen," the new Red Queen drawls.

"Who's the new Storm King?" Freya squeaks.

"It must be Luther. I can't see Maddox siding with the Tide-callers," I say quickly, taking it all in. Zepharion at the hands of the Tidecallers... My father would faint.

"An armada of boats?" Ethan repeats.

"Yes. A fleet of war vessels sailing north from the Breach," Damian clarifies, and the room falls dead silent.

The Breach is a narrow stretch of ocean renowned for its typhoons and the many monsters that hide within them. It separates the continent from the Islandide, but its waters have been deadly since the fall of the Mist King, and the few rebels and pirates who managed to cross it in the last few centuries were almost as violent and merciless as the monsters themselves.

"But— That's impossible," Ethan scoffs. "Any boat spotted crossing the Breach is blasted on sight. The Zepharion fortress's walls are riddled with cannons equipped to do just that—"

Damian cuts off the King of Light. "I think we all have to re-evaluate what we thought impossible. We assumed the Tidecallers were a bunch disorganized rebels— We were wrong." He grips the armrests of his chair.

"Where would they go next?" Freya asks.

The Red Queen plays with the sash of her war tunic. "Even if Luther Storm has been crowned king, the regional Lords of Storm's End are bound to rise up against an insurrection of this magnitude. The Tidecallers can't expect to invade the Fae Continent without being challenged."

Elio nods. "Janina is right. I wouldn't expect the Tidecallers to march onto Wintermere or the Shadowlands just yet. They'll be expecting a challenge from within. But controlling Storm's End's capital legitimizes their rebellion. With Alaveen behind us, we have only a month before the seven crowns need to reunite for Beltane. Maybe Luther plans on strong-arming us in exchange for his participation in the ritual."

The Spring festival ensures fertility on the continent. Botching it could derail birth rates for generations to come. All monarchs must meet for each of the seasonal rituals, or chaos will ensue.

Elio perches on the edge of his makeshift throne. "We're going into this war blind," he adds. "We don't know anything tangible about the Tidecallers, the Breach, or the Mists, aside from what we've read in history books. We need to make contact with the new Storm King and the Lord of the Tides and find out what they intend to do with their newfound power. If we mean to act in any efficient capacity, we have to know exactly what they want."

Janina sneers. "We need to kill them, you mean."

"Killing Willow or Luther or both will not destroy their armies," Damian says flatly.

"But it's a start," Freya sniggers, and a nasty shiver lances up my spine.

"The leaders of the rebellion wear a throng of Mist jewels that amplify their power. They might prove incredibly hard to kill," Elio says. "Diplomacy could save thousands of lives."

His status as the King of Death, combined with the strategic placement of his realm, positions him as a key leader in this matter. Which, judging by the grimace on his father's face, annoys the older Fae to no end.

I stand up, breaking up the bickering. "Do you have a map of the continent?"

Elio walks over to the stacks, pulls out a scroll tube from the bookshelf tucked between the turrets windows, and hands it over.

I unroll the map across the table in the center, pinning its corners with whatever I can grab. The ink is faded, and the cartographer made a few mistakes, but I know this coastline by heart.

"Without using the sceawere, there are only two ways to travel from Wintermere to Zepharion," I say, tapping the border. "By foot, you have to cross the Uaithe, the bolt-shaped chasm that separates the Frozen Hills from the Lightning Point province. The official crossing is here." I point to the Fenrall bridge. "Reinforced. Guarded by watchtowers and too many eyes. If the Tidecallers have taken control of Storm's End, they'll be expecting Elio to send his army there. But" —I slide my finger north, to where the land splinters and twists— "the Deiltine crossing hasn't been used in centuries. There's no gates. No walls. Just a sky that keeps exploding and a dilapidated road leading into the city."

"Deiltine is a dump," Ethan grunts. "And a deadly one at that."

I ignore him and continue with my exposé. "The people who live there are mostly caretakers for the Aeolians, the giant turbines that power the factories, the forges, and everything else. We send our best engineers, technicians, and machinists in on rotations."

I pick up a square-shaped receptacle that holds one of the cameras they use to broadcast the Yule Pageant. "All modern electrical-based technology built in Faerie—the projectors, the screens, etc., are powered by capacitors made in those factories."

I move to the coastline, tapping the map again. "Our only other option is by boat. We could sail from Taiga through the Deiltine channel, but the winds and tides here" —I trace the eastern coastline — "are tricky. Even if we're lucky, it'll take us a week, maybe more, to reach the port of Zepharion."

Freya clicks her tongue. "Not to mention the capital's port is bound to be well-guarded."

"Why would Deiltine even be an option, when it's still eons away from the capital?" Elio asks.

"The city was considered a strategic hub—being so close to Wintermere and exposed to a sea attack. My father needed a way to reach it quickly, so he used his influence over the previous Shadow King and got him to build an obsidian passage."

Damian shakes his head. "All obsidian passages are listed in the Shadowlands archives."

I'm only too glad to be the one to tell him his precious archives are not foolproof. "Not this one, and it emerges directly in the Storm King's study."

Elio's eyes widen. "So breaking into Deiltine could lead us directly to Luther's chambers?"

I flash my audience a confident grin. "New recruits arrive at the plant every week. I could pass for a technician and access the passage."

My mother nods gently at me, the way you smile at a helpful kid —or a particularly bright dog. "Thank you, son. We will discuss this further and let you know our decision."

Ethan Lightbringer cocks his head to the side, studying me like a bird of prey studies a mouse. "Wait a minute. Seth hasn't yet told us what he wants in return? If he succeeds, what does he expect from us?"

You can always count on the most villainous man in the room to iron out the nitty gritty.

"I want Devi Eros to be pardoned. We're engaged."

The King of Light's jaw sets in a hard line, his top lip curled up like I'm a worthless bum who just asked for his daughter's hand.

The horror on my mother's face would bother me if I had any hope of ever making my last remaining parent proud, but that ship sailed long before I set my sights on the woman she hates the most.

Elio's frown deepens, and the ice around the door melts. "Thank you, Seth. Please wait in the hall." He shoos me out with a disgusted grimace.

A fresh wave of frost seals the room behind me as I exit, shutting me out and cutting off any chance of eavesdropping. I pace the hallway, restless. The way my mother addressed me in front of everyone sits like an anchor in my gut. No matter how hard I try, she never takes me seriously. She didn't take my betrothal to Devi seriously at first—just chalked it up to another act of rebellion. But I'm not a teenager anymore.

Luther's words echo in my mind: *Too dark for the Light crowd, and too much of an extrovert to keep to the shadows.* I should be a chameleon, able to move between both worlds with ease. Instead, I'm a contradiction. Not a prince. Not a commoner. Not even a proper bastard. Just the afterthought of a scandal, with enough magic to matter, yet not enough to rule.

Well, I'm going to marry Devi Eros and inherit my mother's crown, and when I do, they won't be able to shut the door on me anymore.

Elio returns before I've settled my thoughts, his expression unreadable. He rubs ice off his neck like he's dusting off fleas, looking more like the Elio I used to know. Keeping company of your enemies does that to a man. It freezes the heart.

"The seven crowns want you to infiltrate the Storm Court and serve as a go-between," he announces. "It's a dangerous gig. Being a messenger between two parties at war means getting caught in the middle."

"A go-between?" I echo.

"Yes. And Devi will go with you," he sighs. "You shared your intentions to marry. As much as that plan disgusts me, you're both old enough to make your own decisions. If you succeed in your mission, you'll be free to marry, and Devi will be granted a formal pardon."

A weird itch weasels its way inside my chest. It's too easy. By my count, three out of six royals were appalled by the mere thought of Devi coming back to Faerie as my fiancée.

"You got my mother to agree to that?" I say, my voice thick with disbelief.

Elio's eyes narrow. "We got a majority, which is enough."

"Who switched sides? You?"

The ice freckles on his neck gleam under the chandeliers, and despite his soothing tone, he won't meet my gaze. "None of your business."

"I could marry her without the crowns' blessing. What are you not telling me?" I ask point-blank.

He opens his mouth to speak, but Mother steps out of the library with her arms crossed, her lips curled in that cruel way she wears so well.

"You couldn't marry Devi without breaking the law. She's still a traitor for now, my precious weed. With enough luck, spending time with her during this foolish mission will make you see how much of a manipulative cunt she really is."

Elio flinches. "Be civil, Freya, or I'll have the guards escort you to your room. Devi is now an agent of the seven crowns, whether you like it or not."

"If you had any children, you'd understand." Her gaze darts to me, and she clutches my arm. "She's not for you, Sethanias. She's only pretending—"

Elio cuts her off. "Devi is not the kind of woman to marry a man she doesn't respect. She's not you, Freya."

I gather my mother's hands in mine and gently but firmly push her away. "I want a crown, Mother. Devi Eros can give me yours, and she happens to be the most clever and beautiful woman I've ever known," I say, trying to appease her. I can't have her trying to murder Devi again.

Elio's fists clench at his sides, but he doesn't say anything.

Mother fans herself dramatically. "Well, as long as you don't forget—that woman is incapable of love."

Something still doesn't add up.

Am I really supposed to believe they've decided to spare my brother and the ringleader of the rebellion after one quick, closed-door meeting? If they think I'm going to play the fool, they're in for a rude awakening. Something else is going on, and I won't let them use me. I'm going to figure out exactly what they plan to do, and why.

I may not have been born to rule. But I *will* be King.

CHAPTER 16
ASSASSIN
DEVI

It cuts that Elio invited Seth and not me. I keep busy after their departure, waving cheekily at my ex-lieutenants from my tall seat at the bar. The members of the Spring Fae delegation stick to their corner, watching me with glum, fearful looks. The lot of them turn my stomach. If I ever take back my crown, I'll make sure they suffer for their betrayal.

Percy stares down my second shadow mule cocktail, arms braced on his hips, wings flicking impatiently at his back. "Is it a good idea to get pissed right now?"

"Good idea or not, it'll be more fun."

He lands on the back of my hand, stopping me from taking another swig. "You're upset they only invited Seth to their little meeting, aren't you?"

He knows me too well.

"It's offensive," I grumble, switching hands to finish the drink.

Percy scolds me. "It's good enough they didn't arrest us."

I open my mouth to argue, but he adds, "I'm not saying we deserve it, but they've never been smart or fair to begin with. Freya downright tried to murder you in front of everyone. I'm not letting you out of my sight again."

Beth sits next to us and hails the bartender. "I'll have whatever she's having," she tells him, and he nods, stealing not-too-discreet glimpses at her.

I tip my glass in her direction. "You're more famous than me, these days."

Beth went from being an outsider to the most famous singer in all the worlds, and a part of me resents her rise to fame, especially since it unfolded in parallel with my harsh fall from grace.

A wry grin curls her red-painted lips. "Are you jealous?"

She's loved and praised for her talents, adored by the masses while I'm being persecuted and feared. You bet I'm jealous. "Jealous of you?" I wrinkle my nose as though she's lost her mind.

She peeks at my flock of haters. "You and Seth... It's all for show, isn't it?"

Why can't anyone wrap their minds around the fact that Seth and I want to marry? He's hot. I'm Devi Eros. He won't rule without me, and I won't be pardoned without him.

"Why do you say that?" I quip. "Is it so hard to believe I'm into him?"

"Don't you think we've had enough of these arranged weddings?"

I scoff at the tiredness in her tone. "Last I heard, your husband was going to marry someone else. That explains your bias, I bet."

Elizabeth Snow spent the last few decades in exile—by choice. She can pretend to be in tune with Faerie politics mere days after her return.

"Call it bias if you want, but it's a recipe for disaster," she says.

I slide to my feet, eager to walk away from this conversation. "Because you have the monopoly on love? I don't love Seth *yet*, but that doesn't mean I couldn't learn to."

Her eyes widen, like she never expected me to mention love at all, and she chases after me. "Aidan wants to save Willow. That's all he's been talking about since the attack on the capital."

"And what if she doesn't want to be saved?"

Beth chews on her bottom lip. "She wants Ethan dead above all else."

"Who could argue with that?" I snicker.

Beth grips my wrists, forcing me to a halt, and scolds me with a stern look. "Willow used to worship you. I know Ethan hurt her, but isn't there a way to bring her back?"

Beth and Willow were close at the academy. She was Willow's kindred at her wedding, and my heart gives a painful, forlorn thud, remembering that clusterfuck.

"Listen, moth. I get it. I want Willow back, too. But if there's one thing I know for sure, it's that you can't heal someone—can't bring them back to life—no matter how much you love them, if they don't want you to."

"If someone could, I think it'd be you. Or Ezra." Her gaze softens.

Ezra again. By Eros, I need to thread carefully. "Ezra can't help us now."

The royals return to the ballroom far sooner than expected, Seth and Elio at the back of the line. My fiancé's bright smile has dimmed to a sullen pout.

"Everything alright?" I ask.

His sharp nod means everything but *fine*.

Aidan hurries to Beth's side and places a hand on her back—his movements subtle but urgent—just as Ethan Lightbringer joins our circle. His arrival steals the oxygen from the air. His bite of power hits like altitude sickness, causing a thin, sharp pain along my ribs, the same breathless pressure felt in his city above the clouds. The hairs on my arms stand to attention.

"Violet. Hi. It's been a while."

"Hello, Ethan."

Few here know why this vicious, soulless king once voted for my exile and not my execution. No one ever entertained the idea that a chalk-white king could sire a girl with dark brown skin, and that failure of imagination turned out to be the best shield I could hope for. Their bias worked in my favor.

They never looked too closely at how I managed to sneak around the Royal Academy unnoticed. Never questioned why I was so good at eavesdropping, or why I was the only one who didn't fawn over his picture-perfect first-born son, while every other girl was desperate to spread their legs for him.

"Aidan. Miss Snow," Ethan says in his usual glacial tone. "I see you two finally got married."

Beth's fists clench at her sides, the siren barely contained. "Yes. In spite of all your *help*."

"It's all in the past now. We have to pull together—" Ethan stops, his gaze landing on Lori. The Winter Queen is chatting quietly with Damian near the exit, the two of them clearly well-acquainted. Ethan drinks in the sight of her and sips his drink with the slow, focused intent of someone who wishes he were draining her dry. "—in these difficult times," he finishes.

Lori turns to look as though she felt him staring, and her bright smile falls from her face.

The dark light in Ethan's eyes, the way he studies Lori, his gaze dipping down the lapels of her pantsuit, dries my mouth. He can surely see the dark soul that has nestled inside her body, and he's not only curious about it, but *thrilled*.

He's found a new prey, and licks his lips. "Excuse me. I need to meet my son's latest wife..."

I could punch him for his gleeful tone and swallow hard at my mistake. I should've stopped them from meeting altogether. I should have convinced Elio to keep Lori locked in her room for the duration of the summit. Because with a dark soul inside her, she falls under Ethan's purview, and he might offer to help her, to cleanse her of it, but Eros knows what he'd want in return.

"She's in danger. We need to run interference." Beth clasps her husband's arm and follows after Ethan, clearly determined to keep him from hurting yet another woman.

"Should we go after them?" Seth asks, but a soft nudge on my shoulder calls my attention away, and my heart somersaults.

"Devi," Damian whispers my name in an intimate, brutal way that flips my stomach. His golden eyes stare into my soul—molten and endless. The dark swirls inked behind his ears are a living picture of the lazy nights we spent back at the academy, sharing secrets and plotting revolutions.

Seth glowers at the Shadow King, his arm snaking around my shoulder in a pointless show of testosterone. "Hey, D. What's up? Where's Nell?"

Damian doesn't even spare him a glance. "Would you give us a minute, Seth?"

Finally, someone from my past who's not miraculously best buddies with my fiancé. I was beginning to wonder if Seth had charmed everyone I'd ever known as part of his evil plan to wed me.

"To do what?" Seth asks, voice tight. "I need to speak with her alone, too. And soon," he warns.

"And I'll be back before you know, *darling*. Let's take a walk around the gardens." I slip from Seth's embrace and hook my arm around Damian's, tugging him along.

The look of betrayal on Seth's face pinches my gut, but he's not allowed to act so territorial. Not when we've only known each other for less than forty eight hours and Damian is happily married to someone else.

Damian and I stroll into the gardens, our boots denting the soft, melting snow. Spring is really starting to break through the frost. Pale shoots unfurl from the Hawthorn's branches, delicate, feather-like flowers daring to bloom at the ends. Above us, silver and gold snowflakes drift in the late afternoon breeze. Puddles stretch between the stones, reflecting a sky the color of thaw. It's beautiful in a quiet, aching way, the way the world tries again after a long, painful slumber, much like the man next to me.

Once we're hidden by the hedges, I squeeze his upper arm over his black tunic. "You look good, Samhain. How did you do it? How did you break your curse?"

"Nell did. She's the most infuriating woman I've ever known, and she changed me. Taught me how to love again, to let go of the past. She's...everything."

I take a good look at his heart. The moving shadow that was there has been replaced by an emerald-green glow, and my breath hitches. He's in love, and not the kind of love that fades. By some twist of fate, he's found the one.

If a part of me was holding onto the infinitesimal possibility that we might ever rekindle what we had, it's extinguished here, seeing his whole face come alive. And I'm glad for him. This beautiful man suffered enough at my hands.

"You married your mystery girl after all."

"Yes."

Last time I saw him, he confided her existence, but we were both pessimistic about his chances.

"I'm happy for you," I whisper.

The light in his eyes speeds up my heart. If Damian managed to rid himself of his curse, if Elio is finally happily married, it gives one cursed Fae reason to hope...

"What about you and Seth?" Damian grimaces like the thought of us together is highly unpalatable, and while the others' meddling irked my nerves, he's allowed to feel this way.

"It's a long story."

He doesn't speak further, and neither do I. He's the one that got away. If I hadn't chased a crown, maybe we'd have built a life. I don't regret choosing my ambitions—I'd do it again—but sometimes I wonder who I'd be if I hadn't been so hungry. A different girl. A softer one.

But the time has come to close that door for good, and it's freeing, really, to turn the page.

We cross paths with Lori. The Winter Queen is fleeing the ballroom, her eyes glassy with tears, though she slows just enough not to crash into us.

"Don't listen to a word Ethan says. He loves to be cruel," I say quickly.

Elio isn't far behind, chasing after her, but she halts him with a teary look and a raised palm, commanding him to stop. "I need a moment alone. I'm going for a run," she mutters, brushing past.

Elio's mouth parts in a silent plea as he watches her go, but I shake my head. "Give her a minute."

The Winter King's fists clench at his sides, opening and closing, his jaw set in a hard line. "I can't imagine what that fiend told her."

I turn to my companion. "Damian should escort everyone back to their kingdoms before night falls, starting with the King of Light."

The Shadow King lets out a tired sigh. "I think it's a wise idea. Be careful out there." he tips his chin in lieu of goodbye, and walks off to take Ethan away.

I breathe easier knowing Ethan won't stay the night, that my mistake in letting him meet Lori won't have immediate consequences. In the meantime, Elio will find a way to protect her.

"Can I have a word with you in my study?" my brother asks.

"Lead the way."

I watch the ice that freckles his neck as we walk. Crowns always come at a price. They break most of us, but Damian and Elio somehow got through the worst of it.

Elio lost his warmth for a time, but love softened his ice. And Damian... He lost his mind. He got splintered into something dangerous and beautiful, but pieced himself back together.

I envy them and their ability to let someone in that close. To love.

They escaped the rot that settles in your heart when you're raised to rule. I didn't fare as well. Most Fae royals don't. We get hardened by power, losing parts of ourselves in the process. Aidan is too green to have felt the brunt of it, but Ethan is a devil, and Freya lost whatever shred of humility she had a long time ago.

Elio and I reach the safety of his study, and he rests a hand on his desk. "I have news." His lips purse as though he's searching for the right wait to put it. From the way he cracks his knuckles, I know whatever he's about to say is delicate, and the evasiveness of his gaze adds a bit of secrecy and scandal. "The crowns have decided that you and Seth should be the ones to negotiate a truce with the Tidecallers."

I arch a brow. "Me and Seth?"

"There's more. Here." He reaches inside his jacket and slips out a small, sheathed dagger. The sheath is made of a delicate weave of dragonbone chain links, supple yet indestructible.

"Is that what I think it is?" I carefully unsnap the holder and tug on the pommel to inspect the blade. The greenish tint along the edge sparks an itch between my shoulder blades.

"An end-all blade, yes. We couldn't send you on a dangerous mission without the means to protect yourself." He hands it to me. "Aidan made it special for you."

The iron and silver alloy is shaped into a narrow, sharp blade, way smaller than the one Freya tried to kill me with, and more practical. Its handle is simple, topped with a small decorative silver heart. The sheath is decorated with gold and silver vines, and the efficient, light grip is a testament to the blacksmithing skills of the Summer King.

"Since you can't use magic outside the sceawere, it'll come in handy. I'll have my best soldier escort you to the end of the Frozen Hills tomorrow morning, so you can cross the Uaithe into Storm's End. Seth will explain the rest."

I shift the dagger from palm to fingertips, testing its weight and balance. "And who do you want me to kill?"

He breathes in deep, a heavy silence settling between us. I study his ice-blue eyes, his disheveled blonde hair, and the worried curve of his mouth. No matter how many of us end up dead, he'll be the one collecting their souls. As the King of Death, he'll feel this war like no one else.

Counting bodies. Gathering souls. Forced to stare at the wastefulness of it all, day in and day out.

"Seth is blind where his brother is concerned. Luther's rise to power will only bring chaos to the continent. He almost killed me. Almost killed Beth. The crowns want the new Storm King dead."

My brows knit together. This Luther guy is really freaking everybody out. "What about Willow? She's the leader of the rebellion."

He wouldn't send me to kill her too, would he? I might have a ruthless reputation, but I'd hardly be the one to ask.

"A compromise is not out of the question where I'm concerned. Talk to Willow. If there's a deal to be made, some truce to be brokered, you're in the best position to find it." He tucks his hands inside his pockets. "And if we get a shot at killing the real monster plaguing this continent, we should take it."

There's no mistaking his words, not when you've known Elio Lightbringer as long as I have. Not when you've seen the mangled scars across his back.

The crowns' sanctioned mission is to kill Luther Storm, but Elio wants our father dead instead.

CHAPTER 17
NO BODY, NO CRIME
SETH

Devi briefly returns to the ballroom after her interlude with Damian, only to slip away toward the guest wing in a hurry.

If I hadn't just seen Sombra leave the party with Ethan Lightbringer through the sceawere, I'd think she was on her way to meet him now. And the image that comes to mind fucking haunts me. I forgot to make sure that the deal we made about not having sex with other people before our wedding went both ways. Major oversight on my part.

I follow her through the empty corridors, her golden, glittering frame casting specks of light along the white halls.

"So...you and Sombra. It was serious," I call after her, my voice coming out far too edgy and judgmental for my liking.

"Why do you say that?" she taunts, not slowing down.

I force my shoulders to relax, aiming for an *I'm-fine-with-you-having-a-royal-ex* attitude, but my next words come out darker than intended. "I saw how you looked at him."

She keeps walking.

"If you liked him so much, why didn't you two marry?" I ask, my mind ablaze with the kind of morbid curiosity that walks hand in hand with jealousy.

"I was queen. He was king. You know the rule."

Kings and queens aren't allowed to marry each other. It would give too much power to one family. Before the Eternal Chalice was destroyed, the other monarchs would never have allowed Devi and Damian to marry. They would have been stripped of their titles if they'd tried, but who knows if that rule still stands now that the chalice is gone.

I expected her to say that Damian was too broody, too self-important, maybe boring—or, better yet, tragically bad in bed. But no. She's basically saying they would have married, given the chance, and the boulder in my chest pulses.

"What about *after* you lost your crown?"

She spins to face me. "You're cute when you're jealous. But don't fret—Damian's already married." She pokes the center of my chest in a playful manner before resuming her escape.

"I know. I was there."

That earns me a sullen pout. "What?"

"Funnily enough, I attended his wedding. And Elio's. Aidan's too. But you're changing the subject. I've heard the rumors. Why didn't you two marry after you lost your crown?"

She shrugs, as though the answer is obvious. "I fell from grace. He got splintered. Two wrongs don't make a right."

We reach her room, and she slips inside, twisting around to block me from following, one arm braced against the doorframe.

"Let me in."

"Why?"

There's no reason why she should. This itch under my breastbone won't let me walk away, but I've never been the type to hold a woman back. If she wants someone else, she can have him. I don't play second.

But this is different. Devi's different.

"I need to tell you about the meeting. The crowns offered us permission to marry, but there's a quid pro quo."

She purses her lips, somewhere between annoyance and disgust. "We don't need their permission, not now that the chalice is gone."

"That's what I said, but hear me out, alright?"

She slams the door in my face. I drag a hand through my hair, swallowing a curse, and stare down the piece of wood separating us. The raw instinct sizzling along my spine screams at me to tear it off the hinges.

Fuck.

How am I supposed to explain what happened if she won't listen? My fists curl, and I knock on the door once.

Twice.

Three times.

"I'm not above trampling down your door if necessary," I announce to the empty hallway, unsure if she can hear me.

Then, with a daring smile, she opens it. A plain black shirt hugs her curves, the loose neckline slipping off one shoulder, with matching form-fitting pants.

"Come in, pretty boy. And tell me what was said during this *so-oh-important* meeting."

The gown I wove for her is in tatters on the floor. I step over it on my way inside the room, a pang of regret squeezing my chest. "They want us to go to Zepharion and broker a truce with the Tidecallers."

Even dressed down, she's a goddess. Her braids fall over her bare shoulder like a river of flames framing her face, and her breasts peak through the black shirt.

"They offered to rescind your banishment and let us marry if we succeed," I add, my tongue parched.

"It's a mission they don't expect both of us to survive," she scoffs. "The crowns don't give a damn about anything but clinging to their own power. What kind of leverage can we offer the Tidecallers when we know the seven crowns will do anything to stop real reform?"

"The destruction of the chalice makes reform inevitable. If we can find a compromise, we could save my brother, save your friend, and lead Faerie into a new age."

"You're being naive. Preventing war now is impossible."

The trivial way she dismisses my point of view strikes a painful nerve, and I pinch the bridge of my nose, turning away to gather my thoughts. "Making the impossible possible is what kings and queens of Faerie are for. You of all people should agree with that. Do you have any idea what it feels like to be dismissed outright—every day, all the time? You might have spent decades in exile, but you used to be *queen*. No one can take that away from you."

She lowers her voice, but it only enhances her mystique. "You think it's easy, losing a crown? It's even worse than never having one at all."

I spin around to face her again. "The grass is always greener, right? You have no idea what it's like to be a bastard, to be ignored and belittled by your own father—"

"Yes I do!" she snaps back.

"You're a legend, a force of nature. Your name is spoken in fear and reverence throughout the worlds while I'm nothing more than the butt of a joke. The prince of nowhere and nothing at all. How could you possibly understand?"

She lifts her chin, tearing off the golden circlet I wove through her braids and throwing it at my feet. "I worked my ass off my whole life, only for your mother to sabotage me at every turn. Excuse me if being prince—if having an endless line of lovers, incredible power over two schools of magic, and infinite wealth—isn't enough for you."

I bridge the gap between us. "Was it enough for you, when you were a princess? You were always hungry for more, no? Ambition is not a crime."

She digs her heels into the ground, not backing down. "It's no virtue, either."

Our chests rise and fall, our faces inches apart, and I forget why we're shouting. The thin cotton of her shirt clings to her forms in a distracting fashion, and I raise a hand to caress her arm from shoulder to wrist. "It's a sin we both share, then. You and me, we're starving for more."

Her eyelids flutter before she suddenly shoves me toward her bed, the back of my knees hitting the mattress. She prowls forward, pushing me to a seat with both hands. I sit on the edge on her bed as she straddles me, and my throat bobs, my hands instinctively finding her hips.

She presses her forehead to mine. "We have to stop quarrelling." Our lips brush, her braids cascading around us, blocking the large windows from view. "Byron's outside, spying on us. That noisy brat."

I tuck a handful of braids behind her ear and cup her face. "Why would he do that?"

She rakes her nails along my hairline. "Elio must have put him up to it. He doesn't believe I'm into you."

"For an ex-boyfriend, Elio sure is awfully invested in your love life," I grumble.

She works my coat off my shoulders and dumps it to the ground, my undershirt quick to follow. "He's not my ex."

"Fine, you might not have *dated*, but you two sure shared *something*."

She pushes me onto my back, climbing over me and nuzzling my neck. "Shh." She traces the ridges and grooves of my stomach. "Let's pretend to like each other for the time being, and give his little snitch a convincing visual, alright?"

My breath hitches as she slips her top off.

A black rose tattoo blooms across her abdomen, its stem winding up along her ribs in precise, deliberate lines. One tendril reaches higher, curving beneath her left breast. The ink is dark and bold, burned into her skin by Eros herself. My muscles cramp, my hands digging into the soft flesh of her waist.

Faint silvery scars fill my vision. She's covered in them. Even her breasts... Her round, heavy breasts, with the most artful peaks, deep brown and aroused, better than the most sinful of fantasies.

Peppered in freckles.

Layered with agony.

Most of the scars are faint, but a mangled, horrific mess stands right over her heart. As though some evil creature has tried to dig it out of her chest. I graze the battered flesh with trembling fingers. The ridges are sharp, the skin twisted and uneven like a wound torn open again and again.

There's no poetry in it. No glory. Just violence.

"Who did this to you?" I choke.

"Who do you think?"

The edge of reproach in her voice is unmistakable, and I shake all over.

The thought that my mother is somehow responsible for this carnage breaks my fucking heart. I've always known she wasn't perfect. I've seen how she rules. Her carelessness, her cunning, always chasing power no matter the cost—but this? What she did to Devi... I can't fathom how that beautiful woman survived, her body torn to shreds a few times over.

I wasn't born yet when Devi fell. Only heard the twisted stories whispered behind closed doors that painted her as the villain. I know better now. My mother might've succeeded in rising to power, but not without breaking something sacred along the way.

Devi's eyes widen, and she holds me down to the bed, her palms flat against my chest. I'm sure she sees it all on my face. The anguish. The hurt. The fucking *shame* of sharing blood and occasional pleasantries with the monster who did this to her. For one quiet second, we just look at each other. No words. Just that raw, unbearable truth.

"Sara told me about your proclivity for beautiful women." She tugs on my lyranthium pendant, hard, forcing me to lift my head and holding me there, inches from her lips. "Everyone expects you to chase me, then move on to greener pastures, but there are no greener pastures where I'm concerned. Are you sure you want to risk it?"

Her nails gauge the flesh over my heart, leaving scratches in their wake.

"I'm a bastard belonging to two kingdoms and yet none, stuck with a name that belongs to neither my mother nor my father. I only became what everyone thought I would be—nothing more than a distraction. I'm not the kind of man women bring home to their parents. I'm the lover they whisper about, the one they take for a night of sin before returning to their safe little worlds. A fleeting indulgence. But I want *more*. I want to matter. To the world. To *you*."

Her mouth parts on a silent gasp. She hooks her small finger around the chain, pulling my pendant into view. "What is this for?"

"It keeps me grounded. My storm magic is stronger without it, but you might get burned."

With a naughty grin, she breaks the chain and throws the pendant to the ground. "Let's test that theory."

Without warning, she bends down and kisses away the anguish, the guilt, the pain gushing out of me—erasing it, replacing it with hunger. There's a wild glint in her eyes, like sex is her way of shattering that moment. Like this is the only kind of closeness she knows how to survive.

My body betrays me, the weight of my thoughts vanishing, consumed by a fiery, unrelenting need. The grief fades into something far more urgent, far more primal. Every inch of me *aches* for her.

I'd theorized that, as our engagement became public, we might share a bed. That I'd have to brush against her body or nudge her cold feet.

But I never anticipated the sight of her moving above me, rubbing herself against my very sensitive, extremely aroused cock. A full-bodied shiver quakes her body, our sex now pressed flushed, separated only by our clothes.

"Have you already forgotten about the rules?" she scolds with a wicked roll of her hips, making me hiss.

I stroke the path between her breasts up and down. "We said no sex. Not no erection. I can't help that part. And not touching you right now wouldn't be very believable." I squeeze her left breast, the glorious feel of it sending a white-hot jolt through my cock. "Why did you insist on this stupid no-sex rule, again?"

She leans down to stare into my eyes. "We both agreed."

"I'm pretty sure I didn't swear to that."

"Mm— Still no."

I grip her hips, holding her still for a moment. "Then marry me tonight."

She snags my wrists and pulls them above my head. "Shut up, pretty boy, and don't move."

I'm used to women chasing *me*, hungry for an unforgettable night.

Devi has perfect control. She's holding me by my literal balls, and I can't do anything but pray she's feeling *something*, because I sure as hell won't be the one to turn her down. She caresses my cock over my clothes with lethal accuracy, dragging her nails from root to tip, then rubbing down the length of it.

"Fuck. Don't stop."

Her eyes dance. "You like that, Seth?"

"Yes," I growl.

She stops abruptly, unfeeling, while I'm about to come from just the touch of her hand alone. "Tough luck. Byron left." She moves to escape, but I roll us over.

"Oh no you don't," I whisper, testing the waters, checking if she'll let me lead.

Our noses touch. I can almost see the war raging inside her beautiful, sexy head. She pats my throbbing length, each vibration reverberating in my spine, my legs, my very soul. "Down, Seth."

Fleeing my embrace, she rolls from underneath me and enters the ensuite bathroom. I fall to the mattress, gloriously unsatisfied, and stare down at the bulge in my pants, gritting my teeth together.

"You're a cruel, cruel woman," I shout after her.

She laughs at that, the sound joyful and mischievous, and my lids flutter.

Fuuuck.

A halo of light frames her naked silhouette as she obscures the doorway. "I'm taking a shower, *darling*. You can show yourself out."

I adjust the pillows behind my back. "I'm not going anywhere. I like to cuddle after fake sex."

She disappears without a word. The door closes behind her, then springs back open by an inch, the inviting gap bathed in golden light.

The shower turns on, and my stomach clenches. The thought of her warm and naked under the spray... How many nights of this sort can one Spring Fae survive? How am I expected to keep my head while Devi fucking Eros grinds herself on me, off-limits, while I'm forbidden from touching her.

That witch knows exactly what she's doing. She hates me. She loathes my mother. And I'd bet it's all part of her evil plan to drive me mad, one "we're just playing a part" at a time.

My hand creeps lower, desperate to take the edge off, but I'm not sure that would help. It's humiliating. Rules or no rules, I won't take this abuse lying down. Two can play at this game. Devi Eros must have a weak link.

And it's up to me to find it.

The inch of empty space at the door wrecks my brain. Was it a mistake? Seems like an odd mistake to make, given the situation. An invitation, then? What if this was an invitation meant to look as a mistake, just so she'd have plausible deniability?

I need... I don't know what I need, but I'm not thinking straight when I curl a hand around the door frame and enter the bathroom. Steam from the shower hangs thick and hot in the air, and I merge with it without meaning to. My senses are different when I turn into a cloud, a mist, or a strong breeze. I can't *see*, exactly, but I can *feel* my surroundings, and Devi's beauty stings my heart. Her long red braids are tucked away under a black, silky shower cap, leaving her smooth, freckled shoulders bare. Rivulets of water roll down her breasts, following the paths laid out by her scars.

A deep sigh shudders through her body as she leans against the wall, eyes closed.

What happens next unravels me. Her small hand sneaks down her body and dips below her stomach.

Fuck me.

I can't stay. Can't look. She doesn't know I'm here. I need to leave before I do something I regret.

"Seth," she says, but her sight travels through me. "Seth," she purrs, leaving no question to what she's doing.

She's moaning my name.

My knees buckle, my hold on the magic wavering. I'm fucking powerless to stop my descent and condense back into flesh on my side of the glass, leaning against it not to topple over.

Devi gasps, and we have a silent conversation. *Are you really spying on me while I shower?* she asks, eyes narrowed.

Are you touching yourself thinking of me? And there's no guile in my question, no cockiness, just pure, unadulterated need.

A sultry chuckle falls from her lips, and she steps forward, pressing a palm to the glass where my left hand is resting, the other still at the apex of her thighs.

"Alright, you can look. But you can't touch." She chuckles again.

The sound wrecks me.

She's all wet and naked. I run my hand down the glass, from her chest to her stomach, and pretend I can feel the heat of her skin beneath my fingertips. I think back to her pebbled nipple inside my palm, to the little moan she gave when I squeezed her breast. I bet I could make her come from that alone.

I feel like a simple mortal, some horny virgin with an overdose of libido and no power at all. I should hate her for making me wait, but instead, I crave her more, the burn of wanting sweeter for it.

With my brow arched, I strip from my undershirt and pants until I'm as naked and exposed as she is. The way she streaks her nails down the glass, her body leaning forward as though swallowed by my gravity, gives me a boost of confidence.

I tuck my bottom lip between my teeth and stroke my rock-hard cock from root to tip. Pre-cum spreads across the head, and Devi's tongue darts out to touch her bottom lip. She draws slow circles across her clit, her breasts now pressed to the glass.

We're playing a dangerous game of tit for tat. I'm entranced by her quickening breaths, and wait for her thighs to quiver, for her lids to flutter on a moan that shakes her entire body, before increasing the pace. I drink her in—every curve, every scar, every flicker of pleasure lighting her face. She's breathtaking, yes, but still hidden behind glass, like a priceless statue or painting.

Untouchable. A relic of a life she barely survived.

Her true self—raw, powerful, wounded—remains concealed beneath the armor of a brave woman who's been betrayed and abused. Admired and revered, but not loved. Not the way she deserves.

I don't want to watch her from a distance, or worship her through glass. I want to strip away her armor. I want to kiss her awake from the long slumber they left her in, until she remembers she's more than what they broke. Not a memory. Not some priceless artifact like the ones she sells in her shop, but flesh and blood and fury.

Not a fallen queen. *My* queen.

To be touched. Cherished. Adored.

I want the Queen of Hearts, the goddess, the legend, to unravel beneath my hands. I want her to tremble in my grip until every wall she's built crumbles. Until she feels as vulnerable, as vibrant, as alive as I do when I'm with her.

I'll count the days, the hours, the *eternities* until I can call her mine. And when I finally get to hold her as my wife, by the spindle, I will love her until her broken, mangled heart beats only for me.

CHAPTER 18
WIND EATER
DEVI

We ride in silence, the wolf-led sleigh cutting a clean path through the snow. Seth sits beside me in the toboggan, nestled close.

"Isn't this fun?" he grunts, as I jab his chest for the twelfth time in minutes, my fruitless attempts to stay on my side of the sleigh felt deeply in my cramped limbs. Each bump sends us crashing into each other—elbows, knees, bruises—until he wraps an arm around me. "Let's try something else."

He slowly, meticulously, shifts me over his thigh until I'm lying between his legs, steadying us both and stopping the jarring back-and-forth.

"Better. Now relax, you're stiff as steel."

"So are you," I quip, rubbing my ass against his erection.

His voice dips into a husky drawl. "Mm. You're not playing fair."

There. While he's busy lusting after me and plotting new ways for us to fuck, he's not asking questions about the mission Elio saddled me with or the secret blade strapped to my thigh.

I press my lips together not to engage further, shutting down any further attempts at conversation, trying to keep my mind as blank and still as the landscape.

But my thoughts keep drifting back to last night.

To his glorious, naked body blurred by the steam of the shower.

How fierce he looked, standing on the other side of that glass pane, ready to smash it to bits. How delirious I was, coming harder than I have in decades as he devoured me with his eyes. The hot curses that spilled from his lips when he stroked himself to completion. The mess he made, ropes of cum splattered against the glass.

All terrible mistakes.

I almost gave in, almost let him touch my body without pretense, and that can't happen again. I can't have sex with him, not if it means feeling that way again, like I could forget what his mother did to me, forget that he's my enemy, forget how much I hate him just to momentarily satisfy the ache in my bones.

Seth Devine is a weed. A beautiful, invasive, *pollinates-everything-in-reach* weed. I won't let him add me to the endless flock of women he polluted with his seed. The way my body answers to his kiss fills me with self-loathing. As though I've become some pathetic, broken thing that craves what nearly destroyed me.

As though my scars, my humiliation, my pain...don't matter.

To open my heart to him would be worse than weakness. It would be an unforgivable betrayal of everything I've fought for and everything I've lost. It would be like handing him the same arrowhead his mother used to ruin me and begging him to cut deeper.

I've been tasked to kill his brother, to betray him, and trade his trust for my freedom. And I will. Because anything else would mean defeat.

"He saved you last night," Percy whispers in my ear.

My loyal Faeling is perched on my shoulder, his gaze glued to the large hand resting comfortably on my stomach. "You don't have to work this hard to hate him, not if you're hurting yourself at the same time."

"Shush."

He only saved me to win my trust, because we're not already married.

Starting the moment this nightmare of a sleigh ride ends, I'm done with fake kisses, convenient cuddles, and impromptu voyeurism sessions. I'm trading all that for locked doors and personal bubbles. Strict boundaries. From now on, every physical touch between us will be strategically calculated.

Seth grazes the hollow of my neck as if daring me to break that silent vow, his other hand heavy on my belly. "Relax, witch," he murmurs.

His command settles over me like a weighted blanket, and I melt against him, my head lolling over his chest. I'm exhausted—from the lack of sleep, the unsated lust, the turmoil I'm hiding behind my blank stares and tired sighs.

I drift to sleep, enveloped in the treacherous heat of Seth's body. Seth's scent. Rain and steel, and the faint, earthy trace of blightroot, a plant that only blooms where lightning has struck.

When the sleigh glides to a sudden stop, I jolt awake.

"Easy, guys. Easy," our guide—the musher—calls to the ice wolves.

He yanks at the reins, but the alpha veers into a half-circle, turning away from our destination. The sleigh tips, and the three of us are thrown into the snow. Seth and I get ejected from our cocoon and land hard on the icy crust of the Frozen Hills. I grunt, crushed by his weight, but he swiftly rolls to stand.

"Are you alright?" he asks, offering me a hand.

I rise to my feet without taking it. "Of course." My boots find traction on the ice. I dust the snow off my pants and coat and untangle a morsel of ice from the bun on top of my head.

The musher spits out a mouthful of snow. "Something spooked them," he mutters, walking over to the lead wolf and petting his head. "You okay there, Ulrik?"

Steam rises from the alpha's black snout as he tosses his head toward the void ahead. The other wolves pace restlessly behind him, claws scraping the snow, and let out high-pitched, nervous coos.

"Good thing the beasts have more instinct than our guide, or we'd be dead," Seth whispers. "We're here."

A hundred feet ahead, the Uaithe cuts through the earth, its depths too far to see. Its signature lightning-bolt shape isn't visible from this vantage point, the span of it too vast to grasp from the ground. This chasm keeps storms from reaching the ice of Wintermere, or vice versa. A narrow bridge without rails stretches across the divide, built by ancient Fae and worn smooth by time.

We say goodbye to our guide and the clever wolves, dig our bags from the overturned toboggan, and finish the rest of the journey on foot.

"Whatever you do, don't look down," Seth says with humor.

No wind stirs near the abyss—only the weight of silence and the echo of distant thunder. Percy cowers under my tunic until he's nestled safely near my heart, and I step closer to Seth. I've never struggled with vertigo, but this is different. Oxygen feels sparse. I can almost hear my name on the wind, its spectral call beckoning me closer to the edge.

All the hairs on my arms stand on end. A strange beat drums at my ears, soft at first, then clearer. Faint whispers of my fears. Of dying before I can reclaim my crown, of being forgotten and erased by time, as if I'd never existed at all. The trench hums a dark melody woven into the wind, and the vacuum left behind it sucking me in.

I stop near the rock base of the arched bridge just as Seth begins to cross. The backpack's straps dig hard into my shoulders, and a trickle of nausea washes over me.

"Wait."

Seth turns around, unbothered by the gaping holes on either side of him, and a prickle of déjà vu sends my world spinning. My mouth goes dry. A vivid image overlaps with my vision—him losing his footing, slipping, then tumbling down to his death.

And dragging me with him.

Cold sweat gathers at the back of my neck. "I need a minute."

Seth returns to my side and raises an arm to pat my shoulder, but

I sidestep away from him, away from the Uaithe, and turn my back to them.

"What's going on?" he asks.

I dig my nails into my palms, eyes screwed shut. "This place isn't natural," I say, breathless. "There's something deep inside that trench— A power."

I tighten the loose scarf around my neck and tuck the ends into my coat, as if it could protect me from a presence that tugs at the very threads of who I am.

Seth nods. "They say anyone who falls into the Uaithe screams for minutes before being crushed at the bottom. That any bird foolish enough to fly into its depths never comes back out. Sound bends in strange ways on the fringes of the chasm. Locals call it the Wind Eater—said to draw in our breaths, our memories, our very souls, and keep them, if we're not careful."

"Well, that cheered me up to no end," I bark, not feeling better about this *creepy-bridge-without-rails* situation.

He licks his lips. "Here, take my hand."

"Stop doing that." I slap his offered hand. "I mean— I'm fine. It's just a bout of vertigo."

I will myself to walk toward the bridge, this time careful not to look down, keeping my gaze fixed on Seth as he strides ahead without hesitation.

"As soon as we're on the other side, stand close to me," he warns, his voice cutting through the eerie stillness of the Frozen Hills. "You wouldn't want to be toppled over by the wind when it comes, and fall into the crack." He spins around to witness my slow, painful progress.

"You're freaking me out on purpose. And showing off, might I add."

The hint of a smile touches his eyes. "Perhaps. Or maybe I'm distracting you from the lure of whatever power lies at the bottom."

My steps are lighter, quicker than before, and I hate that his shenanigans are working.

On the far side of the bridge, hundreds of wind turbines spin slow and steady, their blades slicing through the gray sky. The gigantic Aeolians are scattered along the rugged cliffs, drawing power from the storms that crackle constantly overhead. At the base of the descending valley lies a city beside the sea. Deiltine is an industrial hub carved into the rock, its borders chiseled one violent storm at a time.

We finally reach solid ground, and a blinding sense of relief washes over me. The storm here, though fierce, is not as suffocating as the emptiness of the Uaithe, the fear of being sucked in relenting.

Rain beats at my face, the sudden change in weather blinding me for a moment, before Seth envelops us in a protective bubble, an umbrella of sorts, that keeps us from the fury of the elements.

Only Storm Fae can reach the heart of the valley, making it one of the most inhospitable regions of the continent, second only to the cold, barren peaks of Wintermere's highest mountains.

Seth stands tall beside me, his face lit with happiness as he opens his arms to the violent beauty of the Stormlands. "Welcome to Deiltine."

Heavy clouds make the late morning feel like a moonless night, the only light coming from the erratic bolts of lightning streaking across the sky. It's beauty at its most primal, and my heart pounds in my chest. Whenever I read about this place, I imagined a bleak, gray hole— Nothing like this.

The black-and-purple clouds are alive, pulsing with an energy that makes my skin buzz and my pulse spike. These weather phenomena can destroy everything in their path, yet a part of me aches to step into the heart of the storm. To let it strip me down to whatever still stands after.

"It's...magnificent," I whisper.

"I'm glad you think so." Seth smiles the way a proud mother smiles down at her baby. "The sun touches the city only a handful of hours each year. It's the darkest place on the continent, darker still than the Shadowlands."

"The wind turbines are massive. I can't believe they're still standing."

"Aeolians are titans of industry," Seth explains. "Their blades are forged from lyranthium, a conductive metal designed to harvest the power of the storm. The energy they collect is stored in their bases, then funneled to the city through a network of underground cables."

Each turbine holds three blades, their surfaces absorbing the dim light. The long, sleek, and razor-sharp pieces of machinery are patched up, showcasing hundreds of mismatched repairs, like they've been broken and rebuilt too many times to count. Just like me. Resilient in the face of relentless destruction, despite the sea, the sky, and the very fabric of this world trying to tear them apart.

"The factory packages the energy into capacitors and ships them across the continent," he adds, pointing to the port. "A cradle of rock shields the lowest part of Deiltine from the monstrous waves of the North Sea. The narrow channel forms a hidden bay where boats wait to carry the tech on the rare days the overhead storm calms." Seth tilts his face toward the sky. "We shouldn't stay here long. The storm's picking up speed."

A crash of thunder blares through my chest, shivering through my fingers and toes and raising goosebumps on my arms. Straight ahead, the road ends in a sharp drop, where stockpiles of uneven rocks mark the cliff's edge. From there, the earth falls away into a steep, vertical descent—the cliffside a weather-beaten wall veined with rusted rope anchors and dilapidated ladders.

Before I can unpack my climbing gear, Seth tosses me a coil of rope and an annoying little smirk. "Think you can handle it, witch?"

"I've handled worse," I shoot back, untangling my harness from the ropes, my bag not quite as neatly packed as his.

He shrugs off his winter coat, and I do the same, the heavy fur impending our movements. Next, I slip on the harness. The straps are damp and slippery, the cold metal biting my fingers. I force my hands to keep moving and fasten the loops around my thighs.

Seth is already strapped in, gloves on as he hammers the pitons into the rock with steady, efficient strikes. He clips his rope in and gives it a sharp yank to check the hold, then glances over to me. "Need help?"

"I'm fine."

"You sure?" he asks, stepping behind me before I can answer. He tightens one of the straps I forgot, his knuckles brushing against my ass in the process, and the confident tug radiates deep in my belly. "If I fall, I can turn into a cloud. You can't."

He doesn't need to remind me that we're only doing this because I lack the power to fly down. I wish I could make him swallow his condescending smile—make him green with envy at the truth of it—but he's not wrong. If I mess this up, I die. Simple as that.

He finishes threading my rope in, then checks on my harness again, blatantly copping a feel at this point. "Nice ass, witch." He pinches my butt cheek, and I elbow him in the ribs to get him off me.

A laugh escapes him before he plants his boots on the edge and leans back like he's done this a thousand times. "Would you like me to hold your hand?" he asks, smug and far too amused.

"Offer that again, and I'll push you off this cliff."

"After you, then.""

He motions for me to lead the way, and I turn my back to the foggy void, inching backward until I'm teetering on the edge. Muffling a flurry of curses, I begin my descent.

The first hundred feet are the worst, but the pressure in my ribcage slowly eases.

As a child, I used to swing between the towering trees of the Secret Springs gardens, using vines as ropes. This isn't so different.

Once I get the hang of it, I pick up speed and glide down the rope with grace.

Seth whistles. "You're good at this."

I grin up at him. "Keep up, pretty boy."

He slides down with ease, giving chase—turning it into a competition, which I'm always game for. It makes me forget the wind, the rain, and the deadly rocks waiting below. When my feet hit solid ground first, I tip my chin up and throw Seth a victorious grin.

"Well done, but I gave you a head start. Next round, you won't be so lucky."

With a quick zap of magic, Seth slices off the tops of both ropes, and the protective bubble around us wavers.

A sudden bout of rain beats down my head and shoulders, flattening my hood against my hair and chilling my skin.

I open my arms to the storm. "Are you a sore loser, pretty boy?"

The long ropes fall in tangled heaps at our feet, and Seth bends down to retrieve them. "I haven't lost, yet," he says with a wink. "This was merely a practice round, and you, *darling*, better get used to defeat."

The rain tapers off, and I'm left breathless—not from the cold, but from the raw, electric thrill humming beneath my skin. My heart pounds against my ribs, every nerve alive with a rush I haven't felt in ages.

I've stared down monsters and danced with death. But this easy banter, this comfortable camaraderie, feels like the most dangerous edge I've stood on yet.

CHAPTER 19
WILD HORSES
DEVI

"**A**re we there yet?" I ask after hours of rappelling down cliffs, hiking across rocky hills, then rinse and repeat.

We've been at this for hours, and we're nowhere near the bottom of the trench where the main road leads into the city. I'm sweaty and deliciously sore—meanwhile, Seth doesn't look remotely tired. We're halfway down a particularly steep stretch, and I'm praying this is the last one.

"How come you're so good at this?" I grumble.

"I used to work on the Aelioans, rappelling down their sides for repairs and such."

I stare up at the nearest wind turbine looming above us, wondering how anyone could rappel down those slick, steep metal sides in this weather, while giant, razor-sharp blades slice the air inches away.

"Freya's only son, working in dangerous conditions, risking his life for some power plant? Why do I find that hard to believe?"

He grins from ear to ear. "Believe what you want." He wipes the drizzle from his face, his magic letting more and more rain through.

"We'll have to make camp soon. This typhoon is getting too strong for me to deal with, and by the time it dies down, it'll be too dark."

I look down, but we're still pretty high up, and a cloud of rising mist prevents me from seeing the ground. "I wouldn't mind a break."

A lightning strike booms above our heads, and rubble pelts down the cliff. The rope in my hand slacks. First slowly, then all at once.

I gasp, my boots skidding on the slick wall as I scramble for purchase.

A sickening line of fear sizzles up my spine.

There's nothing beneath me.

Nothing to grip.

Just wet, unforgiving rock and a foggy, dizzying void.

Percy's wings flutter near my heart, his nails digging into my skin as we start to fall.

Next thing I know, Seth slams into me. My forehead hits the rock, hard, and the whiplash dizzies me for a beat. The force of his rescue sends us arcing on the rope in a jarring swing before we crash into the cliffside again. His arms lock under my shoulders, clasped tight across my front.

"Fuck," he grunts in my ear. "You okay?"

My voice trembles. "For now."

A loud, ominous sound grates from above, and I flatten myself to the cliffside. Seth shields me from the incoming onslaught of rocks with his body, his muscles twitching with every hit.

I screw my eyes shut, my nails digging into his arms.

If his rope breaks, too...

The harsh grate of shifting stones crescendos before it ends as abruptly as it began, and Seth moves behind me. "That was the last of it. We're okay, but the rope is stuck between us. It'll be easier for me to get us down safely if you pivot so we're face to face."

The adrenaline in my system screams at me not to move, that I'm about to fall, but I force my fists to open and mold my palms to the almost vertical wall in front of me. "Okay."

Seth slips a knee between my thighs to support some of my weight, but the thick backpack between us makes for an awkward hold. "Spin around slowly, and hold on tight."

The cold wind and rain batter us in relentless, punishing waves. Seth's magic doesn't shield us anymore, and I figure he's too busy keeping me from plummeting to my death to channel it. I'm trembling all over, fingers numb and boots sloshing with water.

I twist my upper body, slipping my right arm under the rope until I can grasp his shoulder, then thread my arms around his neck.

"Easy." He braces his other foot against the cliff to keep us steady. "Now, I'm going to remove my knee. Wrap your legs around my waist, alright?"

I nod, following his instructions. Seth wraps one steady, powerful arm around me, the other one holding the rope, and I muffle a sigh of relief into the crook of his neck, unwilling to show just how terrified I am.

"I got you, witch," he whispers.

Seth maneuvers us so we can resume our descent. My heart beats like a flock of frantic birds in my ribcage—enormous, wild, unsteady —until, finally, my boots touch solid ground. My knees buckle, but Seth catches me, keeping me upright. He leans in, resting his forehead on mine.

"By the spindle," he whispers, "I've never felt such relief."

I don't answer right away. My knees, my arms...my entire body is shaking, and not only from fear, but from his heat.

We're both trembling like lost petals in the wind, his rushed breaths warming my cheek. He squeezes the nape of my neck again, his thumb caressing the space behind my ear. His eyes are almost completely purple, the storm inside them blown away, replaced by something far more dangerous. Want. Need. A desperate softness I don't know how to carry.

He dips his head down to claim my mouth in a bruising kiss, and my brain screams in warning. I sink a hand into his damp hair, nails scratching his scalp, and tug him closer. My other hand slams against his chest, but I don't shove him away. I clutch. Desperate. Frantic. Caught between a hunger to survive and the fire of his touch.

My whole body lights up like I've stepped into his lightning, relief and madness thrumming through my veins. We've been quite literally swallowed by a cloud, the world around us reduced to mist and the rock beneath our feet, and I can't see beyond him.

Beyond this kiss, this moment.

Seth's gaze drifts lower, catching on the raindrop trembling at the edge of my chin before trailing down the length of my body. The way my drenched tunic clings to every curve doesn't go unnoticed. His gaze penetrates me, and this time, there's no glass wall between us, nothing to keep us apart.

"We seem to have a kink for showers," he says, darting his tongue out to taste my neck.

"Hands off, pretty boy," I ground out.

If he keeps touching me, I'll cave in like those damn rocks he saved me from.

I'm shaking, holding myself back from reaching for him, because if we keep tripping into each other's mouths, we'll end up having sex. The temporary indulgence would not be worth the hassle, but gods, wouldn't it be nice to taste every inch of his dark, unblemished skin...

He links our fingers and pins them to the wall above my head, water dripping from his lashes. "You kissed me back," he places a butterfly kiss on my collarbone. "Don't deny it."

"It doesn't count. It was a 'fuck yes, we're alive' kiss."

"Should I kiss him too, then?" Percy squeaks, crawling out from the neckline of my shirt, his wings damp and wrinkly. "Or scold him for getting us into this mess in the first place?"

Seth freezes, blinking down at my Faeling. He'd probably forgotten where Percy was tucked, and I laugh—a dry, breathless sound that tastes of fear and adrenaline.

"Settle down, Perce," Seth says, shaking off the surprise. "I've saved your mistress' life twice, now."

I try to wrestle myself free, but the more I wiggle, the tighter his hold becomes.

"If not for you, I'd be home right now—*not* on some dumb, dangerous mission," I say.

It's technically true.

"You're not sorry to be here, witch. That much, I'm sure of."

He kisses me again, and because I'm apparently still high from the whole rescue heroics, I kiss him back. Tongue and all. That smug bastard. His fingers remain laced with mine, the feel of our hands entwined tethered to the low, aching heat between my legs.

"Can you both stop?" Percy whines as he balances himself from my cleavage to my shoulder. "I'm freezing."

I angle my mouth away from Seth, accidentally allowing him better access to my neck, and he drags his teeth along my pulse point, making my clit throb.

"Get off, pretty boy. I'm losing patience," I croak.

If Percy wasn't here, I'd let Seth fuck me against that wall, and that's the ugly truth.

"So touchy today," he says with a lopsided smirk, finally releasing my hands. "We're near the main road, now, so there's bound to be a cave nearby for us to dry off and spend the night. Come on."

We scramble down the hill until we reach a massive pile of debris —driftwood and remnants of what might once have been a house— heaped against the cliff base. A tunnel just wide enough for us to squeeze through beckons at the bottom.

As a Spring Fae, I'm weary of anything that looks remotely like a lair. "Should we worry about disturbing some creature's nest?" I ask.

Seth shakes his head. "Not much fauna in these parts, aside from rodents and birds."

"What if it caves in?"

"It looks solid enough, and better that than sleeping in the rain and catching a rockfall in the face." Seth ducks beneath the slab with his hands braced above his head.

I follow. The narrow, Fae-made passage opens into a wide, hollowed-out cavern, its ceiling a dome of stones coated in phosphorescent lichen. Water plinks steadily from above in a gentle *plop, plop, plop*, sending ripples across the surface of shallow, rainwater pools.

The floor is wildly uneven, but dry enough in places to sit comfortably, with a few deeper nooks and plateaus. The ceiling is just tall enough for us to stand at its center if we're careful, though Seth has to hunch slightly.

His hands lift to the ceiling to guard his head. "It's not much. But it's shelter."

"I bet you take all your girls here," I tease.

"Never go hiking in Storm's End without someone to keep you warm." He shrugs off his wet shirt. "A nasty piece of rock hit my side. Can you take a look?"

He tugs his white undershirt out of his breeches, revealing his belly button and the top of the V-shaped groove that disappears below his pants, angling himself so I can see better. I school my gaze away from his chiseled abs to check on his supposed wound, wondering if this is all theatrics, but my breath stutters.

A giant bruise has blossomed across the small of his back, spreading over his right hip, with a dark core marking where the projectile struck the hardest. Blood crusts along a series of shallow abrasions, clear liquid and rain coalescing on top. I don't understand how he kept moving—how he got us down the cliff and out of danger—with that kind of injury.

Percy grimaces at the mess. "That's a nasty bruise. Here." He zooms forward, pressing his tiny palms to Seth's skin.

I blink a few times, my lips parted in disbelief.

Percy only ever heals *me*.

Seth's blood leaves a red sheen on my Faeling's hands, but the bruise slowly fades, shrinking to nothing.

"Wow. Thank you, Perce." Seth flashes him an infuriatingly charming grin. "You're the man."

A deep blush warms Percy's cheeks. "You saved us, I'm just doing what I can..."

"It's flawless." Seth pulls out a rag from his bag and sinks it into the clearest pool in an attempt to clean the leftover blood from his back.

After a few inefficient tries, I snatch the rag from his hand. "Let me do it."

I don't even know why I'm angry. Maybe I just want to get it over with, get Seth clean and decent again, so I can stop the wildfire simmering under my ribs. So I can stop feeling like this stranger—because that's what Seth is—has somehow seduced my Faeling.

I don't so much *wash him* as *scrape the new flesh raw*. "There. All clean." I toss the rag back into the nearest pool.

Seth rinses the blood from the fabric and squeezes the excess water out. He proceeds to do the same with his clothes, stripping to his underwear in front of me. "How about we use your light power and my weather-man influence to get a little sunshine in here and dry us off?"

"I can't summon sunlight right now," I grumble.

"Why not?"

A bitter tang floods my mouth. The whole point of us rappelling down the cliffs was because I couldn't fly down to Deiltine, and I couldn't even manage that without a fuss.

"I just can't, okay?" I snap

He meets my gaze head-on. "Funny. Looked like you had enough juice to summon a whole star system the other day."

"Well, I don't have any *juice*. No juice. Zero juice. And you better get used to that."

He blinks a few times before saying, "I'll light a fire, then."

"Don't be ridiculous, it'll suck the oxygen out and replace it with smoke."

He raises a hand in a calming motion. "My wind can tame a little smoke, don't worry. I'll make it work."

The odd word choice bugs me.

"Is that what you're doing? You're trying to *tame* me? I'm not a wild horse, Seth."

"That's right, you're not." He lowers his voice and mutters to himself, "Wild horses are easy."

CHAPTER 20
LITTLE MISS FORTUNE
DEVI

The fire crackles low, its warmth slowly drying our damp clothes. Seth strung them out on a rope, each piece swaying gently above the flames. Smoke clings to the cavern air—earthy, bitter, laced with the sweetness of lichen and char—but it weaves through the cracks above our heads without getting too dense, drawn upward by Seth's magic. Outside, the storm still rages.

Seth sits close enough that I can feel the warmth of him. My muscles ache from the climb, but I keep still, arms wrapped loosely around my knees. The black underwear and sporty bra Lori lent me dried fast, and the fire keeps me from shivering, but I'm still far too exposed.

Every movement is calculated, because if I shift even a little, my knee will brush his. And I don't trust myself not to lean into it. I glance at Seth from the corner of my eye and catch him staring at my bare legs. My breath hitches, and I rest my head on my thighs, erasing him from view.

He rummages through his bag and retrieves a metal flask,

unscrewing the top before taking a sip and passing it on. Nether cider. Nice.

"Truth or dare," he says as I take a swig.

I rub off the taste of oblivion that comes with strong Nether cider, grateful for the familiar sting of the icy drink. "Are we teenagers again?"

Seth pouts in a pleading grimace. "Humor me. I'm not remotely calm enough to go to sleep, and you wouldn't approve of the other way I'd like us to spend our time."

Incorrigible bastard.

"Alright, but I go first. Truth or dare?" I say quickly.

"Truth."

I resent him for how easily he chooses it, when I'm simply bursting with lethal secrets.

"Okay." I untie my bun and let my red braids fall around my face, shaking my fingers through them to dry them off. "Why did your father refuse to acknowledge paternity, even after your Storm magic became common knowledge? The fallout between our courts wouldn't have been so damaging if he'd just admitted to it outright. Disinformation and conspiracy theories just polarized the debate further."

Seth scratches the back of his neck. "Weeds are many in Spring, but infidelity is not viewed in the same light in Storm's End. Before marriage, men can do whatever they want, but after, they're expected to honor their wives. Cheaters get judged pretty harshly. To betray one's mate is viewed as petty and weak."

"Helgar and his all-important cock, right?" I snicker. "How did the legend go again?"

A touch of humor warms his whole face, and my pulse spikes. In this bleak, gray hole, there's nothing to distract me from his beauty. Nothing else to do but admire how the firelight kisses his skin, highlighting the lines of his athletic build. Legs and thighs bare, abs rolling on an easy laugh, the man would have made a killing as an underwear model.

"Helgar, a Storm god reputed for breaking hearts and promises alike, cheated on his wife, Nyssa," he says, his conspiratorial drawl shivering through me. "When she caught wind of his infidelity, she buried him alive, deep beneath the earth, in a cavern as cold and dark as his conscience."

"My kind of gal," I say joyfully, gathering my braids to one side to disperse the heat at the nape of my neck and using them to cover my chest.

Seth drags a piece of wood among the embers. "Before sealing him in, she handed him three gifts: a cracked mirror, a black rose, and a pair of scissors. To break free, he had to sever the root of his sin —his Faehood. But Helgar would rather scream beneath the earth for eternity than give that up. It's a cautionary tale against infidelity, but the hidden moral is that sometimes, the hardest prisons are the ones we build ourselves. And gods are no better than us at cutting their losses."

I blink. "That's not the moral."

Seth lifts a brow. "How so?"

"Nyssa buried her husband alive. She entombed him, plain and simple," I grumble. "It's a story of revenge."

His eyes dance with mischief. "Yes, but he made her do it, so it's his fault. There's no revenge in justice."

Vigilante justice. The fuck-someone-else-and-I'll-make-you-cut-your-own-cock-off moral is terrible. Such a sentence would be unimaginable in Spring, where people step out of marriages every day in the name of passion. But, it's also kind of awesome. Deliciously unhinged.

"Damn. I really like that crazy bitch." I chuckle.

"I thought you might."

I gulp down a few mouthfuls of cider, mulling over the underlying message of Seth's story. By that logic, I could justify anything, but I can't help but be charmed by a Storm legend that puts the woman at an advantage.

"Truth or dare?" he asks.

"Dare." There's no way I'm giving him a chance to pry into what he thinks he heard back in Inverness. If he caught even a glimpse of my cupids, he already knows too much about my curse.

He draws absentminded patterns in the debris beneath his feet before saying, "I want you to...read my future."

"What?"

I expected him to ask for a kiss or something scandalous, so his demand throws me for a loop.

"In your shop, there were plenty of crystal balls and tea leaves. You must be good at palm-reading, too."

"I'm no oracle. I was just pretending for the mortals—"

"Humor me."

I take Seth's hand. It's warmer than I expected—callused, a little grimy, a fading smudge of blood near the heel. His fingers twitch when I trace the center crease of his palm.

"This is your lifeline," I say.

"Looks short."

"Could mean that you fake your death at some point. Start over somewhere. New name, new haircut, terribly boring wife. Maybe you take up some weird hobby, like collecting feathers to make your own quills."

The corners of his mouth tilt upward. "Only if I get to write you love letters."

Shaking my head at his blatant attempt to flirt, I follow another crease. "Here's your fate line. It's...tangled. Means you'll most likely encounter troubles on your way to greatness."

He leans in, eyes fixed on my mouth instead of his hand. "And what about my love line, O' Wise Oracle?"

"A heart line that stretches all the way across the palm is rare. A great love awaits you, one that'll never end, even in death," I answer truthfully.

Blimey.

I don't give much credit to the mortal science of palm reading, but I definitely should have said something silly and mocking instead—poked fun at him for his endless string of lovers.

I find myself hypnotized by the lines of his hand, the shape of his fingers. The warmth of his skin, the weight of his arm pressed close.

The fire pops. The moment stretches.

He cups my face and caresses my lips with his thumb. "What's it like—having everyone you meet fall in love with you?" he murmurs.

"It's horrible," I blurt out, no sarcasm or false pretense shielding me now. Just a raw, brutal ache throbbing in my chest, like my heart was carved out, and the gaping hole where it used to beat was left to bleed. "Because they all leave in the end."

"You're...perfect. Body and mind. Who could ever leave you?"

"But who could stay?" I shoot back. "I'm Devi Eros. Men find an excuse— I'm a queen, or I'm too beautiful, or have too much power, or attract too much attention. I look too young. There's always a reason."

The silence thickens, taking on a life of its own. The dying embers of the fire glow bright orange before vanishing into smoke.

"I'll stay. If you let me in," Seth murmurs.

"I don't know how to do that."

"It starts here. Now." He squeezes my hand, and I let go too fast, jerking away.

Percy clears his throat. "If you're done reading his fortune, we could use more kindling."

"Your fortune," I say, pretending I'm not rattled, "is that Percy's going to murder us both if we don't keep the fire going."

Seth reaches for the ceiling to avoid smashing his head as he stands. "Alright. I'll be right back."

I wait until the sound of his footsteps fade, and check on the blade I crammed under a rock in a hurry while his eyes were closed. I wiggle the dragon sheath out of its hiding place and tuck it away at the bottom of my backpack.

Percy winces, swaying from the balls of his toes to his heels with his hands linked at his front. "Maybe we should tell him about our mission. It won't be easy hiding that blade from him, and the more we wait, the more he'll resent us."

I shoot my Faeling an annoyed glare. "Who's got a crush on Seth now?"

"Me?" he huffs. "You almost slept with him last night."

"I *pretended* to sleep with him."

Percy rolls his eyes. "The orgasms were real enough."

My lips part. "Orgasm. Singular," I correct him. "And I managed that on my own, thank you very much."

"You think I'm going to let you off the hook on a technicality?," he says sternly. "Seth is right, you two should get this nonsense over with. You're grumpier when you're horny."

"You *healed* him."

"He *saved* you."

"But you only heal *me*." I curl a hand over my heart, feeling hurt and childish and yet oddly vindicated in my reaction.

Percy flies up so we're eye to eye and points his index finger at me in a chiding fashion. "Are you trying to pick a fight with me so you don't have to deal with the frazzled way your heart is beating?"

I turn away from his know-it-all grimace. "You bug me."

"Good. Bugging you is literally my life mission."

"Why are you rooting for Seth all of a sudden?" I whisper quickly, dropping the sarcastic facade in favor of the unease and betrayal slowly coalescing in my blood.

"*Diamantay*," he says on a sigh. "I'm only ever on your side. But you won't get better until you let down those walls you've built around yourself. Everyone, you included, keeps worrying about the outside—the scars, the physical proof—but it's your heart that needs healing. And only you can fix that."

"Having sex with Seth won't fix me."

"Not sex. But you have to learn how to let people in again. Seth saved your life twice, and I know what I just saw."

"I hate him."

"Do you really? Or have you forgotten what it's like to feel something other than anger? To crave other thrills than revenge? Are you afraid to learn how to be *you*, without your magic?"

"I don't want to be me without my magic," I deadpan.

"Better living without magic than wasting away waiting for a miracle that might never come."

I'm shook.

Most Fae see Percy as this singular, funny-looking creature that dresses in flamboyant turn of the century fashion while juggling dark humor and sermons, but he's my whole world. He's the only male who's ever cared for me. Protected me.

He's family. A part of my soul. And he *never* gives up hope.

"I only love *you*, Perce. You fix me."

Tears shine in his eyes. "Yes, I do. And that's why you've got to trust me on this."

Seth returns, forcing our conversation a halt.

"Phew. Good thing we got here in time. It's a hurricane out there," he says, oblivious to what he just interrupted.

He resurrects our dying fire, channels the heavy smoke out, and rubs his hands together for warmth. His gaze flicks to Percy and me, both of us with our lips pursed, the end of our conversation still simmering on our downturned mouths.

Seth blows on his cold hands and extends them in my direction. "Maybe you should read my future again. Second opinions are important."

I narrow my eyes. "You just want me to hold your hand."

"I'm cold." He wraps an arm around me and pulls me to him—and to my horror, I rest my head on his shoulder.

The flames dance inside the circle of stones at our feet, and a sense of serenity takes over me. It's easy here. There's no one looking. Nothing to prove.

Cuddling to keep warm has got to be the cheesiest trick in the book, but Seth doesn't kiss me or fondle me—doesn't try to push this further. He just holds me. And I don't know what scares me more: the fact that I'm aching to climb onto him, or this innocent, comfortable embrace... Like we're actually close.

CHAPTER 21
QUIET STORM
DEVI

Warmth cocoons me. Not just from the embers of our makeshift fire, but from the steady rise and fall of a man's chest beneath my cheek. For one long, blissful moment, I let it be. I let the ache in my limbs dull against the heat of Seth's body. The rock bed is unforgiving, but nestled into him, I feel oddly at home.

My leg is flung over his, my fingers curled in the hollow of his neck as though he's my personal, breathing pillow. Skin on skin. Hearts beating in tandem.

Mortification rises sharp and hot in my throat, and I try to extricate myself, hoping he's still fast asleep. But our gazes collide. His eyes are already open, and worst of all, they're sparkling. The sleepiness evaporates from my body in a rush, replaced by a pulse-pounding swirl of heat.

I speak low enough not to wake Percy, my Faeling sleeping soundly in a high nook in the rocks. "Is it morning?"

Seth grins—full-on, blinding, insufferable. "Not yet, no. You know, for someone who claims to loathe me, your unconscious mind sure has a different opinion."

I glare at him and straighten my bra, but he's undeterred.

"You're beginning to like me, admit it."

I sit up to put some distance between me and his ridiculously comfortable chest. "Keep talking like that, and I'll shove you off a cliff tomorrow."

His grin only widens. "Come back here."

Thunder resonates along the surface of the cave, drowning out my outraged gasp as he tugs on my arms and settles me back in his lap. His strong hold on my wrists is gentle, but firm. I squirm to escape his grip only to end up pressing against his erection. My chest heaves, my nipples showing through the plain cotton of my undergarment, my breasts heavy and sensitive.

"Settle down, witch," he whispers.

It's claustrophobic. Intimate. Maddening. We're cloistered in the middle of a never-ending storm inside a cavern that, for all I know, could collapse at any minute, yet I feel perfectly safe. Like the world out there, the enemies that want me dead, and the mistakes I've made, can't reach this forsaken place.

Seth gathers my hands over his heart and holds them there before drawing me in for a kiss. It's not as violent as the ones that came before, but just as passionate. Sweeter. Hotter. He tastes of salt and rain, spiced with an earthy undertone of limestone and metal.

The tantalizingly remote nature of our hideout makes me want to misbehave, and I don't resist when he rolls us over, his weight pressing over me in an eerie, beautiful way. The muscles of his shoulders are well-defined and mesmerizing, and I let my hands travel over the smooth expanse of skin, his strong bite of power crackling under my fingertips.

He traces my tattoo in retaliation, studying its pattern. "I think you like me quite a lot, actually." I open my mouth to argue, but he covers it with his free hand. "Don't worry. We don't have to tell Percy about your weakness toward me. It can be our secret."

I stick my tongue out to taste his skin, the fresh, salty taste weakening my will power.

"I dreamed of you again," Seth emphasizes the phrase with a slow grind of his hips, the hard shape of him rubbing against my core in a wickedly precise and deliberate manner. "I've looked enough. Now, I want to touch," he says on a possessive, *I-won't-be-denied* growl.

It's hot as hell.

He stretches my bra to free my breasts, and they spring out into the cold air.

Bright purple clouds roll in his irises as he tests the weight and shape of them in turn, teasing them, playing with them, studying my reaction to each graze and rough touch. It drives me wild that he doesn't shy away from the scars, worshipping even the broken parts of me.

A zap of electricity spreads from the tip of his fingers, pinching my nipple before travelling south. I sink my nail in the nape of his neck at the unfamiliar caress, and my eyes widen.

"Don't fight it, trust me."

The intense flare hits again, the current scurrying to a spot inside me that both hurts and soothes. My back arches in response, his hand still covering my mouth. "Oh, fuck," I groan against his palm.

"Let's be quiet, queen of my heart. So, so quiet." Seth bites his bottom lip at the sight of me writhing beneath him, slowly increasing the bite of his magic. The Storm touch heightens the sensations, like he's got not one, but five or six hands massaging, plying, exploring my chest and stomach, and my lids flutter.

The pressure of his hand over my mouth increases, but I can't hold my noises in.

I've never felt anything like this. Seth's magic takes me right there to the junction between pleasure and pain. I should stop this before we go any further, before I break every promise I made, but this is too different. Utterly new. Wickedly exciting. I want *more*.

I rub myself over his erection. It's still captive in the confines of his boxers, but the two thin layers of fabric between us don't mask the violent throbs of his cock.

"So fucking beautiful," he growls. "I need you to keep your hands where there are, flat against the stones, and think about how engorged and painful my cock is for you and your fucking perfect tits."

I obey, loving his foul mouth, and how he takes charge.

A low, masculine sound escapes him before he dips his head down to lick my aching peaks. I moan. The touch of saliva allows the electrical current to sink into my flesh in an entirely different way. My inner walls throb. Every brush of his tongue somehow tugs at a deep, sensitive spot inside me, like his magic created a tangible, physical link between my erogenous zones. I've been with a few Storm Fae, but none of them knew this trick. It's criminal, but oh-so-good.

I can only imagine what will happen when Seth turns his attention to the place between my legs, my core drenched with arousal.

He seems to be thinking the same thing, his dark eyes drifting to the narrow path of lace still covering my pussy. With a shuddering breath, he pulls down his boxers, and the thickness of him fills his hand. The raised veins along his shaft melt my brain, pre-cum leaking from the tip.

"Look at what you've done to me, witch. I'm about to come from the sight of you alone. Fucking hells." He rubs his crown over the drenched fabric covering me, and—

Tap. Tap. Tap.

Each time the swelled tip of his cock hits my clit, my belly fills with liquid fire. I gasp, so fucking turned on by his wicked acts of worship that I tether on the edge of a blinding orgasm.

"Shh. It's too soon for that, yet." Seth slides down into the deeper nook in the rock.

He places a tender kiss to my inner thigh, drinking in the sight of me spread for him, his pupils dilated, and peels off my underwear. My belly clenches in anticipation.

I brace myself on my elbows to look at him. His sweet, talented tongue finds my heated core, hard and soft all at once.

His growl of approval rumbles across my clit. "You taste so good, witch."

The tip of his tongue is imbued with a hint of magic that wreaks havoc on my nervous system in the most maddening way possible, and I fall to my back, overwhelmed.

The link from before works in reverse. Each time his tongue traces a soft circle around my clit or dips inside me, the hard pinch at my nipples returns. My breath quickens, and my blood spikes, my fingers digging into the rocks for support.

Seth wraps an arm around my thighs to steady me and waits until the orgasm tapers off again. That devil.

I grip his hair and grind myself against his mouth, but he just laughs. "All in good time, darling. I want your hands on those beautiful tits, now. I want to see you play with them as you wait for your reward."

I release his hair and coo, the sound bringing heat to my cheeks, my hands slithering up, up, until I reach my chest.

"That's it, beautiful. Show them to me."

I'm panting, as though my body is no longer my own but Seth's toy. The aureoles are thick, the peaks so hard and sensitive that I cry out as I roll the heavy flesh in my hands.

"Don't you like the games we play together?" He laps at my lips again, taking his sweet time.

I'm used to men going down on me in a hurry, impatient to fuck me, not this slow, tortuous dance. Seth shies away from the pulsing bundle of nerves, denying me my release in trade for a divine haze that stretches and expands, slithering inside my lower abdomen. He slips a hand between my butt cheeks, spreading my wetness over the ring there, and taps his index finger over it, circling, drumming, and teasing the tight hole.

I tense up, my muscles clenching. It's been a while since I've been touched *there*.

"So tight... We have to get you ready for my cock, my queen."

My eyes widen. Is he joking? He's *huge.* "You're not getting in there."

Seth blows on my clit, and my body gives a lovely shudder. "You'll love it, just as you love *that.*" He spears his tongue deep in my pussy, his lighting reaching deeper still, tendrils of electricity tingling all over.

I feel so full, so deliciously stretched, so impossibly fragile, like he could shatter me with one word. The savage ache pulses without mercy, expanding, rumbling, *growling* between my thighs.

"Now, palms flat to the rock, or my thunder will burn you on its way out," he warns.

My eyes widen. *Fuck, I never thought—*

I force my palms to kiss the ground, my chest rising and falling in rapid, uneven breaths, the electricity in the air creating bright sparks over my bellybutton.

"You're so close now. Can you feel it? So fucking close to the edge."

He sucks my clit inside his mouth, and I inhale sharply, my legs tightening around his face. The storm obeys his command, and his command only. I've never felt so helpless or delirious, or greedy for release.

"Come for me, witch. Make a mess, and whatever you do, don't resist."

I'm falling. Flying. Crashing down.

I bite the insides of my cheeks not to scream, caught in an endless high that marries tingles of delight with harsh, violent clenches. Seth holds my hips in place, driving two fingers in and out of me in quick, repetitive bursts. "That's it, ride the storm, darling. Surrender to it."

The voltage imprisoned inside me sizzles through my spine, my legs, my toes. It makes me see stars, filling me with indescribable rapture as the orgasms hit, one after the other, tearing me asunder.

The lightning leaves my body one blissful heartbeat at a time, slithering like serpents returning to their nests.

And leaving me hollow.

I blink my eyes open, a tortured groan tearing out of my throat. Somehow, the chain orgasms only made me crave his cock more. My pussy clenches around emptiness, over and over again, searching for him, my whole body shivering for more.

"Has anyone else made you come that hard?" Seth asks huskily.

He already knows the answer, and his smug grin adds insult to injury.

The game of cat-and-mouse we've been playing the last few days has deepened the emptiness I carry with me, and his Storm touch wrenched every nerve ending to the surface. I desperately need him to fill the void inside me. Even if it costs me what's left of my pride and self-respect.

"What was *that*? Gods! You're so—" I fight to catch my breath and try to sit up, but Seth drags his finger over my darkest hole again, dipping in, the ring of muscles tightening. It's a most intimate place, and I almost come again at the unfamiliar invasion. His cock would never fit in there, but maybe...

I relax and wiggle my ass to take his finger deeper, the leftover ache soothed by what he's doing.

He grins, stretching me wider, pushing deeper. "You're so fucking hot for it. Now, answer me."

"No," I begrudgingly admit. "No one."

He gives a long, hard lick to my overly sensitive flesh. "See how good things can be between us? You were made for me, darling. Made to rule our kingdom while I serve you, and your greedy little cunt."

"Blimey. Does your filthy mouth ever stop?"

I *hate* what he's saying but *love* what he's doing, and there's no denying that.

Seth nuzzles my core like it's his own personal playground, the fullness in my crotch returning full-force. "You love it. Now, come for me again, my queen. I need more of your honey."

Another wave crests at his command, and I suck in air, taken by surprise. Pleasure rips into me, making me cry out in bliss and defeat. I don't bother biting back my noises this time, singing his praise to the wind.

Seth drinks the gushing pleasure in. "Such a lovely taste."

I grip his hair and tug. "Enough games. I need you to fuck me. Now."

"Next time, I'll fuck you long and hard until you can't walk, but I need you on your feet today."

"You think you can stop now?" I scoff, matching his grin.

"This demonstration was merely an argument in favor of dropping your no-sex rule. Consider it carefully."

"Because that wasn't sex?"

He just laughs, "Not strictly sex, no. I was merely training you for what comes next, so you can take more thunder in."

The nerve— Wait. More?

I rake my nails over his erection. If it was angry before, it's seething now. Pre-cum drips along the side, right up to his balls. "You can't stop now. You think you can, but unless you want to knock on Deiltine's door with cum leaking into your breeches, you'll give me what I want."

He moans as I wrap my hand around his shaft, the raised veins pulsing with blood, signaling how excited and vulnerable he really is.

"You probably won't last a second, not without *training*, but that's okay."

His cock is perfect. Smooth, large, and long, with a few dark freckles over the glistening crown. I run my fingers over the slit in the middle, and spread the bead of moisture there across the head.

His hips jerk forward and into my hand. "Maybe I'll surprise you."

"Shut your beautiful mouth and fuck me, pretty boy."

He laughs at that, the sound low and ominous. "At your command, my queen." He works both my legs over one shoulder, and kisses my ankle, positioning himself.

The length of him glides over my lips, from tip to root and back again a few times, the hard ridge pressing down on my clit without entering me.

The cheater is trying to last longer.

I shift my hips to meet his next thrust, and his girth stretches my entrance, his crown dipping in.

"Oh, fucking hells," he breathes.

Then he finally, *finally* slams all the way inside me. He's hard as stone, throbbing in a devastating rhythm, and I moan at the violence of the thrust. *Yes.*

He's talking a good talk, but he's wild with lust, his balls tight in their sack, abs clenched, teeth grounding together, soul in pieces. I don't need my magic to know his heart belongs to me in that moment. It shines like the fucking sun, almost blinding. I've never felt more powerful—or vulnerable—all at once. I've tried to dismiss his attraction to me as nothing more than desire or infatuation, but whatever Seth feels for me, it's not small. Not meaningless. And it's not going to go away so easily.

Seth hisses. "Fuck. What magic is this?"

"What? You're not the only one with a special talent. Tell me how it feels." I dip a finger inside my mouth and suck on it.

"I can feel your walls pulsing, your heart beating, the clench of your puckered hole... I can feel the back of your throat against my crown without ever entering your mouth—"

He moves in and out of me, stretching me in all the right ways.

"I'm impressed, other men—"

He bites the soft skin of my calf and bands an arm around my thighs to shut me up. "Stop talking about other men. You're mine."

"Not yet."

"But you will be my wife, queen of my heart. And I will kneel for you in public, while you kneel for me in the dark."

He's lost his grip on his magic, his moves, his sanity, enduring one more thrust before he surrenders. A frustrated groan tears out of him, his hot seed spilling inside me, filling me, *soothing* me. I grin, feeding from it, my inner walls quaking around his cock and holding it there until I've milked every drop.

Until I've absorbed his seed, feeling satiated for the first time in a long time.

Seth slips out and searches for his cum, testing my pussy but finding no moisture there. "What the— That's a devious trick."

I spring to my feet and grab my tunic off the drying line. "Says the guy who used my body as a lightning rod."

Seth chases after me, scurrying to the center of the cavern with his arms braced over his head. "How did you do that? What does it mean? Could you be pregnant from this?"

I pull the dry tunic over my head, and it shimmies past my ass. "Calm down. Do you need a calendar? Or a knock on the head? I'm a Spring Fae, I won't be fertile until Beltane. Beltane is this major Spring holiday—"

"I remember what Beltane is, thank you." Seth snaps his pants off the line. "Gods, you're so hostile when you want to be."

"I take that as a compliment."

It's almost impossible to reconcile his intensity in bed with his childishness in life, and just like that, we're back to quarrelling.

"I thought we'd worked past that," he says, the disappointment and judgement in his tone palpable.

I pull out fresh socks and underwear, feeding the little ball of arousal-soaked lace to the dying fire, averting my gaze. "Sex is sex, Seth. It's a basic need we have. It doesn't mean anything more." I snuff out the urge to add something to soften the blow.

Long seconds pass before he nods, turning his full attention to his clothes. "Duly noted."

I clench my teeth until the meteoric flare of guilt passes, and force a deep breath down my lungs. Now that the haze of pleasure has lifted, a terrible bout of anxiety blossoms at the pit of my stomach. A sore of weakness and betrayal. I let myself down. But sex doesn't have to mean anything more, and now that I'm no longer starving after months of celibacy, no longer hypnotized by the novelty of Seth's body, I won't let it happen again.

I sit on a rock to lace up my boots, pleasantly surprised that his wind managed to dry them through, while Seth repacks his climbing gear neatly into his backpack.

"It's almost dawn," he says, his voice tight.

I dismiss the tremor in it, reasoning that my comment—my attitude and my refusal to fawn over him like he probably expected—must've bruised his pride. Nothing more.

"We're about an hour from the city. Only Storm Fae are allowed in, which means we'll have to change our appearance. People around here aren't used to folks like us," he says.

I fail to mask my surprise. "Are you saying Storm Fae can't be dark-skinned?"

"No, I'm saying we can't show up at the gate looking like Devi Eros and Seth Devine. We have to look *normal*."

I chew the insides of my cheeks, unable to mask a wince.

"Is there a problem?" he asks.

I can't use my magic to do my hair, let alone glamor myself to look ugly and pale. I rake a hand through my loose braids, wondering how to phrase it. "I don't like the idea of passing as someone else. Sara gave us black, hooded tunics for a reason. We'll be fine."

"Fine?" Seth snorts, shaking his head. "Okay, the way I see it, we can argue about this for hours, or you can admit outright that you can't use your magic, and I'll draw a few glamor runes on your body to take care of it for you."

"Have you lost your mind, comrade?"

He's right, but hell if I'm going to admit it. It's bad enough that I let him touch me.

He puts on his best condescending smirk. "Don't bother, I know I'm right. You used your light magic briefly in the sceawere to fight the wolf, but not once since. You're holding back your bite of power like it's some kind of disease. And Elio slipped you an end-all blade to defend yourself."

My jaw drops. "You pat me down in the sleigh while I was sleeping?"

"By accident. The hard shell of a dragonbone sheath isn't exactly discreet. Why would the great Devi Eros need a weapon like that unless she was otherwise defenseless—or hired to kill someone?" His eyes narrow, studying me.

He's treating this like it's an either-or situation. Either I can't use my magic, or I've been hired by the crowns to carry out an assassination. The only question is: which one do I admit to?

"Alright," I say, swallowing the lump in my throat. "I can't use my magic. Not outside the sceawere."

A full-blown frown spreads across his features. "Why? Does it have anything to do with that strange buzzing sound I heard back in Inverness?"

"It's none of your business."

"We're traveling through the most dangerous Faerie province undercover," he says, pulling a small vial of ink and a fine paintbrush from his bag. "I think it *is* my business."

As if I'm going to give him any more power over me after the cave sex debacle. Never. I need to establish those boundaries I've been daydreaming about, and soon.

"What happens if we're caught sneaking into the city?" I ask.

He shrugs and dips the brush into the ink. "We'll be taken straight to the Warden of Lightning Point."

"Is he an enemy?"

"Oh no. My uncle is not so bad, for a Storm Lord."

Seth traces a delicate rune along the curve of my ear. The gentle tickle of the brush raises goosebumps all over.

"Then why don't we ask him for help? He must control the access to the obsidian passage," I say.

"My uncle is unfailingly loyal to the crown, so we have to assume he's now under Luther's command,"

"That's not the reason."

"The Warden isn't the problem," Seth murmurs, his eyes flicking to mine, "but his sons... they hate me. It'll be better for all of us if we don't cross their paths."

"Why do they hate you?"

He grins. "Oh, because I'm a bastard who dishonored my family name. That, and the other thing. But don't worry, I have other friends here that can help us."

I raise a brow. "What *other thing*?"

His brush hovers in mid-air near my throat for a moment, before he grins. "To quote you: it's none of your business."

I grit my teeth as he finishes the last rune. The faint shimmer of magic settles on my skin, a subtle glamor taking shape.

Seth steps back to admire his work. "There. Now you look perfectly ordinary."

I square my shoulders, a bitter taste stuck at the back of my mouth.

Seth draws a similar series of runes on himself. "Dragonflies—common Storm Fae—are pretty traditional when it comes to gender roles. The only women allowed in Deiltine are the wives of technicians, machinists, and engineers. So play it docile and quiet, alright?"

He throws his bag over his shoulder, all packed up and ready to go.

I huff at his last-minute instructions. "You mean dutiful wives for cooking and cleaning *and* wild prostitutes for the brothels, right? I've heard about this place."

He shrugs. "Many workers are still single, that's true. Would you rather pass as a prostitute?"

"Playing the role of your quiet, dutiful wife is my literal worst nightmare."

"Ouch. I'm happy to go with the alternative, if you prefer."

"Yes, I'm sure you'd enjoy that."

A smile tugs at the corners of his mouth. "I might. Now, all we have to do is wake Percy." His gaze flies to the ceiling, searching for the nook Percy slept in.

I grin at the idiocy of his delusional comment. "Be realistic, pretty boy. We woke him up *ages* ago. He's waiting for us outside."

CHAPTER 22
STOP THE FEELING
SETH

Deiltine's gates rise at the end of the winding road. The steep cliffs we rappelled down cradle the left side of the path, while the downhill slopes across from us drop into a frothing sea. Wind howls as it blows past the surface of our bubble, but here, in the middle of the storm, I feel steady. Whole.

I feel more at home here than I ever did in Spring. It almost compensates for the burn of Devi's rejection. The steel in her eyes cuts after the night we had. I thought I was tearing down the walls between us, but kindling our physical connection only amplified her resistance.

She's holding back. Not just keeping secrets—though gods know she has plenty—but parts of herself. Her magic buried deep. Her heart locked away. She flinches at my attempts at small talk and stiffens when I get too close.

I want to believe it's fear. That she's afraid of feeling.

Maybe I'm being naive. Maybe she's already decided I'm not worth it.

She warned me not to fall for her, certain I was too reckless and immature, and now she's filing me away as just another lover. Another mistake.

But it's too late for me. I've already fallen.

Ahead, wooden palisades block our path. Deiltine's walls aren't made of clean-cut timber, but of driftwood from shipwrecks that floated into the bay centuries ago. The wood is held together by time, salt, and spells older than memory.

We climb over the occasional pile of scree until we reach the gatehouse's studded door.

"Here goes," Devi grumbles, raising a hand to the knob, but I grab her arm.

"Wait. There's still one more thing."

I shrink the protective bubble around us to mimic the kind of barrier a run-of-the-mill, weaker Storm Fae could manage.

"The guard can't see us looking so dry," I explain.

"Are you kidding?"

"Just give it a minute."

When we're reasonably damp, I tap the round, metallic knob to the lyranthium plate below it. The peep hole in the door opens from the inside, revealing the face of a worn-down, bearded guard.

"We were not expecting anyone today. Who are you?"

Fuck. I've never seen him before, so I'm not sure if he's part of Horace's crew or not. Horace's guys are always open to a little gold in exchange for a favor.

"I'm the best technician you'll ever get," I say, imitating the local accent. "Horace can vouch for me."

A sarcastic chuckle pops out of Devi's throat, drawing attention to her.

"Who's she?" the guard asks.

"My woman," I grumble. "Come on, let us in. It's pouring out here."

"Just wait. And ask your wife to keep quiet."

Devi's eyes narrow, her lips parted in outrage. "What if they don't let us in?" she whispers in a rush. "We're not equipped to climb the cliffs back in reverse."

"Patience."

"And for the record, I'm not your woman." She mimes air quotes, her top lip curled in disgust. "I'm baffled you could even get the words out."

I crack a smile, loving how angry she looks. Anger I can manage. It's eons better than the stilted, tensed indifference she saddled me with on our walk over. It tells me I can still crawl under her skin.

"I can say it because it's true," I say, grinning.

"Only in your skewed, distorted brain." She paws at the blade hidden beneath her tunic. "What if they attack us first?"

"Then I'll die as I lived. Drenched and under-appreciated," I crack. "Look, even if we had reason to push in, we wouldn't make it to the obsidian passage. Not with your current limitations. What exactly is going on with your magic?"

She fidgets, weight shifting from one foot to the other. "You're awfully noisy."

"I've been called worse."

Devi crosses her arms tightly, like she's holding herself together.

"Your magic worked in the sceawere," I press her. "What was different there? Why could you use it there and not here? Is it Faerie? Is that why you stayed away so long? After they banished you?"

She doesn't respond, focussing on the lightning storm above our heads instead. Even though I glamored away her silver stare, high cheekbones, and delicious freckles, I can't help but admire how her wet clothes hug her curves.

What kind of magic could muzzle someone like Devi Eros? I've read the stories—accounts of her turning the Royal Academy, the Spring Courts, even the Eternal Halls on their heads. And yet here she stands beside me in the rain, an end-all blade tucked in her tunic, as if her magic—her infamous bow and arrow—have never existed at all. It wouldn't take just an enchantment to do that. It would take immense power. I wonder if that's why she stayed away so long. Maybe Faerie itself is what binds her. Maybe returning here is not a homecoming, but a prison sentence.

She turns to me. Her eyes are darker.. "I wish it were that simple."

The peep hole snaps shut, interrupting our conversation. A breath later, the palisade groans open. The door drags against the earth, sending ripples across the puddles.

"Come with me," the sentry says flatly.

A second guard holding a double-edge axe motions for us to follow his colleague, the sharp blade decorated with runes.

"We don't need a guide," I grit my teeth. "I know this place like the back of my hand. I'll report to Horace immediately."

"Horace isn't in charge anymore," the guard with the flail replies, his leather gloves creaking as he tightens his grip on the hilt. "Since the old king's death, all strangers must be taken directly to the warden."

My jaw clenches, but I will myself not to spark into a one-man storm, unable to hide the frown that overpowers my face at the notion that our stealthy operation has just lost all discretion.

"Smooth," Devi mutters, just loud enough for me to hear.

Fuck. My past is about to bite me in the ass.

Last time I saw my uncle and cousins, the warden asked me never to return—and his oldest son, Alaric, wanted my head on a spike. He'd drowned in his own hubris. The thought of him curdles my blood. I don't know what he's become in my absence, but I doubt he'll welcome me with open arms.

I watch Devi, rain dripping from my lashes. Her true beauty is still veiled behind my glamor. I reach up, wipe the rune from my neck, and discreetly rub off the ones behind my ears. Glamor or no glamor, my uncle will recognize my bite of power, and I don't want him suspecting I've altered our appearances at all.

If they don't realize who Devi is, we might be on our way within the hour with minimal fuss. If they do, I know in my gut that Alaric will fight to take her from me.

I brought her here. And now, it's on me to protect her.

"We're going to have to negotiate our way into the citadel," I admit grimly, "even if that means begging my uncle for help. Because my cousins would gladly throw us off a cliff instead."

A dry chuckle slips from her mouth. "Noted. If negotiations fail, you can go first."

CHAPTER 23
UGLY DUCKLING
DEVI

The citadel sculpted into the cliffs of Deiltine looks inhospitable and bleak—some windowless, grimy factory with angular walls and spires spurting black smoke. The wet stones of the staircase leading to the entrance scrape my boots, too coarse to be slippery.

Seth and I are sandwiched between the guards, one out front and one at the rear as they herd us in for an audience with their boss. The guards' dark gray uniforms have no sleeves, showcasing their many scars and tattoos, their buzz cut and pointy ears enhancing the tough-guy quality they share.

Many similarly dressed workers carrying supplies or traveling between the different neighborhoods that make up this place glare at us as we pass under a covered porch. The static electricity in the air—amplified by the presence of so many Storm Fae in one place—tickles my insides. Nothing says 'welcome' like bulging biceps and dubious intentions.

Thunder clings to my skin and bristles down my spine, but the workers track me with cool disinterest. I'm not used to being seen and then immediately dismissed. For men to turn up their noses at me as though I'm nothing more than a stupid, useless female. I've suffered through many forms of sexism, but to be so easily written off... that's a first.

We walk through a series of sliding doors designed to crack open just enough to let people through, then seal shut behind them—layer after layer protecting the interior from the weather. There's no signage, no directions. This place isn't meant for visitors.

A sickly trickle of claustrophobia takes hold of me, the thickness of the walls meant to protect us from the outside caging me in. Even though the citadel is big—its many hallways and corridors forming a kind of beehive—it feels oddly small and small-minded. Like any idea that doesn't fit the mold, anyone who challenges the status quo, anything that isn't anchored in tradition and beaten down by years of hard labor, comes here to die.

At the core of the citadel, the air remains damp, and the hairs on my arms rise with the static charge humming through these ancient, square-cut tunnels.

This isn't a land of pleasure or lazy afternoons wasted on wine and sunshine. It's a world of hardship, lit by lightning and ruled by thunder. Tough. Grueling. Gray.

There's no real light, only the occasional torch, and the rumble of storms is near constant—like the halls themselves are growling.

No wonder the darklings of Storm's End are so rough around the edges.

At the center of the main hall, a raised platform allows the Warden of Lightning Point to preside from above. A throne of rock, accented with lyranthium, stands at its center, and two enormous Aeolian blades form an X behind the chair, their tips licking the ceiling. The whole setup feels too elaborate for a Shadow Lord and looks ancient and worn, a reminder that the citadel of Deiltine once served as Storm's End's capital during the war. Zepharion had been deemed too close to the Breach and the Islantide to protect the royal family.

"Fuck. We're in trouble," Seth grumbles, earning himself a shove from the ax-wielding guard escorting us.

"What kind of trouble? Let's-start-killing-people trouble?" I whisper.

The guards snicker, as if the idea of someone like me fighting them is laughable.

Three black wolves prance inside the room and sprawl at the base of the throne. They are flesh and bone like the ice wolves that led our sleigh, but meaner and leaner, each rib a mark of the scarcity of raw meat in these parts. Their canines peek from beneath their lips. They don't snarl or growl, but watch us with the focus of animals taught to wait for a command before ripping you open.

Three men enter the room behind them, dressed in finer clothes than the guards and workers we've seen so far. Not the silks and leathers typical of the High Fae, but the newer fabrics developed in the new world. The dark woven material is designed to dry quickly and wash easily, with accents of metal and leather buckles. I gather they must be the cousins Seth mentioned.

The Fae in the center wears a golden lightning-shaped medallion on a chain around his neck and a matching signet ring, both marking him as the warden of the province. His bite of power crackles through the air, strong but strangely contained—like thunder on a stick.

The other two are taller by a few inches. One is built like a thug, with broad shoulders, a thick middle, and a heavy beard. The other is muscular, too, but more refined. His hair is just as black, matching scruff lines his jaw, and his piercing mismatched eyes make my stomach twist with unease.

So far, none of these men have spared me more than a passing glance, which is bizarre, but probably for the best.

"Sethanias Devine... I didn't think you'd have the gall to show your face here again," the warden hisses.

A dark cloak billows behind him as he slouches into the throne, legs spread, his energy a cross between *fuck-boy* and *gothic martyr*. Dark circles drag his gray eyes down, while his thick, unkept black hair and pale skin emphasize the brooding edge of his presence.

"Alaric Rayne. What happened to your father?" Seth asks, clearly disappointed and a little freaked out to find his cousin wearing his uncle's mantle.

Alaric grins from ear to ear. "Dead. We're all sons without fathers now, cousin."

"Which means you're no longer the Warden of Lightning Point. Not until the new king legitimizes your role," Seth says calmly. His voice holds no taunt, no snark—just quiet resolve, like it belongs to someone else.

Alaric flexes and cracks his knuckles. "Haven't you heard? The chalice is gone, so the strongest wolf gets to lead the pack." His cold, baring gaze flicks over to me. "Who's your friend?"

"I'm his woman," I grumble, and true enough, it's not a lie.

I expect Seth to beam at that, but he grimaces instead, like I just said the wrong thing.

"Is that so?" Alaric jumps from the ledge of his raised platform, landing right in front of me. He braces his knuckles under my chin, forcing my head to turn. "She's not much to look at, cousin. Strange. You're not usually one to settle for ugly ducklings."

His brow furrows as he wraps a hand around my throat.

"Get off me!" I head-butt his face.

The wolves leap to their feet, barking along with a crash of thunder as their boss stumbles away, holding his nose. His fingers are covered with a mix of blood and dark ink.

The guards raise their weapons, but Alaric grabs his subordinate's double-headed axe and gestures for them to stay next to Seth.

His brothers flank me instead, grabbing an arm each.

"Who are you, little duck?" the brother with the mismatched eyes whispers nefariously in my ear. He's oddly cold to the touch, his grip firm enough to incapacitate me without causing lasting harm— holding me right at the edge of pain.

The thug clamps a hand around my upper arm and presses his rough palm flat on my shoulder, pinning me in place, both my hands now held behind my back.

"What do we have here?" Alaric inches closer, more careful this time. "Looks like Seth's girlfriend is hiding her true appearance with a glamor rune. Let's see."

He grabs a dirty rag from his pocket and scrapes the coarse, unrefined piece of wool from my chin to my cleavage, then rubs behind my ears, all the usual spots where glamor runes are typically hidden. The magic starts to fade, and the two men holding me swallow hard, not giving me an inch to spare.

Mismatched eyes sinks his nails into the flesh of my arm, marking it with half crescent grooves, but it's the way he dips his head to sniff me that turns my blood to ice.

Alaric whistles. "Brothers...we have a legend in our midst."

"You're—" the big one stammers.

I hold Alaric's stare, unflinching. "I'm Devi Eros."

He flattens the blade of the axe against my cheek. "And how are you supposed to shoot me with a love arrow with your hands held behind your back, luv?"

I give him an impish smile. "If I wanted you to fall in love with me, I wouldn't need any arrows."

Alaric tucks his chin, laughing, and scapes the hair from my face with his blade. "Take Seth to a cell. I need to speak with his woman alone."

Seth shoves the guards off—something he could have done easily before—and marches closer, his sword taking shape inside his palm.

Thunder quakes the room. Magic hangs thick in the air, heavy and electric. A creeping shadow gathers above our heads, blotting out the already faint light. It feels as though I'm suddenly being held twenty feet under water, caught in the eyes of a storm. The air around me presses down on my legs, my arms, my throat, making it awkward even to breathe.

Every nerve ending begs me to flee and take refuge, and a tickle of warning cramps my gut. Mismatched eyes presses a wave-bladed dagger just below my ribs, the blade angled upright, toward my heart. "Calm down, Seth."

Alaric faces my fiancé, unbothered to draw his weapon. "Have you known me to be anything but a gracious host? You never wanted for anything when you last visited. I'd even say I shared everything a host could share."

"As I recall, you turned on me the next morning," Seth says.

"Well...your woman should take that as an incentive to stay on my good side."

I meet Seth's gaze and give a slight nod. "You go. I'll be okay."

Seth raises his sword toward Mismatched eyes. "If you touch her—"

The creepy man holding a blade to my side snickers. "And what could you do? You're our prisoner."

Seth's nostrils flare. "I'll slice off your balls, Nate. I swear it."

"That's enough," Alaric barks. "Take him away."

His features twist when he glares at Seth. He hates him much more than I do, most likely for more than just being Freya's son.

The two brothers and guards leave with Seth, and I narrow my eyes at the warden. It's bold of him to ask to be left alone with me, especially since he doesn't know I can't use my magic. But maybe women are never taken as threats around here.

A three-foot-tall white sprite with leathery wings, pink eyes, and floppy ears inches into the room once we're alone.

"Wine for me and my guest in the study, Brel."

"At once, Your Highness," the sprite answers in a thick accent.

Alaric's mouth purses at the overly formal address. "I told you to call me warden," he barks unhappily at his servant, but the female sprite is already gone.

He walks toward the hallway behind the throne, motioning for me to follow, and whistles a high note. The three wolves rise to their feet. They stretch and yawn, pink tongues and gleaming teeth on display, before silently bringing up the rear.

No one thought to search me, so my end-all blade remains tucked safely inside my tunic.

Inside the study at the end of the hall, a cart near the hearth holds a jar of wine and two cups, waiting for us. Alaric pours both drinks with slow, deliberate grace.

The study feels like the back room of a rugged tavern. Wood-paneled walls frame a worn dartboard marked by countless throws. Heavy leather chairs circle a low, battered table. Shelves overflow with dark liquor and scattered trinkets. A faint haze of Storm magic lingers in the air, as if we're standing inside the belly of a cloud, mixing with the scent of aged wood and spilled ale. Altogether, the room carries a volatile, masculine edge.

Alaric hands over one cup. "Here."

Now that the others are gone, the bitterness and rage have lifted from his demeanor. His shoulders hunch as he sinks into one of the big leather chairs, and if anything, he looks a bit worn down.

I sniff the wine, making sure nothing's been slipped into it. It's classic Brimvale wine. The neighboring province is famous for its magic that clears the skies just long enough each day to ripen those tiny, fragile grapes grown in glass greenhouses. It's expensive and bitter, like the Storm lords who flaunt it, proving they can command both the nature and wealth of their inhospitable lands.

Alaric clinks our cups. "So, why is the great Devi Eros lowering herself to the likes of a dual-wielding bastard? Is my cousin really that good in bed?" He grumbles the last part without passion before taking a sip.

I shrug. "Politics."

"That's interesting."

"And you're here because you're hoping to get into Zepharion without using the sceawere?"

Smart guy.

"Yes."

"Is that all?" He stares at me with a slight squint, like he's certain there's more to it.

A glimmer of thirst, or perhaps lust, behind his gray eyes sparks a swell of unease in my gut, but it's there one second and gone the next.

I swirl the wine in my cup. "I don't want any trouble."

"What about Seth? Is he here for the same reason as you?"

"You'd have to ask him."

He licks his lips, pausing for a couple of breaths. "I'm asking you."

"And I'm choosing not to speak for him."

He shrugs, gulping down the rest of his wine and pouring himself a second glass. "If you refuse to cooperate, you'll end up in a cell, too. Are you two married?"

I take a quick sip of wine. "No, not yet."

He squints, the corner of his eyes upturned, as though he's both surprised and thrilled to hear that. "But you love him?"

Percy's wings flutter against my heart. I press my palm over his shape through the tunic, commanding him to stay put. In hostage situations, Faelings are liabilities, but as long as he remains hidden, he could break us out of here, should the need arise.

"Our engagement is purely political," I finally answer.

"Shame," he leans back in his chair. "Would've made seducing you more interesting if he loved you." He studies me carefully. "Why do you want to sneak inside the capital?"

I take the seat next to him, unwilling to set us up as two opposing sides or show any kind of fear. "The crowns want Seth to serve as an envoy and negotiator between the seven crowns and the Tidecallers. They believe Luther Storm, the new Storm King, allowed the Tidecallers to set up base in Zepharion."

I test the words, unsure how to phrase them to appease his suspicions without revealing I was sent to assassinate his new king.

Alaric's gaze flies to the many old-fashioned portraits hung on the walls. "Luther is not the new Storm King."

"No?"

"No. And I've heard on good authority that he's pretty upset about it."

I watch Alaric's mouth as he speaks, the wry grin tugging at his lips making me nervous. "Do you mean to join them or kill them?"

"I've been in exile for decades..." I trail off, wondering how much to share.

"Yes, the great Queen of Hearts, traitor to the crowns, banished to the new world and living there as a mortal. I've read about it."

"Then you can imagine I'd do anything the crowns asked if it meant earning back my freedom."

"Even if it means marrying Freya's son..." he trails off, misconstruing my words, probably thinking Freya is eager for me to wed Seth, to keep the power in the family.

I give him a quick nod. "Yes."

He combs his long black hair back and gulps down the entire glass, his Adam's apple bobbing with every lustful swallow, like the wine is meant to soothe some raw ache in his soul. "As long as you're here, I'd love to pick your brain about something..."

His true feelings are veiled, but I can see he's hurting. If I had my magic, I could search the depths of his sorrow and find out exactly what he's grieving—find out what kind of man he is, and what kind of love he craves—but without it, I can only see what pierces the clouds.

"There's this *girl*..." he says.

"Let me stop you right there. This girl—she loves someone else, doesn't she?"

He leans forward, emphasizing the hunch and hides his face in his arms. "Yes."

"Then I can't help you."

"And what if I kept you here until you became more...helpful?" he suggests with a raised brow and a schoolboy look, like he didn't just threaten to keep me prisoner.

I'm still wary of this man, but so far, this little *tête-à-tête* feels like a consultation. He's not the first to come to me, desperate for a solution to cure a one-sided obsession. Male Fae—especially powerful leaders—suck at accepting rejection. They keep chasing the object of their fantasies until they get what they want. Or until they get gutted, metaphorically or not.

"I couldn't carve a forbidden arrow to make this girl fall in love with you even if I wanted to," I tell him honestly.

"Why not?"

"Many reasons, but mostly because it would destroy her. Love is a tricky disease, Warden Rayne. You can't infect someone who's already sick."

"What about me? Could you cure this love I suffer?" he negotiates.

"Not without destroying you, too. I've tried to carve my arrows just right to free the most unhappy Fae from the ailment of unrequited love, but alas, the ones who responded to the treatment became immune to love altogether."

"So my choices are to continue to love someone who doesn't love me back or forget how to love altogether?"

I nod. "If I tried to cure you, you might never love again."

He exhales loudly, then sets his cup on the table. "There's a ball tomorrow night. You'll be my companion for the evening. Maybe if Tatiana sees the most beautiful woman in the worlds by my side, she'll think twice about rejecting me again." Alaric gives a low whistle, and one of his wolves runs out of the study. "I'll have Brel escort you to your room so you can rest and recuperate. I'd love it if you could join us for dinner later tonight."

It's not an invitation, but a command, and I nod. "What about Seth?"

The corners of his mouth quirk. "Let him stew in his own filth for a while."

CHAPTER 24
THE WORM, THE RAVEN, AND THE LORN
DEVI

Brel escorts me to a guest bedroom with an arched window overlooking the sea. A bench with plaid pillows is perched on the windowsill and allows for one person to lie down and admire the violent scenery. Thick checkered glass warps the view of lightning zigzagging through the purple-streaked sky.

"Is it always like this?" I ask, in awe of a world where the sun never shines and the thunder never stops.

"Oh no. It's usually much worse," the sprite says without entering the room. "His Highness expects you to dine with him tonight. I drew you a bath, and there's a dress for you in the wardrobe. I'll be back at seven sharp."

She closes the door, and the click of the lock raises goosebumps on my arms.

The air is dryer in spite of the close proximity to the outside. I suspect this room is part of the old royal apartments, so its walls must be lined with stronger magic than the rest of the citadel.

Rows of dusty books are stacked below the bench. There's a thick fur on the bed, a fire in the hearth, and a steaming copper tub, but this room lacks true warmth. A wardrobe towers along the back wall.

I open it, and sure enough, a cocktail dress is hanging there. The big chest in front of the bed is full of spare linens, and the hand mirror on the bedside table is small enough to ensure no Fae could fit through it.

Percy flies out of his hiding place and inspects the room. "I don't like it here," he declares.

"It's a fancy prison, nothing more." I dump my backpack to the ground and stop in front of the hearth for a beat, letting the heat of the flames kiss my skin.

Percy lands on the bench of the reading nook and braces his hands on his hips. "I'll check on Seth first, then try to learn more about our hosts."

Faelings can pass through glass or let others do the same. Unfortunately, there are only cutting rocks and angry waters below my window, so there's no question of me escaping with him, but he can slip through the citadel unnoticed and find out what happened to Seth. He might even eavesdrop on our host, his staff, and his brothers.

"And I'll make myself pretty," I say, unbuttoning my tunic.

The mud from our climb, the cold rain, and the dust from the road stick to my skin. Grime and humidity have crept under my nails, inside my clothes, and into my very pores. I sink my hand into the tub and hum at how delicious the warm water feels.

"Not too pretty. I'm wary of these men, *diamantay*," Percy breathes, flying over to the bed.

I retrieve the hidden blade tucked under the tunic's sash and slip it under the nearest pillow. The silver heart on the pommel catches the firelight for a second before it disappears from view.

"Promise me you'll be careful," Percy adds.

"I should be safe enough here, but same can't be said for you." I rest my index finger on his shoulder and give it a heartfelt pat. "Beware of the wind and rain. Your wings aren't made to withstand a monsoon, and the weather here is an enemy in itself."

He bows, all serious. "I won't be captured, that's a promise."

There's nothing that tickles the loyal soldier in him quite like the thrill of *espionage*, and I watch him leave with an amused smile.

When he's gone, I finish undressing and climb into the tub. My muscles hum in pleasure when I lower myself into the water. I rest my head on the cool copper and close my eyes. It's been such a hectic day and a short night that I drift into an unplanned nap.

A loud thunderclap shakes me out of my slumber, and I open my eyes just in time to see Percy reenter the room through the window-pane. A spray of rain follows him inside.

"You're still in the bath?" he asks.

I check the clock above the mantle and jump out of the water, my fingers all wrinkled. "Fuck! I have to get dressed."

The towel rack next to the tub is full of coarse, gray towels, and I pat myself dry in a hurry. "What did you find out?"

Percy lands on the bed. "The workers are chatty little devils, and rumors of your visit have already spread. Now that they know Devi Eros is here in person, they can't shut up about it. There are a few travel-ready mirrors in the citadel. Not a lot, but enough to be sure the Tidecallers' new mirror-shattering policy hasn't been enforced here. Whatever rebellion took control of the capital hasn't spread to this province, yet."

"That's good. It means they won't send us directly to Luther Storm," I say.

Percy clears his throat. "There's more. While the late warden was considered by most to be a level-headed leader, his sons are not. They call the Rayne brothers the Worm, the Raven, and the Lorn."

A big frown overpowers my face. "The Lorn?"

It's not a word used in Faerie without thought, as Lorntre Hollow is haunted by one of the darkest powers in existence.

I grab the dress from the hanger and slip it over my head. "Mis-matched eyes gives me the creeps. Which one is he?"

"Nathaniel Rayne, the Raven. He's the youngest, but according to the kitchen maids, he's a real devil and starving for a change in the pecking order."

The skirt of the gown slides over my hips, and I adjust the neckline, feeling more naked and vulnerable than when I started. "Well, his older brother has outrageous taste in hostage clothing."

The color of the chiffon shifts between black and seafoam, depending on how the light hits it. The neckline dips into a scoop, modest enough, but I resent the softness and femininity of the design. I like my dresses and pantsuits ready for battle, with straps to hide my weapons, and army boots to support a quick escape. This piece of lingerie would better fit some whimsical, imaginary woman. The A-line clings to my waist before drifting out, the hem longer in the back. There's a pair of black stilettos in the wardrobe, but no underwear.

It might be a test. I'm supposed to be able to weave my own dress, after all, but I'm so sick of these games. Without my magic, I'm nothing but a doll for men to dress up.

Percy flies down to retrieve the high heels, setting them down in front of my feet. "Nathaniel is the official patron of the brothel in town, and there's a naked woman chained to his bed as we speak." Percy raises his hands in a calming motion. "Now, before you go berserk, I'd say she's there of her own free will, eager for him to return."

I step into the heels, and Percy fixes the straps.

"Alaric is in charge, but I heard he hasn't been himself the last few days. And the third brother, Salazar, is secretly into men," he says.

"You got all that from less than an hour of snooping?" Percy is a talented spy, but this sounds like the luckiest reconnaissance mission in history.

He bites his bottom lip. "Alright, I got most of it from Seth."

"You should have led with that." My voice grows a little breathless. "Is he alright?"

"He's being kept in a cell usually reserved for the occasional drunk and disorderly worker. Fancy enough to block his magic, but he's fine."

My chest heaves in relief.

"He's mostly worried about you," Percy adds, watching my reaction. "He thinks his cousin might try to force himself on you." His gaze falls to the chiffon dress. "Which, given the way Alaric chose to dress you for this dinner, is a clear possibility."

I open and close my mouth, the discomfort between my shoulder blades growing into an itch, and play with the uneven hem of the dress. "This dinner is an opportunity for me to persuade Alaric to let us use his secret passage. I can't refuse to go."

"Are you planning to seduce him?" he asks, now hovering at eye-level. "He's in love with someone else."

"Men thwarted in love are the most hungry for validation," I mumble.

"What about Seth?"

"What about him?" I shoot back.

Percy shakes his head like I'm being a difficult child, and he doesn't know what to do with me anymore. It soothes my nerves that he was able to talk to Seth so quickly, but my fiancé not being in mortal danger doesn't change the fact that the quickest way through his cousin's citadel is probably to buy Alaric off with a one-night-stand.

I used to be above such machinations. As an idealistic kid, I never used my magic or my body or a combination of the two to win favor or get myself out of a bind. I was always being pursued by the wrong men, and so I vowed that I'd never marry for duty, never lay with someone I didn't choose. Then, I lost everything and got banished, without money or magic, to a different world at a time where women had very little rights.

I'm not that kid anymore, but my stomach is iffy about the mere idea of seducing Alaric Rayne.

I've been with plenty of dangerous men.

In fact, I usually prefer them as far as flings go. Even Seth fits that description, his bad boy persona probably to blame for all my indiscretions. There's no real love between us, and our engagement is only for show.

Sleeping with Alaric in exchange for our freedom might be the easiest play.

So why do I feel so queasy? Why is my heart beating so furiously?

"What's the story between Alaric and Seth? Did he tell you?" I murmur, the sickness in my belly taking on a life of its own.

"Unfortunately, I had to leave before he could say more."

I bite my bottom lip and check myself in the hand mirror, adjusting a few loose braids.

"Will you promise not to do anything rash? There'll be time to seduce the warden tomorrow—once we've exhausted our options," Percy negotiates.

"I've never known you to be so judgmental about whom I fuck."

"It depends. Are you only considering it because you want to punish Seth?" His mouth curls down, and I know he's disappointed in my answer. "If you sleep with Alaric tonight, you'll only hurt yourself."

"I'm a big girl."

"Are you still lying to yourself about how you feel about him?"

My mouth opens in outrage. "Percival Arthur Batten!"

The nosy, overbearing meddler... Ever since Seth saved me from that end-all blade, and again on the cliffs, it's been one allusion after another, but this takes the cake.

"I'm off. Be good," he says in a pointed manner, warning me off myself.

He slips through the glass and flies off into the stormy night, leaving behind a knot in my stomach the size of a moon.

Misplaced loyalty grates on my nerves, as though some part of me actually bought into the whole engagement lie. It's preposterous, because I never had any real intent to marry Seth.

Right?

I might have briefly imagined what it would be like, but I'd already decided it wouldn't happen back in Inverness. Maybe the quickest way to burn through this tangle of impetuous feelings, would be to fuck Alaric's brains out tonight.

And I've got half a mind to do it just to shut Percy up.

CHAPTER 25
A SIMPLE FAVOR
DEVI

The citadel's dining hall is a cathedral of shadows.

Vaulted arches stretch toward a high, concrete ceiling. Chandeliers dangle from heavy metal chains, the flames cradled inside geodesic crystal cages. Long windows line the far wall, showing off dark skies slashed by lightning.

A long obsidian table dominates the center of the room, veins of lyranthium zigzagging across its surface. Two lines of high-backed chairs dressed in gray velvet flank both sides. The table could host thirty, yet only two places are set, while the rest of the enormous table remains empty and silent. Alaric stares at me with one hand tucked beneath his chin from his lonely seat at the end.

"Come in," he says, patting the seat next to him. "I saved you a seat."

The storm picks up as if he summoned fresh lightning just to silhouette my entrance. My heels click across the polished stones, each step echoing in my spine.

The chiffon dress hugs my waist, then floats down both sides of my body like spilled ink, the shorter hem in front offering a scandalous view of my bare thighs. My cold, peaked breasts, the absence of a weapon, and Alaric's scrutiny all contribute to my restlessness as I stop across from the Warden of Lightning Point.

"Your brothers?" I ask, chin high. "They don't eat with you?"

A slow smile unfurls across his face, more ominous than thunder rolling in. He stands but doesn't answer right away. Instead, he rounds the table to pull out my chair.

"I don't like to share," he says at last. "Not food. Not wine." His eyes rake down the dress. "And certainly not the most beautiful woman in the worlds."

I sit to his right, close enough for him to touch, and my pulse spikes.

There is no orchestra here. No gathered court. Just the clatter of silverware, the eerie sway of the firelight pendulums above our heads, and a man who would rather feast alone with a stranger than the people he's known all his life. Which means either Alaric Rayne doesn't have any friends, or he doesn't want any witnesses.

Brel carries in the wine and entrees as soon as my ass touches the chair. The ingredients are not fancy, but a lot of thought has gone into the presentation. Stacked potatoes with buttery cream wrapped with ribbons of cooked leeks, seaduck meat, and root vegetables to the side. These shadowy parts of the continent are ill-equipped to grow food. The Storm Court relies mostly on imports from Spring and Summer, as their greenhouse efforts in the Brimvale province are nowhere near enough to sustain their population.

My mouth waters at the pleasant aromas rising from the offered meal as I pick up my utensils, my ankles crossed and spine straight.

Alaric devours me with the intensity of a bird of prey, his gaze fixed on the asymmetrical cut of my dress, all the more scandalous now that I'm seated. The velvet cushion rubs against my inner thighs, and I simply have to break the charged silence before I do something rash.

"The citadel is a lot grander than I expected. Must be a pain to maintain a building of this size in a land that consistently tries to chip away at it," I say.

"That's the beauty of it, no? Things that withstand adversity become even more precious." Alaric finally stops staring long enough to cut his meat.

I mask a sigh of relief as I do the same.

"The late Storm King didn't like it mentioned, but way back when," he says, his gaze drawn to the flicker of candlelight against the shiny black table, "during the Mist Wars, the royal family lived here—at the heart of the storm."

"And now it belongs to the powerful warden of a forsaken city," I say in a cajoling tone.

He glances at me with something like amusement—or warning. "You truly don't know, do you? When you and Seth first appeared, I thought for sure you were sent here to kill me."

I arch a brow. "I wasn't sent here to kill you."

"Then how do you explain this?" He slides the sheath of my end-all blade from his belt and slams it on the table. "Brel found it in your room."

Bloody hells.

"Now, one would wonder why you'd leave such a weapon sheathed under your pillow if you were indeed sent to kill me, but it's rude to carry such things inside one's home."

"It wasn't meant for you," I blurt out, eager to disperse his suspicions.

"I'm inclined to believe you."

"So I can have it back?" I joke, the duck and potatoes long forgotten.

His eyes flare up. "Not just yet."

Instead of answering, he stands and shrugs his dinner jacket off, discarding it over the blade. My face crumples when he starts unbuttoning his shirt, and my breath catches.

I force a bit of warmth into my voice as I say, "A woman likes to be wined and dined first, my lord."

Alaric discards his dress shirt and peels his undershirt over his head in one smooth motion.

The air shifts. *By Eros!*

A jackal is inked into his side. The black tattoo undulates under the flames, the eyes of the animal glowing like it's watching me. But it's not just the lifelike creature that steals my breath—it's the chaos surrounding it. Pale red tendrils stretch out from the mark, webbing over his torso, his shoulders—even his arms—like bolts of lightning are trapped beneath the skin. Not scars, but raw, throbbing, flesh.

The mark dips below the leather at his hips.

I suck in air. "You're the new Storm King."

Alaric smiles a small, infinitesimal smile, his lids fluttering as though the words are impossibly sweet. He dumps his undershirt over the jacket and sits back down.

"But why hide it? Your girl—Tatiana, right?—she'll change her tune fast once she knows."

His jaw flexes. "I'm in uncharted territory. My brothers...they obey, but only because they have no other choice. I have to be careful with how I play my hand. The mark didn't come, it *struck*. I haven't entirely recovered. I'm vulnerable, and now that the chalice is no more, they might think they're next in line and try to kill me to steal my crown."

"And you're telling *me*? A prisoner?"

"You're my guest, remember?" He leans close, the scent of pinesap soap tangled with char rising from his burnt skin. "If not my brothers, then Luther and Maddox Storm will come for me. I need to get my affairs in order before they realize who wears the crown. I need to marry as soon as possible."

I can understand his rationale for wanting to marry. It'll solidify his power and influence.

Before the destruction of the Eternal Chalice, someone chosen by the gods to rule—like Alaric—would have been reviewed by the seven crowns. A period of about ten days would have been set aside for official challengers to come forward before the new king was anointed and allowed to claim the magics of his lands.

With that ritual came the reveal of their full name. Names and magic go hand in hand, so for a king to rule over his peers, he had to reveal the entirety of his name. Once the challenge period ended and the seven crowns stood behind a new king, that vulnerability no longer mattered.

Now that the chalice is gone, things are different. Anyone could convince themselves they're next in line and try to use that knowledge to tip the scales in their favor.

"That's where you come in," he adds, sitting back down.

I fight to keep a straight face.

This completely shifts the outlook of our escape from Deiltine. Alaric is king, and even if he's green, wounded, and hasn't figured out the kinks of his new powers, he's now the most powerful being in Storm's End. The end-blade he just confiscated was the only weapon that could've harmed him—our one shot at leveling the field, and now it's gone.

A bone-deep fear shivers through me. He could do anything. With me. With Seth. There's no court to answer to, no higher power looming over his shoulder. He's no longer just a charming predator playing at power. He has it. And I'm not a guest. I'm a hostage wrapped in chiffon, with no way out but through him.

"I need a favor," he says, voice soft, almost thoughtful, as he trails a finger along the rim of his wineglass. "Tatiana will attend the ball tomorrow with her father. If she can't love me, then I want her to agree to marry me."

"And if I succeed?" I ask, keeping my voice cool. "Will you let me go?"

He leans in again, his breath warm and sea salted. "Yes. I notice you didn't mention Seth. Not once. Don't you want to know if he's still alive?"

I tilt my chin higher. "I'm good."

A hint of approval warms his eyes. I pray he doesn't hear my wild heartbeats.

"Then tell me. Who were you supposed to kill?" he asks.

"Luther Storm. Seth's mission to broker peace with the rebels was only a way to get me near his brother, but he has no idea," I breathe, lacing my words with smugness.

Alaric whistles. "Oh, I'm almost enamored with you, Lady Eros." He rubs the arch of his brow back and forth. "If you succeed with Tatiana, I'll allow the both of you to go on with your mission, so you can kill my competition, and break Seth's heart in the process."

My smile doesn't falter. "I'm going to need some supplies..."

"Supplies? Are we talking about love arrows or witchcraft?"

I shrug. "Do you care?"

He holds my gaze for a moment, and I wonder if I've revealed too much, but he finally mirrors my nonchalance. "No. Get me Tatiana, that's all I want."

"You have a deal. This way I can finish my mission. With Luther dead, the seven crowns will find it easier to secure peace and stability across the Continent—and you'll be the uncontested king of Storm's End."

It might be a little much, but in my experience, buttering up a Fae King is never done in vain.

Alaric laughs, and the sound mirrors the rumble of thunder teasing the horizon. "Careful, Lady Eros. Keep talking like that, and I might decide to marry you instead."

The flames flicker.

The storm outside builds.

And I honestly wonder if he's teasing...or warning me.

CHAPTER 26
VISITING HOURS
SETH

Letting my cousins imprison me was a mistake. The cell is too quiet. Unrefined lyranthium deposits line the walls, and the reflective stones glimmer with hints of blue and purple, the color of old bruises. Even the bars are threaded with lyranthium, the metal feeding on my magic and draining it to the dregs. There's no possible escape from this fancy cage dressed down as a drunk tank—not for a Storm Fae.

What is Devi doing? Is she safe?

I see her face behind my closed lids—those striking silver eyes, and the mocking tilt of her mouth when she teases me. The way she gets quiet and bites her cheeks when she's thinking. The shimmer of her faint scars.

Alaric took her prisoner, and I know he won't pass up the chance to avenge his wounded pride. The realm is in chaos, and Devi is branded a criminal and a traitor. He's got *carte blanche* to do what-ever he wants to her.

A cold, sinking sense of dread licks my ribs.

Even when we were friends, Alaric was vicious. And he always lusted for what he couldn't have. The Royal Academy. Being a dual wielder. His father's love. Whatever Devi is to me now... I shouldn't have brought her here.

I should've known better, but I never imagined Alaric could have already taken his father's place. My uncle was young and strong, unlikely to die this century.

My hands curl into fists, useless without magic.

Lyranthium saps more than power. It strips away distraction and leaves you alone with your regrets, your mistakes. It takes away your hopes and dreams, and every single one of my doom-laden thoughts leads back to Devi Eros.

If Alaric touches her—if he lays a single hand on her, with that sly, calculating smile—I'll burn through every layer of this prison to avenge her. Even if it kills me.

The soft flutter of Percy's wings stirs the air, and my heart booms at the now familiar sound.

I jump to my feet and clutch the metal bars in front of me, my knuckles white at the strain. It was reckless for him to sneak in once, let alone twice. It would only take one flick of a Storm Fae's wrist to scorch him, and yet, I'm glad to see him. When he's here, I'm no longer drowning in catastrophic scenarios. I have a thread back to Devi, a chance to warn her, to plan an escape.

"Percy?"

The Faeling wiggles through a narrow crack in the outer wall.

"*Urfpth*," he grunts, halfway through. "I should really lose weight."

I let out a small chuckle, relieved to see his sense of humor is still intact. If he's making jokes, it means Devi's safe.

"Is she alright?" I breathe.

"By Eros," he mutters, "you two sound exactly the same."

A smile tugs at my lips. "She asked about me?"

He lands on the bracket of the lone torch lighting the prison and fixes his clothes, dusting off grime from his purple tweed jacket and hair. "She's been summoned to dinner."

He opens his mouth, then presses his lips together, like he was about to add something and thought better of it.

My brows furrow. "Should you be here, then? Devi might need you if anything happens."

"I need to know exactly what happened between you and Alaric, why you think he poses a danger, and what kind of man we're dealing with."

By the spindle, recounting my twisted history with Ric would take hours.

"It's a long story," I say.

Percy's wings twitch. "I need more. Tell me everything you know about him. In detail."

I hit the bars with my opened palms. "It's hard to think about. I was young, I—" I exhale hard through my nose. "It's not pretty."

"As mistakes so often are," Percy cracks.

A wince wrinkles my face. "It might alter your opinion of me."

"As secrets so often do." He waves off my concerns. "Don't hold back, pretty boy. The more I know about the vendetta linking you two bums, the better I can advise my mistress."

I walk away from the bars, threading deeper into the cell. "After I graduated from the Royal Academy, I was desperate to be accepted by my father. It was a fool's quest, but I didn't know it yet. I came to Deiltine under an assumed name and worked as a technician, until my uncle figured it out. He wanted to send me straight back to the Secret Springs, but I begged him to let me stay, to earn my place here. No nepotism—I worked. Day and night, fixing the wind turbines on the western cliffs. The ones that get the worst of the wind."

I rub my hands over my face. "I'm not proud of all the choices I made back then, but I'm happy with the work I did. The effort I put in. It was potatoes and leeks nearly every day, and a cot that barely counted as such. Alaric was a few years younger than I was—he'd just failed the Royal Academy trials, so he was just as desperate to prove himself. And a little unhinged."

My eyes dart down. *Unhinged* is not enough of a word to describe

Alaric, and my throat burns. I couldn't see it sooner, young as I was and so desperate to belong. So happy to get a real Storm Fae on my side... I didn't want to admit, even to myself, how cruel he really was.

I swallow back a sigh. I dug my own grave where Alaric was concerned, and I should be enough of a man to own up to my mistakes. It's cathartic to confide in Percy, to *confess*. I just hope he won't hate me for it.

"Alaric hated me, at first, but we were the only high-borns. I was a bastard, sure, but I had the education, the accent, the posture. To the common folks, I was still a High Fae. We got bullied for it. Hazed. Relentlessly. In between black eyes and ritual humiliation, we became friends. At the end of our year-long posting, he invited me to spend Scebaan with his family. We were to attend the royal ball in Zepharion, where my father would finally see me as a man."

Scebaan. The wild end of the Fae year.

I pause, the memory worming its way through my heart. "I've learned since then that less is more, and that no amount of hard work can make up for being an unwanted and unloved child."

"Go on," Percy says.

"If Beltane is meant for fucking your spouse and St. John's Eve gives you an excuse for fucking anyone but, then Scebaan is a break from traditions. A respite from social norms. One long night when Fae are allowed to get lost in the storm, before we start the year anew."

Percy raises a brow. "Yes, as Spring Queen, Devi used to attend the Storm King's ball on Scebaan. Partied a little too hard, did you?"

"As the firstborn son and heir to the warden, Alaric was engaged to Katia Brimvale, the eldest daughter of Lord Brimvale, my father's right-hand man." My fists clench at my sides. "I was angry that night. My father wanted nothing to do with me—even after I'd wasted a whole year trying to prove I was tough enough, clever enough, and dark enough to be his son.

"I left the ballroom and found Katia trying to sneak into the cata-combs. She kissed me, and I was wasted, so I took her where the young, single Fae from the different courts had gathered. Maddox had arranged for a night of debauchery, and Katia, Alaric, and I ended up celebrating Scebaan in a very...deliberate fashion."

"Is that all? You had a threesome?"

He's missing the point. "This isn't the Secret Springs. Storm Fae are weary of these sort of things, especially when an unmarried woman is involved. Maidens aren't allowed to take part in the celebrations. Alaric expected Katia to save herself for him, and in the morning, he accused me of using my powers on her. Publicly. He said that my magic was to blame for her weakness, and that without me there, she would have had the sense to say no. He demanded reparation from my father."

"He could have married her, still."

I bite the inside of my cheeks, debating whether to elaborate. "He thought she'd been... spoiled."

Percy grits his teeth. "What happened to her?"

He clearly resents me for relaying Alaric's views, even though I don't share them.

"I have no idea," I admit. "My father relinquished a hundred acres of land in the Brimvale to the Raynes and sent me back to Spring. I was forbidden from setting foot in Storm's End for decades after that, until the Storm Queen passed away."

"And your pal, Alaric? He's still angry about something that happened almost half a century ago?"

"He's not a forgiving person, but I'm valuable to him. My brothers would most likely be inclined to confirm Alaric's command of Deiltine if I was returned to Zepharion in one piece. But Devi's another matter."

A metallic groan echoes down the corridor, followed by the heavy clink of boots. My pulse swirls.

"You have to go."

Percy curses under his breath and scrambles up to the ceiling to wedge himself back into the crack in the wall, wings tucked tight.

The door opens without jangling keys or clanging chains, just the creak of metal on stone. Footsteps follow.

Alaric smiles.

I brace against the bars once more. "Where's Devi?"

He cocks his head. "Still obsessed with pretty women, I see. Or is this one special?"

I should keep my feelings close to the vest, but I can't help myself. "I'm supposed to bring her back in one piece," I say instead, trying to hide my concern under a veneer of duty.

"Don't play with words, Sethanias," he says with an overdose of pep. "Your Devi has agreed to do me a favor in exchange for your freedom, so she's accompanying me to the ball tomorrow night."

"A ball?"

Whatever deal he dangled in front of her, I don't trust it.

Alaric would rather cut off his own arm than let me walk away scot-free. Devi is about to walk straight into a trap.

"You're still single, I hear," I taunt him.

"And I have you to thank for that."

It's dangerous, poking the unstable bear that now rules the grittiest province of Storm's End, but I have to figure out his real plan, and Percy is probably still within earshot. "It's rare that Deiltine hosts a ball...especially in Spring, when the storms are most active. Are you planning on getting engaged tomorrow?"

Alaric is the oldest of the three Raynes, but his brothers have just as much magic—if not more. If Alaric wants to remain warden in a difficult political climate, if he hopes to win his family's seat, he's going to need somebody else's magic and influence.

"That's the idea. For your sake, you better hope your Devi is as powerful as the legends say..." he trails off, and my pulse picks up.

"Who do you have in mind?"

"Luckily, you wouldn't know her. Lord Grimmage keeps his daughters on a tighter leash than Lord Brimvale did."

The name rings a bell... He couldn't be talking about Tatiana

Grimmage? Is he serious? She must be twenty, at most, though rumored to be the strongest of the bunch, and incredibly beautiful.

"Isn't Tatiana Grimmage betrothed to my brother Maddox?"

"Engagements can be broken. You taught me that lesson the hard way."

Fuck. Judging by the villainous grin on his lips, he asked Devi to shoot the girl with a forbidden arrow. It doesn't surprise me—Alaric would rather manipulate an unwilling woman's affection than settle for a less-powerful bride. Under different circumstances, Devi might even acquiesce to his demand, but the renowned archer has no bow, no quiver, and no arrows. She can't use her magic. Alaric doesn't know that, which is good. But how long can she keep up the charade?

With the end-all blade in play, Devi might get a chance to kill him. She's ruthless when she wants to be, faster than her size suggests, and unpredictable enough to catch him off guard. Let's just pray he's not smart enough to search her.

CHAPTER 27
THORNS
DEVI

The wind howls outside the narrow windows, pressing through the cracks in the stone walls. The fire in the hearth has dwindled to embers by the time Percy flutters through the glass and lands softly on the mattress. I sit cross-legged on the bed, arms wrapped around myself. My heels are off, abandoned by the rug. The bare skin of my back is cold from the lingering bite of storm-drenched air, but there's nothing to sleep in except this damn dress.

"Seth is alright," Percy whispers. "Alaric just came to speak with him, so I left."

I open the covers to make space for him. "Stay close to me, tonight. We can't risk you being seen."

After Alaric confiscated the blade, I won't lose Percy, too.

My Faeling hops closer.

"Aren't you going to ask if I slept with him?" I say flippantly.

"I already know you didn't."

"How?"

He taps two fingers to my heart. "Your heartbeat is peaceful."

A shiver rakes through me, and I tighten the covers around my frame. "Then why do I feel so empty?"

"Excellent question."

"What's the answer?" I plead.

He sways from his heels to his toes. "You've been lonely for decades, *diamantay*. Since your guy came along, you've felt connected to him. Even though you're fighting it, you don't feel quite so alone when he's around."

I meet his eyes. "What are you talking about? I'm not alone, I have you. And Seth's not *my* guy."

Percy sits down fully and folds his hands in his lap. "You haven't felt that sting of loneliness and despair in days. Not since Seth *rained* into our lives," he says, doubling-down on bugging me, his eyes wrinkling at the corners.

I hold my forehead and shake my head at his stubbornness. "He's not for me, Percy."

"Maybe he's the *only* one for you," my Faeling replies softly. "Because of how Freya hated you, how badly she treated you, even as a kid. Because of everything that made you *too much* for other men. Seth's seen all that, but he's not afraid."

I press the flesh of my palms to my eyes. "You gave me hell for accepting his offer."

"I gave you hell because I could see how much you wanted to hurt him." Percy lets the silence settle between us before adding, "What happened at dinner?"

I exhale slowly. "Alaric wants to force Tatiana into marriage. He offered to free us if I manage to get her to agree. He'll even grant us passage to Zepharion so I can kill Luther."

"How are you supposed to sway Tatiana's heart without magic?"

"Well, I didn't lead with that. But it gets worse. If I refuse to help him, Alaric could keep us here for as long as he wants." I play with my braids, stroking them down in a nervous, restless fashion. "He's the new Storm King."

Percy's eyes widen. "Bloody fucking hells."

THE NEXT MORNING AND AFTERNOON IS SPENT IN LOCK-UP, TOYING WITH THE supplies Brel fetched for me and the ingredients from my backpack. I might not be able to carve forbidden arrows, but I've got a few tricks up my sleeve. Decades alongside Mabel taught me a lot, and Seth's not entirely wrong when he calls me a witch.

Blood magic is not needed to brew a love potion.

A small blackened cauldron dangles from a rack above the fire, swaying in the heat. Dried damiana leaves coat my fingers with sap, their peppery aroma sticking to the roof of my mouth. The water comes to a boil, unspooling a tangle of scents.

"I should go and warn Seth," Percy says. "Explain to him what's happened."

"I told you. I can't risk you being found."

I gather the next ingredients.

Red lotus for a pliable mind, angel trumpets for a lush, heady high, and wild tuberose to induce obsession. Add a few drops of honey to sweeten the taste, and some hair Percy stole from Alaric's pillow, and voilà!

One *fall-for-the-villain* flask, ready to serve.

"Seth needs to know that Alaric is the new king," Percy insists.

"Then you'll tell him tonight, *after* the ball."

The mixture simmers into a thick, fragrant steam that curls into my hair and clothes.

I bottle a dose. "Here. Its effect should last about a day, enough for Alaric to be satisfied. If everything goes according to plan, he'll never suspect that I used a cheap trick, and not my magic, to win over his bride."

Percy sticks out his tongue, retching like he swallowed a handful of hair. "I can't stomach the scent."

"Me neither." Shame pools low in my gut. This isn't me. Love potions are superficial and short-lived. They don't bind souls or form real attachments—just drug the mark long enough to make them pliant. I'm trading another woman's right to choose for my own survival, and that sits foul on my tongue.

I used to abhor these tricks. Seduction by witchcraft always felt like a coward's route, a step too far. But here I am, brewing a cliché. If I ever get my magic back, I'll teach Alaric a lesson he won't forget, but for now, he's the one in power. And saving Percy, Seth, and myself has to come first.

"I've got only one shot at making our host happy, so wish me luck."

I add enough water to the potion to destroy what's left of it. With spells of the sort, you can never be too careful.

Percy flies up to the window. "It's almost sundown. I better hide before that ghastly sprite comes in. Don't do anything I wouldn't do." He kisses my cheek and disappears under the bed.

Brel comes into the room minutes after sundown to get me ready, just like she'd promised. Two of her subordinates fly in holding a hanger.

A strange, unusual dress dangles from their grasp, but before I can take a closer look, Brel hands me a black, see-through thong and a matching strapless bralette.

"Put this on, please," she says, and I nod, quickly putting on the mesh lingerie.

Underwear is progress.

"And remove your necklace," she adds.

I clutch the Aurelian talisman. "I need it for the task Alaric assigned me."

"So be it, then kneel and hold your arms over your head. This dress is a little tricky to manage."

I raise a brow but obey. In Spring, we weave our dresses directly around the body, a feat that permits risqué cuts and patterns, but the gown Alaric wants me to wear pushes the limits.

The dress is made out of a series of diamond-shaped pieces of lyranthium. The plates are strung together by delicate silver chains, the design fragile in appearance, yet heavy. It offers no coverage, no warmth, just the illusion of luxury.

"Don't move." Brel, with the help of her two assistants, pulls the dress over my head carefully. "The outer edges of the fragments are sharp enough to cut skin."

The straps are minimal, with no sleeves, no back, and a hem that barely covers my butt. The small pieces of metal hug my curves, their inner surface polished to a smooth, cold gleam, and it feels like I'm wearing man-made scales.

It's not the most outrageous dress I've worn, and it suits me far better than the soft, feminine gown Alaric had me wear last night. This one is made for a goddess. The dark lyranthium looks either pitch black or deep purple, depending on my movements, and a tangible magnetic field hums against my skin.

"Well done," Brel says.

Her two helpers leave as soon as the gown is out of their hands, and Brel places a pair of black flats on the ground. Their style is similar to the thong and bralette, but with thick leather soles.

Alaric must have noticed that the heels made us the same height last night.

Brel studies me, her ears held back. "His Highness wants you to wear your hair up."

I toss my head forward and gather my braids together, quickly tying them in a high bun on top of my head. "If his Highness wants a messy bun, a messy bun he shall have," I say, full of snark.

Brel clicks her tongue. "Couldn't you braid it in a more appropriate fashion?"

"Not before dinner, no."

She grunts. "Then come."

I follow the sprite through the various hallways of the citadel until I spot a mismatched stare in the dark.

"Thank you for your service, Brel," the Raven says to my guide. "I'll escort our guest, now."

The sprite bows before flying off.

Nathaniel Rayne's mismatched eyes—one light gray, one cerulean blue—aren't natural. I've never met a Fae with eyes like that, not even in the underbelly of the Spring Court where beauty turns monstrous. It feels like they shouldn't exist in the same face.

He's perfectly shaven today, with no imperfection. His youthful skin is balanced by a strong jaw and a muscled physique, but something about him sets my teeth on edge. He's too pretty, too clean, too symmetrical.

There's always something wrong beneath that much perfection.

And I should know.

He circles me, his voice smooth as glass. "Let me see you, little duck."

The nickname hits harder now that he knows my true name and fame.

The nerve.

I spread my arms out, bored and unamused. "There. You've seen me."

"Yes, a dress fit for a black rose. Thorns and all." He extends his fingers toward the dress but thinks better of it, his hand retreating back to his side.

The cold weight of the metal protects me, the sharpness of my see-through armor preventing him—or anyone else—from touching me without getting cut.

"Brel will leave your door unlocked tonight, after the ball," he says. "Ric will use it as a test, to see if you try to find Seth, try to escape, but you should come to me instead."

My gaze snaps to his. "What?"

"Come to my bed tonight, and Alaric's interest in you will wither."

My jaw hangs open. "You're offering to fuck me so your brother doesn't?"

He nods, calm as a cucumber on ice. "Yes."

"That's obtuse."

"You don't want him to like you any more than he already does. Believe me."

My fingers curl at my sides. "Oh?"

"He's the Lorn," he says, the word flat and obvious, like I should already know what it means.

"And you're the pimp, right?"

His smile thins as he traces my necklace with his fingers, the chain dipping low between my breasts. "Indeed I am."

I take a step back, not because I'm afraid, but because Alaric has just rounded the corner, and I don't want him to get the wrong idea.

"Nathan," he says, his voice firm but quiet. "Aren't you supposed to be downstairs, greeting our guests?"

Nathaniel doesn't blink. "I'm on my way." He pauses as he brushes past me, his hand settling on my elbow for a split second. "I will leave my door open, just in case."

Watching Nathaniel's retreating back, I straighten my spine and wait for Alaric to catch up.

His evening jacket showcases the same diamond pattern as my dress, and he offers me his arm. "What did my brother want?"

"He tried to seduce me," I answer honestly.

I'm used to men fighting over me, but this time, they're not arguing about which one of them could fuck me better. It's about power, and Alaric is king.

He licks his lips. "Did he succeed?"

"It takes more than a pretty face to sway me, Your Majesty," I say, stroking his ego.

He grins. The expression looks awkward on his face, like the only smile he knows how to manage is joyless.

"Is Tatiana going to accept my proposal?" he asks.

I answer with a solemn nod. "Yes. But check with me before you ask."

CHAPTER 28
DREYAH
DEVI

Alaric leads me to the second-floor entrance of the ballroom, where a long hallway lined with tall windows overlooks the space below. From here, we can observe the guests unnoticed, watching the gathering unfold before we step inside.

The High Fae wear dark tones, the Storm Court's seamstresses favoring metal over gem. Women drape themselves in platinum, silver, and tungsten necklaces, cuffs, and rings. Smooth metal polished to a ruthless gleam. But none of them wear lyranthium.

Only me.

The skirts are short, with no trains, no fabric dragging across the floors. I suppose such things would be soiled within a minute in a land ruled by storms.

"It's not very...festive," I remark.

"It's a *dreyah*, a special funeral in which we are mourning the loss of the king. It's customary in Storms for the new king to stick to the shadows until the ninth night after the old king's death—after the provinces have celebrated their departed leader. I used to think it was out of respect for the departed—a tradition meant to keep the

Chosen of the gods and his possible challengers from the spotlight while we mourned, but given the burns I suffered, I think it's out of necessity."

He's probably right. "So these are the High Fae of Lightning Point?"

Alaric's mouth tenses. "The Raynes have ruled over this citadel for centuries. I'd argue the Raynes are the only true High Fae of Lightning Point, but yes, the influential families of the province are here."

"And where is your beloved?"

"She's standing next to her father, Lord Grimmage." Alaric points to the line of courtiers waiting to pay their respects to a statue of the late king.

At the base of the effigy, a giant stone bowl holds water, and the guests dip their index and middle fingers in it before touching their foreheads in reverence.

Tatiana holds the arm of an older man midway through the line in a perfect picture of courtly grace. I'm a sexy tin man to her Snow White, her glittering black gown leaving her delicate shoulders exposed. Every inch of her is composed—chin lifted, back straight, hands folded *just so* at her waist, but something dark is tucked behind her eyes.

Nathaniel walks up the line and stops to greet her, all wet and disheveled. The predatory stance of the Raven is gone, like he can turn it on and off at will. Alaric tenses beside me as his brother kisses Tatiana's hand.

Nathaniel bows low, all charm and honey, and brushes his lips against her knuckles. Smooth bastard.

She blushes, like she wasn't expecting the touch to land, and Alaric's younger brother speaks with her father for a moment before he disappears into the mass of courtiers.

Alaric stiffens and guides me past the door to the top of the stairs. The onlookers gasp and elbow their companions, all eyes turning to us as we descend the regal staircase.

Storm clouds frame our entrance. The glass dome overhead is most inconvenient and must be a nightmare to maintain, but to my astonishment, there's no rain blurring the view. As dramatic scenery goes, it beats even the mural of the Fall of the Mist King.

Goosebumps tickle my spine.

Alaric leads me to the front of the line, and we both pay our respects to the late king's statue. Excited whispers and murmurs follow in our wake. I put on my best queen mask, holding their stares with a crafted air of superiority and mystery I mastered back at the academy.

"Look at them. They're practically drooling over you," Alaric notes quietly, frowning like he didn't expect their reactions to be so intense. "When are you planning to act?"

I pat his arm in a soothing manner. "A woman needs her secrets, Your Majesty. I'll act when the time is right. Introduce me to your court, and enjoy their envy, for now."

Alaric's jaw clenches, but he nods in agreement. He makes the rounds, greeting his unsuspecting guests as the eldest son of the late warden, and not the king.

None of them dares to address me directly. I'm still a criminal, still in exile—but no one dares speak out.

Tatiana and her father approach next.

"Warden, may I compliment your companion?" Lord Grimmage asks Alaric.

"You may."

Lord Grimmage gives off a stern, grandfatherly energy as he bows to the waist. "You're a vision, Your Highness. For as long as they live, the High Fae of Lightning Point will never forget the sight of you in that dress."

"It's an honor to meet the famous Devi Eros." Tatiana curtsies in a meek, respectful manner, but there's a definite edge to her voice. "Alaric deserves such a beauty by his side. A Spring legend is more fitting of his appetites. I hope this means you've forgotten about me, Ric?" She asks him through her lashes.

"Tatiana," her father clips, scolding her for either her taunt or familiarity—probably both. "Excuse my daughter, milord. She feels emboldened by the recent death of our king. It's widely accepted that she should be queen soon..." the man trails off, beaming.

"Heard from your royal fiancé, lately?" Alaric shoots back.

Tatiana's brows knit together. "He's still mourning his father."

Alaric smiles a cold, humorless smile. "And you think that's why he stayed away?"

"Have you heard from the capital since the Chalice was destroyed? From our new king? Do you know what he plans to do about your father's seat?" Lord Grimmage asks in a way that spells out both his devotion for the hierarchy and his low opinion for my companion.

Alaric grinds his teeth together. "Yes. He'll be here tomorrow, as a matter of fact."

Lord Grimmage's dubious, wrinkled expression matches his daughter's.

"Here, milord?" he asks.

"Yes. Here. Spread the news, Grimmage. All of you are expected back here tomorrow night, to pay your respects to your new king."

I can't tell if Alaric is improvising or not, but he keeps his composure, the tick in his jaw the only clue that he's not in perfect control.

"We'll be here, milord."

Grimmage and his daughter bow, and Alaric guides me over to the next group of courtiers.

"Make it happen soon, yes?" he mutters under his breath. "I want to see that snobbish man's face decompose when he realizes his precious virgin daughter will be mine. That she'll have to kneel for me at the altar tomorrow and take my cock in her tight little cunt, for everyone to see..."

The joy boiling in his voice brings a chill to my spine, and blood drains from my face. By Eros, I'd assumed my love potion would be enough to sway Alaric, and convince him to let us go. I'd never expected him to actually marry the girl *tomorrow*.

We join the next circle of guests, and Alaric serves them the same enigmatic invitation. Come tomorrow and meet the new king. *Fuck.*

No one seems to suspect the truth.

"Won't they figure it out now?" I say quietly.

Alaric shakes his head. "These idiots wouldn't recognize raw power if it cooked their own balls. They all treat me with condescension—heeding my invitation, but no more—because they think I won't be confirmed as warden."

"Why give them the opportunity to humiliate you?"

"I want them to dig their own graves. Believe me, they will fear me more for it."

I've played at politics long enough to know he's right, and if an unsuspecting woman wasn't standing between Alaric and his demented revenge, I'd gladly let him have it. The courtiers grin knowingly at our quiet chat, my presence not enough to sew a seed of doubt and alert them that something is amiss.

"Wouldn't it be simpler for you to reveal yourself now and demand Tatiana as a bride?" I suggest.

It'd spare us the unpleasant aftermath of the love potion.

"I want her to beg for it," he clips. "To beg for more as I tear her open, so her father always remembers how much of a whore she really is. Lord Grimmage might be stupid enough to betray me. He's the only one in this province connected enough to try, but seeing his daughter squirt around my cock... That'll haunt him."

I bite my cheeks hard, holding my fists close to my body.

There's no point arguing with a psycho king, no point picking a fight I can't win, so I switch my focus to the sprites carrying trays full of canapés and drinks through the ballroom. I inventory the offerings with care, scanning past the sugared tarts and candied éclairs until I see stemless metal flutes of Feyfire wine heading our way. The bronze and tungsten design showcases the Rayne sigil.

They are only now being passed around, and Alaric grabs two flutes off Brel's tray.

"You're serving Feyfire wine?" I ask loud enough for everyone in the circle to hear.

Alaric raises his cup in cheer and hands over the other. "In your honor."

Feyfire wine is strong enough to mask the taste of my brewed potion, fragrant enough to cover any bitterness, and an aphrodisiac in its own right, which can bear the blame for the aftermath. It's like Alaric knew I'd be using a love potion instead of arrows.

I squeeze his lower arm for his guests' benefit and whisper, "I need a minute alone."

He nods, and I skip out of the room through the nearest door, exiting to an empty hallway. Once there, I reach for the clear glass vial tucked between my breasts, my hands trembling.

I tug on the Aurelian talisman to get it out of my cleavage and activate it. The disk is cool against my skin, its crude chain matching the gown in an oddly perfect way.

If I had my magic, this would be easy. Instead, I'm stuck relying on a third-rate invisibility enchantment. My heart pounds. I have to move fast, before any of the Fae have time to notice my shadow.

As I return to Tatiana's side under the spell of the talisman, my steps are quick and silent. The flats were a stroke of luck.

I twist the seal off the potion, and my fingers turn white around the vial. I don't want to do this. Gods, I really don't. It goes against everything I believe in. Everything I've fought for.

Tatiana doesn't want to marry Alaric, but like most well-born daughters, she likely didn't get to choose Maddox, either. And Alaric will marry her tomorrow one way or another, so the love potion is kinder than the alternative.

That's how I try to rationalize it, but my hands shake.

It's disgusting, plain and simple. I should stop. Right now. Dump the contents of the vial, let the plan fall apart, and face the consequences.

But if I do, it's not just me who suffers.

I pour the potion in Tatiana's wine, right before she picks the cup off the tray. The liquid vanishes instantly, and a tight knot curls under my ribs.

I slip out of the room to click the talisman off.

When I return, my shoulders are squared, my face composed. There's no applause for this kind of trickery, no glory. Just white-hot guilt.

My eyes lock on my mark. I know better than to assume she'll drink the poisoned wine without a hitch. She wets her lips on the rim of the flute just as Nathaniel approaches and steals it from her hands.

Bloody hells.

I'm too far away to hear his words, but I'm good at lip reading. "May I have this dance?" he asks.

Tatiana curtsies, smiling from ear to ear.

Nathaniel hands the metal flute over to her father. "I'll bring her back shortly, Your Lordship."

Does he know? Did he see me spike her drink?

The couple takes to the dance floor. For a woman engaged to Maddox Storm, Tatiana Grimmage certainly enjoys the company of the youngest Rayne. He holds her close, and the way she blushes tickles my curiosity.

Are they lovers?

But if that were true, wouldn't Alaric be ticked off by it? Unless Nathaniel is making a play for her, like he did for me? Alaric did mention she was a virgin.

As Tatiana stares up at Nathaniel, the storm over her heart thins long enough for me to glimpse at the truth. She's engaged to Maddox, coveted by Alaric, but she *loves* Nathaniel. It's right there, in the glow of her heart as he holds her.

Alaric weaves his way through the dancers to tap his brother's shoulder.

"Can I step in?"

Tatiana's eyes widen, and she shakes her head. "No."

I slip closer.

"You're here, in my home," Alaric hisses. "You can't refuse your host a simple dance."

So much for patience. Is he such a glutton for punishment that he couldn't wait for me to act before he picked a fight with her? What is he trying to do?

"Now, brother. The lady said no," Nathan says, but the admonishment sounds like a taunt.

Tatiana grabs a fist of her dress, standing taller, her eyes narrowed. "If I have any say in it, Nathan will be warden of this province, not you."

Alaric grips her elbow to keep her from retreating. "Believe me Tatia, *I* will lead this province. Wouldn't you prefer to wed me? To stay close to your beloved raven?"

Tatiana struggles, wriggling in his hold but failing to break free. "You're a monster, Alaric. I'd never lay with you—not even if you were the last man in Faerie."

Everyone stops dancing and drinking, and Lord Grimmage hurries to his daughter's side.

Fuck. Where did he put the wine?

Luckily, both flutes—his and Tatiana's—are still tight in his grip, and he slams them on Brel's empty tray before taking his daughter's hand. "Alaric Rayne. My daughter is engaged to our new king—"

Alaric's voice crashes through the ballroom in a thunderous boom. "And where is he, eh? Your supposed king? It's not like Maddox Storm hasn't broken an engagement before. Who's to say he's our new king at all?"

Tatiana's brows furrow. "Maddox is the Jackal's son. He'll be king."

"Gods are powerful," Alaric replies, "but their affections are fickle at best." He finishes his wine and discards his cup. "Be careful, Lord Grimmage. Or your daughter will end up bouncing on my cock as one of my brother's whores, not as a wife. And certainly not as a *queen*."

Lord Grimmage swings at him.

Alaric shoves him aside, sending the man straight into Brel. The flying sprite, Lord Grimmage, the tray—including the two wine flutes—stumble, fall, and clatter to the floor.

Burgundy wine splashes across the marble, staining it deep red. Gossip thrums through the air, the guests absorbing the scene.

Alaric has gone nuclear, electricity sparking off him in all directions. A thunderstorm obscures the glass ceiling from the inside of the ballroom, the somber specter gathered right above his head. His power crackles at the heart of the storm, putting the subterfuge to bed.

Now, there's no doubt who wears the crown.

Every hair on my body lifts in warning, and my nipples chafe against the cold metal of my dress.

Lord Grimmage crawls to his feet, his sneer melting into a horrified grimace. "You..."

Alaric doesn't look angry. In fact, he's smiling. "That's right, I am now King of Storm's End. And you're all expected here for my wedding tomorrow. Especially you, Tatiana."

With that, Alaric vanishes in a flash. His electricity merges with the clouds overhead, and chunks of hail hit the ground. Guests cry out in surprise, raising their arms to shield themselves, helpless against the incoming storm.

Nathaniel shrugs off his coat and uses it to shield Tatiana's head. "We should leave. Now."

"Poor boy," Lord Grimmage says darkly. "There's nowhere to run where he can't find you."

Tatiana clutches Nathaniel's chest. "Did you know?"

"No. If I had known, I would have warned you, somehow."

I turn away from the distraught couple. A strange tickling spreads across my shoulder blades, chest, and neck. The metal pieces of my dress begin to vibrate, warming against my skin, and I realize I've been spared the worst of the blizzard. The lyranthium shields me from the storm, but Alaric is calling me to him.

And I must obey.

CHAPTER 29
HEARTBREAKER
DEVI

Cold air slips between my legs and numbs my fingers while the body of the dress hums with energy. Alaric's power coils around me like a leash of wind and static, guiding me through the thunderous halls of his citadel. I thread deeper and deeper into the dark until I pass under a wide stone arch and emerge into an ancient arena.

The amphitheater rises from the cliffside. The tiered seats curve beneath the overhanging ceiling, hewn directly into the rock. One wall is missing—by design, not decay—opening the place to the sea, where lightning dances across black waters and the cliffs plunge without mercy. The salty tang of brine presses inward.

It's a chapel built not for prayer, but performance. Not to worship saints, but to satisfy gods who crave a barbaric spectacle. The vacuum of Alaric's presence makes the oxygen feel thin, like we've climbed too high, too fast.

"Forget love," he snarls, hands clasped behind his back. "I want you to make *her* as indifferent to him as she is to me. Make sure she never loves anyone else."

I hesitate. "I can't do that."

He narrows his eyes. "I know about your pet Faeling waiting in your bedroom. He's the one you truly care about, isn't he?"

Heat drains from my face, my heart, my stupid, dumb brain. *Percy.*

"Now you'll carve that arrow for me. Make her numb forever."

My hands shake. "I can't."

His voice drops. "I'm getting real tired of hearing those words from you."

"I've been cursed. I can't use my magic anymore," I roar over the wind.

He spins around to face me. "Cursed?"

"Yes. If I were to craft a forbidden arrow for you now, I'd be dead within the hour."

His eyes are black, but he's listening. The scales of lyranthium bristle, one end tipping inward to bite my skin, the other hovering in mid-air. They no longer offer any coverage, but threaten to slice me open instead. A thousand tiny diamond-shaped knives, poised to strike. They tickle my flesh—my collarbone, my ribs, the swell of my breasts—ready to kill at his command.

I must look like a sacrifice laid bare at his feet, dressed in nothing but two strips of black mesh. My nipples are hard in the cold, outlined clearly beneath the mesh, my stomach bare, rising and falling with shallow breaths.

Alaric stares at my body beyond the spikes. His teeth are clenched, his nostrils flaring, but his gaze lingers on my chest. On my hips.

He hesitates, lips parted in a mix of cruelty and sexual arousal. "I love her, and she just...dismisses me. Insults me. She doesn't deserve to be queen."

The Storm King doesn't like being rejected. His feelings for Tatiana make him vulnerable, and that's the part he can't stomach.

"To love someone is to hand them a blade, hoping they don't twist," I say. "Loving Tatiana means giving her the power to hurt you."

His tongue darts out to touch his bottom lip. "I'm no good at giving away power, I'm afraid."

"We have that in common."

Alaric disgusts me, but in his darkness, his desire for revenge, his hunger for power, there's a piece of my reflection. Everything I hate about myself is in there, magnified tenfold.

He spins around toward the sea, and the dress sighs, its links and pieces trembling over my skin as it settles back into place.

A long outcropping juts from the center of the concentric stone floor, narrowing as it stretches over open air. At its end rests an altar of lyranthium. No railings, no steps, just a smooth, wet stone that rises up to my midriff.

"What is this place?" I ask.

Alaric runs his hand over the slab, caressing it. "Do you know what a traditional Storm's End wedding looks like?"

"I never had the pleasure, but I would assume the bride and groom have to fuck, like everywhere else."

A slow, wicked smile spreads on his lips. "That's right. No musicians. No silverware. No tarps. No pretending this ritual is anything but primal. The groom claims his bride right here" —he slaps the slab— "in front of his peers and under the fury of his gods. Seth might talk a good game and look the part, but he's no true Storm Fae. He's soft, like you." He walks over to me and grazes the flesh of my arm from shoulder to wrist. "You need a man bold enough to possess you, Lady Eros."

Behind his heated words—phrased to appeal to women in search of a passionate lover—I hear a different truth. This man wants to own his wife.

He motions to slab again. "There's no silly phrases or sugary vows. Only a willing bride surrendering herself to her husband."

"Glad to hear she's got some say in it."

"No blade, either. Just the scarred edge of our most precious metal."

The lyranthium altar looks like it might detach from the stone floor and plummet down to the sea at any moment.

I picture her—the bride. Hands flat against the altar, back arched, hair caught in the gale. Holding still. Waiting. She's not meant to see the crowd, or the arena behind her. There are no candles here, no flowers or music, just the thrum of magic rippling across the sky. As if the storm itself demands her complete submission, while the ocean below swallows her screams.

Along the front edge of the slab, where her fingers might curl to find purchase, the metal forms a broken ridge.

Alaric gives an amorous sigh. "Yes, it was made to cut. To mark the mating couple as love does. Uneven. Unclean. A place to grip when her knees buckle, when her husband's cock enters her body like lightning breaking open the sky. The sharp edge here allows the male to cut himself, too, so the storm takes their blood in equal measures. A union of pain, power, and sacrifice. Beautiful."

My heart hammers.

And I thought Spring Fae were into some twisted shit... Whatever happens here is elemental, and the weight of it kisses the stones. The memory of bodies bent, of vows never spoken aloud, but witnessed by hundreds.

"I've been too sentimental." Alaric finally stops pacing, towering close. "Who needs a rude, stubborn Storm Fae when they can have you?"

My blood rushes at my temples.

The horror of the statement sinks in. I've seen that kind of measured amusement combined with a thirst for a 'yes' before—on Seth's face, the first time we met. He wore that same half-smile, that same studied calm, like he was peeling me apart, dissecting my psyche to his advantage. But Seth's curiosity came with reverence.

Alaric's attention tastes like control.

Fucking hells.

There I go again, being blackmailed into an engagement, but

Alaric's intrusive hands at my waist highlight the differences between my two suitors.

"The Queen of Hearts on her knees... That's better than any stubborn, foolish young virgin," he says. "I want you to marry me, Lady Eros."

I keep my face as neutral as I can manage.

I've been blaming my attraction to Seth on his looks, his confidence, his overall darkling-ness, but if that were true, I should be swooning right now.

Alaric has a strong jaw, chiseled abs, and darkness pulsing in his bones—yet everything about him sets my teeth on edge. His arrogance reads oily and overdone. His innuendos turn my blood to ice. His proposal makes me want to crouch and snarl.

But I don't. Instead, I take a deep, cleansing breath and push my hips forward, bumping into his erection. Because what he's offering is aligning with every raw, dark fiber of my soul.

And he's not truly asking.

"And what if I say no?" I say in a teasing tone, tracing the ridges of his chest.

His pupils dilate, his eyes glued to my hands. "If you refuse to bend for me at the altar of your own free will, then I will throw you over the ledge. And Seth and your winged servant will be fed piece by piece to my wolves."

Just as I thought.

I despise this man, but he's not pretending to be someone else, not using tricks. A part of me always knew it'd come to this. That marriage would be my undoing.

The ultimate instrument of doom.

"I'll marry you, but only if you promise not to harm them."

I planned to only include Percy in this deal, but somehow, I fucked up.

"*Them*?" Alaric shows his teeth. "Plot twist. You care about the little shit after all."

I keep my cool. "Going once..."

He sucks in air through his teeth, his fists curled.

"Going twice."

The tension in his arms eases, and he unclenches his hands one at a time, the sly curve of his mouth going from *dangerously annoyed* to *mildly amused*. "Oh, alright. It'll be fun anyway, to see Seth squirm, knowing what he missed out on."

"Then I agree to marry you, and stand by your side, for as long as they're safe." I hold out my hand for him to shake, and he does so with a dry giggle.

"You're a shrewd business woman. I like that," Alaric whispers as he bends down to kiss me.

His hand squeezes the bottom part of my jaw between his thumb and index finger, and his tongue spears inside my mouth with no true rhythm or instinct, just the push of his will past mine. The bitter taste of salt and the tangy, earthiness of decaying moss invades my senses.

I can almost see the rest of my life pan out before my eyes, see the bottom of the trench coming from me as I tether over the edge of this catastrophe.

My hopes shatter. My ambitions gnaw.

Something in my chest snaps, then hardens.

I focus on the rationality of the agreement, not the gaping hole in my soul. I think of a strategy to distract myself from his disgraceful tongue pressing against the roof of my mouth, his slimy hands sliding beneath the metallic hem of my dress.

I'll take this forlorn king—so clearly starved for attention and loyalty. Betray Seth, become the Storm Queen, and when Freya dies and my rightful crown reverts to me, I'll rule both kingdoms.

Something that's never been done.

More forbidden and legendary than my arrows are.

I'll have more power than even my grandsire did, enough to beat Freya's curse, I'm sure. All feelings aside, two crowns are better than one, and I'd rather be queen than dead.

Rather cut out my own heart than leave it for someone else to break.

CHAPTER 30
ROXANNE
DEVI

To my extreme surprise, Alaric sends me back to my room without pushing his advantage further, but the unexpected mercy feels hollow. Dangerous. What kind of maniacal king kisses his new fiancée once, gropes her like a trophy, and then simply sends her to bed? Especially when she's wearing the most outrageous dress known to man—a dress clearly designed to be peeled off by outside help.

The imprint of Alaric's fingers throbs on my asscheeks, a phantom reminder of the humiliating tap he gave me in lieu of a proper goodnight. A crude little pat, like I was a horse he owned.

Brel doesn't offer any assistance with the dress and closes the door like she did last night, but the click of the lock never comes. Nathaniel was right.

Percy leaps out of his hiding spot, and my heart caves in relief. "The sprite left the door open. We have to get out of here," he says quickly.

I release my hair from the bun. "Nathaniel warned me this would happen. It's a test. Alaric will be watching me."

"Why?"

"He wants to see if I'll try to escape," I avert my gaze. "Before the wedding."

Percy gapes, his face decomposing into a horribly twisted grimace of fear. "What wedding?"

"I know." My eyes fly to the sky as I try to make light of it. "Another handsome, arrogant Storm Fae who only wants me for my magic. Draw a number, please—"

Percy cuts me off. "Do not insult me by comparing them."

"No?"

Failing to catch my gaze, Percy lands on my shoulder and pinches my neck.

I wince at the pain, but in all fairness, I deserved that.

"Be honest, *diamantay*," he scolds me. "From the moment Seth Devine knelt in front of you, a piece of your heart has belonged to him. You can't marry anyone else, and especially not Alaric."

A tear weasels its way to my cheek, and I rub it off violently. "Not an important part. Barely a shard. My heart is useless. *Broken*."

"And if you marry that Rayne King, you'll never find out what that shard could have become, had it been allowed to heal."

"I don't have a choice. It's the only way I can protect you," I explain. "Besides, it's not such a bad idea. Who knows? Maybe his magic won't trigger the cupids. Why would it, when it's not truly mine? I'll finally have magic again, and if things get a little too dark, I can always fry his brains out. I'll at least have the option. It isn't so different than marrying Seth, and you'll see that when your silly crush on him fizzles out."

"*Diamantay*! Don't do this. It'll destroy you." His voice is high and urgent, like he didn't really believe me before. "Alaric is like Ethan. You can't marry a man like that."

The mention of my father brings acid to my mouth. A dark hole inside me pulses, aches, *throbs*.

"I've been fighting all my life, to belong only to myself, to be queen in my own right, to *matter*, and for what?"

"For what's right."

"Seth is Freya's heir, Perce."

"Children shouldn't be blamed for their parent's sins."

I shake my head. "Even if I could find a way out of this, Alaric is too strong, and Seth is his prisoner— He'd hurt him. And you."

"Then fight! Raise hell! Recruit this creepy Nathan guy to help, if you must. Be Devi Eros!"

"I'm not the Devi you used to know. I faded away, day by day, month by month. I'm tired of running, Perce. I want it done."

"You've given up?"

"It's no use. My heart is unfixable." I tear at my fiery locs, wishing I could erase them—erase the woman, the myth, the legend. "The girl you were born to protect is *gone*."

He presses his palms to my mangled heart over the diamond-shaped plates. "No, she's here. She's right *here*."

"I'm sorry." I turn my back on him and squeeze my eyes shut. The panicked edge of my voice withers into a decisive drawl. "I need you to stay here quietly until I return, Percival Arthur Batten."

The words hang in the air—more hurtful and damaging than if I'd sucker-punched him.

"Don't you d—" His voice wheezes out, cut off mid-sentence.

"It's only for a little while..." I don't turn back to see the betrayal on his face, the disappointment, the hurt.

I can see them perfectly in my mind.

Somehow, this night has gone horribly, horribly wrong. I slip out of my room, each painful step leading me to Alaric's bedroom.

Nathaniel's offer might've been well-intentioned, but he made it before he knew his brother was king, and going to Seth? That would sign his death warrant. He's stuck in a cage, powerless, so there's only one option left that keeps us both alive.

But as it turns out, I'm not the only prisoner running loose in this cursed citadel.

A flicker of movement. The softest exhale in the dark.

"That's"—the voice scrapes through the silence, hoarse and far too familiar—"quite a dress."

Seth.

My steps falter. I thought I could slip into Alaric's bed unnoticed and bury my shame in silence and silk sheets, but fate's got other plans.

The damp air of the citadel crawls along my spine, up my legs and exposed thighs. The metal bodice of my dress bites into my ribs with every breath, and I stand there burning. Unraveling.

Seth is still wearing the same clothes he had on when we arrived, his shirt torn at the front like he fought his way past a few guards. Dirt smudges his jaw, and his dark curls are damp with sweat, stuck to his forehead. He smells of despair and humidity, raw magic and blightroot powder, but he's still the most attractive man in the worlds.

Relief floods me so hard, I nearly drop to my knees. I drink him in like a starving woman, my eyes tracing every familiar line—his large shoulders, his witty mouth, the shape of his arms. I want to run to him, bury my face in his chest, and disappear in his embrace.

But I can't.

Terror coils low in my belly. He has no idea what's coming. No idea what I've promised to keep him alive.

Seth searches the dark corridor ahead. "Where were you headed?" His eyes rake over me, and he takes a step forward, arm extended. "Come on." He reaches for my hand. "Let's leave this place together."

My body tenses, and I jerk away before he can touch me. "We can't."

I know better than to fail this test. Alaric is nearby—I feel it in the prickle across my skin, in the way the dress hums in warning, and in the chill that hasn't left my body since he proposed.

Seth doesn't back down. "Between the two of us, we can fight our way to the warden's chambers—"

"Our intel was wrong. Luther might have ordered all mirrors shattered in the capital and allowed Tidecallers boats into Zepharion, but he's not the new Storm King." My voice falters. "Alaric is."

Seth opens and closes his mouth. "Then we have to escape *now*." He shackles my wrist. "I know him. He will hurt you to get back at me."

"Why would he think I mean anything to you?"

He blinks, stunned. "Because you do."

He steps closer, both hands on my arms, grounding me.

"You know you do," he says again, softer this time. Pleading.

I try to lift my arms, to push him back, but they don't listen. They're desperate to hold him instead.

I force a shrug. "You said you'd never fall for me. So that's a gross mistake on your part. Our arrangement doesn't serve us anymore. Consider it done."

His breath catches. "You don't mean that."

But I do. There's no way to warn him, no way to explain that death is skulking in the dark. The only way to keep him alive is to convince Alaric that I'm truly done with him.

Something twists in my chest, cold and broken, but I press on.

"The crowns asked me to kill your brother," I say, the words bitter in my mouth. "That's the real reason they sent me with you to Zepharion. They made it a condition for us to wed. But you wouldn't have married me after I'd done it, so we were doomed long before we ever set foot in this place."

I let the revelation simmer.

A flurry of emotions twist his face like a storm trapped in a bottle. Fury, betrayal. Doubt.

So I remind myself who he is. Why he came to me. What he truly wanted.

My magic. My body. Nothing more.

There can't be more.

I have nothing else to give.

"You leave if you want. But I'm staying." I lift my chin, each word another nail in the coffin of our budding romance. "I'm sorry, Seth. Our little scheme has run its course. Alaric asked me to marry him."

He chokes on a strangled breath. "You'd...sell yourself to him like that?"

"How is that different than selling myself to you?"

The blow lands. His mouth parts, but no sound comes out.

I deserve his obvious disgust. Every bit of that and *more*.

"I could never have loved you, Seth. Your mother grabbed one of my arrows and rammed it straight here." I hit the space over my heart, hard. "She drove it deep and raked it around. She doesn't deserve to die knowing her son and heir will be king after her."

A strange heaviness settles in my ribcage, like my soul is slowly leaking out. *Drip. Drip. Drip.* Only the knowledge that I have used and abused Seth remains.

And then—

Clap. Clap. Clap.

A slow, cruel applause echoes off the stone walls.

Alaric steps in, all teeth. "You heard her, Seth." He drapes an arm around me. "She doesn't want you. She'd rather marry a true king."

Seth summons his blade with a flick of the hand, but Alaric clicks his tongue.

"Calm down, Sethanias."

The Storm King doesn't need steel. His power drums down the corridor in a violent gale, slamming into Seth hard enough to blur his shape. His blade is blown out of his hand and vanishes into thin air before it hits the ground.

"But you'll be her kindred, yes?" Alaric tilts his head, waiting for an answer as though his offer is overly magnanimous. "You're the only friend she has in these parts."

Seth struggles to stay upright. His eyes—those beautiful, purple-flecked eyes—hit me one last time. A goodbye wrapped in disbelief and heartbreak. "Do I have a choice?"

"Not really." Alaric chuckles. "Let me escort you back to your cell. You wait for me in your room, Lady Eros."

I can't look at Seth. Not now. Not ever. I'm just glad he gets to live.

CHAPTER 31
FIRE
SETH

"You wait for me in your room, Lady Eros," Alaric says.

The cold, guarded glint in Devi's eyes turns my stomach, and bile fills my mouth.

Alaric is king, which means he's more powerful than I could have imagined. He probably blackmailed her, but her expression—cool, unreadable, fills me with doubt. It's the mask she wears when she's protecting something. Or hiding who she really is.

The gown reveals the dark peaks of her breasts, the aureoles peeking through the gaps between the clusters of diamonds. It's a deliberate, provocative design—her body both on display and untouchable.

Alaric knew exactly what he was doing when he gave her that dress, her beauty fashioned into a hook and strung up as bait. He wanted me to find her, and now he's sending a clear message that she's his to unwrap.

My fists clench at my sides, and I taste blood when she walks away without a word.

No apology. No excuse. No real explanation.

The woman who once kissed me like I was her beginning and her end is walking away from me, ready to plan her wedding to someone else.

It can't be real. It can't be her choice.

Her words echo in my ears—words that couldn't have been lies. *I could never have loved you, Seth.*

Zeus knows I want to believe she's still on my side. That she's not looking forward to this sham wedding, that she's not hungry enough for power to choose Alaric over me. But I'm not sure. That's the tragedy.

Alaric walks ahead, silent. He doesn't need to guard his rear, his wind snaking around me, pressing tight against my ribs and dragging me along like a dog on a chain. I can barely move, barely breathe. The bastard's thorough, I'll give him that.

We descend into the lower halls, to the cell that was conspicuously unlocked at just the right time.

I fight his magic, trying to slow things down, to no use. The more I fight, the more his wind squishes my chest. Black dots dance in front of my eyes. "It was all a trick, no? For me to see her heading to your room?" I ground out.

"She's a vision in that dress," he says, voice heavy with desire. "I can't wait to tear it off her."

My spine stiffens. "You're disgusting."

"And you're jealous."

The burn in my throat says enough. "How did you blackmail her into this?"

"Are you so sure about her? Isn't she a criminal? A traitor? Do you really think her feelings for you are stronger than her ambitions? Be honest, Seth. Isn't this the perfect revenge on your mother—marrying me instead of you?" he taunts me.

My nails bite into my palms, leaving crescent-shaped grooves. "Is that what she told you?"

He laughs. "She didn't have to say it. Everyone in Faerie knows how your mother treated her. You're too much of a hypocrite to admit it, but your intentions aren't pure, either. You want the shiniest toy in the store, the one Mommy told you you couldn't have. That's what this is. Rebellion dressed up as romance."

He pauses just long enough for the sting to land. "Deep down, you're still that boy starving for your parents' attention. And this bogus engagement between you two? It was fake as hell, at least where Devi's concerned. This is strategy. Survival. She's playing the long game—and she found a better card to play."

The "come-to-Zeus" moment crawls under my skin.

Alaric snorts. "Come on, Sethanias. You would've grown bored of matrimony within a year. It's in your nature to fuck anything with legs. And Devi? She's not the kind of woman who tolerates competition."

We reach the cell. The metal door groans open, controlled by his magic, and his wind plies me into submission, tucking me back inside the cage.

"It's better for everyone that I get to have her instead," he sums up.

The claustrophobic pressure of his magic leaves me.

"You don't deserve her," I say.

He meets my gaze head-on. "Neither do you."

In his eyes, I'm nothing but a screw-up, womanizing prince of nothing.

The air changes. Thickens. Hums. My instincts scream a second too late. Power coils in his hand, and lightning hits me square in the chest.

It burns.

I fall flat to my stomach, my muscles useless under the onslaught of bolts ravaging my nervous system.

There's no respite—just fire. My body jerks off the floor, my vision whites out. I can't even scream, not at first. Every inch of me contracts in on itself, nerves flaring, muscles locking. The metal walls of the cell glow faintly, drinking in the charge and throwing it back like an echo of agony.

It ends. For half a second, I think I can breathe.

Then the next strike comes.

The bolt slams into my side and drags me back into the inferno. My limbs convulse. My jaw snaps shut so hard I taste blood. My heart stumbles in my chest like it's lost its rhythm. Instinctively, I try to fight, but the bars, the floor, even the ceiling are designed to punish power, reflecting back my own magic. The lyranthium acts as a feedback loop, cycling any attack or counterattack back to me.

"Careful. You'll hurt yourself," Alaric snips.

Ashes of regret clog my throat. "I'll kill y-you. If y-you h-hurt her," I stutter.

He kneels down beside the bars. "What was that?"

"I-I'm s-serious."

Another bolt. I scream. The sound is full-throated, guttural, primal. It tears out of me like it's trying to escape the pain, but there's nowhere to go. My back arches off the stones. The lightning doesn't just burn. It scrapes along every nerve ending, pries into my spine, yanks on my thoughts, contorting my body, burning, melting.

But Alaric is not done.

The next surges come in smaller, surgical waves. He's experimenting. A zap to my shoulder. A snap against my thigh. A full blast. I'm twitching on the floor, my skin blistered.

"I'd gladly rape your fiancée while you watch, Sethanias. But I'd rather fuck her as she begs for more, her perfect body hungry for my cock. Trust me, the sight of her wet and willing will hunt you for much, much longer than if I take her by force."

"She won't beg for you, Ric."

"Oh, but she will. Because she hates you, hates your mother—hates herself—much more than she hates me."

Another bolt.

My thoughts fragment into broken flashes of her laugh.

Random memories fill my brain. The way she rolls her eyes when she's pretending not to care. The brush of her hand. The taste of her kiss. Until I'm nothing but charred flesh and shattered breaths.

And when the black finally takes me, it's a mercy. My last

thought is of Devi—and how I failed her. Because no matter what she said, no matter how Alaric's speech fed my fears, she sure as hells isn't marrying that demented king of her own free will.

I cling to that fleeting hope to keep despair from pulverizing all the little pieces of my heart.

CHAPTER 32
CAGED
DEVI

Percy ambushes me the moment I return to my bedroom, bouncing off the mattress. "What happened?" he asks.

My command for him to stay here quietly and wait has expired, but I stare at my feet to hide from his disappointment. "I told Seth it was over."

He hovers closer, bracing both hands under my chin to lift it. "What is going on with you?"

The numb ache from before has spread through my entire body. "Maybe I've reached the end."

I was always swimming against the current, always pretending to be some indomitable force. Strong. Untouchable. A queen, even after they exiled me from my court. But the truth is, I was just good at posing. Good at hiding the cracks beneath the crown.

Now, I can't even pretend. My limbs are heavy and unwilling. Every breath is borrowed. There's no magic left in me—no clever scheme waiting to be deployed, no spark to chase.

I feel...estranged from my own body.

Like someone scooped my soul out and left the hollow shell behind to fester.

The dark thoughts I've nurtured in exile haunt me. They scream through the silent room, cruel and familiar. I killed my mother. I abandoned my people. I lost my power, my pride, my essence.

I'm nothing.

I used to drown that dark little voice in whatever distraction I could find. Lovers. Drama. Friendship. But there's nothing left to fight for. No crown worth the hassle. I'm not powerful, or cunning, or brave. Not anymore.

I'm truly worthless.

The door creaks open, and Alaric strolls in with a genuine smile on his face. He deposits a show-box sized cage on the mattress, and I blink at it a few times. His proximity makes the little voice echo even louder.

"Here. It's for your pet. You can get him back after the wedding."

The birdcage is made of sleek lyranthium bars, welded close together—the kind of old-fashioned design you'd find in Spring, meant to catch a singing bird.

Alaric hands it over, and I fumble with the latch for a second before opening the small door.

My Faeling crouches and snarls, digging his boots into the mattress.

My throat bobs. "Please, Percy. I don't want to fight with you."

The words feel foreign on my tongue. I don't usually beg.

"You want me to get in there?" he barks, eyes wide.

"There's no other way."

He buzzes closer and grips one strap of my dress. "This dress— it's the lyranthium! It's making you act this way."

Alaric sends a burst of power forward, and the hollowness inside my chest throbs.

"Get in, Percy," I command.

Percy flies up to Alaric, teeth bared. "You're controlling her, somehow."

"I'm not." Alaric slithers to my side and brushes my braids away from my neck to plant a kiss there. "She's exactly herself, but without hope. Without joy. The Queen of Hearts in her purest form."

"Release her!" Percy claws at the scales of my dress, but even though I understand what he's trying to do, I know it's pointless.

"Don't worry. I'll take the dress off her soon enough, but it won't change anything. Lyranthium doesn't create agony. It only amplifies what despair or regrets are already there. It doesn't summon emotions from thin air, but shines a light on what she's kept buried. If she's drowning now, it means she was already neck-deep before I ever touched her." Alaric licks his lips. "Your mistress is darker than even I am, pet. Now, get in the cage, or I'll cook you through."

Percy purses his lips, but obeys.

I can breathe again.

Alaric melts the latch with a zap of magic, and I open the wardrobe.

I don't want Percy to see me this way. He's better off in the dark.

Once he's safely tucked away, Alaric's middle brother, Salazar, wheels a drink cart into the room. "I have what you asked for, Ric."

I haven't seen him since I first arrived, but he must have been at the ball, too, because he's dressed in tails. His thick beard is at a sharp contrast with his brothers' sleek, aristocratic looks.

"Come in, Sal." Alaric picks a familiar cup from the cart and skips over to me. "This is a little keepsake from the ballroom…"

The bronze and tungsten wine flute looks awfully familiar, and my throat itches at the heady scent rising from the wine.

"Brel managed to keep your little potion safe. I want you to drink it."

The empty shell in my chest shrinks. "No."

"You're not as good an actress as you think, and I don't want to fuck a woman who wishes Seth was there instead." He sniffs the potion. "How long does it take to work?"

I pick up the flute. "A couple of minutes."

The scales of the dress expand like the skin of a snake coiling around its victim. I want to dump the wine, but somehow, I can't.

The liquid swirls in a dizzying spin, and I feel as though I was always meant to drink it. I betrayed myself. Denied my conscience. Betrayed the only man my broken heart beats for. It's only fitting I should suffer for it.

Alaric raises a brow. "And how long does the effects of your elixir last?"

My ribs cramp. "A day."

Alaric shrugs off his jacket. "That gives us plenty of time to practice before our wedding tomorrow."

I pull the cup to my lips, and Alaric tips it toward my mouth.

The sweet taste brings tears to my eyes.

"Drink it all. That's it, good girl." He brushes a drop from my chin and licks it off his little finger. "Now, we're going to play a little game."

Salazar sits on the bench by the window, his large frame obscuring the sky.

"What is he doing?"

Alaric tugs on his belt. "He's the Worm. He likes to watch me play. Don't worry, he won't touch you."

An all-consuming desire to please my king assaults my senses. I go from disgusted and panicked to anxious and willing in the span of one breath. I long to be his queen. To quench his thirst.

It's unstoppable.

I make potent love potions, a talent that Alaric congratulates me for all night, as I suck his cock. Sing his praises. And disappear.

CHAPTER 33
WEDDING MARCH
SETH

Is it morning? Night? I wouldn't know. Time doesn't pass in this cell, but curdles. Folds in on itself until all that's left is pain. I think I slept, but maybe I just fainted.

A bruise pulses along my ribs, while another throbs behind my eyes. The dull scream of muscles and tendons contracting into themselves sears my brain. I'm nothing more than cooked meat in a gilded cage. Every joint aches.

Only my face has been spared.

Because that's the part Alaric wants intact when he parades me around as Devi's kindred. Marries my girl. Claims his realm.

My mind mirrors the state of my prison.

Quiet.

Dark.

Hollow.

Until the flutter of wings breaks through the stillness.

Percy's voice trembles. "Oh, pretty boy…"

I try to stand up, but it's no use, so I push to my elbows instead. Sweat gathers on my forehead, my limbs shaking. Weakness seeps into every bone in my body. I'll be surprised if I can make it to the wedding.

"Is Devi alright?" The question tears out of me.

Percy doesn't answer, and the grayness of his skin gives me pause. She's not alright—not at all.

"Don't come too close," I rasp as he flies closer to the bars. "What if you get trapped in here?"

"I'll risk it," he says, slipping between the metal rods.

His wings—gods—his wings are shredded at the edges.

"What happened to you?"

"I had to squeeze out of a cage."

Bile burns my throat. "Alaric got to you too, didn't he?"

He nods.

A black hole forms in my chest. I can't protect anyone. I'm useless. And soon I'll be forced to stand witness for the one thing I can't stomach.

"Why didn't she fight?" I whisper. "Magic or no magic, we could've fought."

"She's lost hope." Percy lands near my face. "You can imagine what that feels like. Always trying, always ramming your head against the same invisible wall."

Gods help me—I get it.

"Why bother, eh? I'm never enough. No matter how hard I fight, no one thinks I'm worth their trust. Or their time. And especially not their love."

The words fall out of me, bitter and cold. I didn't mean to say them aloud, but Percy doesn't flinch.

"You fight the Alarics and the Ethans of the world because you don't want to become like them," he says softly. "Empty souls, content only when they're stealing from others." He presses both hands to the singed cut splitting my chest in two and heals it, one inch at a time.

"Cruel kings always end up on top," I choke.

"Then it's up to you to take away their power—and make them small."

"What if I can't?"

"You must." He moves to heal my arms next. "I'll make it so they don't immediately realize what I've done."

I watch him survey my wounds. He heals the deep bruises and lacerations, but leaves the superficial abrasions—and their layers of blood and grime—intact.

"You used to hate me. What changed?"

Percy sucks his bottom lip inside his mouth, remaining silent for a while before he finally says, "Devi's heart is a dark place most of the time. Full of regret. A lust for revenge. A desire for self-destruction. It's been brighter since you came around. She thinks your mother destroyed her ability to love. She refuses to see what I see: that a broken heart loves just as fiercely, if not more. Scars only make us wiser in choosing whom we love."

I roll to a sitting position, my ribcage no longer burning, each new breath coming in easier. "You heard her: she's marrying Alaric, not me."

"It's the lyranthium fucking with both of your heads. Devi needs you to fight for her now, when she's done everything in her power to push you away. The dress—"

The main door of the prison block whines on its hinges, and my eyes widen. "Hide. Quick."

Percy takes refuge behind the chamber pot, and I turn to the entrance.

It's not Alaric, but Brel. She's hauling a bushel of clothes in her hands, two of her subordinates following behind her. "We brought you an evening jacket and some decent pants. For the wedding," she explains.

I bark out a laugh. "You're too kind."

I pretend to need help getting to my feet, Brel and her helpers buzzing around me until I'm dressed. I let them work, wincing and groaning at the appropriate times, hiding the fact that I'm well enough to do this on my own. The pain's still there, but it's bearable now.

Percy's a magician. He healed everything but the outer shell. As long as Alaric thinks I'm a walking bruise, I hold the advantage.

Percy's right about the dress. How did I miss it? I've been blinded by my own fears.

Even though I've built up a tolerance to lyranthium during my years here, the walls of the cell are affecting me gravely. If Devi's dress was forged from pure lyranthium—refined, not alloyed—that would explain the symptoms. Even a small amount, worn so close to the skin, could've overwhelmed her.

WIND CUTS ACROSS THE OPEN WALL OF THE ARENA, CARRYING THE SCENT OF salt, brine, and anticipation. The constant roar of the sea below matches the pounding in my skull.

The seats are already filled. The High Fae from Lightning Point sit out front in private booths, acting stern and serious in the face of a wedding they didn't expect. Behind them, the common folk of Deiltine flood the bleachers. Mainly the men working on the Aeolians and in the factories.

They came for a show.

For the disturbing spectacle of a traditional Storm wedding.

To witness the moment the woman I've fallen for is claimed by another man.

I search the arena, but Devi isn't here. Before I forfeit my life for a woman who might never love me back, I need to see her.

Brel ushers me forward, toward the edge of the arena where the stone underfoot is slick with rain, and orders me to wait there. She flies ahead to meet her king near the altar.

The Rayne's green and black sigils snap in the storm.

The ground is marked with three concentric semicircles with the altar at their center. The innermost ring is meant for the bride and groom. The second is for the kindreds. The third encompasses the spectators.

I wish it would all crumble to ash.

Nathaniel joins me along the rim of the second circle, his top lip curled in a snarl. "Is Devi Eros meant to strike Tatiana with a love arrow in front of everyone? Tell me!" he whispers in a rush. "Could that work? Can Devi really make her love him?"

The youngest Rayne is dressed in a tailored black evening coat and crisp white undershirt. His eyes are cloudy—almost enough to mask their mismatched colors.

"You're missing the point of this wedding. Devi is the bride," I say quickly.

His jaw hangs open, his gaze searching the bleachers, focussing on a booth at the front, where a thick man is standing alone, flanked by guards. "No. I saw Tatiana head off with Brel earlier..."

"Devi is the bride."

"How can you be sure? Is she that hungry for power?"

My teeth grit together. "He's forcing her, you idiot. Just as he planned to do with your Tatiana."

Nathan huffs. "Like Devi Eros couldn't overpower a newly-minted king? Alaric's no match for her."

"Alaric wanted us here as his kindreds to salt the wound. Me because he gets my girl. And you, your dream of becoming king. If he was marrying your friend, I wouldn't be here."

His face slowly falls. "Fuck. If you're right, then where is Tatiana?"

Deep, guttural notes grate through the air, ancient and dissonant, before the organ's music swells. The mournful melody sharpens into a primordial dirge, announcing the start of the ceremony, and Devi steps into the arena.

My pulse stumbles and spikes. Rushing. Swirling. *Screaming.*

She wears a simple white dress with no corset or embellishments, but the simplicity of the silk gown only makes her look more ethereal. She walks with purpose to the inner circle, eyes glued to the ground.

Gasps erupt from the crowd.

The outcropping of the altar is the only part of the arena that's directly exposed to the elements, and she crosses into it at Brel's silent command, following the swirled pattern etched into the floor with her back to the spectators. She stops just before the slab of lyranthium where she's meant to kneel.

Rain hits her in waves, soaking her wedding dress until it clings to her body. The fabric molds to her deep brown skin, revealing the swell of her breasts, the line of her thighs, and the shape of her ass. Her braids are woven into one thick side braid that hangs heavy with water, strands of red hair plastered to her cheeks and collarbone.

She doesn't flinch, but stares at the stone slab in front of her, arms limp at her sides.

Percy pinches my neck, voice thick with urgency. "You've got to stop this."

"Patience, little man."

Gods help me, I need her to look at me. Just once.

Alaric steps into the circle, standing dry beneath his magic shield. "Under the watchful eyes of the gods, I claim this woman as my one and only wife," he declares, licking his lips in triumph. He unbuckles his belt, and for a moment, the only sound is the pitter-patter of rain on stone.

The spectators hold their breaths, waiting for Devi to kneel. A sharp pain at the center of my breastbone chokes me.

"The bride must kneel for her husband," Brel whispers, just loud enough for Nathaniel and I to hear.

It's a reminder that's rarely needed, and the sprite's worried gaze flies from the bride to her groom.

Devi's top lip curls in disgust as she contemplates the slab, and she digs her heels into the ground. Brel flies closer, motioning softly, unsure whether to coax her or beg.

Alright, that'll do.

"Wait! I challenge your claim to this woman!" I roar over the wind.

Gray clouds gather overhead. A heavy shift in pressure rolls through the arena, the air thick and unstable. Too many Storm Fae are packed into one place, heating the atmosphere with their presence. It's volatile, electric, ready to break. There are a few boos, some fists raised—but mostly, silence. Trepidation.

I circle around Nathaniel, putting distance between myself and the ledge, then step into the third circle.

"Did you hear me?" I call out. "I challenge you, Alaric Neptune Rayne."

He thinks I'm broken.

Bruised.

Barely standing.

Easy pickings.

He's king. I'm nothing. And that's why he laughs, even though I know his name. "You challenge me?"

"I invoke the ancient rite of *rakvir*," I say, my voice raw, cracked. "A duel to decide who gets to wed this woman."

The laws of the Storm Court are older than any crown, and if he insists on this ancient, barbaric wedding, dusting off some forsaken part of our history, I can only repay the favor.

"You insisted on a traditional Storm wedding. Challenges are allowed, and to the death," I add.

Echoes and shouts ripple through the amphitheater. No one invokes those laws anymore, not since the Mist Wars ended, but they're still written. Still binding. It's not a wedding arena for nothing, and for once, Alaric's arrogance works in my favor, because he can't imagine losing.

Nathaniel walks offstage in a hurry, the tails of his coat flying behind him.

Devi's lips part in surprise, the first sign that she heard me. That she even knows I'm here. She cranes her neck around to glance past

Alaric and meets my gaze. The cold in her eyes, the tightness in her jaw... those aren't just signs of lyranthium poisoning. They're signs of suffering.

"You'd die for her?" Alaric drawls, mocking. "Even with my seed still leaking out of her sweet cunt?"

Devi's silver gaze drops back to the ground at that, but I don't miss a beat.

"I would."

Rage floods my blood, chest, and ears. That monster.

I swallow the acrid swell rising in my throat, forcing it down before it can poison my thoughts. He hurt her. Violated her. And that breaks me more than any wound Alaric could ever inflict. No wonder she's given up—she's in shock.

"Very well," Alaric purrs, rolling his shoulders. "I accept." He strips off his jacket and undershirt and throws them both to the ground.

I do the same, revealing my bruises, lacerations, and burns.

Devi stirs. Her now translucent gown gleams like frostbitten snow in the night, but it's the heat in her cheeks that quickens my pulse. A flicker of life. Defiance. Her fists tighten against the silk at her sides.

"You promised he'd be safe," she whispers. The words are barely audible, but the ache in her voice is sharp enough to pierce stone.

Two sprites fly to keep her from getting involved, one on each arm. They turn her back around and force her to her knees.

"The bride must wait for the victor at the altar," Brel says mechanically.

Devi retreats back into whatever hell she's buried herself in—chin lifted, face blank, eyes dead, but everything is different.

The pain fades. The unbearable weight pressing down on my ribs eases. Because if there's even a sliver of her left in there, if she's still fighting in her own, hopeless way, then I can fight, too.

I will kill Alaric Rayne if it's the last thing I do.

Alaric raises his hand, and sparks race along his fingers, waiting to be unleashed. Wind gusts into the arena. Thunder cracks above us. The stone under my feet vibrates.

The rules are clear. No armor. No weapons. No tricks. Only Storm magic and brute strength. Nothing else. I can't rely on my mother's gifts. This fight is on his terms.

I set my feet. My knuckles tighten.

Alaric drinks in the sight of my wounds. "Look at you. You're already broken."

He doesn't wait. The wind slams into me. I slide back, boots scraping on stone, but my balance holds.

I send a blast of lightning into his chest. He takes it in stride, inflating his pecs to receive it, then laughs. "You think you can over-power your king? I'm a vessel for Zeus himself. He chose me to repre-sent him on this earth—"

I leap forward, closing the distance in three strides. My fist connects with his jaw, and a dark satisfaction rakes through me as the hit lands hard. His head jerks, and blood sprays the floor.

"You talk too much," I say.

With a snarl, he punches my side. My vision flickers. My legs weaken, but I stay upright, avoiding his next two strikes as I try to immobilize him in a rear chokehold. He grunts and grasps my arm, keeping it from strangling him.

Another flash blinds me. Lightning hits my shoulder, and heat surges through me. My muscles scream. The scent of burned cloth and skin pervades the air.

I land a few quick blows, but his wind acts as a shield, keeping the other kicks and punches from landing, until it gathers below him. He lifts from the ground and hovers a few feet into the air.

Alaric's power threads through my body like marionette strings, and I fall to my knees at his feet. Thunder pounds through the arena, each crash counting down the last seconds of my life. Rain whips across my skin, soaking me through.

My arms are scorched. My knees are bleeding. I can't breathe right.

A powerful lash knocks the wind out of me, and my vision sways. The sky deepens to black, lightning gathering at his fingertips as the crowd roars his name in cheer.

He's going to win.

And then, I see Devi.

She's no longer held at the altar. She's wrapped around Alaric's neck, her fingers clawing at his eyes, her weight throwing him off balance. He staggers, and they both crash to the ground.

The crowd barks in outrage as the storm dies for a beat.

The pressure lifts from my chest, and I suck in air. The taste of blood and burnt stone fills my mouth. Then a flash of metal catches my eye to my left—a heart-shaped hilt, its greenish sheen promising certain death.

Devi's end-all blade.

How the hell did it get here?

Doesn't matter.

I lunge for it. My fingers close around the hilt just as Alaric slams a bolt where I stood seconds before, heat scorching my back.

I rise, blade in hand.

Screw the rules.

This ends with him dead.

Alaric spots the weapon and scans the crowd, nostrils flaring. His gaze locks on Nathaniel. His younger brother is leaning against the stone arch of a side passage carved into the arena wall. The first few rows of seats curve over it, casting deep shadows inside the alcove, hiding the narrow passage from view of the spectators. It's meant for dramatic arrivals or exits, but today, it hides a quiet rebellion.

Nathan prowls forward, revealing his presence to the crowd. "Where is Tatiana? What did you do to her?"

Alaric's jaw ticks as he glares at his brother. "You never loved her, admit it. Only toyed with her because I wanted her. Well, I got to her first, Nate, and she was good. Maybe now that she's worthless, her father will let you play with her too."

Nathan spits at Alaric's feet. "Zeus made a mistake, choosing you."

The sky rumbles, Alaric's knuckles overrun with yellow lines of electricity.

"You will all kneel for your one true king." He joins his hands to concentrate his power into a giant flare of lightning, and I brace myself for the strike. The bolt hits me square in the chest, short-circuiting my heart and my breath. The forced reboot of my nervous system sends me crashing to the ground, and I drop the blade.

My clothes ignite before the lightning arcs, snapping to Nathan and blasting the man back several feet. His skull emits a sickening crack as it hits the rock.

Alaric's lightning chains toward Devi next. It slams into her chest, hurling her backward... straight over the ledge.

CHAPTER 34
FALLING
DEVI

I'm falling.

It's a sensation I've grown used to. After all, I've been falling for the better part of eight decades. Fallen Queen. Ever falling. Never reaching the ground. Never hitting bottom. Still waiting for the inevitable crash, for my body and soul to finally be *crushed*.

Only this time, I'm falling faster than the storm.

The wind tears past me, tugging at my burning clothes, tangling my hair, roaring loud enough to drown out everything else. Fire bites my ribs. Rain stings my eyes. The sea below swells like a dark, furious beast foaming at the mouth, ready to swallow me whole.

Maybe I should let it.

My fingers are numb, my soul even more so.

The last twenty-four hours are a blur. A cold, gray place I don't want to revisit. The kind of memory you look away from.

Humiliation.

Self-loathing.

Despair.

I'm not sure how I survived any of it.

I went so far inside myself, I might as well have left my body behind.

But I'm back.

I remember how I got here. The mistakes I made.

I remember who I am.

A tremor of magic crawls through muscle and bone. The first sharp, aching pinch between my shoulder blades burns hot and raw. The truth of my flesh, the secrets of my birth, and the tragedy of my fate stir and stretch deep within me.

I wrap my arms around myself, tears mixing with the onslaught of rain, as the tender skin of my back pulses and folds outward. The feathers grow, soft at first, then exploding. A liberation.

Black feathers. Strong bones.

They're not just wings.

They're part of me.

Part of my destiny.

A brutal reminder that I am my father's daughter.

These wings are the only truth my mother could not face nor endure. The ultimate proof of paternity that drove her to suicide.

I was proud of them once.

Proud when they saved me from a cliff not so different from this one.

Proud when I discovered I could fly.

I remember grinning down at my mother as she knelt at the edge, screaming for help, for the healers, for anyone to come and save me...

But when she looked up and saw them—saw me—she smiled.

Dried her tears.

Told me she loved me.

Then stepped off that ledge, and never smiled again. I killed her by showing her I could fly. And still, despite all the horrors they've brought, my wings are mine. I grow them in defiance. In grief. In quiet rage.

They are both my most profound shame and my salvation.

CHAPTER 35
MALEFICENT
SETH

I race toward the ledge, my feet hammering against the ground. My chest burns, my blood slick and hot at my temples. I should turn back, get the blade, and kill Alaric, but victory means nothing if Devi dies. I reach the edge of the arena and peer down.

Percy's wings and my own heartbeat slam into my ribs. She's already so small, falling fast, shrinking against the backdrop of the waves frothing below. Without thinking, I jump after her.

I'd do anything to slow her fall. To catch her. Or die trying.

I swallow hard, scanning the churning sea. If I could dive close enough to where she falls, I could swim to her, drag her from the current, and get her to the healers in time—maybe.

Percy slips out of my jacket and disappears into a burst of Faerie dust, zooming past my feet to reach his mistress. She's seconds from impact, but suddenly, she stops falling. Her silhouette grows bigger below me.

Sleek, black wings unfurl behind her, and then, with the grace and fury of a reckoning, she starts to rise. To *fly*.

Her virginal wedding gown is in tatters, shredded by wind and fire. The threads weave themselves to cover her intimate parts, making my heart thump at how beautiful and badass she is.

Fierce.

Unstoppable.

Magnificent.

She flies directly for me, and I melt into a cloud to avoid a hard collision, then condense back into flesh. She catches me in her arms, the added weight dragging us down for a moment before we rise again. Devi's powerful wings are strong enough for two.

"You jumped," she stammers, like she can't quite believe how silly I've been.

"I wanted to save you."

Her gaze softens, her silver irises clearer than I've ever seen them. "Let's cancel this wedding."

CHAPTER 36
BURNT WINGS
DEVI

S eth jumped.

He *jumped*.

He doesn't hate me for what I did. There's a chance to put everything right, but first, I'm going to kill this brute of a king. This horrible man who almost extinguished my will to live.

Seth cups my cheek, his eyes wide with surprise and devotion and something else—more potent than relief, and purer than pride. "You..."

"We still have a king to kill."

I don't care how many cupids come for me this time, I'm going to kill Alaric Rayne.

"I'll see you up there." With a solemn nod, he melts back into a cloud.

I rise into the sky and summon my bow and arrows, flying up, up, up, until I pass the ledge of the arena.

Percy flies up beside me. It's been ages since we've flown side by side, my feet rooted to the ground for too long. Just like that, the shadows and doubts worming through my heart evaporate.

He's here. He always is. When the world turns against me, when I lose sight of who I am, Percy never loses faith.

"We should leave. The cupids—" he starts.

"One enemy at a time, *diamantay*," I say with a smile.

"But you could die."

"Death is part of life. I just need to do what's right, here."

He nods. "I know you. By heart. You're thinking this is your last stand, but it doesn't have to be."

He does know me better than I know myself. Every broken edge. Every shard of the queen I used to be and the woman I've become. I want to tell him thank you. I want to say I'm sorry. I want to promise we'll survive this.

Instead, I just say, "If it's our last fight, let's make it a good one, alright?"

The sky above ignites, lightning flaring in scattered bursts. Alaric stands at the ledge behind the altar, fists buzzing with electricity. He must have looked down to savor the moment my body would break on the rocks.

Now, he sees me.

Thunder tears through the clouds.

White-hot bolts strike left and right, but I swerve between them and wrap myself in a protective sphere of light magic. A rainbow of colors swirls along the walls of my translucent shield. The rain hisses and turns to steam on impact as the bubble swells, stretching outward until this land of drear and darkness is flooded in sunlight.

I draw a crystalline arrow from the ether and aim right at Alaric. Not a love arrowhead, but one meant to cut flesh.

One arrow to his groin.

Another, smack-dab in the middle of his chest. Alaric gurgles, hand flying to the shaft, eyes wide, knees buckling. I'm not the most renowned archer for nothing.

"You kneel, you fucker," I declare, my words swallowed by the wind but no less satisfying.

Alaric opens and closes his mouth, his hand clutching the base of the arrow embedded in his heart as if he might try to tear it out. It's a grave wound, but not fatal. Not for a Fae king.

A small group of Storm Fae stalks in from the side, axes in hand, Salazar at the head. I could shoot them down—in fact, I'm itching to —but spilling more blood will likely push the rest into action. Most of the High Fae stay rooted in place, apparently torn between rushing to their king's aid or waiting a little longer to see if he remains king at all.

Seth condenses into form in front of them, blocking their path. He stands tall, his back to me, arms spread wide. A long sword shines in his hand, my prince poised to take on the entire population of Deiltine.

Alaric lifts a hand to the sky, and the clouds split open again. Power churns in a growing tempest overhead.

I land and focus my magic on my shield. Lightning crashes against it a second later, crawling across the surface like fiery lines of ants—alive, relentless, but unable to pierce through.

Nathaniel prowls out from behind his brother, blood matting his hair and running down the slope of his neck. His white-knuckled grip tightens around the hilt of my end-all blade.

Alaric senses his approach and laughs. "You're never going to be king, Nate. You're a pet. A broken-winged raven."

Nathaniel steps around him until they're face to face. Seth moves in from the side, closing the circle.

Alaric smiles through a mouthful of blood, red trickling from the corners of his lips. "There's no ever after for you, Seth. Only death. And you, Nathan... mark my words. You'd have to kill a hundred kings before the gods looked at you twice."

Nathaniel matches his grin. "Only ninety-nine left to go."

A red-orange bolt of lightning bursts across the sky just as Nathaniel drives the blade into his brother's heart. It zigzags as it falls, bright and violent, hurtling straight for Seth.

"Watch out!" I scream.

The bolt halts midair—suspended, crackling—then veers toward the back of the arena. The ground convulses, a crevasse the size of my head ripping through the seats, the far wall, and part of the ceiling. Chaos erupts. The bold few who stayed until now push and stumble over each other as they flee. The rock slab beneath our feet tilts toward the ocean, debris crashing from the arena ceiling and tumbling past the ledge.

I search the sky for an answer, trying to understand where that eerie bolt came from, whether there's another behind it, and why it missed.

Where the bolt diverted, where the lightning veered off-course, a small blur plummets toward the arena floor, leaving a trail of Faerie dust behind it. The iridescent shimmer stops me cold.

No. Nonono.

"Percy!"

I fly to catch him, cradling his little body in my palms, shaking so hard I can barely hold on.

Percy's once-purple suit is charred black, threads melted into his skin. His melon hat is gone, his hair singed down to the roots, scorched red patches peppered across his scalp. His skin, where it's not blistered, is ashen. His wings—those strong, beautiful wings—are nothing but crumbling bone and dust. Gone.

His eyes stare straight ahead. Glassy. Empty. No mischief. No glint. No clever retort on his lips. Just stillness.

"Come on," I whisper. "Come on, please..."

I press my index finger over his chest, but there's no faint heartbeat to find. No pulse. No spark of magic humming beneath his skin.

He's gone.

The best part of me. The part that made me laugh when everything else hurt. The only one who never asked me to be more than I am. Who loved me as I was. My only companion. My heart.

I shake my head. "You weren't supposed to do this. You were supposed to *live*." Messy sobs distort my voice as my wings curl around us, my knees sliding to the ground. "Don't leave me, *diamantay*."

Tears scorch down my cheeks. I bend over him, nose pressed to his forehead. The scent of singed fabric and Faerie ash twists my stomach. The weight of him, already cooling in my hands, makes me retch.

This is the price for living.

My most precious friend—the last part of my heart that wasn't all dried and shriveled—is dead.

CHAPTER 37
SHATTERED GLASS
DEVI

"Devi... I'm so sorry," Seth whispers, his hand warm on the nape of my neck.

I can barely hear him over the staccato of my heart, but he squeezes my shoulder again. "It's dangerous to stay here."

I want to claw his eyes out. Stomp over his body. Tear off his limbs.

As I glare at Seth through angry, bitter tears, I can only see my own pain. "Why? Why would he sacrifice himself for you?" I roar.

Seth inches closer, holding his hands out in front of him. "I'm so terribly, terribly sorry. If we could only—"

"No." I cradle Percy's tiny body, shielding him from Seth's gaze.

It's been seconds since he died. Or hours. I lost track.

Seth's hand presses hard on my shoulder. "Something's happening. We need to leave."

I glance past my wings to see what he means.

Behind us, electricity slithers out of the hole in Alaric's chest, coiling around the blade and hilt before spreading through his lifeless body. The iron-silver alloy sparks, then begins to melt, the current spilling outward like a swarm of yellow serpents trapped inside him and desperate to escape.

Alaric crumbles to ash as the strange, living power crawls away. At the center of the mound, what's left of the end-all blade gleams— no longer a weapon, just a puddle of molten iron and silver cooling on stone.

The serpentine bolts of electricity merge together to form bigger, longer shapes that hiss from puddle to puddle, turning water to steam and creeping away from the dead king's ashes.

Nathaniel leaps back from the phenomenon, spooked. The swarm of electricity responds quickly, picking up speed to stop his escape, slowly snaking around his ankles, wrists, and neck.

The Storm Fae screams, and Seth's fingers digs into my shoulder. "We have to leave *now*."

I don't care if Alaric's remains spread everywhere and obliterate what's left of me.

Percy is dead.

Nathaniel leaps over the tilted ledge of the arena, dissipating into a cloud of rain that *tsst* and tssak as the electricity gives chase, turning parts of him to steam.

Above us, red clouds bleed into the sky, stark and furious against the ever-churning blacks and purples of the storm. I know the sound that rides the wind just before my cupids arrive. Their laughter is monstrous and gleeful, loud and close. It echoes in a place deeper than my ears, somewhere inside my ribs, where my broken heart now stands, emptier than it's ever been.

My monsters are coming, drawn to the scent of my magic, my blood, my grief, and they're ravenous for the kill.

They say once a beast has tasted you, some part of its primal mind will always remember. Will always hunger.

I've spent a lifetime running from them. I've tried to meet them head-on, tried to destroy them with an end-all blade. I've even hired others to do it for me, but nothing, no brand of magic or weapon, ever worked.

I've carved wards into too many rowan thresholds, invoked every kind of protection known to the Fae. I've whispered spells in a dozen languages, traded my pride for safety, and tested which lines I couldn't cross—each experiment taking its pound of flesh.

I've played at being mortal, tried to blend in. I've hidden both in plain sight and in the dark, under false names and dishonest pretences.

It's always the same. No matter how fast I run, this moment always comes. When I wield the magic I once took for granted to save myself or someone else. When I fight to make a difference.

But my curse is not something I can outsmart or dispel. It's one I have to endure, until the end. No matter where I go, the sky always turns red.

I'm done running. I'll die here, standing my ground. With Percy.

"This storm... like the one in Inverness. It's coming right for us."

I breathe in deep. "Let them come."

Seth narrows his eyes as the first wave of monsters detach from their blood-red clouds. They fall fast, forming blurry, black, earth-bound cannonballs. "What are they? What do they want?"

"When I say *cupid*, you picture a cute cherub in a diaper with a heart-shaped arrow, right? Curly blond hair. Cheeky smile." I grind the words out. "Well, think again. *Those* are cupids, and they're here to carve out my heart."

"How do we fight them?"

"We don't." I fall to my ass on the stones and hunch forward. "I'm ready to die." The corners of my mouth twitch. "Your mother will have my heart at last, pretty boy. Maybe keep it to yourself, if you can."

"I'd rather it stays inside your chest," Seth says, his Storm sword held tight in his grip, ready to greet our attackers. "Please, Devi. We have to leave."

I close my eyes. "I can't live without him. Now go, before they kill you, too," I say, my voice tired and listless. My heart is cold, and my eyes are dry. Like I'm already dead.

"I won't. Not without you."

I curl my wings around myself as four or five cupids hit the ground around me like enormous balls of black hail. They snigger as they land, the wind they carried with them blasting Seth back several feet.

Sharp claws tear at my feathers, plucking them out, the cupids jumping in victory, like they know I've given up.

"I didn't know him well, but Percy would want you to live," Seth shouts, slashing my abusers one by one.

I can't hear him clearly. I'm stuck inside a storm of claws, teeth, and grief.

"It's no use," I whisper. "Another wave will come. Then another. That's how the curse works. Without Percy here to fix me, I can't heal. Can't survive."

Two monsters grab the top of my right wing and gauge their nails in at the root in an attempt to scrape it off the bone. Seth's lightning cooks them through before they succeed, and they fall to each side of me with resonant thuds.

Another wave hits the ground, now focussed on Seth. They want me dead, but he's an obstacle to that, and they don't discriminate.

I blink my eyes open. He looks so fierce, battling my demons, taking care not to burn me with his magic, fighting for me when all hope is lost. No wonder Percy had developed a soft spot for him. If he was alive, my Faeling would have faced these beasts head-on before letting them kill me, much like Seth is doing now.

Stab. Kill. Repeat.

His stamina is impressive.

His tolerance to pain even more so.

The wet sound of chubby bodies hitting the ground—the absence of the familiar crunch of broken glass—pulls me out of the haze. I dismiss my wings, the feathers shimmering back to the ether, and take in the scene before me.

"Are there more?" Seth stands tall over my prostrated body, eyes wild, searching the black and purple sky for the next wave. But there's no more wings beating on the wind. No demented laughter. Just silence.

Blood, bite marks, and lacerations cover his body, and his breath is rushed. "Is that it? Are they dead?" he croaks.

I gape at the mess of mangled bodies—a hundred cupids strewn across the broken slab of the arena in twisted positions, oozing dark, tar-like blood. Eyes glassy. Guts spilling. But no shattered glass. "You... How? What did you do?"

"What do you mean? I killed them."

I stand up and shake one with my bare foot. Its plump black flesh wiggles under the tip of my toes. By Eros, he's right. They're dead.

He holds out his hand. "Let's get out of here, alright?"

He killed them. My demons. My monsters. I slip my hand in his, clutching Percy's body with the other, holding my poor, lifeless Faeling close to my heart. "Alright."

CHAPTER 38
FORSAKEN FORTRESS
DEVI

The obsidian passage ripples within the confines of a dark, oval-shaped onyx slab. It's a void meant to take us to Zepharion in the blink of an eye. No address needed, no skill or runes required. Just one step forward.

It's a step I'm not sure I'm strong enough to take. I grip the burial shroud wrapped around Percy's small body. It hurts to hold it, yet it would destroy me to let it go.

I wove it from my own plucked feathers and a dozen braids cut from my head, and I inscribed his name in dark ink. Spring Fae are never buried in wood, glass, or metal caskets—only fabrics. We return to the earth faster this way. The nutrients from our decaying bodies nourish the plants and trees that feed us and shelter us, creating new life.

Nature gives birth to us and welcomes us back in death. That's how it should be. I'll bury my Percy at the heart of the Secret Springs, where the two Amouran rivers converge, just the way he would have wanted.

But to do that, I have to live on, and travel through this tenebrous passage.

I've never seen one before, let alone used it. The Shadow King is the only one who can create them, and he does so reluctantly, since the comings and goings allowed by an obsidian passage are separate from the sceawere and therefore beyond his influence and power.

"You're sure this thing leads to Zepharion?" I ask Seth, wary of such magic.

He hasn't left my side since we left the arena. He hovers like a big bear, unsure where to put his hands, which gives an accidentally clumsy quality to his demeanor. One moment, he's got a hand on my shoulder or on the small of my back. The next, he steps away to give me room. Then he drifts close again, fingers flexing at his sides, like he's not sure what they're meant to do, or how to help.

Again, his hand grazes my spine with butterfly touches.

"Yes. It'll take us directly into my father's private study," he says.

My brows lift. "Convenient. If it's so easy, why didn't Luther use it to attack Deiltine? From what I've heard, he's not the kind of man who scares easily. Especially not from someone like Alaric Rayne."

Seth tilts his head, considering the question. "My father was a bit paranoid, and warded his study with a blood lock he bought from an old witch of the Red Forest. I suspect Luther never got inside the study to begin with."

"How did your father manage to get Ferdinand Nocturna to build him a private, unregistered passage? The previous Shadow King didn't lift a finger unless he was getting something out of it."

Seth's lips press together. "Blackmail, I suppose. You ready?"

"Let's go." I nod.

Seth's shoulders hitch. "And we're agreed?" he purses his lips. "There's no secret assassination in the cards?"

"I won't try to kill your brother. Unless he gives me good reason to."

Seth pries one of my hands away from Percy's shroud and laces our fingers, taking ownership of it and squeezing it tightly. "Let's go together."

I step forward.

The sensation of traveling through an obsidian passage is similar to the one we experience when we get our Shadow masks, like stepping into liquid darkness. The shadows slip inside every orifice, smooth and warm as butter. The feeling is strangely serene, yet similar to drowning, though it only lasts a second.

The room on the other side is furnished with thick leather pieces and a marble desk. The hearth is dark. A fancy drink cart stocked with some of the most expensive brands of wines and hard liquors known to Fae is set next to the cushy leather chairs. The desk is pristine, with no trace of dust or clutter. Thorald Storm has been dead for less than a week, so the cleanliness of his study neither confirms nor denies Seth's hypothesis that it's been sitting empty since he died.

I tiptoe to one of the turret windows and risk a glance outside.

We're on top of the Zepharion Tower, the highest point in the fortress. The sea below is much like it was in Deiltine—foaming and dangerous—but this stronghold sits higher, with four hundred feet of rock beneath our feet. More than enough to give anyone a bout of vertigo.

On the horizon, the south-eastern window offers a soul-shattering view of the sunrise, while the distant silhouette of the Islantide, the infamous island beyond the Breach, is covered in mist.

"Damian was right. The Tidecallers' army is here." Seth waves me over to the northern window, where the port of Zepharion sprawls along the secluded bay.

Hundreds of ships are anchored in the dark, icy waters—sleek vessels with tall masts and black sails rippling in the coastal wind, their hulls reinforced with dark metal fittings that gleam beneath the bright orange glow of the sunrise in the East.

"Should we look quietly for Luther or Willow? Or announce ourselves?"

I click my tongue, stepping away from the window. "Breaking in is fair game. Skulking around? Not so much."

If we'd come here to kill Luther, I might've tried stealth, but sneaking into Luther or Willow's private quarters would only tele-graph dark intentions. We're walking straight into the wolf's den as a sanctioned peace delegation, and we need to act like it. No games.

I move to the door leading outside the king's office and knock loudly on the metal. If it's known to be a way in and out of the fortress, it must be guarded. "Hello? Is anybody there?"

One gasp, and then—

"Who's there?" an urgent, masculine voice asks.

"Devi Eros. I want to speak with the Lord of the Tides."

"Open the door," the voice orders.

I press my palm to the cold metal. "No, not until she stands before me. Be warned, I will not open the door for anyone else."

Hurried footsteps echo in the distance.

Seth leans closer, his breath stirring the hairs at the nape of my neck. "Is this how you usually act during dangerous and delicate covert operations, or should I be worried?" he jokes, trying to take the edge off.

I'm not sure if I want to punch his face for teasing me at a time like this, or thank him for shaking me out of my grief.

"We're one end-all blade short and bleeding through our clothes. Let's not beat around the bush. If Willow and Luther decide we're worth more to them dead, there's not much we can do," I say.

"You'd have enough magic to fight them now that the cupids are gone."

A shiver quakes me. It hurts to contemplate the possibility that my curse has been vanquished, that I'm finally free, when the only soul I wanted to share that joy with is no more. "And what if they're only momentarily deactivated? What if, as soon as I use magic again, another red cloud forms above our heads?"

"What if it doesn't?"

Two sets of loud footsteps echo from the other side. "Shush, someone's coming." I press my ear to the door.

"Devi, it's me." A melodic voice says. "Open up."

The sound of my name tingles across my neck, warm as those

endless summer nights spent by the sea, where we became more than friends or family. Where sisterhood blurred into something deeper.

We're bound, Willow and me. Not by blood, not by love, but by a common goal: to dethrone the man who ruined us and bury him six feet under.

I wrench open the door.

Brown hair. Pixie haircut. Amber eyes that gleam with new magic, old trauma, and a shimmering hunger for revenge.

Willow's Tidecaller uniform hides her curves, her Mist jewels the only thing that separates her from one of her underlings. The brown leather is the antithesis of what Fae royals usually wear on the battlefield. Simple, inexpensive, and unremarkable. The Tidecallers are warriors of the people.

One corner of her mouth curls up. "I'm not sure whether to thank you for opening that door, or scold you for never answering my letters."

"Willow..." I breathe.

Seth draws back as Willow strides forward and pulls me into a hug, his lips pursed like he's not sure whether to let her or not.

"It's been too long, sister," Willow murmurs, rising to her toes to hold me close.

The greeting carries a tacit trust that I didn't expect, but it's also a show of power.

We're not a threat to her, and it shows.

The jewels embedded in her skin have multiplied in our time apart, like her hunger for power grew restless without me to temper it. Mist jewels are dangerous but beautiful things. They bestow and amplify magic, yet they're known to be addictive, like most potent substances. The more you wear, the more you want. The more they give, the more they take.

If I had been able to use magic when I was at my lowest, I'm not sure I would have had the strength to walk away from such a power.

Willow looks radiant in them, and sure of herself in a way she never used to be. But something's different. Her eyes hold the same fire, but it burns colder now. Calculated. Controlled.

Seth's brows lift. "Sister?"

I shake my head. "It's a long story."

Willow crosses her arms and looks him up and down. "You're Seth Devine, I suppose?"

"You suppose right."

"I'm the Lord of the Tides. You already know my second-in-command, Luther Storm."

A man appears behind her, shimmering out of the shadows.

"Luther, Devi. Devi, Luther," Willow says.

Despite his young age, Luther Storm is a very attractive man. Soft black locks curl around his pointy ears, and aside from his pearly-white skin, he looks much like his brother. Their eyes are oddly similar, the familiar purple-flecks peppered among heavy grey clouds.

He squares his shoulders and faces me. "It's an honor to meet you, Lady Devilyne Eros." He bows his head in greeting, but there's a rugged, impulsive quality to him, like he's merely making fun of court customs. His eyes drift to Seth. "So...you found me again, brother."

Seth matches the spark in his brother's eyes as he answers, "I hope that this time, you won't be so quick to tie me up."

"It depends. Are you ready to join the Tides?" Luther says, the half-smile on his face leaving me in doubt as to whether this is just a joke between them or a real threat.

"The only thing I feel ready for at the moment is a long, long rest."

Luther squeezes Seth's upper arm in a soothing, brotherly manner. "That'll do for now."

Willow's gaze falls to the burial shroud still tucked in my grip. "Oh no." She sucks in air, her face slowly decomposing. "Is that Percy?"

I give her a reluctant nod.

In that brief flash of grief, I glimpse at the girl I used to know.

"How did it happen?"

"Alaric Rayne is dead. The Seven Crowns sent me to kill the new Storm King in exchange for ending my banishment. I never should have agreed."

"You've done us a favor, then." She rests a hand on my shoulder. "I'm sorry this happened to you, my old friend. You, of all people, deserve better than to bury a part of your soul."

Luther's expression grows somber, and he offers me a respectful bow. "I'm sorry for your loss. After you're rested, we'll hold a *vala* for the fallen warrior."

Vala. As in, a wake. My heart hammers.

Willow ushers me forward. "Come on. Let's clean you up, first."

She sends the boys away and takes me to her private quarters. Her bedroom is situated in front of the king's, but it looks like it had been empty before their arrival, so it was probably the late queen's apartments.

She skips over to the copper tub in the back of the room and twists open the water spout. "I knew the destruction of the Chalice would facilitate your return. Freya is vulnerable now. I'm glad you came to me." She watches me from the corner of her eyes, the way you would a frightened golden-horned deer during a royal hunt.

I clear my throat, still holding on to Percy. "From what I've heard, you tried to kill all the kings and queens of Faerie—and nearly succeeded."

"A necessary evil." She slips out of her uniform and changes into a form-fitting tan leotard.

The stiffness in my spine doesn't relent. "It was a necessary evil to try and kill my brother? And yours?"

"Elio wasn't my target. I never expected him to die with the others. And Aidan wasn't supposed to be there." She clicks her fingers, and a strong fire appears in the hearth.

I look out the small, vertical window.

The fortress defies gravity, its battlements built right at the edge of the continent. At Storm's End, literally. While Deiltine was mostly hidden inside the cliffs, this place rises in a series of skewed, uneven towers reaching toward the sky—the highest of which we're occupying. The last glimmers of dawn burn in the east in bright shades of purple, orange, and pink.

I press my lips together. "You still went on with your plan and almost killed them both."

"I had to. I'd been waiting for a chance to melt that dreaded Chalice for decades."

"And Damian?"

"I never much cared for that crow, but the target was always the Eternal Chalice. And in that, I succeeded." Willow pats my arm with one hand and gently tugs on Percy's shroud with the other. "You should get in the water while it's warm."

I don't want to let him go. But no amount of blood or grime will bring him back, so I tuck him safely on the nearby table and begin to undress. The wound the cupids carved into my back is still oozing, and Willow steps forward.

"Here, let me."

She heals the fresh gashes, leaving me dressed in nothing but my old scars.

"You've become quite the healer since I last saw you," I remark, grateful for the ease of movement.

"The jewels are limitless. I could teach you how to use them."

To everyone else, Willow is the big, bad rebel. The new, unlikely leader of a centuries-old cult responsible for countless uprisings. A threat. A symbol of a faction of Fae most royals would rather exterminate.

But to me, she's just Will.

The girl who had a crush on me for ages before she finally became my friend. The sister I never had. The broken woman I helped to fake her own death, the one I sheltered in my rowan house while she patched herself back together.

There's been many, many evenings like this, spent between a bottle of wine and a steaming tub. I sink into the warm water, trying to see past my grief and exhaustion—to her heart. The last time I looked, it was a dark and frightening place. Now, it's hidden beneath a cluster of gems. Emeralds, onyxes, amethysts, rubies, opals, diamonds, and garnets shimmer against her skin, each one drawing power from a different realm, a different school of magic.

I'm vulnerable. And part of me wants nothing more than to let bygones be bygones—to call her a friend again, to cling to the last scraps of familiarity in a world that offers less and less of it. But I can't forget she set a plan in motion that killed her own mother. She tipped Faerie into chaos.

I have to keep a cool head.

"Your Luther tried to kill Elio twice. Wasn't he acting on your orders?" I ask.

She joins me by the tub and dips a hand into the water. "Luther is a good soldier, but he's young. He's got a skewed, somewhat romantic view of the future. He thinks he can save the world from many ailments, including grief."

"But you don't approve?" I press her.

"A world without pain is impossible. I think we both know that."

A heavy sigh whizzes through my lungs. "Aidan wants you back."

"Aidan wants *his* Willow back, but she's gone." Willow wets a piece of cloth and uses it to wash my back, wiping the last remnants of the attack from my skin. "Even if he was manipulated and brainwashed by our parents, he still stood by while that monster of a king used and abused me. I resent him for it."

"I don't blame you."

She braces her chin over the copper rim of the tub and draws absent-minded patterns in the water near my feet. "Freya will eventually succumb to the wounds she suffered in the attack, so once Ethan is neutralized and killed, only the Red Queen will need a good spanking. After that, the new order of things can finally prevail."

"What about Alaric Rayne? Was he part of your new order?" The water sloshes around me as I bend forward to hold my knees. "With the Chalice gone, anyone can be chosen—even the most devious psychos."

"The Chalice never kept psychos from the throne. Alaric would've been neutralized within days, had you not intervened. We were preparing to sail to Deiltine. Destroying the Chalice was only the first step. The seven crowns were holding an entire realm's magic in it, preventing its people from rebuilding, forcing them to stay in hiding. That's not right."

For a moment, it feels like we're two best friends at a sleepover, gossiping about boys and planning our futures.

Before her marriage, she was a fierce Summer Fae—sun-bright and clever, always busy planning a secret get-together or a grand, public gala. But after she wed Ezra, she absorbed something of him. His light. His lure. His cunning. That maddening quality that made him seem dangerously approachable. Sweet, yet lethal.

From that day on, she carried it too—that same glittering charm. That quiet, compelling power to make me feel like I was her one true friend. Like everyone else either didn't matter...or answered only to us.

Like I was the most badass Fae in all the worlds.

The rubies on her knuckles shine under the firelight as she unravels my braids. She cleans my hair, threading her delicate fingers through to massage my scalp and style my red mane into soft, smooth curls.

"What I want is a Faerie government that exists independently of the crowns. Using the Mist Jewels, the Tidecallers can hold royals accountable for their crimes or inadequacies," she says.

"You have that power?"

She holds out a clean towel. "I've taken on all the kings and queens of Faerie at once. I could easily kick your ass."

I step out of the tub. "Could you take on the new Mist King, too?"

"Yes." She punctuates the statement with a wink. "I'll have rooms prepared for you and Seth, and we'll discuss the next steps in the morning."

I couldn't bear to be alone tonight, and my eyes dart down. "One room will suffice."

Embers flicker in her gaze. "Ooh, I thought I got a vibe, earlier. Good for you. Well, good for Seth, really. You're the catch of the century."

I raise my brow, feigning to be offended. "Century only?" I tease.

She laughs and pinches my arm. "Oh, I've missed you, sister. I want you by my side, and Luther... He still hopes his brother will come around. If you found each other on your own, maybe we're finally getting what we wished for. Like it was written in the stars."

"The stars can be deceiving," I murmur.

"But they light the way," she says with a wistful smile. "Always."

CHAPTER 39
BROTHERS
SETH

I hover near the bedroom door Devi just disappeared through, reluctant to leave her alone. The obvious familiarity between her and the Lord of the Tides sets me on edge. Willow Summers waved me off like it was no big deal, but she has no idea what Devi endured.

Luther waits for me at the top of the staircase. "Come on."

My fists are clenched at my sides. "Promise me your boss won't harm her."

"Willow is fond of Devi. Besides, you're very important guests."

The humor in his tone warms my chest. It feels like old times, before Morrigan and the tides took him away from me. "Is there honor among rebels?" I ask, mirroring his cheekiness.

He grins, his eyes wrinkled at the corners. "Only for family."

I fall into step with him.

"So...you and Devi Eros, huh?"

"I love her," I admit freely. It's much easier to say the words out loud to Luther than to find a way to break it to Devi herself. I'm terrified of smothering her, of running her off by being too much, too fast. "She's all I can think about."

He rubs his thumb across his bottom lip. "Are you sure she didn't shoot you with a love arrow? Falling in love... It's not your style."

His skeptical, sideways glance rubs me the wrong way.

"Oh, stop being a jerk. If you can join the Rebel League of Evil, I can fall in love."

He raises his palms in front of him. "Alright, alright. Just saying —a couple of weeks ago, we were two chumps on a boat, dying to fuck a manipulative, dark-haired siren. In that moment, I would have betrayed my comrades in arms, betrayed the gods of the tides themselves, just so that Elizabeth would kiss me again. Love and lust, by my count, are never to be trusted. Especially not together." He pauses for a good second and a half before adding, "And we prefer to be called the Tides of Justice."

I hold his gaze, lips pressed together, trying to discern if he's yanking my chain. That bum is totally fucking with me.

"I know my own heart, Luther, and this is not a siren song situation. I've never felt anything like this before."

"You and Devi Eros..." he repeats, shaking his head. "That will drive your mother mad."

"I don't care what she thinks. That woman is dead to me."

He nudges my arm. "See? You're already rebelling, cavorting with a known traitor and criminal. Freya will try to make it impossible for you two to be together, but here, with us, you'd be free to do whatever you want."

When he asked me to join him on the boat, I never could've imagined saying yes.

But after seeing the damage an unchecked king can do in so little time, I wonder. The Tidecallers might have been wrong to destroy the Eternal Chalice, but now that it's gone, we have to rethink the way Faerie works. And seeing what it did to Devi—allowing my mother to steal her crown because of her political sway over the seven crowns—I'm not so sure it was the neutral, balancing force it was supposed to be.

But without it, the kings and queens will hold too much power over their respective realms, and the continent will stay locked in endless war, any Fae in line for the crown ready to assassinate the current ruler, hoping to take their place.

"I'll think about it," I finally say.

Luther squeezes my shoulder. "That's all I want. For you to give us a real chance."

He leads me to his bedroom—on the second highest floor of the tower, just beneath the king and queen's apartments. I pause before entering, my gaze drawn to the other door across the hall.

"Where's Maddox?"

"In a cell, downstairs. I found him after our father's death. He was drowning in a Nether cider bottle, whining about not being king."

Our eyes fly to the sky in sync. Maddox was the golden son, but that made him insufferable. While Luther and I always got along, Maddox treated me like my father did—like I didn't exist.

"So he's not the new Storm King..." I trail off. "No mysterious bolt of lightning striking the prison about an hour ago?"

"No."

I look him up and down. From what I've heard from the battle-field, Luther can heal fast, so he might have been able to hide his injuries. "And you're not either?"

He shakes his head. "No."

"Then who?"

Luther raises his brows. "That's an interesting twist, isn't it? It would've driven Father mad to know that none of us were chosen to succeed him."

I grin at his logic and step inside his quarters.

Luther's rooms used to be a teenage prince's den, and looked the part. I remember the first time I stepped in here: curtains torn down to let the wind in, runes scorched into the floorboards, smuggled trinkets from the new world, and crude drawings of our father.

Now, it's eerily neat. The rebel clutter is gone, the only remaining legacy of his youth the painting of the Islantide on the far wall.

Luther was always obsessed with the island. The sting of vinegar and jasmine—typical Storm's End cleaning products—clutters the air. The walls are bare stone, the floors scrubbed clean, and the bed is made with military precision. The space has been emptied out, like he boxed up every part of who he used to be to become who he is.

"Willow is wonderful," he says, settling into a leather armchair by the fireplace. "She's going to change the world."

"But?"

"You know me too well." He licks his lips, swallowing back a faint smile. "She doesn't think suffering and grief can be avoided. She doesn't approve of my experiments."

My gaze catches on an odd shape in the next room—no doors separate the different spaces of the apartment.

"Is that a spinning wheel?" I ask.

"Yes. One of many."

A peculiar bite of power ripples from the wheel, luring me in, and I walk closer to it.

"Why? Have you taken up knitting or something?"

The charred, blackened wood is smooth and warm, as though kissed by dragonfire. Golden-foiled Fae runes run along the outer edge of the wheel. The twin spindles are nerved with lyranthium, their pointy edge impossibly sharp.

Luther joins me in his study, hands tucked inside the pockets of his gray breeches. "They say the right combination of spindle and wheel can spin a Golden-horned deer's fur into a fiber strong enough to link a soul back to its body. Replace the missing tether. I've been tinkering with different materials and shapes."

I walk to the desk and squint at the dozen open leather-bound journals cluttering the space. Their delicate pages are filled with meticulous calligraphy.

"By the spindle... These are the Mist King's journals." I flip through a couple of pages, uncovering detailed drawings of Mist jewels and advanced Mist technology lost to this world for centuries.

"Where did you find them? I thought all his work had been destroyed."

"We found them on a remote island in the Breach." He glances down at his collection with pride.

I brush my fingers over the soft paper. "And what do they say?"

"They talk about the Lake of Souls, the power of the Frost Peak mines, and a disease that spread from Wintermere's glacier and infected the population, transforming Winter Fae into reapers. The jewels in the mines fuel the Winter King's power and make him stronger than his peers. He gathers souls to boost that power even further, which allows him to become immortal. The journals give specs for the weapon needed to contain his ice."

Ever since his mother died, Luther has harbored a profound hatred for the Fae king who came to collect her soul.

"You're not just hating on Elio Lightbringer because he's holding your pal Morrigan captive, are you?"

He gives a dismissive wave. "Forget Rye. She was playing her own game and let herself be captured. Come on, you always thought Elio was a dull, grumpy, better-than-thou asshole. Your words."

"I don't deny it." Devi's mysterious and intense connection to the man gets on my nerves, I'll admit. "But it's a stretch between 'mightily self-righteous' and 'maniacal king who schemes behind everyone's back'. I don't buy it. Maybe the old Winter King cooked something nefarious on that mountain. If he did, I bet Elio doesn't know a thing about it."

Luther's eyes darken. "You can't deny he's nearly unkillable. If the Mist King found a way to bring his loved ones back from the dead —to reattach their souls without losing their essence, to stop the inevitable rot that usually takes over a dark soul—who's to say death can't be avoided entirely? That a reinforced tether, similar to the one the Winter King has, couldn't prevent the bond between soul and body from snapping in the first place?"

The clear-cut longing in his voice brings chills to my spine, but alas, I fear this is a hopeless crusade.

"That's a fever dream, Luther. A sales pitch Armand Moonreaver used to rally his army and launch an attack on the continent. He dangled immortality like a worm on a hook to justify his war."

Luther taps the closest journal with his fingers. "Not according to these texts. They've been lying to us, Seth. The old Mist King wasn't insane. He didn't want to become the one true king—not at first. He just wanted to vanquish Death."

AFTER MY CHAT WITH LUTHER, HE TAKES ME TO THE GUEST ROOM BELOW HIS floor.

I pause in the doorway, holding my breath.

Percy's body is set on the mantle above the hearth, while Devi stands in front of the window. She's fresh out of the bath, wrapped in a soft black robe that hugs the swell of her hips and slips just enough to reveal her collarbone. Her long brown legs shine in the light, and her red curls frame her face like a halo. My pulse swirls. The way her robe hugs her slender waist, the gentle rise and fall of her breath, the strength in her posture even in this intimate moment...

Her beauty stings my heart.

I make my way to her and try to wrap my arms around her, but she sidesteps. "Wait."

My chest is about to burst. She didn't ask for us to sleep apart, but she seems untouchable just the same.

She points to the bathtub. "Your turn. You're filthy."

If that's the reason she rejected my embrace, I can make peace with it. Her eyes are clear, her posture relaxed, so maybe there's nothing more to it, but I just can't shake the feeling that some invisible wall still stands between us.

I'm beginning to understand just how much she loathes her

queenly mask. Her independence, as she calls it, is bred out of necessity—from a world that didn't allow her to show weakness.

I've seen her eyes light up under a rainy sky. I've seen her smirk when someone underestimates her. She wants a man who sees through the illusion, who won't back down when she lets him see the hurt, the violence, the parts of her she keeps locked away. And Zeus help me, I want to be that man.

She sees every part of me—the bastard, the outcast, the fuckboy—and prompts me to become more.

Steam rises from the tub, the water crystal clear. I unbutton my torn shirt, pull off my breeches, and step inside. The warm water soothes my aching joints, but it does nothing to ease my troubled mind.

She sits on the nearby ottoman and passes me the soap. The intimacy of it all, the sash of her robe loosening, the slippery soap in my hand... My cock swells under the water. I shift positions, trying to conceal just how aroused I am. This hardly seems like the appropriate time for sex, but gods, she's so fucking beautiful.

It's so quiet. The only sound is the swirl of water in the tub over the furious beats of my heart.

She leans forward and wipes the leftover blood from the biggest and most debilitating lash Alaric's lightning drew across my chest. Her brows rise—the skin underneath unblemished and untouched. "Luther healed you?"

"Not Luther. Percy."

Her lids flutter shut, and she shudders.

We ran out of Deiltine while everyone was still trying to figure out who was in charge. There was no time to talk, no time to exchange notes.

"He snuck into my cell and healed me before the arena," I say softly. "That's how I was able to fight Alaric. Percy wanted me to save you—"

She covers my mouth with her hand. "Stop. I don't want to hear any more."

Be still my heart. She drops her robe and climbs in the bath with me. The smooth skin of her bare stomach, breasts, and legs is interrupted only by her original scars. The wounds she suffered in Deiltine have been healed, but the emotional ones, the ones I can't see, are what worry me.

She straddles me and sinks her nails into my hairline, swallowing my next sentence with a kiss. It's not soft. Not gentle. It's desperate, like she's trying to cut herself on my mouth. Like she wants to bleed out everything she can't say. It's a command. A plea. A way to shut me up.

And I almost let her.

Because I want her. Gods, I want her, but I feel...guilty.

"Not like this," I murmur against her lips, bracing my hands on her shoulders.

"Please. I need it." She shifts her hips, my crown bumping against her inner thigh.

The water makes for an easy glide, and I grip her waist to avoid accidentally slipping inside her.

"I don't want to take advantage—"

She holds my gaze. "Take me, Seth, or don't—but never treat me like a victim. I'm your queen, or nothing at all." The heartbreak in her voice stirs something in me, but she quickly shakes it off in favor of a seductive smile. "And I want you to fuck me. From the way your cock is throbbing against my thigh, I'd say you want to fuck me, too."

Sex is the most efficient way for a Spring Fae to turn the page, and I know what she's trying to erase. Percy's death. Alaric's hands. The lingering bite of lyranthium on her soul. She's trembling, eager to light a fire big enough to burn the memories of our journey here.

"I'd rather be worshipped at the wrong time than lonely when it hurts the most." She explores my chest with both hands. Her bite of power drums in wild waves, snapping against my skin. "I need you, Seth. It's a mercy."

Mercy. I can give her that—let her bury the pain, let her use my body to silence the screaming inside her head. I'd take it all. I'd carry it for her. I'd break myself a hundred times if it meant she didn't have to suffer any longer.

Gods, I'd do anything to soothe her, however ephemeral the cure might be.

Because I love her. Zeus help me, I love her.

And if this is what she needs to crawl out of a dark place, I'll give it to her. I'll fuck the sorrow out of her bones. I'll replace every haunting trace of Alaric with a bruise that says mine.

I pull her down, impaling her onto my shaft.

Her mouth parts around my name, and I graze my thumb across her pebbled nipple. She rocks against me, rising until I'm all the way out of her and crushing back down, sheathing me to the root.

My hand travels down her stomach, down the seam between her thighs to the sweet bundle of nerves there. I press on it with my thumb and a hint of thunder.

"Oh, fuck." Her high-pitched groan vibrates against my shoulder, and she nibbles the skin there in retaliation. "You're awfully good at that."

The water makes the electric current radiate outward, and my balls tighten, tickled by the charge. I grab the side of her face. This thing is moving fast. I need to see her face before I fuck her senseless.

Her round, heavy breasts fill my hands, and I take her nipples inside my mouth one at a time, the taste of them so fucking sweet. I could spend a lifetime worshipping her body, and still groan at the mere sight of them. "What do you want?" I rasp, lifting her off me and bringing her back down again, hard.

She fucking purrs. Her walls tighten, wrapping around my cock and holding me there. She craves as I crave. Loves as I love. An all-consuming, ruinous love.

Her nose bumps against mine. "I want you to make me see stars."

I bite down on her earlobe. "Then I shall do what my queen commands, of course."

CHAPTER 40
CATACOMBS
DEVI

Seth carries me out of the bathtub bridal style and spreads me down on the bed. The way he stares down at me, like I'm the most precious treasure he's ever claimed, lights an inferno in my belly. His kisses are tender. His bites are possessive. Together, they wreck me in the best way.

He treats me like I'm his queen—yet makes it clear my body is his to worship, to unravel, to ruin with pleasure. It's hot as hells.

He massages my breasts, rolling and teasing the peaks until I arch into his hands.

"You're obsessed with them," I tease.

"With good reason." He chuckles, but it comes out low and husky, like he's too busy imagining how to make me scream his name to bother joking. His hands stroke my hips, slow and deliberate, before he flips me onto my stomach.

"Now, I want you on all fours, witch. I want to give that gorgeous ass of yours the attention it deserves."

He was careful in the tub. He's not careful now.

And gods, I could cry from the relief. His filthy mouth. His rough touch. That's what I need. For him to fuck the trauma out of me.

I crawl to my hands and knees, heat pooling along my ribs.

Seth kisses a fiery path down my spine, hovering above me, caressing every inch—my sides, my arms, my shoulder blades—before turning his attention to my rump. His magic coats my skin like a hot towel, warm to the point of near pain. He tests the limits of my patience like some wicked deep-tissue masseur determined to make me beg for more.

Then he shifts to his knees, grips his length, and presses the head to my clit, then lines himself up with my soaked entrance.

"Do you want my cock inside you?" he asks, pushing in an inch.

"Yes."

"How much?"

I adjust my hips in response, taking him deeper, and we both groan.

His thunder scatters across my skin like vines crawling up to my front, circling my breasts, zapping my nipples before it slithers across my stomach to hit my clit. The sensation booms like fireworks exploding in my core, and a gush of arousal squirts out of me.

"That was fucking hot." He gathers my mane in one hand and tugs. "Keep those palms nice and flat to the bed. I'm not going to go easy on you."

He rushes all the way in, and I gasp.

He's bigger and thicker than I remembered, the angle far more delectable. Primal.

He sets a delirious pace and keeps me right there on the edge, his thick cock hitting that impossibly needy spot inside me with every thrust. The roots of my hair tingle deliciously as he tugs and releases my hair in turn.

Then, he stops and spreads my arousal from front to back, gently teasing my dark hole with his thumb.

"I like what I like, witch, and I will have your beautiful ass."

The crown of his cock presses against the tight ring, and I exhale, shaking in anticipation. He pushes his hips forward, forcing past the tight muscles there.

A burst of fire slithers up my spine, but Seth pauses, letting me adjust around his bursting-hard shaft. He's too big, but the pain of the invasion soothes my aching heart. His thunder delicately sparks in my pussy, making me hum, my clit now throbbing, begging for mercy.

He kneads the flesh of my ass with both hands. "Relax your muscles. Yes, like that. Take it all."

I suck in air as he pushes deeper, filling me in ways I never even dreamed of, like he's claiming my soul at the same time. I cry out his name in praise, but he slips a finger inside my mouth, filling me further.

Another thrust—quicker, rougher—and a low grunt escapes him. "See, witch? See how much you love my cock?"

He sounds close to unraveling, and I grin, sucking on his finger, salt and soap lingering on my tongue.

"So fucking tight and greedy, squeezing my cock like that. I could spend an eternity inside you. I can't wait to try your mouth."

His hands tighten around my hips as he sets a slow, controlled pace. The thunder writhes against my skin. I feel it inside me, too—something swelling, stretching me wide, pulsing right where I need it. My nipples ache. My heart beats between my legs like it's a live, desperate thing.

Seth purrs in satisfaction, his big hands keeping his thrusts impossibly precise, despite all my moaning and writhing.

"Come, darling. Let me see how high my dark angel can fly with my cock deep in her ass."

That sentence alone sends me over the edge. My name vanishes. My pain, my grief—all of it recedes to the depths of my subconscious. I plummet into white-hot oblivion, my arms and legs quaking, my toes curling. I'm falling, my dark hole pulsing around his shaft, demanding every drop of his seed.

I see a whole sky full of stars. Galaxies.

He curses under his breath, riding out the high until my arms shake.

His eyes glow with mischief as he rolls me over and kisses me languidly, my walls still pulsing. He drags his hand down between us and rubs my clit with the rough pad of his thumb. Once, and I'm falling again. Just like that.

"Let's count together. Two." His brows knit together as I grip his shoulder to steady myself through the orgasm. "Tut-tut. Palms to the mattress, remember."

He barely gives me time to recover before thunder surges through me again.

"Three."

The soft duvet tears in my grip.

He gives my left breast a punishing lick. "Four."

I scream, but he covers my mouth with his palm.

"Who's the best lover you've ever had?" he asks, all smiles.

"You, damn bastard. Must we do this every time?" I mumble.

His mouth opens, lips forming an F as though he's about to send me spinning for the fifth time. My knuckles flex. My toes curl.

"Until I tire of hearing it," he says instead. He shifts over me, pinning me to the mattress, until his cock teases my entrance. It's rock-hard again. "Five."

He feeds me his cock inch by inch, and I quake all over.

The duvet is wrecked. My mind is wrecked. Seth's special brand of dual magic has forever ruined me for other men.

He's the only thing grounding me to this earth, thrusting all the way in and out, over and over again, but excruciatingly slowly. He praises every gush like his favorite fetish is watching my juices drip from his cock before pushing back in.

By the end, he doesn't even have to move. My body obeys the slow drawl of his voice, clenching and pulsing until I'm begging for mercy. Until I'm drunk on a string of orgasms I've completely lost count of. Until he's all but painted me with his seed.

Everywhere but inside, where I could absorb it, no, he revels in the sight of me covered in ropes of his cum.

I'm gasping for breath by the time he's done, and yet I feel like I could cry from the loss. I'm usually the kind of gal who sends a man packing after I've had my share, but I find myself already daydreaming about our next time—about how it'll feel when he uses my mouth and comes deep in my throat. How much I'll enjoy the next round.

"Fuck, you really know how to create an addiction."

He smacks a kiss on my belly button. "I love you, witch."

I curl into his side and sigh, hiding my face in the crook of his neck, inhaling him deep. He smells like soap and musk—and a new scent we've made together. He traces his fingers up and down my spine. I snuggle closer and pray he'll be patient enough to stay— because I can't say it yet. But I feel it. I'm terrified by how much.

I WAKE UP TO AN AWFULLY COLD AND EMPTY BED AND SLIP ON THE FITTED black clothes I find in a drawer and fix my hair as much as I can without using magic. Stopping by the hearth, I press a quick kiss to Percy's shroud and tiptoe out of the guest quarters to explore.

The tower of the fortress is only narrow at the top five floors, and it begins to widen as I descend. When I reach the first broader level, two large double doors stand wide open. I expected guards—or Willow herself—to stop me from wandering alone through the castle, but I enter the bibliotheca without a hitch.

The long, diamond-shaped windows offer an unobstructed view of the bay below, where workers bustle along the docks, loading crates into ships. I stride deeper into the room.

At the heart of the stacks, where tables and desks once stood, dozens upon dozens of spinning wheels—of every size, style, and material—are arranged in neat rows. The original furniture has been shoved into a corner and stacked to make room for the map. Only one table remains upright, cluttered with a thick, geodesic Shadow mask, electrodes, rods, fluxes, woodcarving tools, and transparent cases filled with materials and fine wires.

I graze the edges of the mask, the likes of which I've never seen. Shadow masks are usually thin and elegant, molded by shadows themselves, but this looks like a piece of metal that was beaten to submission by a hammer. In fact, many of the materials and instruments are new to me.

This must be where Luther and Willow tinker with their jewels. They use metal to mount the gems and fuse them to their bodies, which demands some serious craftsmanship and expertise. But some of the gear can't be explained by that alone. A few half-finished spindles lie in a separate box, while one sits at the center of the worktable, inlaid with amethysts and gold.

"Lady Eros. I see you've found my collection." Luther greets me as he enters.

He says the title with a hint of impertinence, like he's above such things but plays the game for my benefit. There's no anger or suspicion in his tone for finding me away from my bedroom.

"Just call me Devi."

"Alright, Devi."

Against all odds, I'm not a prisoner, though I didn't see any mirror, so there's nowhere to go.

I brace my hands on my hips, contemplating his rather peculiar collection of spinning wheels. "Seth told me you want to vanquish death?" I say, keeping my voice from sounding too judgmental or doubtful.

"You just lost someone dear to you. Wouldn't you do anything to get him back?" Luther says softly, walking to the nearest wheel to pry off the spindle.

"Death is part of life."

The corners of Luther's mouth quirk. "Only because we allow him to be."

He walks to the working table and sets down the spindle.

"Don't listen to Luther, he's very angry with Elio." Willow says, prancing into the room like a mystical creature crawling out of the ether. She drums her fingers across Luther's fitted black shirt in a teasing fashion. "Are you trying to rope my friend into your experiments?"

Luther doesn't answer her question but holds my gaze instead. "In our world, there are only two types of rulers. The ones that try to double down on the mistakes of their predecessors—usually a parent—and the ones that challenge the status quo in order to provoke change." He sits at his workstation, turning his focus to his current project as he adds, "You've always been a destroyer of traditions. You would fit well within the tides, so why don't you join our ranks?"

I suppress a smile. "You never stop pitching, do you?"

He slips on the geodesic mask and lights a solder rod with a grin. Flashes of light and flame dance across the worn metal. "I never give up on anything before I've succeeded."

Willow gestures toward a table laid with a steaming pot of coffee and a plate of biscuits. "Coffee? I remember you don't like honey. Would you prefer sugar instead?"

They act like it's perfectly normal for me to stroll around the castle, inspect the wheels, and make small talk while Luther tinkers with arcane machinery. It's too easy. Too trusting.

I observe Luther again. "Where's Seth? I thought he was with you."

"He wanted to see his father's grave," he answers, not looking up. "Down in the catacombs. I can take you there, if you want."

"Not quite yet." I fold my arms. "I've spoken with Seth. We agree —Ethan needs to die. I propose we join forces for that. Afterward, I'll consider your offer to join the Tides."

Willow straddles an empty chair, coffee in hand. "Fair enough. Is he vulnerable somewhere? Grooming a son—some bastard he decided to legitimize after Ezra's disappearance? Is he searching for a new wife?"

"He wants Lori. I saw it in his eyes back in Wintermere—he was looking at her the same way he used to look at you..." my voice cracks at the end.

Her eyes shine with tears and something else, something hungry and dark, like a beast she caged inside. "Then we don't have to get to Ethan. We only have to wait. If he wants Lori, we'll give him an opportunity to get close to her—and strike when he least expects it."

"Elio will never go for that," I say quickly. "Couldn't you just take her place and deal with him yourself, like you did in Eterna?"

"Even if I could emulate her stance perfectly, Ethan won't be fooled by that scheme a second time. Now that he knows I can change appearances, he'll be more careful." She shakes her head. "No, it should be Lori. As a Shadow huntress, she's the most likely to hit her mark."

"If she manages to kill Ethan, I'll free her of Iris's soul. I saw them in Eterna, before the attack, and that dark soul is ingrained pretty deep inside her. I'd rather not be the one to destroy Iris for good, but if Lori gets me Ethan, I'll do it. I promise."

What Willow is offering is massive. I suspect Elio wants Ethan dead so he can bargain with his successor to save his wife. But Willow is not just admitting she has more power than the King of Light, she's offering to save Lori. The promise soothes the raw ache in my chest. Maybe I've had it all wrong. Maybe she veered off the path of self-destruction she was on the last time we were together. Maybe I've been on the wrong side of this fight.

Doubts worm into my brain, but I can't deal with a crisis of faith at present. A temporary alliance will give me time to test if Willow's ambitions have cooled enough to convince me she's not about to set the world on fire...again.

"You might be her best chance, so I'll take your offer back to her. But I can't agree to join you yet. Not before I bury Percy and think it over," I say with a sad but hopeful smile.

"Killing Ethan is the goal for now," she takes my hands in hers, "but think about the world we could build together. No elitist rules at the academy. No more keeping women from their rightful thrones.

Picture Mabel's witches back in power. The Red Forest restored to its former glory. The Mist Fae no longer in hiding but home again. We could right a thousand wrongs in our lifetime."

Her enthusiasm is infectious, but I can let my guard down.

"Very well. Seth and I will return to Wintermere and speak with Lori. Since I killed the Storm King, as the crowns asked, they might allow Seth and me to wed. That would give us the perfect opportunity to strike. But first—I have to bury Percy in Spring, under the Hawthorn, as is custom. He would have wanted that."

"I've thought of a way to honor Percy here," Willow says softly, "but I figured you might say that." She squeezes my lower arm. "You have our blessing to cross into Spring, but be careful. Freya may be weakened, but she still rules."

"My wolves will not hunt you in the sceawere. You have my word." Luther rises and sets his mask on the table. "I'll take you to Seth now."

"When you're ready to leave," Willow adds, "come find me in my room, and I'll take you to the mirror."

Luther grabs a cloak from the hook outside the bibliotheca. The dark fabric billows behind him as he leads me down the main staircase, across the hall, and through a hidden door that opens onto yet another set of stairs. The spiral staircase curves downward, taking us deep into the heart of the rock beneath the fortress.

The catacombs beneath Zepharion's stronghold are cool and still, the silence broken only by the steady drip of water from the stalactites above. A dark underground lake shapes the cavern, its waters lapping gently at the black sand. Torches cast a soft golden light across the nature-made mausoleum, where rows of metal coffins rest in alcoves along the far wall. The air smells of salt and mineral stone, and the slightest hint of decay.

Luther pauses on the last step and spins on his heels. "I'll give you some privacy."

Thorald Storm's coffin lies atop a glimmering slab of lyranthium in a prominent spot by the lake, and the lid depicts the likeness of the dead sovereign. A narrow well of light above allows the moon to shine directly onto the king's effigy, the pale gleam reflecting off his sculpted face.

Seth stands quietly in front of the grave. "It's stupid. He's not even in there, his body burned in Eterna," he murmurs.

He glances toward the far end of the chamber, to the nearest row of tombs. "Luther used to sneak down here all the time to visit his mother. I never thought I'd get sentimental about Thorald fucking Storm. I never thought that fucker would die—honestly. I thought I'd spend my entire life disappointing him—never meeting his standards, always speaking out of turn. We didn't have much of a relationship, but I could count on that, at least."

He huffs a shaky breath, and a single tear slips down his cheek.

"I never thought I'd cry for him. Must be the sleep deprivation or something—"

"Shh. It's okay." I pat his shoulder blade.

"Death really does meet us all... despite what Luther thinks."

"Your brother makes me nervous," I admit. "A lot of Fae try to cheat death, and it always ends badly. I'm afraid he might try to hurt Elio again."

Seth tenses, his knuckles flexing. "You really care about that ice dude."

I blink at him a few times, biting back a smile. "Seth. He's my brother."

His entire face blanks out for a beat. "Wait. What?"

"Ethan Lightbringer sired me. That's why I have so much light magic. Why I have wings." I avert my gaze. "He raped my mother, and she never truly recovered. She killed herself when I was seven."

"By Zeus, I'm so sorry..." He rubs down his face, his jaw slightly askew. "So you're..."

"A closeted bastard, yes."

A sheepish grimace twists his lips. "I was going to say you're not still hung up on Elio."

"Were you jealous?" I tease him.

He hooks his little finger around mine. "Immensely."

"And now?"

His lips press together. "Now I fear we're stuck in a world where my brother plans to kill yours, and I don't know what we can do to stop him."

I straighten his collar and gently tug at the lapels of his jacket.

"Let's cross that bridge later. I want to go home to Spring and bury Percy." My voice falters, and my mouth hangs open for a moment before I find the strength to whisper, "And... I want to do it with you."

CHAPTER 41
SECRET SPRINGS
DEVI

Mist obscures the scea(were, the heavy white flumes sturdier than they were the last time we traveled through the space between worlds. I can't see anything, so I slip my free hand into Seth's, the other holding Percy close to my heart.

There are no nightmarish wolves leaping at our throats, just as Luther promised, but it's nerve-wracking to know we wouldn't see them coming this time around. If some monster prowled this white, cottony blur, we'd be sitting ducks.

"Ominous, no?" Seth cracks.

"Very."

"Luther wasn't nervous—like he didn't even consider the new Mist King a threat."

A shiver slithers through me, the icy kiss of the mists on my cheeks like being smothered by a very soft, inviting pillow. "Willow thought she could take him."

"I almost flunked history, but I'd still be wary of a Summer Fae going up against a Mist King. Not after what happened last time."

A small chuckle grates my throat. "Willow hopes to right that wrong. She's a Summer Fae in name only."

"I'm not sure any Fae alive could right a wrong of such biblical proportions," Seth grumbles, hastily drawing runes on his lower arm.

"Freya must've warded all the mirrors in the Secret Springs against me," I warn him. "It might take a while to find one that wasn't properly maintained."

He smirks at that. "There's no mirror in Spring I don't control. My mother doesn't do subtle when it comes to enchantments or wards, and as the only living relative who shares her blood, I can get anywhere I want—from the prison to her chambers." His voice brims with that signature cockiness that makes me want to kiss him and slap him in equal measure.

"And she has no idea?"

"None."

The charming quip coaxes a reluctant smile out of me as he flicks through a dozen possible entry points into a land I haven't stepped foot in for eight decades.

Freya was never the most talented spellcaster. Or arrow carver. Or anything, really. She always valued showmanship over efficiency, and alliances and sexual favors over talent.

Now, I finally see the truth behind her well-crafted but crumbling mask. Everything she has depends on others' willingness to let her keep it, and that's no place to rule from.

Back at the ball, it was fun to pretend Seth was on my side, but now that he'd actually burn the world down for me, it's even sweeter. Freya's only son is the one taking me back home—against her will and her wards—all because she never contemplated the possibility that her own blood might turn on her.

I might have given Seth all the pieces of my broken heart.

But I still feel like a criminal and a goddess wrapped in one, that he'd be the one taking me home.

Revenge is sweeter for the wait.

"Freya's archers are doing a very poor job in the new world. My mortal goddaughter fell in love after a split-arrowhead hit her, and she has no idea she's about to marry a man who won't love her for more than a couple of years," I say, revealing a piece of the exiled life I never thought I'd share with any man.

Seth purses his lips to the side, still searching for a mirror that suits him. "Sucks for her."

"I used to think it was none of my business, but maybe I should tell her. Percy would say—" I stop abruptly, tears flooding my eyes.

Seth finally lands on the desired entry point. "I'm so sorry for your loss, my darling."

The mirror spits us out into a place I recognize. The distant memory of my time here screeches my heart to a halt. Humidity assaults my senses. It's still winter on the Continent, but it's always warm in Spring, the tropical air seeping into my pores.

"We're already in the inner cloister of the castle. Near Eros' forest," I gasp.

"Yes," Seth says proudly.

When he told me he could access any mirror, I didn't have time to contemplate that we'd come out so close to our destination. The Spring Castle is the only way through to the sacred forest from the south. Our northern borders are guarded by a beautiful but deadly jungle that stretches for miles, all the way to the border of the Summerlands.

My hands shake as I pull off my black boots and socks. I dig my bare feet into the grass, then spread my toes and let the earth spill between them, moaning under my breath.

The ground hums beneath my feet, warm and alive—like a welcome home. A deep vibration rocks the soles of my feet. I brush off tendrils of lingering mist from my black dress, the collared neckline, and the sleeves that stop at mid-arm. The single row of gold buttons down the front shines under the moonlight.

Up above, the two Amouran rivers carve a heart-shaped groove through the land—one flowing through a natural tunnel beneath, the other gliding overhead, their waters close but not mixing yet.

After crossing paths, they spiral around the most sacred ground in the Secret Spring: the Rond-de-l'Âme, a small island dominated by our Hawthorn. Its long, trailing branches stretch beyond the circle, brushing the land across the rivers.

At the point where the twin rivers finally meet, they merge into a single, roaring waterfall that spills over the edge of a three-hundred-foot rift. We stand at the bottom, where the water crashes into a wide lake near the castle.

The moon is enormous above, bathing the scenery in soft, silver rays.

"We'll have to fly up there," Seth declares.

"I know. I'm ready."

A sigh whistles out of my lungs as I summon my wings, spreading them wide on each side.

It's such a relief to have them again, yet it hurts to fly without Percy by my side.

Seth sucks in air. "Wow, you look like a dark, avenging angel, witch."

"You must say that to all the girls," I joke.

We fly up to the Rond-de-l'Âme, landing on the only part of the island not shadowed by the Hawthorn. I watch the sky closely for signs of red, and my stomach cramps as a small cluster of burgundy clouds amass overhead.

"Here goes."

Seth's lips curl downward. "I thought they were gone for good. Honestly."

"Apparently not, but you can kill them. That's good enough for now."

Four cupids detach from the cloud, that number downright ridiculous compared to the throng of winged cannonballs that rained down on us in Deiltine. Seth quickly tears them down with his lightning, and sure enough, they die rather than respawning, bleeding instead of breaking into glass. No second wave comes behind them, but their disgusting bodies mar the pristine, sacred island with their dark, viscous blood.

"Why were there only a few this time?" Seth asks.

"I didn't use much magic," I explain. "But you figured out the loophole. And now I know exactly what thread still holds my curse together."

He arches a brow. "I'm the loophole, right?"

"Not quite. You said it in the sceawere—your mother doesn't do subtle."

We pass beneath the trailing leaves of the Hawthorn, where a burst of color awaits us—dozens of blue, red, and pink lotus flowers blooming on the surface of a shallow pond. The water comes from Eros' Fountain, the purest spring in all of Faerie, nestled at the base of the tree. It gushes up between two thick, exposed roots before spilling gently into the crystal-clear pond below.

Garlands of pink and purple moss fall from the Hawthorn's primary branches, the substrate allowing veiled violas, white plumerias, and ghost orchids to flourish in the shade.

I stride over to the trunk of the trees and press my palm to it. "On that first night, before the cupids hunted me down and tried to tear out my heart—before they chased me out of Faerie—Freya cut herself to seal her vow. She rammed a special arrowhead into my heart to take my crown, and she must've used her blood to weave the curse, too. Her blood is the loophole. You can kill the cupids because you share her blood."

Seth's jaw clenches. "But if you're right, they'll keep coming until she dies."

"Willow told me your mother only had weeks to live. Does that upset you?" I watch his reaction closely, and to his credit, he doesn't brush off the question. He doesn't shrug. He just holds my gaze without fail.

"Not if it means you're safe," he declares in a solemn tone.

But that's beside the point, I realize.

If he can harm the cupids—if the curse sees Freya's blood and his as the same—then they won't vanish until every last drop of her blood is gone from the worlds. Including his.

Unless...

"If we marry, maybe they'll disappear," I murmur. "Marriage is a sharing of flesh, blood, and bones. Maybe then, I'll finally be free of them. I'll at least be able to kill them, I think."

I kneel down to the earth and focus back on the reason why we came.

It's customary to bury Faelings under the protection of a realm's sacred Hawthorn, and Spring has the best, most beautiful one. Percy loved it here. It was our secret place to chat and work out difficult decisions when I was queen. We shared many picnics in the shadows of those branches, admiring the heaps of tumbling moss and the flowers that nestled and thrived within them. When the ugliness of court politics became too much, we escaped to this little cocoon of beauty.

I peel away the crust of moss at the back of the tree and dig a small hole in the earth with my hands, right between two roots, just large enough to cradle Percy's shroud.

A sob quakes my chest as I tuck him safely inside. One handful at a time, I fill the hole, each grain of earth striking the shroud like the last sand falling through the hourglass of our time together.

"Do you want to speak?" Seth asks.

"I can't."

I lost a piece of myself I can't replace.

"Can I say something?" he asks, kneeling beside me.

I hold back a sniffle and nod.

Seth doesn't hesitate, his voice confident, yet soft.

"The tiniest man I've ever known turned out to be one of the grandest. No taller than my hand, but he walked into cages and stared down monsters. I've seen High Fae with mountains of power cower when it mattered, but Percy never did."

My bottom lip trembles, and I cross my arms over my chest. "I don't know how to say goodbye. I've been lonely, but never alone. Percy was there, by my side, since I was born. How am I supposed to face life completely alone?"

Seth slides closer until our legs touch and wraps me in his arms, pulling me against him. I breathe him in. He smells of warm skin and morning rain, wrapped in a sizzle of crushed leaves.

"You don't have to be alone," he murmurs against my ear. "By the spindle, I'll be right here—for as long as you'll have me."

I kiss him, unable to put into words all the things I want to say.

Mostly: thank you for being here, for being you. I hope you'll stay with me forever.

The kiss is chaste, but deep—like the end of one chapter and the start of a new one. Percy knew, all along, that my heart belonged to Seth.

He knew me better than I know myself, but the time has come to say goodbye.

I press my palms to the thin cover of overturned earth. "I will love you forever, diamantay," I whisper.

Eros help me, I cry.

I cry for all the times I didn't. The dams in my soul break wide open. Salt and sorrow fall to the earth, gliding between the dead leaves before being absorbed by the sponge of moss covering the ground.

Seth holds me. Helps me carry the weight of this grief that would've toppled me on my own.

I feel different in his arms, like I might survive this. Like I can go on.

Even if it hurts like the fires of the seven hells.

When the sobs have dwindled, I slap my knees to summon the strength to speak again. "We shouldn't stay too long, or we might risk being spotted by a patrol."

Seth threads his fingers into my flamboyant curls and forces me to look at him.

He's been crying, too—though his eyes now shine clear and purple.

"What?" I ask.

"Devi Eros. Will you marry me?"

CHAPTER 42
BODY AND SOUL
DEVI

I wipe the last of my tears and smile. Deep down, my Storm prince is a romantic.

"Aren't we already engaged? I thought we were," I tease.

"I mean here. Now."

My brows furrow, and I search the heavenly scenery. The moonlight plays with the shifting branches and leaves, streaking through the canopy with every gust of wind. It's true that it'd make for a wonderful setting for a wedding, but alas... "We have no officiant, no kindreds, no ceremonial knife—"

"We're in Eros' sacred forest. We don't need any of that. A couple who drinks from Eros' Fountain is immediately wed under her eyes. No witness needed."

I gape at him. This isn't the kind of marriage we're used to in Spring, or anywhere else on the Fae continent. No, it's rare because it demands something almost as impossible to find as it is beautiful. Something Spring Fae whisper about when they're intoxicated or yearning.

A legend every other realm dismisses as a foolish myth.

"But the Fountain doesn't allow just anyone to marry, only—"

"Fated mates." He pecks my lips. "I love you, witch. And I'm not ashamed to say it. I never loved anyone else as I love you. You were made for me, and I was made for you."

My heart somersaults, but I shake my head. "The crowns will punish you. If we come back from our mission already married, they'll brand you a traitor."

He nuzzles the back of my ear, his hot breath making all the hairs on my neck stand at attention. "If you're a traitor, then so am I. If you're exiled again, I will go with you. Besides, even if they gave permission, do you really want to get married in front of the seven crowns? With my mother there, ready to stab you while no one's looking? With your father watching us as we consummate our love?"

I grimace at the thought.

"No, but we need the excuse of a wedding—or at least the threat of one—to lure Ethan in," I stammer, holding on by a thread, ready to abandon the whole plan.

"No one has to know. When the time comes, we can stage a wedding. But for now, I want it to be just us."

I rest my forehead on his. If it were up to me, I could drown in those purple depths of his, and be perfectly content. "I love the sound of that."

"Then the only question is: do you love me? Because this fountain will know the difference between a fake engagement and true love."

I tiptoe over to touch the bark of the tree, sliding my palm across the rough edges, down and around to the place where the sacred spring water rises from the ground.

I run my fingers through the sparkling water, marvelling at its freshness. "According to my grandfather Oberon, Eros' own daughter, Hedone, drank from the water with someone she mistakenly thought was her mate. Drinking the water with the wrong person not only caused the union to fail but also prevented her from finding her one true mate. And so, the young goddess spent her life chasing pleasures instead."

"Are you worried I might not be the one?" Seth croaks.

"Not at all. In fact, I always suspected that part of the legend was tacked on so that young lovers wouldn't defy their parents and elope here..." I meet his gaze head-on. "I love you, Seth. With all that's left of my heart—but it's not much. It might not be enough for the Fountain to work its magic."

He bridges the gap between us. "Gods know it's enough for me."

He claims my mouth again, but this time, the kiss is anything but chaste. It devours, wrenching my soul out to meet his.

We kiss hard under the canopy of the Hawthorn. Suddenly, the wind stirs, rustling the leaves and making the branches sway. A flurry of birds bursts from the branches above, tweeting in warning. The earth vibrates faintly beneath our feet, and we reluctantly pull apart.

Seth's eyes flash with worry. "Mark my words," he growls, "I'll kill anyone who dares—"

"Shush. Look."

A ball of light rises from Percy's grave. A soul. But not like the souls of the Fae. There's no reaper waiting for him, no one tasked with reaping the Faeling's light and gathering them to be later released to the sky, because their souls are merely borrowed pieces.

The little sphere of golden light rises from the earth and hovers at eye level.

Percy's voice echoes in my mind.

"We've made it home, diamantay."

I choke on a sob at the sweet caress of his voice, one I never thought I'd hear again. "I miss you, Perce."

Two delicate wings appear from the ball, the golden glow dwindling to reveal Percy's entire shape, right up to the curve of his melon hat. He's smiling.

"Be happy. Marry your guy. Save the world. I'll be with you. Always."

He flies forward, zooming directly into my chest. My ribcage rises on a deep breath, as though Percy is breathing for me. The light spreads, igniting my whole body, flesh and bones. I press a hand over my heart, to the scarred, mangled flesh. It's now as smooth as it was... before.

"Your scars are gone..." Seth trails off, caressing my arms up and down.

We rise to our feet, the golden glow beating in sync with my heart.

A thousand other spheres of light rise from the earth around us, gleaming like fireflies in the night. I stand, ready to flee if needed, but feel nothing but comfort radiating from the orbs. No threat. Just peace.

They wiggle up and down in the air before crashing into me, all at once.

What the—

I feel different as I bring a shaky hand to my head.

An intricate gold crown sits there, my thick mane braided around it. The golden glow coats my skin, sparking in and out of view a few more times before it's gone. The branches of the Hawthorn blow in the wind, revealing the rest of the island, where the cupid bodies are gone.

Seth kneels in front of me, one arm braced across his chest. "At your service, Your Majesty."

"Did Freya die?" My nose wrinkles. "No, that's too coincidental. Do you think Percy did this?"

Seth licks his lips, considering my question for a long time before he says, "I think Percy's soul enacted Eros' will. Gave you back what was stolen. I'd expect Freya to be shouting at her lackeys right about now, but they won't answer to her anymore. The common folk never liked my mother, so there'll be people dancing in the streets tomorrow. We'll have to be careful. If she's alive, she'll be even more desperate to kill you when we face her again. But I won't let her anywhere near you." His voice trembles, but not from doubt or grief. In fact, it's brimming with happiness.

I flex my knuckles, my toes digging into the earth. "Stand up, pretty boy."

He obeys, and I cup my hands to gather spring water inside my palms.

"Now that you're queen, should we still do this? We won't be able to keep our marriage secret—not with you wearing the crown," Seth says quietly, his gaze glued to the ground.

I raise his chin with one finger. "If you're a traitor, I'm a traitor," I arch my brows, daring him to contradict his own plea. "If you're exiled, then I'll come with you. And if I'm queen—" I grin at the word, my breath shaky as hell, unable to keep it all in, my grief momentarily eclipsed by Percy's final act of healing.

In the end, he did it. Percy fixed me, body and soul.

Relief pulses through me. I'm finally reclaiming my crown, filling that aching emptiness inside—replaced by the hope of a future free of curses, and my love for Seth burning bright, eclipsing everything else.

It's fucking fabulous.

I was withering before we met, a rose sealed under glass, petals dropping one by one. Safe to a point, but not living. Drowning in regrets, surrounded by the wreckage of everything I thought I'd be. Then Seth tore me out of that glass prison, and loved me even though I fought him every step of the way. After decades in limbo, I've lost plenty—endured more than I thought possible—but I'm still here.

The hole left behind by the dreaded arrow that almost carved out my heart has been filled, and the gash in my soul, too. I'm ready to love again. To risk it all. To *live*.

"And if I'm queen, you're my king," I finally say, tipping my chin toward my palms to prompt him to drink, too.

He gathers spring water in his cupped hand. "On three. One."

"Two."

We share a solemn, yet mischievous grin that lights up his eyes all the way through.

"Three." Seth drinks the water from the fountain, and I do the same.

The branches go still. Lotus flowers bow against the pond's surface, as if leaning in to listen. Moonlight turns the droplets sliding from our fingers into strands of liquid silver.

Seth blinks, once, twice. His gaze roams the small island—the mossy ground, the flowers tucked in the tree's shade, the canopy overhead, and even the clear waters of the pond.

"Did it work?" I ask, wondering if he feels different at all.

He squints at me, then steps one leg between mine, leaning forward and gently pinning me to the trunk of the Hawthorn at my back.

A storm gathers in my stomach, rumbling low, swelling with the promise of bloom after a monsoon. Static electricity prickles along my skin, hairs standing on end, the bond between us snapping into place. The tempest belongs to us both, shared and carried. A piece of him takes root inside me, undeniable, eternal. I feel lighter, my body trembling, like I could turn into rain myself and drip into the earth.

"Shouldn't we... I don't know...consummate this marriage?" Seth suggests with a kiss, grounding me.

"Here? Now?" I try to keep a straight face, but a big smile spreads across my lips. "That part wasn't covered in the legends."

"Yes, but Eros wouldn't content herself with a gulp of water, no?" Seth unbuttons my black dress, one button at a time, and spreads it until I'm exposed to him. The gentle breeze tickles my breasts, making them peak, as he explores the places where my old scars used to be, then traces the lines of my tattoo.

The ink glows with a faint golden sheen under his touch, my new skin even more sensitive than it was, like it's never been touched before. The matching glow of his skin steals my breath. He looks different, yet the same.

He was always meant to wear a crown.

"She's the goddess of love, but also desire." His nose drags down the slope of my neck, and my lids flutter, the sensations multiplied tenfold. "Lust." He plants a hot kiss at the angle of my jaw. "Sex." He dips a hand under the lace covering my heat, sinking two fingers inside, and groans at the wetness he finds there.

"She'd need more proof. More...worship," he adds, bringing his fingers up to his mouth to taste my arousal. "Let me show you how much I love you, my queen."

I hum at the sight and link my arms around his neck. "Yes. That makes sense."

He rips my underwear off before his hand moves between us. His breeches slip down, and I wrap my legs around him, pressed between the rough bark of the tree and the greedy proof of his desire.

"It appears I'm your fated mate after all," he murmurs in my ear.

I meet his eyes and smile. "Now worship me hard, king of my heart."

CHAPTER 43
FROZEN KINGDOM
SETH

Tundra is unrecognizable. Devi and I step out of the sceawere hand in hand, but this is no place for a honeymoon. The guardhouse, the castle gates—even the sky—are blurred by a raging snowstorm.

"By Eros, what happened here?" Devi says, her lips tight. The beautiful, otherworldly glow of her skin and the crown on her head vanish.

We exchange a heavy glance.

I motion to the castle up the hill with my chin. "Let's find out."

Something bad happened here.

Bad enough to reverse the change in season.

Faerie weather is usually consistent. Spring had been spreading to Wintermere, melting ice and coaxing blooms unseen in decades. But ice has taken it all back in the days since we left.

The low temperature numbs my fingers and prickles my ears. My breath puffs in white clouds in front of my face, each inhale burning cold in my chest. I taper down the storm, failing to shut it off entirely, but the heavy snow dwindles enough for us to fly to the parapet.

I let myself turn into a cloud, the change blocking the cold.

Up on the hill, the Lake of Souls is hidden behind the thick veil of snow. We pass over the maze on our way to the inner gardens. Every dead plant is encased in ice, dusted with snow. The flowers are frozen mid-bloom, petals and leaves still vibrant in color, as if the change happened in an instant.

The three towers looming above the garden are sheathed in thick ice, their spires glistening like the tip of a sharp, lethal blade. The entire castle appears to be entombed, checkered windows and ancient stones sealed under a heavy, gleaming crust. Everything is still. Silent. Frozen.

Devi flies beside me, her bottom lip tucked inside her mouth. I can't hold hands with her in this form, but I feel her so clearly. Even with the storm clawing at her, snow tangled in her hair, and ice dusting her lashes, she's the most breathtaking thing I've ever seen.

Without the crown, she looks a little more like the woman I met in Inverness. I want to steal her away, lock us in somewhere warm, where we could spend days—weeks—just the two of us. A real honeymoon. But the realm doesn't wait. At least I know we'll face this new crisis together.

We land inside the courtyard, snow crunching under our boots. The Hawthorn fared much the same as the gardens, its handful of blue apples encased in ice, their peels already turning brown.

Sara comes running out of Elio's study, her short blond hair pulled into a severe bun at the nape of her neck. Her eyes are puffy and red.

"Where's Elio?" Devi croaks, striding over to meet her. "What happened?"

Tears shine in Sara's blue eyes. "Elio left for the Solar Cliffs. I couldn't stop him." She hesitates, her throat bobbing. "Lori's gone," she finally says. "Ethan... He took her."

TO BE CONTINUED.

LOVELY READERS

I really enjoyed writing Devi and Seth's love story. In many ways, this book felt like a departure from the previous ones, whether because both characters were Fae royals already, or because Devi was a very different FMC. I cried when Percy died. I'm not sure why, since I'm the psycho who killed him, but I had trouble sticking to that decision.

I left a few breadcrumbs for you in this book about our next MMC, and I'm so freaking excited! I'm sure you've guessed we're going to explore Ezra's story next. Who doesn't love a villainous shadow daddy?

But have you guessed where he is and who cursed him? Or who he might be falling in love with? Read the blurb on the next page...

See you back in Inverness,

xoxo

Anya

CURSE OF THE FAE CHARACTERS AND MAPS

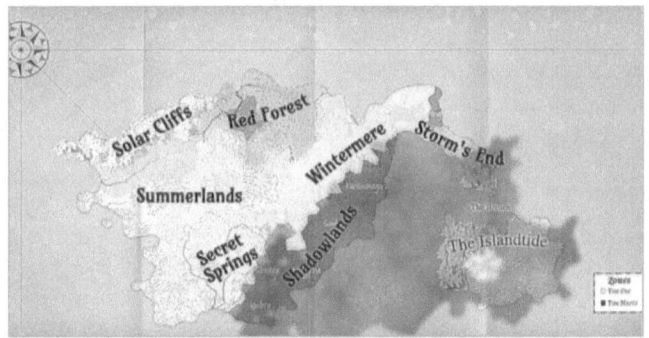

Map of the Fae continent

Current Rulers of the Fae continent (and their spouses):

Solar Cliffs - Ethan Lightbringer (twice widowed)
Secret Springs - Freya Heart (twice widowed)
Summerlands - Aidan Summers (Elizabeth Snow)
Red Forest - ?
Shadowlands - Damian Sombra (Penelope "Nell" Darcy)
Wintermere - Elio Lightbringer (Lorisha Singh)
Storm's End - ?

Recurring Curse of the Fae characters:

Mabel Bloodsinger, the last queen of the Mists by marriage
Seth Devine, Freya Heart and Thorald Storm's illegitimate son
Violet "Devi" Eros, granddaughter of Oberon Eros
Iris Lovatt, Freya Heart's niece
Morrigan "Rye" Quinn, Granddaughter of Mabel Bloodsinger
Maddox Storm, Thorald Storm's oldest son
Luther Storm, Thorald Storm's youngest son

THE SHADOW OF A VICIOUS KING

Villains have more fun. Even the broken ones. FREE ON KU

I'm a ghost.
A shadow stuck on this earth, cursed to rot.
No escape. No mercy. Just a gilded cage I call home.

Until she moves in. Little Fox.
Hair red as flame against the pillow she clutches at night.
Skin pale as the moonlight spilling through her window.
Lips red as blood, parted in sleep.

I want to touch her.
Crawl into her bed.
And drink her tears.

Bad men want her dead, and I'll kill anyone who tries to hurt
her. I'll save her. Or ruin her.

I only break the ones I love.

But I crave her beyond reason.

This novel is a full-length romantasy with a happy ending, and though it's part of an interconnected series, it can be read first.

Steamy. 18+. Full list of triggers inside.

Invisible Shadow Daddy
Hidden Identity
Forced proximity
Forbidden Love